CAN'T TAKE MY EYES OFF YOU

A SMALL TOWN ROMANTIC SUSPENSE

KAIT NOLAN

For Allen,

My personal hero, who proves daily that opposites attract can totally work.

I love you.

K

A LETTER TO READERS

Dear Reader,

This book is set in the Deep South. As such, it contains a great deal of colorful, colloquial, and occasionally grammatically incorrect language. This is a deliberate choice on my part as an author to most accurately represent the region where I have lived my entire life. This book also contains swearing and pre-marital sex between the lead couple, as those things are part of the realistic lives of characters of this generation, and of many of my readers.

If any of these things are not your cup of tea, please consider that you may not be the right audience for this book. There are scores of other books out there that are written with you in mind. In fact, I've got a list of some of my favorite authors who write on the sweeter side on my website at https://kaitnolan.com/on-the-sweeter-side/

If you choose to stick with me, I hope you enjoy!

Happy reading!

Kait

"Hey, hey married lady." Miranda Campbell grinned as her best friend slid into the opposite side of the booth.

"Someday that will probably get old, but it is not this day," Norah declared. "Sorry I'm late. Meeting ran over."

Miranda noted her faintly mussed hair and rosy cheeks and smirked. "And did your *meeting* come to a satisfactory conclusion? Judging from your glow, I'm gonna guess it did."

Norah cast a frantic look around, her just-had-a-quickie-with-my-new-hubby glow being replaced by a ferocious blush. "Keep your voice down!" she hissed.

"Hey, at least one of us is being kept satisfied. I just try not to think too hard about the fact that it's my cousin putting that look on your face. Did you and Cam at least remember to lock the door this time?"

"That was *one* time."

Miranda just arched a brow.

"Okay, maybe two." Norah dropped her voice. "He has a thing about desks."

Lifting a hand Miranda shook her head. "Stop right there. I don't need to know this." At Norah's chagrinned expression, she added, "But it's awesome to still see you blissfully happy. You're practically radioactive with contentment."

Norah unwound her scarf and shed the red wool coat, running her hands through her dark brown hair to neaten it. "I'm going to credit the happy for making me susceptible to crazy proposals."

"Is that a euphemism for something?"

Norah laughed. "No. But somehow I find myself chairing the committee organizing the Valentine's Dance this year. Because I have so much spare time, right?"

And then it all came suddenly clear. Bracing both hands on the table, Miranda stared her down. "You invited me to lunch to talk me onto that committee, didn't you?"

"It'll be fun!"

Unamused, Miranda just continued to stare.

"What's that face, Dr. Campbell?" Mama Pearl, the much-beloved heart and soul of Dinner Belles Diner, slid their customary sweet teas onto the table.

Miranda gestured at the sneak she'd roomed with in college. "Norah here has been whacked upside the head with the love stick and thinks she's gonna talk me onto the Valentine's Dance committee."

"If I had to judge by the smile she was wearin' when she walked in here, I'd say there was definitely a love stick involved."

Norah's mouth fell open. "Mama Pearl, hush your mouth!"

Miranda snickered and a grin creased the older woman's dark face.

"Usual?"

"Yes, ma'am," they chorused.

As soon as she shuffled off, Norah resumed her campaign. "Anyway, it'll be the social event of the season."

That wasn't saying much. With a population just edging toward six thousand people, Wishful wasn't exactly a hopping, happening place. Social gatherings down here tended more toward church potlucks, football parties, and chilling out at The Mudcat Tavern. Miranda was totally okay with that. Transforming the community center into something out of a John Hughes movie prom set for a town-wide dance was not her idea of a good time. Or maybe that was just a little sour grapes because she wouldn't have anyone to go with.

"I already made my contribution to the Wishful social calendar for the year with my annual New Year's Eve bash. Literally last week."

"And that bash was awesome," Norah conceded. "But come on. It'll be like the old days back in college, when we were planning sorority mixers."

"I do not have the enticement of half a dozen cute Sigma Chis doing setup for this."

"So, if I can load the setup crew with hot single men for you to ogle, you'll do it?"

Miranda knew she'd make it happen. She also knew Norah would just keep pushing until she got what she wanted. "It is my busiest season at the clinic. Flu is horrific this year, and I'm trying to control an outbreak of strep. I cannot commit to committee meetings. But I'm available for brainstorming, and I promise to clear the decks as much as I can for actual setup. Final offer."

"Deal."

"Hey, y'all."

Miranda looked up to find her administrative assistant hovering at the edge of the table. She braced herself. "Please tell me Shelby didn't send you to fetch me for an emergency at the clinic." She desperately needed this hour to check out with her best gal pal and breathe something that wasn't disinfectant fumes and illness.

Delaney laughed. "Nope. Here to pick up takeout for me and Keisha. Did I hear y'all talking about the Valentine's Dance?"

"Oh girl, you have made a grave error," Miranda told her. "Run, run now, before you get sucked in."

Norah beamed a bright smile Delaney's way. "You sure did. Are you interested in joining the committee?

"Um, I don't know. What would it entail?"

Miranda just shook her head as Norah cheerfully and skillfully herded Delaney right where she wanted her. Which was what Norah Burke Crawford did. Nobody ever saw it coming. At her high-powered marketing firm in Chicago, that talent had earned her the moniker The Closer. It was a skill Miranda both abhorred and admired. Since Norah used it to the benefit of the town these days, Miranda was hardly in a position to complain. At least until Norah turned those skills on her. Thankfully, long familiarity gave her some measure of immunity.

Amused, she watched Norah go in for the kill.

"It's a great way to give back to the community."

Delaney grinned. "Sounds great. Sign me up."

"Wonderful! We'll see you on Tuesday for our first meeting."

"Okay then. Bye, Miranda."

"See you back at the clinic."

She and Norah both watched as the younger woman headed for the counter to pick up her order.

"Never even saw what hit her."

"How's she working out for you?" Norah asked. "You've had her—what?—three months now?"

"Really well. We had a few hiccups that first week, but she's a quick learner and a hard worker. Shelby's ecstatic to have help running the office. Especially somebody to take over the onerous management of the computer system. You know how Shelby hates that thing."

"—just can't believe she has the nerve to walk around with her head held high after what she did."

Miranda didn't even have to scan the busy diner for the speaker. Clarice Hopper Morris was a bitch on wheels and had been since elementary school. If there was something cruel to be said about someone, she or her sister had no compunction in saying it. At the counter, Delaney's shoulders tensed and rounded, as if she could make herself a smaller target. Miranda's temper bubbled and snapped on the girl's behalf as Clarice and her companion just kept right on talking.

"I'm surprised they didn't run her out of town on a rail after it happened."

"Didn't she get arrested or somethin'?"

"Well, you know she did. It was all over the paper. Don't know what she's doing back in Wishful."

Miranda's fists clenched as Delaney paid for her lunch, took the takeout bag, and all but ran out of the diner.

Mama Pearl shook her head as she slid two plates onto the table and looked after Delaney. She shot a fulminating look at the gossipers and announced in a voice they couldn't fail to hear, "Anybody can change."

Clarice didn't pay any attention to Mama Pearl. "I can't imagine what she's doing for work. I mean, who on earth would hire her after everything she did?"

Temper bubbling, Miranda shoved out of the booth and marched across the diner. "That would be me, and I'll thank you to stop spreading malicious gossip about my employee."

Clarice and her companion, Karen Alberson, looked up in shock.

"Why Miranda Campbell. I didn't realize your charity work ran to your employees, too. How…magnanimous of you."

Steam was most certainly coming out of her ears. Miranda itched to plow her bunched fist into Clarice's face. "I suppose you would think it magnanimous to recognize that sometimes people make mistakes and deserve a second chance. The fact of the matter is, she's a smart girl and a hard worker, and she deserves better than to be maligned by the likes of you."

"It's a free country. There's no law against talking."

"Sadly, no, there's no law against being hateful. If there were, you and your sister would both have rap sheets taller than either of you." Disgusted, Miranda shook her head. "Are your lives so bad, you feel the need to talk down about everybody around? Tearing down good people and perpetuating rumors and half-truths about the mistakes they may have made to make yourselves feel better?"

"I hardly think our topics of conversation are any of your business."

"I think you know you're making it everyone's business by talking loud enough for the whole diner to hear you, just to get attention. Grow up, Clarice. And maybe you could find a scrap of humanity while you're at it." Miranda swung around to go back to the booth for the lunch she no longer wanted and plowed straight into a brick wall.

The wall gripped her elbows and drawled, "Steady there."

Startled, she looked up…and up, into the clearest gray eyes she'd ever seen.

CHIEF OF POLICE Ethan Greer had dealt with a lot of angry people in his lifetime. It wasn't generally an attractive state, often involving red faces and flying spittle—or fists. But Miranda Campbell, in full temper, facing off with a couple of women he'd already learned were bitchy gossips even in his short three months on the job, was one of the most unaccountably sexy things he'd ever beheld. Ethan had no idea who she was defending, but those changeable hazel eyes still flashed with a righteous indignation as she looked up at him. Stunning.

As they stood there, the indignation faded and something else pulsed between them. It had been so damned long, Ethan barely recognized it for what it was. Mutual attraction. And wasn't that interesting?

"Excuse me, Chief."

"Doc."

Her eyes widened slightly at that. Yeah, he knew who she was, even if they'd barely spoken before. At 5'10", with a fall of thick, honey blonde hair a man could lose his hands in, she was a hard woman not to notice. And he'd done plenty of noticing in the ambulance bay of the hospital the first time he'd seen her. She'd been in a fine temper then, too.

Ethan released her, edging back so she could get by him. He shifted his attention to the gossips, leveling them with the flat cop stare that tended to make hardened criminals break. The side-kick's cheeks reddened, and she looked down at the table. The ash blonde with the pinched face, who'd been doing most of the talking, just lifted a brow. Supercilious bitch. He knew the type. For the sake of whoever she'd been maligning, he wished he did have something he could arrest her for. She needed to be knocked down a few pegs.

"Hey Chief. Are you meeting somebody or sitting at the counter today?"

He found a smile for the fresh-faced waitress, who'd arrived in Wishful not long after he had. "Mornin', Hannah. I'm meetin' Clay."

"There's a booth right over here." She led him to the opposite side of the diner from Miranda. "I'll just get your tea."

As he sat, studying the menu, conversation started up again. That whole confrontation was gonna be all over town by dinner. Probably faster. He'd learned that viral social media had nothing on the gossip network in Wishful. Especially when it started here, at Mama Pearl's place. If you wanted to know anything, Dinner Belles was the first place you started.

Clay wandered in and worked his way toward the table, pausing in time-honored, small-town tradition to greet everyone he knew. Given Wishful was his hometown, that was most of them. The delay was fine with Ethan. It gave him a chance to surreptitiously watch the good doctor as she conversed with City Planner Norah Crawford.

Clay slid into the other side of the booth. "See somethin' you like?"

Or maybe not so surreptitiously. "Hello to you, too."

Hannah came back with his tea. "Hey Clay."

"Miss Hannah Wheeler. And how are you this fine day?"

Ethan wondered if there was a woman between twelve and eighty in this town that his best friend didn't know by name.

"Doing fine. Caught your show last weekend. Nice to know the rumors are true. You're good."

He grinned. "Glad you enjoyed it. You know, I used to be a part of a duo."

Her brown eyes brightened with interest. "Yeah? What happened?"

Clay turned a bland stare on Ethan. "My partner went off and joined law enforcement."

"And you became a high school math teacher," Ethan shot back.

Hannah stared. "You, Chief? Really?"

Shifting in the booth, Ethan shrugged. "It was a long time ago."

"Well, that is a thing I'd like to see." She lifted her order pad. "What can I get you?"

"What can you do about a bacon cheeseburger?" Clay shot her the twenty-four carat smile that girls had been fawning over since he was a cocky nineteen-year-old. It hadn't lost its potency.

Hannah blushed and batted her eyes in his direction. "I'll get Omar right on that. You want onion straws on it like your usual?"

"That'd be great. And a Coke."

She made a note on her order pad. "How 'bout you, Chief?"

Mentally adding an extra mile to tomorrow's morning run, Ethan stuck the menu back between the napkin dispenser and the ketchup. "I'll have the same."

"You got it."

As soon as she'd wandered away, Clay started in. "So, when am I gonna get you back up on stage?"

Here we go again.

"I've been trying to get settled into this new job, establishing myself in the community. I need people to see me as Chief of Police before they see me on stage."

"It's been three months, man. You're in it, you're settled, and I promise you everybody knows exactly who you are."

"Yeah, the new guy." The new guy who was still in a probationary period for another nine months. Despite the fact that his transition had gone pretty smoothly, Ethan was sure the jury was still out for a lot of people. He was an outsider here.

From the corner of his eye, Ethan noted the gossips packing up and heading out. His eyes slid to Miranda. She scowled after the pair, muttering something under her breath and stabbing at her lunch with more savagery than necessary.

"Getting your ass back on stage and showing folks you can be approachable would go a long way toward being something other than the new guy."

Ethan dragged his attention back to Clay. "Yeah, I remember how people treated me when we performed back in college. That's not the kind of approachable I want to be."

Clay laid a hand over his heart. "Those were the days. But unlike you, I've been performing all the years in between, and it's been at least a few months since anybody threw their underwear on the stage." At Ethan's cop stare, he sobered. "Seriously though, Wishful isn't a college town, so people aren't gonna behave like they did in Austin. The Mudcat is the kind of small, intimate venue you used to love to play."

Back when it had been entirely about the music. Yeah, Ethan couldn't deny that had some appeal. He still played for himself and had occasionally stepped out for open mic nights in Dallas, but it had been years since he and Clay had performed together. He'd be lying if he didn't admit he missed it. Hadn't he taken this job so he'd have the chance for more of a life outside work? Part of that life ought to include taking back up hobbies that didn't involve honing his skills with a gun or attending training seminars.

"All right. I'll think about it. We can at least set up some rehearsals."

Clay smirked. "Think you remember how?"

"Smartass. I may not have been on stage in ages, but I can still keep up with you."

"Great! How about you prove it Saturday?"

"Can't. I'm running a bowhunter's safety course Saturday. Maybe Sunday afternoon?"

As Hannah slid their burgers onto the table, Clay nodded, satisfied. "I can work with that."

Across the diner, Miranda and Norah rose, shrugging into coats.

"Getting back into music isn't the only thing you've been avoiding."

"What are you talking about?"

"Dating, my friend. You haven't done any of it since the divorce."

Yeah, he'd been busy trying not to die, then changing his entire life. Women hadn't exactly factored into the equation. And Ethan had been fine with that. Nobody had sparked his interest anyway.

Miranda's laugh rang out, rich and unabashed. The sound rolled over him like warm molasses.

Until now.

"She's single."

Ethan jerked his attention back to Clay. "Who?"

"Miranda. I assume you weren't eyeing the new Mrs. Crawford."

"I'm not eying anybody." But he couldn't stop himself from glancing back as the two women got to the door.

Clay continued as if he hadn't even spoken. "She's a lot of fun. Helluva dancer."

Something in the casual tone had Ethan's hackles rising. Still, he kept his expression bland and reached for the ketchup. "And you'd know that why?"

"We dated a while."

The bottle jerked in his hand, making his fries look like the victim of a particularly gruesome homicide. Stupid. He'd exchanged all of five sentences with the woman, and two of those were today. He certainly had no claim on Miranda Campbell, and he sure as shit had no right to be aggravated that she'd gone out with his best friend. "I expect you've dated damn near every single woman who's breathing in Wishful at one point or other."

"My streak isn't near as wide as you seem to think."

Ethan just lifted a brow at him.

"Not since I came home, anyway," Clay amended, grinning. "Anyway, it wasn't recent. We had some fun together, but we just didn't click."

Ethan didn't want to think about what kind of fun that might've been. "Doesn't matter one way or the other."

"So, you think being Chief of Police means you don't get a love life either? Man, why did you move here again?"

"You know why."

"Yeah, and I remember something in there about having a life while you still had one. You're falling down on that, brother."

Ethan scowled at his friend. "I'm easing in at my own pace."

"Yeah, the Geriatric 500." Clay leaned closer, lowering his voice. "Look, I know Becca did a number on you. But it's time to get back out there."

The flash of honey gold hair had Ethan looking up.

As if summoned by Clay's words, Miranda stood there, those hazel eyes snapping, her long, surgeon's fingers balled to fists. "Chief Greer, I'm really sorry to interrupt your lunch, but I need to report a crime."

∽

As Wishful's not-quite-brand-new police chief turned those clear gray eyes to hers, Miranda couldn't help but hear Clay's words repeated in her head.

It's time to get back out there.

For the barest instant, she forgot what she'd come here to talk to him about because her long neglected lady parts were busy standing up and waving. *I volunteer as tribute!*

"What happened?"

Those three little syllables pulled Miranda out of her nanosecond's fantasy about what those big, warm hands that had steadied her earlier would feel like somewhere more interesting than her elbows. She didn't have time for tributes or fantasies.

"My car's been vandalized."

He didn't look annoyed, didn't even look at his food. He just slid from the booth. "Show me."

The position put him inside her personal bubble again, and Miranda took an instinctive step back, glancing at Clay. "Sorry to borrow him."

Clay waved that off. "Nature of the job."

Ethan followed her out of the diner and halfway down the block to where she'd parked. He didn't make casual small talk. Miranda had no idea what to say, so she said nothing at all, just pointed him to her driver's side door where *Nosy Bitch* had been scratched into the paint. He still didn't speak, just slowly circled the vehicle snapping pictures with his phone and, presumably, looking for more damage.

Eventually, he brought that laser focus back to her. "Do you have any idea who might do this?"

Why did his attention make her want to shiver?

"I know exactly who did it. You walked in on the tail end of our argument earlier. Clarice Morris."

"The blonde in the diner?"

"That'd be her."

"What was the argument about?"

The temper that had dropped to a simmer cranked back up to boil. "She was maligning one of my employees. I called her out on it."

"Is this your first run-in with Ms. Morris?"

Miranda snorted. "Hardly."

Ethan's eyes sharpened at that. "You have history?"

"Going all the way back to first grade."

A flicker of surprise cracked the serious cop mask. "First grade?"

"Not an exaggeration, actually. It's a small town. Most of us go back a long way. In this case, Clarice and her sister, Amber, have a history of tearing people down. I abhor bullies, so I have, over the years, intervened to defend people. And before you ask, no, it's never led to any kind of physical blows or retaliation in this particular fashion."

"So why do you think it was her this time?"

Miranda frowned at him. "Because I literally just dressed her down in public. She left first, and I come out to find this. Two and two equals four."

He glanced back at the door. "She only had a couple minutes' lead on you. A message like this would take a little while to carve in.

I'm not sure she had enough time to do it. Is there anybody else who might have a grudge against you?"

"Contrary to the evidence of the moment, I don't make it a habit to fight with people. I don't have enemies."

That focus came back to her, feeling almost like a physical touch. When Ethan Greer looked at her, he really looked *at her*. No glancing at her shoulder or the bridge of her nose. He made full, unabashed eye contact. It was both disconcerting and strangely intimate.

"Everybody has enemies, even if they don't know it."

"That's a pretty cynical point of view."

"What you call cynicism, I consider realism. Realistically, unless somebody happened to be driving by, or walking on the green and glanced over at the right moment, nobody actually saw this happen. There are no businesses with security cameras along this stretch. There's not really any way to prove who did this. You can believe down deep in your gut that this woman was behind it, but without any corroborating evidence, I can't charge her with anything."

"You're not even going to talk to her?"

"Oh, I'll talk to her. But unless she spontaneously confesses, I don't really have anything else to go on."

"So basically, I dragged you away and let your lunch go cold for nothing." Scooping a hand through her hair, Miranda felt stupid. Of course, there was nothing he could do about this. It was minor vandalism. He probably had more important things to be worrying about.

"Not nothing. I'll write up a report to document it. If you plan to file a claim on your insurance, you'll need that."

She blew out a breath and looked at her Jeep. Having the door repainted wouldn't eat up her deductible for the year, and reporting it would probably just make her rates go up. With the burden of her mortgage, student loans from med school, and the business loan on her practice, that was the last thing she needed.

It's an inconvenience. An irritant. Clarice just wanted to get to you, and you're giving her exactly what she wants.

With effort, Miranda tamped her temper down. She had patients to get back to, and she needed to be calm when she saw them. "Thank you."

"I'll need your number."

She blinked at him. Had he just asked her out?

"To let you know when the report is finished. The forms are all in my patrol car."

"Right." *Idiot. He's just doing his job.*

He punched the number into his phone. "It should be ready for pick up in a day or two, after I've had a chance to talk to Ms. Morris."

Not, *I'll call you.*

"I appreciate it, Chief Greer. And I apologize again for dragging you away from your lunch."

He angled his head and started to lift his hand before stopping himself, as if he was accustomed to having a hat to tip at a lady. "No problem. You have a good day now, Doc."

Miranda climbed into the driver's seat and watched him go.

Maybe she'd completely misread that frisson of attraction when they'd bumped into each other in the diner earlier. She'd been out of the dating game entirely since she came home to Wishful, and her last relationship had left her singed enough to be okay with that state of affairs. But Ethan Greer made her wonder. Worse, he made her want things she hadn't wanted in a very long time.

Doesn't matter. He's not interested, and you don't have time for a guy anyway.

But as she drove past the diner on her way back to the clinic, she couldn't stop herself from taking one more glance at the way those broad shoulders filled out his uniform shirt.

CHAPTER 2

"It was just an accident. I tripped and ran straight into the door frame." Rene Forbes gave a nervous laugh. "I'm such a klutz."

Miranda looked down at the hand-shaped bruise darkening Rene's wrist. "And when did the door grow fingers?"

Had she not been holding the hand and wrist to examine it, Miranda had no doubt that Rene would've tugged her sleeve down to cover the injury. As it was, she dropped her gaze to somewhere around Miranda's left shoulder.

"Rene." She kept her voice gentle. "You didn't fall into a door. You didn't step in a hole last time or have a box fall off the top shelf onto your head the time before that. Let me help you."

"I just need to know if my wrist is sprained or broken."

Miranda resisted the urge to grind her teeth. "All right. I'll get Keisha to take you back for an x-ray."

While her nurse ushered Rene down the hall, Miranda slipped into the break room and called the police station. Inez Barlow, the dispatcher and admin who'd been running the place for thirty years, answered the phone.

"Hey Inez, it's Miranda Campbell. I wondered if you could send an officer down here to take a statement about a domestic abuse case." She didn't know if she could convince Rene to cave and report Harley, but there needed to be some kind of documentation of his escalation on file.

"Is there any danger presently at the clinic?"

"No. The victim is alone. Could you ask whoever shows up to be circumspect? I want to protect her privacy as much as possible. Have them come to the back door."

"Can do, Doc."

As soon as she ended the call, she sent a text to Shelby Abbott, her office manager. **Called Theresa's Mom.** Theresa Hammond had been the first domestic abuse patient Miranda had treated when she moved back to Wishful. She and Shelby had established a shorthand around that to let the rest of the staff know, per their established protocol for this kind of situation, that they'd be sneaking police in the back and to keep all patients out of the halls as much as possible.

That done, Miranda continued seeing patients.

She'd just stepped back into the hall and ordered a strep test for little Rachel Keeney, when Ethan Greer came through the back door of the clinic.

Of course, it would be him. After she'd damned near knocked him over at Dinner Belles earlier in the week. Well, no, he was incredibly solid. She hadn't been able to avoid noticing that when she'd been pressed up against him for that all too brief encounter.

He hadn't called about the report on her car. His dispatcher had. She refused to analyze the flare of disappointment she'd felt at that.

Focus.

He strode down the hall with a long-legged swagger that reminded her of a cowboy in an old Western, an impression helped along by the well-worn boots on his feet.

"Chief." She took him into one of the empty exam rooms and shut the door for privacy. "Thank you for coming. I'm gonna be honest with you—my patient probably isn't going to be willing to report her husband today. But I have a documented escalation of injuries in her medical records over the past year, and I want to make sure that the police are aware of it."

"Sensible."

Did it take a crime of some kind to elicit more than three syllables at a time?

"Can you wait here, while I go over the x-ray with her? I'm going to make my case. If she'll agree, I'll bring you in. If not, I'll make the report myself after she goes."

"I've got time."

Not sure what else to say for the moment, Miranda gestured to a chair. "Make yourself comfortable."

Keisha met her in the hall with the radiograph and followed her back into the exam room. Miranda slid the x-rays onto the lightbox to view them. The hairline fracture wasn't a surprise. Perhaps the bigger shock was that it wasn't any worse. Given the bruising, he'd cranked his hand around her fragile wrist like a vise.

"Well?" Rene asked softly.

Miranda used a capped pen to point. "It's fractured. See that line right there? You'll need a cast for a few weeks."

"Can you do that here?"

"Yes. The bones aren't separated or out of alignment. If it was any worse, I'd have to send you to an orthopedist." She glanced at Keisha. "Non-displaced wrist fracture."

"On it."

As her nurse slipped from the room to retrieve supplies, Miranda spoke again. "Rene, I want you to look here, too. See that?" She pointed to several thick, white lines across the ulna. "Those are previous healed fractures. This has happened before."

Rene hunched her shoulders. "I told you, I'm clumsy."

"I'm sure that's what he tells you." Miranda dragged a stool over to the exam table and sat. "Are you aware you've been in here seven times over the past year for injuries? Three times since Thanksgiving. And I know I saw you in the emergency room once last year. Your records at the hospital indicate that wasn't your first visit. Harley is getting violent more often."

"Holidays are hard. Since he got laid off from the factory, he hasn't been able to find steady work."

The fact that Harley was seldom sober probably had a lot to do with that. "You don't have to stay with him. You have options. The women's shelter out at Hope Springs has both room and resources." Well, not as much room as they needed, but they were nearly done constructing an expansion, and Miranda knew that Lily Mae Pollard, the woman who ran Monarch House, wasn't about to turn away anyone in need.

"I took vows."

How many times had Miranda heard that from Rene and others like her? "So did he. And he's breaking them. He assaulted you. You need to report this."

"The police can't do anything. What happens in a man's home—"

"That's where you're wrong. The law doesn't stop at the doorway to a residence. Assault inside the home is still assault. Now you can ignore this like you've been doing. You can go on home and tiptoe around his moods, hoping you can anticipate what will set him off. But one of these days he's going to snap, and it's going to be worse than a fractured wrist and some bruising. Based on the escalation I'm seeing here, that's not far off. He could kill you, Rene."

Miranda's hope that the words would shock her patient into action were dashed when she only lifted a stubborn chin. "He wouldn't. Harley loves me."

Maybe he had once, though Miranda questioned how much a man like that could really love. She chose her words carefully. "He probably wouldn't mean to, but he gets aggressive when he's been drinking. He's not in control of himself. He needs help."

Rene brightened somewhat at that. She wouldn't reach out to take help for herself, but she'd think about it for him? Miranda didn't like what that said about the woman's self-esteem, but she pushed for whatever advantage she could get.

"If you report him, a judge could order him to counseling, to treatment for alcohol addiction, if he thinks it's necessary."

The woman chewed her lip. "Harley would be really mad about that. He doesn't trust therapists and head doctors."

"Maybe not. But if a judge says he has to go, he doesn't have a choice. And while he's there, he could deal with his anger issues and get the drinking under control." Miranda knew perfectly well a hostile, court-mandated patient wasn't a good candidate for any of those things, but if they could get him out of the house and away from Rene long enough, they could maybe finally convince her to leave his ass and go to Monarch House.

"You really think it could help?"

I really think it could help you. "Yes."

"Then I'll do it."

Repressing the urge to do a victory dance, Miranda rose. "Okay. I know you don't want to go into the station, so I've called someone to come take a statement. Meanwhile, we'll get started on that cast."

In the hall, she snagged Keisha. "She's agreed to report it."

"Praise Jesus."

"I'm not taking any chances that she'll change her mind. If you'll set out the casting materials, I'll do it when I bring in our guest."

"You got it."

After putting Delaney on duty in the hall to see that none of their patients left their exam rooms, Miranda went to grab Ethan. "She'll talk to you. She doesn't have the self-esteem to pursue it for her own sake, but I convinced her it was in Harley's best inter-est. I may have implied that a judge could order him to treatment."

His dark brows winged up faintly and an expression of respect crossed his face. "Not inaccurate, even if not guaranteed. Good move, Doc. I can work with it."

Wow, three whole sentences.

He followed her back down the hall to room three.

"This pink wrap is gonna look so nice and cheerful," Keisha said as they opened the door. "Doctor Campbell is gonna put this on you now." She'd already fitted Rene with a plastic drape to keep her clothes dry during the process.

"Thanks, Keisha."

With a raise of her eyebrows that clearly said *good luck*, the nurse stepped out.

Ethan stepped quietly into the room in her wake. Rene's eyes went wide at the sight of him. He shut the door and nodded at her. "Ma'am."

Again, Miranda had the ridiculous notion that he ought to be wearing a cowboy hat so he could take it off in the presence of women. His pause had that air of polite respect.

"Rene, this is Chief Greer. He's here to take your statement. Chief, this is Rene Forbes, Harley Forbes's wife."

He kept his focus on Rene as he came over, folding himself into the visitor's chair as Miranda started the casting process.

Good move. Make yourself look less intimidating.

His eyes fell on the bruises as Miranda tugged up her sleeve. "I understand you've had a little trouble."

Rene instinctively clutched her wrist against her chest, covering the bruising with her other hand. But Ethan had already seen. Gently, Miranda nudged the wrist back down and slipped the stockinette over her hand. "I need you to hold your thumb and forefinger together. Yes, exactly like that."

"No, no trouble."

Ethan just offered a reassuring smile. "You know, I've met your husband."

"Oh?" Rene's eyes flickered back and forth between them, as if she couldn't decide who was the greater threat.

"Hauled him in a couple times for drunk and disorderly. Once for simple assault in a bar fight. Not a new thing based on his record. I'm guessin' the bar isn't the only place he gets aggressive after he's had a few."

"A man has a right to a few drinks in peace." The words fell from her like rote. Clearly a common phrase in the Forbes household.

"Not everybody can drink responsibly. Some people get foolish. Some get mean. It's not their fault. Just how they're wired. Those kinda people need help learning how to handle it."

"He's not gonna want help. If I wasn't so stupid all the time—"

"You're *not stupid.*" Miranda snapped the words like a bullwhip. She cursed herself as Rene flinched back at the tone.

Chill out. You're not the one being called stupid. But Miranda couldn't stop the instant flash of temper that particular term engendered, no matter who it was directed at. Gentling her voice, she repeated it as she wrapped the arm with cotton padding. "You're not stupid. Don't let him tell you that you are."

Rene's throat bobbed. "How…how would this work?"

Miranda all but held her breath as she began to wrap the Scotch-cast around Rene's wrist.

"Well now, I'll take a statement about what he did to you. I know that's likely to be difficult. Dr. Campbell will stay right here with you, if you want."

"Of course, I will."

"Given Harley's history, I'd then have to bring him in to the station to talk to him about what happened. And chances are, I'd have to arrest him."

"Arrest? No. No no no. You can't do that."

"I'm afraid that's how we'd get him in front of the judge. He's the only one with the power to order Harley into treatment."

"I'm not doing that. I'm not. I won't turn in my husband." Rene's breathing went short, her voice rising.

Miranda choked back a curse. But Ethan stayed steady as a rock. "It's a scary thing going up against somebody who's got power over you. Someone who's hurt you. Nobody can make you do it. We won't push you about it today. But I'm gonna give you my card. It's got my number at the station and my cell number. If ever you feel ready to press charges, or if you need help, or if you're just scared and need to talk, you call. All right?"

Rene didn't answer, so he just tucked the card into the purse by her side.

"I'll just let y'all finish up with that cast. I hope you feel better soon, Mrs. Forbes."

With one last look at Miranda that told her he'd be waiting when she was through, he slipped out the door.

Miranda took a hard grip on her temper. She finished up the cast in silence, with her patient staring at the floor. Once she'd applied the final wrap, she stayed calm and professional as she gave Rene her discharge instructions. As the woman slid off the exam table, Miranda stopped her. "Chief Greer is a good man. He wants to help you, just like I do. We're here whenever you're ready."

Rene jerked a nod. "Am I finished?"

"Yeah."

The woman couldn't get out fast enough.

Miranda stayed where she was. A minute later, Ethan came back into the room.

Frustrated and heartsick, she scooped a hand through her hair. "I thought I'd convinced her this time."

"I wish I could say this kind of thing didn't happen all the time. I expect you know that."

"Yeah. Yeah, I know. It's always so hard to balance walking the line between HIPPA regulations and duty to report. And worrying over whether they'll stop seeking treatment if the incidents *are* reported."

"Hey, you tried. That's more than a lot of people would do. Plenty of others look the other way."

Miranda lifted her gaze to his. "I have never been that person."

His lips curved, just a little, as if he appreciated that about her. Then he sobered again. "She wasn't going to press charges. Not when she got up close and personal with the idea. But I'll still make a report, add it to the file. Every little bit of evidence helps."

"I'll write up what I saw. I have no problem testifying about it, should it come to that. He's escalating."

"That's my read, too. Believe me, I'm keeping an eye on Forbes. He does anything else I can put him away for, I'll do it."

"Let's just hope nobody else ends up in the hospital when he does it."

"Your mouth to God's ear." He shifted, reaching into his pocket for something. "Speaking of reports. You haven't picked yours up."

Miranda reached automatically for the folded paper he offered. "We've been swamped this week. Thanks for bringing it by."

He shrugged. "Since I was coming over anyway." His radio crackled. Without breaking eye contact, he answered the call. "Greer."

The dispatcher came back. "Chief, we've got a report of a theft off of Buddy Dibley's grill."

"You mean somebody stole his grill?"

"No, sir. Somebody stole the ribs he was cooking right off it."

Ethan's face went slack with shock. "Come again?"

"You heard me. Texting you the address."

Clearly baffled, Ethan looked to Miranda. "I used to track dangerous fugitives for a living. This is my life now," he muttered.

Miranda hadn't thought she could smile again so soon. "I'm sure Buddy would appreciate those investigative skills being put to the cause of locating his ribs. He's spent the last five years trying to beat Abe Costello in the annual summer barbeque cook-off."

His lips twitched up into an answering grin and wow. It transformed his sober face into something that set her pulse tripping. "So you're saying it's prospective espionage in the name of barbeque?"

Miranda shrugged. "It could happen."

"Never a dull moment." He nodded at her again with that hat tipping motion. "See you around, Doc."

SATURDAY MORNING, as he was setting up for the hunter safety course in the community center gym, Ethan was still thinking about Miranda Campbell. Big-hearted, beautiful Miranda Campbell, who wanted desperately to help a woman who was so entrenched in the cycle of abuse, she wasn't likely to ever listen. A foolhardy effort maybe, but Ethan had to admire her conviction in doing what was right.

He'd been on edge the last couple of days, fully expecting a call for another domestic disturbance or a bar fight in conjunction with Harley. But all had been quiet. The guy was bad news. In his career as a U.S. Marshal, Ethan had chased the worst of the worst. He knew the type. It wasn't a question of if Harley would go over the edge, but when. The waiting made him twitchy. As a Marshal, it hadn't been his job to build a case to confirm someone's guilt. By the time they'd been brought in, someone else had already done that. He'd had a warrant and a fugitive and a mission of bringing them in before they had a chance to hurt anyone else. He didn't have that liberty here. Without Rene being willing to press charges, his hands were tied. Even if everybody in town knew he was beating his wife, without witnesses willing to testify about it, he couldn't get the bastard off the streets.

That didn't sit well with Ethan.

He needed a new angle. With that in mind, he joined Clint Yarbrough, the officer who'd agreed to help him teach today, at the sign in table.

"You ever had any run-ins with Harley Forbes?"

"Don't think there's a one of us in the department who hasn't."

"You ever get wind of him being involved in any illegal activities? Beyond what's in his record."

"Can't say as I have. What are you thinking?"

"Guy's been unemployed a long time. Wondering how they're getting by."

"Unemployment for him. And his wife cleans houses."

"She's gonna have a damned hard time doing that with a broken wrist."

Clint's eyes went hard. "It's a shit situation. You expecting something?"

"Don't know. I just want everybody keeping their eyes and ears open. He steps one toe out of line, I want to know about it." The doors at the end of the gym opened and the first of their students arrived. "We'll talk about it more at next week's briefing."

Ethan worked up a good-natured smile for the late-twenty-something guy who got there first. "Mornin'. You here for the bowhunter safety class?"

"Yep."

"Name?" Clint asked.

"Sean Murphy."

"I'm Ethan Greer, and this is Clint Yarbrough." Ethan approved of the man's firm handshake. "You ever shot a bow before, Sean?"

He accepted the clipboard with the release and course contract. "A bit as a kid. Been a long time. I thought this would be a good refresher."

"Should be. Hope you won't be too bored." Ethan passed him his course materials and moved on to the next person in line.

People trickled in for the next fifteen minutes. With each one, Ethan took the time to introduce himself and learn their names. When the clock ticked on to 10:10, Ethan figured they had all the students they'd get.

"Reckon we're about ready to get rolling here."

The door squeaked open and a petite woman with dark red hair slipped in, hurrying toward the table. "Is this the bowhunter safety course?"

Clint eyed her with obvious surprise. "It is."

"Great. Sorry I'm late."

She was the only woman who'd shown up. Not that Ethan hadn't known women who could and did bow hunt, but this girl hardly seemed the type. Still, looks could be deceiving. "Name?"

Pink crawled across her fair cheeks. "Delaney Newell."

Clint handed her the clipboard with the paperwork, and Ethan racked his brain for why she seemed so familiar. As she handed the clipboard back, it popped. "You work at Dr. Campbell's clinic."

Delaney's eyes widened and her hands began to twist at the strap of her purse. "Yes. I'm the administrative assistant."

Because she seemed unaccountably nervous, Ethan offered her an easy smile. "Saw you when I was in earlier this week. You ever shot a bow before?"

She shook her head.

Only woman, never shot a bow, so what had prompted her to take the class? "This will be a good starter for you."

The three of them strode over to join the rest of the class. There were fifteen students in total. Most claimed to have some experience with a bow. Ethan figured they'd see about that. "All right," he began. "Let's get started with a little bit of history."

Jordan Linley raised his hand. "Not to be rude or anything, but a few of us were wondering, you being a city guy and all, what your qualifications were for teaching this class? Can't be too much cause for bowhunting in Dallas."

Ethan wondered if he'd still be called the City Guy in fifteen years. "Fair question."

Instead of laying down the history of his youth in rural West Texas, he opened his bow case and withdrew the compound bow. Picking up one of his own practice arrows, he nocked it and verified no one was in the vicinity before he drew back and anchored, sighting the foam deer target about seventy-five feet away. He released on an exhale and the arrow hit the target in with a *thunk*, dead center mass. The whole shot took only a few seconds.

Jordan was staring at the target, brows up. "Well, all right then."

"I didn't always live in the city." Ethan replaced his bow in the case. "Now, as I was saying, we're gonna start with a little history."

Over the next few hours, he took them through it. There were grumbles as he went over the development of the sport and basic bowhunter education. Even more when he talked about wildlife conservation principles. Probably most of them had been through that with their regular hunter ed course, but it was a mandatory part of the state-approved curriculum. They perked up when he finished the unit on safe and responsible bowhunting and started on the segment about the weapons themselves.

"You've got three different types of bows to choose from." Ethan picked up the first. "This is the longbow. It's the traditional bow. Simple, elegant, requires minimal additional equipment." He swapped for the next one. "This is the recurve bow. It's another more traditional bow. It's smooth, quiet, fast shooter. It's got shorter limbs than the longbow and tends to provide more power in a shorter package. This is what I grew up shooting. And finally —" Ethan picked up the compound bow. "—this is a compound bow. Far and away the most popular type for hunting or target shooting, the wheel and cam system can reduce the draw weight by at least fifty percent."

He went through an explanation of arrows, covering the different types of shafts, heads, and fletching.

Dave Lautner's hand shot up. "When do we get to shoot?"

"Not for a bit yet. We've still got more to cover, and I want to make sure the track and gym are cleared of people before any of you takes on a target."

The other man's expression turned mulish. "Some of us have done this before."

"But not all. Now, let's talk about how you match arrows to your bow."

By the time Ethan made it through a description and demonstration of all the accessories, he could sense the mood of the group turning restless, so he sent Clint upstairs to clear all the walkers off the track.

"We're gonna divide into three groups. Each of you will have a chance to try out each type of bow, to get a feel for what you like, what the draw weight feels like." He demonstrated proper technique for each, noting Clint in intense conversation with one of the blue-haired ladies on the track above. He made a mental note to reserve the entire space next time, as he went from student to student, correcting their form.

Delaney frowned as she struggled to pull back the recurve bow. "It's heavy."

Stepping behind her, Ethan adjusted her stance and hold. When she still had trouble pulling back, he took the bow from her hands. "It's got a heavier draw than you need. This one's intended for a much bigger person." Picking up the compound bow, he handed it over. "Try that."

With minimal coaching and correction, Delaney managed to pull it back much more easily.

"All clear!" Clint called.

"Okay then. We're going to get started with some actual target practice."

There was a bit of jostling as everybody lined up.

"We're going to let the lady go first," Ethan announced. She was the most likely to accept instruction.

Setting her at the line, he handed over one of the arrows with a practice tip. As he began to explain to the group proper technique, Delaney nocked the arrow, drew it back with perfect fluidity, and let it fly. It hit the outer edge of the red center. Her lips curved in a satisfied smile.

Ethan arched a brow. "You sure you haven't done this before?"

"Nope." The answer rolled out easily, but she didn't quite meet his eyes.

She was lying. He didn't know why. Maybe it was a flirtation tactic? Trying to get him to show her up close and personal how to correct her form? Not that it really needed correcting. He reached for a second arrow.

"Dude, I don't think you should—"

"Dave, put that down right now!" Clint snapped.

Ethan started to turn. White hot pain erupted in his ass, and he went down to his knees. "Son of a *bitch!*"

As he looked over his shoulder at Dave Lautner, who stood with a stunned expression on his face and Ethan's recurve bow in his hands, he officially decided he did miss the Marshal Service. Because he'd just been shot. Again.

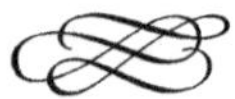

CHAPTER 3

"What have we got?" Miranda asked, stepping out of one hospital room and preparing to go into the next. Her weekend rotation in the emergency room was keeping her hopping.

She didn't mind. Between that and periodic surgical assists, she kept her skills sharp, and, up until recently, she'd enjoyed a flirtation with the sexy Dr. Phillips—dubbed by many as Wishful's most eligible bachelor. It had never gone anywhere, and, in the last month or so, he'd started dating Mary Alice Reed. Miranda couldn't get herself too worked up over the idea that that ship had sailed. She'd dated another doctor during her med school and residency days, and it simply wasn't for her.

The nurse, Corinne Dawson, met her in the hall. "Patient is a white male, thirty-six, with a puncture wound from an arrow."

"Well, that's a new one."

"Oh, it gets better." Corinne grinned. "He got shot in the ass."

"The ass," Miranda repeated, shifting mental gears from considering damage to major organ systems.

"Skewered right through his left butt cheek."

"I assume he's conscious then?"

"Oh, yes."

Picking up the chart, Miranda reviewed the triage notes as she stepped into the room. Her patient lay face-down on the gurney, the neon-green-and-white-fletched shaft of an arrow protruding from his backside. Blood had seeped from the wound, staining his khaki cargo pants, but sufficient shaft protruded that she knew nothing vital had been hit, so she allowed herself to feel some amusement at the situation. What kind of story was she gonna hear about this one?

"Hey there. I'm Dr. Campbell. Why don't you tell me what happened, Mr.—" She paused to check the name on the chart. "Greer?" She hurried to the head of the gurney. "Ethan?"

The Chief of Police turned his head to look at her, irritation written in every line of his face. "Doc. It's been a shitty afternoon."

"I can imagine. Were you in a hunting accident?"

"In a manner of speaking. One of the idiots in the bowhunter safety class I was teaching didn't follow directions and shot me. With my own damned bow." Ethan narrowed his eyes, as if daring her to so much as chuckle.

Miranda pressed her lips together to keep her expression neutral. She absolutely should not laugh.

"What are you doing here, anyway?" he asked.

"I have one Emergency Department rotation a month. This happened to be my weekend."

"So that's why you were here when I brought in Autumn Buchanan last fall. Is that normal? The whole splitting time between hospital and practice?"

"In small town hospitals, yeah. Anything truly serious comes in, we'll call our head of emergency medicine or the necessary specialist, but for the run-of-the-mill stuff, we're more than qualified to handle it. Not that I can say this is run-of-the-mill. In Chicago, I saw stab wounds, gun shots, car accidents, burn victims, any manner of construction accidents, and even a few bombing victims. But I've never seen an arrow before. Do you know what kind of tip is on it?"

"Bullet tip. Thank Jesus, I don't store my arrows with the broadheads attached. You were in Chicago?"

Bullet tip could cause some damage, but extraction would be much simpler than any of the alternatives. She probed around the injury, refusing to pay attention to the firm curve of his ass, an effort made more difficult by Corinne's silent "Damn!" and eyebrow waggle. Thank God they were both well behind Ethan's line of sight. "Mmm, before I came home. I was doing a surgical residency. I'm going to have to cut your pants to get a better look at the wound."

Ethan laid his head back on his arms, effectively muffling his voice. "Fine. I don't think this situation can get any more mortifying. So, you're a surgeon who practices family medicine?"

She used scissors to cut the fabric free, folding it back to reveal a truly superb backside. It was really too bad someone had shot it. "No. I'm certified in family medicine. I knew halfway through my residency that I wouldn't be happy as a trauma surgeon, which is what my mentor was convinced I should be. The way he saw it, I had a gift for it and doing anything else was wasting my abilities.

He still hasn't forgiven me for getting out and coming back here. You're gonna need stitches."

"Figured. Won't be the first time. Beats recovering from a gunshot wound. I figure you were in that residency long enough to be better at them than the Army medic who stitched me up in Afghanistan."

She asked the patiently waiting Corinne to prep sutures. "You were Army?"

"Yep. Enlisted when I turned eighteen. Got out at twenty-one and went to college on the G.I. Bill."

"And from there into the U.S. Marshals." She kept talking as she slowly extracted the arrow and tossed it onto a tray. Grabbing a gauze compress, she covered the freely bleeding wound and applied pressure.

Ethan grunted.

"So, what makes a big city guy move to a small town?"

"Why does everybody assume I always lived in the city?"

"Probably because you've played your personal history close to the vest. You're new in town, so you're a hot topic of conversation. Mostly all people know is that you were a federal Marshal, and you came from Dallas." She certainly wanted to know more about him than that.

"I'm not in the habit of talking about myself."

"I expect that's the law enforcement training. Makes sense," Miranda admitted, "but in the absence of the truth, people will make up their own stories." She irrigated the puncture with disinfectant. "So why Wishful?"

"Clay's my best friend from college. And I wanted to slow down some. Work a job where not everything is high stakes life and death."

Miranda wondered how the fun, flirty musician had gotten to be friends with the very serious Ethan Greer. "I get that. It's part of why I walked away from being a trauma surgeon."

"Yeah? What was the rest?"

"I cared too much." Glancing at Corinne she asked for a local anesthetic.

"I don't need anesthetic."

"I'm about to be sewing up a hole in your backside. You're gonna want a local."

"I didn't have one in the field in the Army."

"Well, bully for you and your manliness, but this is not the Army, and we are not in the middle of a war. I need you to stay still and a local anesthetic ensures you will be."

"I can hold myself still," he insisted.

Miranda looked at Corinne. "Can you give us a minute?"

"Of course, Dr. Campbell."

She waited until the nurse slipped out of the room. "Okay, what gives? Your chart doesn't list any allergies."

"It's not an allergy." Ethan's voice was tight. "I just…don't like needles."

"You got shot in the ass and barely did more than blink, and you've got an issue with a little bitty needle?" She didn't know why she was pressing him. It wasn't as if he was the first person she'd treated with a needle phobia. But it was just so…unexpected.

He was ex-military, a former U.S. Marshal who'd spent a decade facing who knew what. He wasn't lacking in courage.

"I didn't say it was rational."

She'd done a pretty decent job of putting Ethan out of her mind the last few days. Of reminding herself that he fell firmly in the category of *look, don't touch.* But this tiny show of vulnerability tugged at her, reminding her that underneath the alpha-male exterior, he was a man with fears, desires, and complexities. Damn if she didn't want to know more of them. Know more of *him.*

Miranda circled around to the front of the gurney and crouched until she was at eye level. His eyes were darker today, like rain-washed slate. "Ethan, you've got a puncture wound. Whether you have a local anesthetic or not, you're gonna have to have a tetanus shot."

His face went a couple shades paler before he pressed his brow to the gurney and swore.

She couldn't stop herself from laying a hand on his shoulder in comfort. The muscles beneath her palm were hard as iron. "Try to relax."

He sucked in a breath and seemed to force the tension out on a slow exhale.

"Better. I'll be fast. Just…don't look, okay?"

Taking pity on him, she used some numbing agent at the site to minimize the stick. Maybe she could distract him with conversation.

"So, what happened with the Great Rib Caper? Or are you at liberty to say?"

He snorted. "By the time I got out there, Buddy had already called the station back. Apparently, he fell asleep in his recliner, and his wife took them off the grill to keep them from burning."

Miranda laughed and slid in the needle, injecting the anesthetic. "I gotta say, I was hoping for the barbeque espionage version of things. It'd liven things up a little."

"I'm okay with the real resolution. He was so embarrassed, he sent me home with some of the ribs for dinner. I haven't had Abe Costello's, but I'd say Buddy stands a fighting chance in the cook-off. They were damned fine ribs for not being from Texas."

She began carefully suturing the puncture. "Are you telling me you've got barbeque prejudice, Chief?"

"Damned straight. Barbeque is meant to be beef, with sweet sauce. Nobody does it right this side of the Mississippi River."

"That is not gonna be a popular opinion."

"I'll concede pulled pork can be tasty, but it doesn't hold a candle to a good brisket."

"I do love a good brisket." Miranda snipped the end off the last stitch. "All done."

Ethan turned his head to look back at her and cracked an eye. "Really?"

She smiled at the look of suspicious hope. "Really."

"Damn, Doc, you've got quite the bedside manner."

Okay maybe it was the fact that his very fine ass was exposed, but that sounded suspiciously like flirting. Miranda liked it. "I try. You're gonna be fine in a couple of weeks. It should go without saying that you should avoid any heavy lifting, unnecessary bending or squatting, or anything that might strain your stitches.

I'm prescribing you a course of antibiotics. I'll want to see you in two weeks at the clinic to check on how you're healing, but barring complications, you should be back to normal in no time."

"Appreciate it."

"I'm gonna round up some scrub pants for you. These are a loss." She started for the door.

"Doc?"

"Yeah?"

His sheepish expression made him look younger, more approachable. "I'd appreciate it if you could maybe not mention the needle thing."

Her lips curved in a slow smile. "Doctor-patient confidentiality. Your secret's safe with me, Chief."

~

"I swear to God, I'm gonna kill him this time."

"Now, Mrs. Ramsey—" Ethan began.

The older woman interrupted, "How many times do I have to tell you? Call me Maudie Bell."

"Miss Maudie Bell," he corrected. "I understand you're frustrated—"

"Frustrated? *Frustrated?* That...that jackass trampled my prize roses!" She gestured to the offender, now nuzzling at winter grass on the far side of Miss Maudie Bell's yard. The jackass in question was, in fact, a shaggy-coated gelding named Houdini, who had a tendency to go walkabout.

"He's a menace," Miss Maudie Bell declared.

Did she mean the horse or his owner? "I'll round up Houdini and go have a word with Chester." Again. This was the third time in as many months he'd had to get involved, and that was just counting the times he'd lost at Rock, Paper, Scissors with whichever of his officers was on duty. More often than not, calls from Miss Maudie Bell and her friends—affectionally known around town as The Casserole Patrol—were minor matters, excuses for the trio of blue-hairs to ogle "those fine lookin' boys in blue." But not today.

"A word is not gonna cut it, Chief. Not this time. Do you have any idea how much time and effort I put into those roses? The Belle Doria is extremely rare! I grew those from cuttings from my own dear mama's garden. It's not like I can just go down to Wishful Nursery and Garden Center to get replacements."

Ethan winced. "I'm sorry to hear that, ma'am."

"I want to press charges for destruction of property. If Chester can't get his fence fixed, he's got no business keeping horses."

"On that we agree." It was a damned miracle none of the horses had been hit by a car yet. "Let me catch Houdini first and get him secured, make sure none of his buddies got out this time. Then I'll see what's what and take whatever steps are necessary to see this doesn't happen again." He had no idea yet what that would be. First time had been a warning. Second had been a fine. Obviously, neither tactic had been sufficient to motivate Chester Harkin to take care of business. Ethan didn't think charging the man was going to make a whit of difference either, so clearly, he was going to have to engage in some creative policing to keep the peace.

Returning to his police cruiser, Ethan popped the trunk and pulled out the lariat. When he'd taken the job as Wishful Chief of Police, he hadn't imagined the roping skills he'd honed in his youth would come into play, but after the first call about Chester's horses, he'd learned to be prepared. Stretching out the loop, he made his way across the yard to where the gelding continued to graze. If he were lucky, he'd be able to walk straight up and slip the lasso over Houdini's head.

He wasn't lucky.

As he got within about twenty feet of the animal, Houdini lifted his head, ears quivering. Ethan began to murmur in a low voice. "Easy. Easy now. Adventure's over. Time to head on home."

Houdini's ears twitched, and he snorted, his breath clearly visible in the frigid January air.

He was gonna bolt. Ethan could feel it. He kept talking in that soothing tone, even as he began to swing the lasso. When Houdini wheeled, he let it fly. The loop settled around the horse's neck and Ethan pulled it taut. Houdini reared, dragging Ethan a few stumbling steps forward that sent pain shooting through his injured butt cheek. He prayed he hadn't popped his stitches. Much as he wanted to see Miranda again, anything involving more needles was a hard pass.

"Settle down, you big bastard." Ethan moved with the animal as he danced in place, making a half-hearted bid for control. But Houdini knew the jig was up. With a few stomps of irritation and a toss of his head, he subsided. Ethan closed the distance between them, until he could lay a hand on the muscular neck. "There now. That's the way."

From somewhere behind, Miss Maudie Bell clapped. "I didn't know I'd be getting a show!"

Ethan hoped that didn't mean he'd just upped his chances of being asked for by name for future incidents. Tipping his head to Miss Maudie Bell in a nod, he led the horse down her drive and along the county road to his proper home a quarter mile away. It was pretty country out here, with all the rolling, tree-studded hills. So different from the wide-open expanses of Texas. Once everything greened up in the spring, it would be quite the view. Maybe he'd look for property out this way, once he was settled and in the market to buy instead of rent.

He noted that wherever Houdini had escaped from this time, it wasn't the same patch of fence as before, though the patch job Chester had done wasn't going to hold for any real length of time. The fence needed serious work, period. The barn and house were in better shape. Both worn around the edges and in need of fresh paint and some touch ups, they seemed to be solid. Still, the place was riddled with signs of neglect.

Turning Houdini loose in the paddock by the barn, Ethan trudged up the porch steps and knocked on the door. Chester took a long time to open it, and when he did, Ethan immediately noticed the slow, pained movements.

"Mr. Harkin, do you know why I'm here?"

He sighed. "Expect that woman down the road's got it into her head to complain again."

"Your horse got out again. And this time it wasn't just a matter of public safety. He destroyed Mrs. Ramsey's roses. She wants to press charges."

Chester blustered. "They're just flowers."

"They were extremely rare roses she grew from clippings her mother gave her."

Something flickered in the old man's gaze. Regret? "I didn't intend that." Absently, the old man rubbed at the knuckles of one hand. Each joint was swollen, the unseasonable cold, no doubt, causing a pretty vicious flare of his arthritis.

Ethan didn't want to charge the guy. "I know you haven't intended any of this, but the fact of the matter is, your fence needs serious repair. So, here's how this is gonna work. You're going to pay to replace Mrs. Ramsey's roses."

"You just said they were rare."

"I expect Cam Crawford down at the nursery can help us track some down. Meanwhile, I'm going to come out on Saturday and help you fix your fence so it'll keep your horses in."

"You'll do what?"

"Fixing fences properly takes two sets of hands. I don't see another one hanging around here, so I'll do it in the name of keeping the community and your animals safe."

The radio at his shoulder crackled. "Chief, we've got a robbery in progress at the salvage store."

"Acknowledged. I'm en route." Ethan looked back at Chester. "I'll be here Saturday. You'd best be ready to work. And keep your horses up in the meantime."

CHAPTER 4

The Mudcat Tavern was packed. It always was when Clay Turner performed. Every unattached female in Wishful under the age of fifty seemed to be crammed into the bar. Miranda cast a glance at the stage, where Clay was already wowing the crowd with a David Nail cover. He was a total heartthrob with that gorgeous voice, that twenty-four carat smile, and those bedroom eyes. They'd had a helluva good time dating back in high school. It was just too damned bad they hadn't had any real chemistry. Still, he put on a great show, so she'd come out tonight to meet Norah and Cam for dinner.

She found them bent head-to-head, his light to her dark, at one of the high-top tables toward the back. With eyes only for each other, they didn't even seem to notice all the patrons around them. The romantic heart Miranda pretended she didn't have turned over at the sight. They were so good together. She couldn't be happier that they'd found each other, but she still felt a pang of envy. It'd been forever since she'd been in a real relationship. Not since she'd left Chicago. She didn't actually miss Stephen—after the things he'd said, she was still inclined to plant a foot up his ass —but she missed having someone to hang out and share her day with.

That's what friends are for. She plastered on a smile. "Hey lovebirds."

Cam slid off his stool and slung an arm around her shoulders, pulling her in for a squeeze. "Hey there. Got you a beer, and there's an order in for chili cheese fries."

"Aww, you love me." Slipping an arm around his waist, Miranda squeezed back.

"You are my favorite cousin."

"Because I introduced you to the love of your life?" She winked at Norah, who still sported a sappy grin.

"Well, you were already my favorite, but that pretty much sealed the deal."

At only three months apart, she and Cam had been more like siblings than cousins growing up. Cam had a tendency to look out for her just like her actual brother, but unlike Mitch, he managed to do it without trying to run her life. It was a gift she didn't overlook.

Sliding onto a stool, she angled to where she could see the stage and took a swallow of Yuengling. "So, what has Wishful's power couple been up to this week?"

"I am on the hunt for rare roses for our new police chief," Cam said.

"Roses? Why?" Ethan hadn't struck Miranda as the type who'd be into gardening. Gardening took time, and best as she could tell, he was as much a workaholic as she was.

"Something to do with a case, apparently. He said a man's life was prospectively at stake."

"His or someone else's?" Miranda asked.

"Chester Harkin's, apparently. He told me to expect Chester to pick them up whenever they came in."

The level of relief she felt that it wasn't Ethan himself trying to get into some woman's good graces left her feeling ridiculous. It wasn't like they had a Thing.

"Pretty sure he's not seeing anybody." Norah's lips curved in a knowing smirk. "I'm sure we'd have heard about it if he were. He's a pretty hot topic of conversation."

Miranda thought of his poor, abused, yet still magnificent ass. "He's pretty hot, period." But that wasn't the appeal. Or at least, not all of it. Deciding to throw caution to the wind—Norah would end up discussing this with Cam through spousal privilege or whatever—she fixed her gaze on her cousin. "You were part of the hiring committee. What do you know about him?"

"And why would you be asking, Cuz? Idle curiosity?"

"A bit more than idle, considering I had my hands on his ass last weekend. Sadly, it was in my ED rather than more interesting circumstances."

Cam covered his ears. "I don't want to hear about wherever your brain is going. You're my cousin."

"Hey, if I can get over the fact that you're sleeping with my best friend, you can get over the fact that I am a woman with needs."

He went pale.

Shaking her head in pity, Norah leaned over to kiss him. "Go get me another cider from the bar and see if Adele will put in an order for some nachos, while you're there."

"You'll be done with this conversation when I get back?" he asked, a hopeful expression on his face.

"Get gone, Leonidas."

Miranda couldn't decide whether to be amused or annoyed at how fast he booked it away from their table. "Okay, what do you know?"

"That you two were setting off sparks at the diner when you ran into him last week."

"Good to know, but not what I was asking. The man's been a closed book since he got here three months ago. The gossip train is failing me on this one."

"He's ex-military. Army, I think."

Miranda waved a hand. "Yeah, yeah, I already know that. Army. College on GI Bill. Then the last decade with the Marshals. BFFs with Clay from college, which is why he wanted to come here in the first place. Tell me something I *don't* know."

Norah laughed. "It sounds like you may be better informed than I am."

"Y'all hired him based on that alone?"

"Well, that would've been plenty—his record is nothing short of impressive—but when Judd stepped down as Interim Chief, he threw his support fully behind Ethan. He was instrumental in rescuing Autumn when she was kidnapped last fall. It says a lot about a man that he'd throw himself into pursuit of a fugitive, when he wasn't even part of the department."

So *that* was why he'd been driving when Judd brought Autumn in last fall. He'd been a stranger, albeit one whose gaze packed a helluva punch, and her attention had been focused on her patient. She'd put him out of her mind until running into him at the diner.

"From what I've seen, he's a man of great integrity."

"That sounds like the voice of observation."

"Nothing I can talk about." He was a man who'd no doubt seen some serious shit, between his military service and his time with the Marshals. But the experiences hadn't led him to dehumanize people. If anything, he'd gone the extra mile to try to make a connection with Rene Forbes. It was *that* more than anything else that had Miranda intrigued. Because it made him Stephen's polar opposite.

"Been a long time since I've seen you interested in anybody."

"Been a long time since I was."

Norah propped her chin in her hands. "So, what are you gonna do about it?"

"Nothing for the moment. He's a patient."

"Oh, please. If you cut out everybody you've ever treated, you'd never have anyone to date."

A fact Miranda was more than a little aware of. She tipped back her beer. "He won't always be a patient. Once he's healed up, I'm in the clear. For what, I have no idea. I don't have time for anything serious, but I'm ready to open up my options."

Cam returned with Norah's cider.

"I'll drink to that," she said.

"To what?" he asked.

His wife pressed a smacking kiss to his cheek. "Nothing you want to hear about, baby."

Laughing, Miranda clinked her bottle to Norah's.

"So, this teenage kid approaches Delia Watson while she's browsing and asks if he can help her. According to Miss Delia, she recognized he was 'trying to case her,'" Ethan emphasized with air quotes, "and told him in no uncertain terms, 'No you may not.' So, she goes on to browse. A little while later, somebody starts shrieking 'Stop him! He's got my wallet!' Some quick-thinking employee locks the front door so nobody can leave, and the entire store gets in on this whole game of chase, trying to stop the thief."

"Even though there are laws about locking the doors during business hours," Judd observed.

"That's what I said. Anyway, Miss Delia and Miss Betty go on and keep browsing, as this whole insanity takes a while, right? And then she sees him out of the corner of her eye coming up her aisle. She turns on him, points her finger like a gun and says, 'Stop right there!' And he actually *does* for long enough for Miss Betty to whack him with her purse. He tries to run, but Miss Delia heads him off, until Liam Montgomery actually takes him down and holds him until Clint and I can arrive."

Judd snickered. "Trust the Casserole Patrol to be all up in the middle of that."

"Oh, there's more. So, I'm taking everybody's statement and as she's telling me about Liam doing the take down, Miss Delia insists, 'Well, I could've taken him.' And then Miss Betty pipes up, 'I lost my chance! I had a taser in my purse!'"

Judd had to grab onto the edge of the desk to keep from sliding to the floor, he was laughing so hard. "Man, I love my job as investigator with the Sheriff's Department, but I do miss those crazy calls. I'm surprised Miss Maudie Bell wasn't with them."

"I'd just come from her, actually. She's on the warpath against Chester Harkin and his horses. And I don't blame her. Her roses got trampled. I'm making him replace them."

"Not gonna do much good unless he gets that fence finally repaired."

"Yeah, I'm helping him do that, too, on Saturday."

Judd angled his head. "Look at you getting all into small-town policing. Sounds like you're settling in just fine."

"I'm sure as hell trying. You working on anything interesting right now? I'm living vicariously through you."

"Got a drug ring I'm trying to bust."

"Meth?"

"Prescription stuff. There's been a string of robberies at pharmacies and doctor's offices all around Lawley over the past six months. Spread out, but same MO every time. Gloves, mask. After hours. Guy's fast. He's in and out before police can respond to stop him, and he knows what he's looking for."

"Any connection to the robbery at the pharmacy here from year before last?"

"Not as far as we can tell. Those guys were put away."

"Is it just in Lawley or do you suspect something broader?"

"The robberies seem localized, but there's been some evidence of sales around the county. If you bring anybody in on drugs that aren't prescribed to them, I wanna know about it."

"I can do that. I'll have Rowan go back through the DUIs we've brought in during that span and see if she can't find out who was on something other than alcohol and whether they had a valid prescription."

"I appreciate it. How's she working out for you? She been able to shake the city off enough to settle into small-town policing?"

Another Texas transplant, Rowan Beale was the only member of Wishful PD newer than Ethan himself. The great niece of Robert Curry, the long-time Chief who'd stepped down after a heart attack last fall, she'd blown the door wide on corruption inside her home department in Houston and wanted a change. She'd moved to Wishful to be closer to her great uncle, and to escape the fallout from that scandal.

"She's a good officer. Solid. Steady. Eager to prove herself. She's settled in well, and the others seem to be good with her."

"I expect the fact that she's dating Nash Brewer helps with that."

Yeah, it hadn't hurt that one of their reserve officers was vouching for her. "You're not wrong. So, how's married life treating you?"

Judd's expression softened. "Better than I could ever have imagined. I owe a great part of that to you."

"You'd have found Autumn without me."

"I found her quicker with you. I know I've said it before, and I'll say it again. Thank you. You ever need an assist for anything, you let me know. I'm there."

"God willing, I won't ever have to call in that marker, but I certainly appreciate the offer."

A tap sounded on Ethan's office door, and Autumn poked her head in. "Sorry I'm late. The book was really cooking."

Judd hauled her in for a thorough kiss. "Hey, Firefly. Good day?"

Autumn sighed. "Good day. Better now." She tipped her head to her husband's chest.

They made a picture of marital contentment that had Ethan's gut twisting. Had he and Becca ever been that easy together, even at the beginning? It had been so damned long and there'd been so much contention at the end, he couldn't remember.

Autumn straightened. "Y'all ready to head out? I'm starved."

Ethan checked his watch. "Clay ought to be just starting his second set by the time we get there."

They caravanned up to The Mudcat. The parking lot was so full, they had to park down the block and walk a bit. In the seemingly wall-to-wall people, Ethan expected to be able to slip in unnoticed, but from his position on the stage, Clay was apparently watching out.

As he wrapped an old Sammy Kershaw number, he called out. "There's my brother from another mother. Ethan, get your ass up here and play one with me."

All eyes turned to him. He pointed to his duty belt and shook his head. "Still on duty, bro."

Clay sighed, hamming it up for the crowd, who'd all turned to gape at Ethan, but Ethan recognized the legitimate disappointment in his friend's face. "Fine, fine. How 'bout some Clapton, y'all?" It shocked Ethan not at all when he immediately launched into "I Shot The Sheriff."

With an eye roll, Ethan lifted both middle fingers in a salute that had Clay grinning. He was really gonna have to break this streak soon. Making his way over to the table Judd and Autumn had managed to snag, Ethan's gaze zeroed in on a familiar blonde head that had his mood shifting. Miranda was out of the lab coat, perched on a high stool, in jeans and a gray sweater that clung in all the right places.

"So that's the way the wind blows," Autumn drawled, as he sat and tried not to wince at the pull of stitches. "I totally called it at the ER last fall."

Ethan swung his head around to face her. "Huh?"

Laughing, Judd said, "Don't even try to hide. She has a sixth sense about these things. She's won more pools down at Dinner Belles than anybody else in town."

"Pools about what?"

"Who's gonna end up with who," she explained.

"Y'all bet on that?"

"Honey, we bet on everything. Not a lot going on in our sleepy little town, in case you hadn't noticed. Don't know if they've started one up on you yet."

"You can always call Omar and get a head start on that," Judd pointed out.

"I just might."

Recognizing the futility of protest, Ethan said nothing, glancing back at Miranda. She looked his way and lifted a hand in a quick wave. He couldn't even stop the curve of his lips. What was it about this woman that pulled him?

"You should go talk to her," Judd said.

Ethan didn't need to start anything. He needed to focus on the job.

"She's single," Autumn added in a sing-song voice.

Clay's words from last week echoed through his head. *You need to get back out there.*

What the hell? It can't hurt to test the waters. "Order me a Coke, will you?" Ethan slid off the stool and headed across the bar. "Cam, Norah, Doc." He nodded at each of them in turn, eyes lingering on Miranda.

"Unlike you, I'm off-duty. I think you can call me Miranda." Her lips curved in an inviting smile.

"Fair enough." Ethan managed to shift his attention to her cousin. "Cam, are you having any luck tracking down those roses for me?"

"Got a couple leads. Should know something by the end of the week. They're pretty rare, so gonna be pricy."

"Still cheaper than the fines Chester keeps racking up, and more likely to keep the peace with his neighbor. Anyway, that's not actually why I came over here." He swung his gaze back to his quarry. "Miranda, you want to dance?"

"I'd love to dance, but as your doctor, I don't know if that's such a good idea, what with the stitches. I did tell you no exertion."

"Then I guess it'll have to be a slow one." He didn't know what had gotten into him, but flirting with the pretty doctor was more fun than he'd had in ages.

"Clay doesn't tend toward the slow," she observed.

Turning toward the stage, Ethan caught Clay's eye and shot him the hand signal they'd developed as wingmen back in college. *Help a brother out.* Clay winked, wrapped the Clapton, and launched into the intro for a slow Chris Young cover.

Ethan turned back to Miranda and held out a hand. "Problem solved."

Her smile turned feline, and his blood leapt as she placed her hand in his. "Let's see what you've got, Cowboy."

CHAPTER 5

*A*s Ethan led her through the crowd to the tiny patch of dance floor not already packed with Clay's fangirls, Miranda felt all the eyes in the room fall to them. She wondered if Ethan knew what he'd done by asking her to dance here, now, with most of Wishful's single gals present to see. His intention might have been a simple dance, but he was effectively declaring his interest in the most public fashion possible. Since it was exactly what she wanted, she wasn't going to complain.

He pulled her into his arms with an easy twirl that said he'd done this many times before. She bumped up against him and was reminded of that day in the diner. She'd thought way too much about the feel of his hands on her since then. As they curved around her waist and her hand, she knew that wasn't going to change anytime soon. He had good, strong hands.

"Sorry about the belt."

Miranda tipped her head back. At 5'10" it was exceptionally rare for her to have to look up at a guy. Ethan had a good five inches on her. She loved that. "Small-town cops are never really off duty."

Those gray eyes seemed warmer under the lights of the dance floor. "Neither are small-town doctors."

"True enough. There tend to be a lot of blurred lines." She felt pretty good about those hazy boundaries just now, pressed close enough she could feel the heat of him. It started a hum in her blood she hadn't experienced in far too long. She wanted to get to know this man. "So, *are* you gonna play with Clay?"

Ethan gave a half laugh. "Is he looping you in on this campaign, too?"

"There's a campaign?"

"We had a duo back in college. Did pretty well on the music scene in Austin. He wanted Nashville. I... didn't."

"Nashville? Y'all were that good?" She couldn't quite reconcile the serious cop with country music star.

"We could've been. But it was a long time ago."

She wondered what he'd been like back then. "You don't feel the pull to play?"

"Sure. But I'm still establishing my reputation in this town. I need people to respect the badge."

"Blurred lines, Chief. Just because you can perform isn't going to make people respect your authority any less. And I, for one, am now insanely curious what you'd sound like."

The smile hit his eyes first and slowly curved his mouth, and all she could think was *Damn.*

"Maybe you'll find out one of these nights."

As the song ended and Clay swung into something more upbeat, Ethan gave her a twirl and started a two-step. That was just fine with Miranda. She wasn't in any hurry to sit back down. Two dances turned into three, three to five. Ethan Greer was a hella good dancer. If she had some concerns about his stitches, well, it wasn't like she couldn't fix them. By the time they stopped to hydrate, Cam and Norah had pushed the table together with Autumn and Judd's. The chili cheese fries were almost all gone, and she didn't even care. When was the last time she'd had this much fun?

Judd nudged a glass in Ethan's direction. "You got some moves there, Chief."

"A few. Got some better ones when I don't have a hole in my ass." He tipped the glass back and drained it.

Miranda guzzled a glass of water instead of the rest of her beer. "You realize you're never going to live that down, right?"

He heaved a beleaguered sigh. "I have resigned myself. Dave Lautner is banned from any more classes I'm teaching, that's for damned sure. I'm surprised your admin didn't give you a blow-by-blow of how it all went down."

"Delaney?"

Ethan nodded. "Only woman in the class. She's a damned good archer for an alleged newbie. Girl's got impressively steady hands."

"Alleged?" Cam asked.

"She said she'd never shot a bow before, but her form was too good. I figure she was keeping prior experience quiet so as not to threaten the men. Or maybe it was a bid at flirtation." He shrugged. "I was setting her up for another go when the idiot shot me."

Fake inexperience so the big, strong man will get up close and position you properly? Classic tactic and one Miranda might have been tempted to use herself in a similar situation. But she didn't see Delaney going for a guy ten years her senior. "Delaney never said a word. She's not one for gossiping." Lord knew, she'd been too often the victim of it herself.

"Then she's a rarity in this town. Far as I can tell, it's the professional sport around here."

Autumn laughed. "You aren't wrong."

Ethan glanced at the stage then back to Miranda. "One more dance before he finishes his set?"

Chili cheese fries be damned. "Love to."

"I think we're about to call it a night," Cam announced.

"Early meetings tomorrow," Norah added.

Miranda didn't want to think about the price she'd be paying tomorrow morning. Right now, she just wanted to spend some more time with this interesting, attractive man. Preferably with his hands on her. "See y'all later."

"C'mon, Legs." Ethan grabbed her hand.

Norah shouldered her purse and made Eyebrows in their direction, clearly demanding details later. Miranda just smiled and followed Ethan back to the dance floor. Clay transitioned into another slow song, one that had been a favorite of hers back in high school.

"He's pulling out old school stuff tonight," she observed. "Slow's not usually his speed these days."

"That's because I was the balladeer of the two of us."

Now she *really* wanted to see him with a guitar in his hands. "Yeah? You're not doing anything to dim my curiosity."

"A healthy curiosity is a good thing, to my way of thinking."

"Only if you're planning to satisfy it."

His only response was that slow, molasses smile. The one that said he knew plenty about how to satisfy a woman. The idea of it sparked off needs she'd too long denied. Well, they'd just see who got satisfied, wouldn't they?

Game on, Cowboy.

"So, what do you usually do when you're not working, Doc? How do you relax? Are you a go out with friends or stay in at home sort of woman?"

"There's a time and place for both. When I've had a really hard week, and I'm too tired to face another soul, I like to order Chinese and binge watch old westerns."

Ethan's eyes brightened. "You like old westerns?"

"Love 'em. My granddaddy hooked me when I was little. Spent most of my childhood sitting with him in his big old recliner, watching *Gunsmoke*. It was how the family dealt with my horse-crazy phase. He died when I was in high school, but I like to watch the reruns, still. They remind me of him."

"You're gorgeous, smart, compassionate, and you're a *Gunsmoke* fan," he said in wonder. "Doc, you may be the perfect woman."

Miranda laughed. "I guess you could say my fascination with the U.S. Marshals started early."

Another beat of attraction pulsed between them, and this time Miranda knew she wasn't mistaken.

"Was Matt Dillon on *Gunsmoke* what got you interested in being a Marshal?"

"No."

When he said nothing else, Miranda lifted a brow. "That's it? Just 'No'?"

His lips curved in amusement at her frustration. "Maybe I'll tell you the whole story one of these days."

Did he always play this hard to get?

When the song ended and Clay took his break, they returned to their table, scooping up the drinks that had been delivered in their absence.

Determined to be properly sociable, Miranda eyed Autumn's ginger ale. "How are you feeling?"

She laid a hand over the barely perceptible swell of her belly. "Good. The morning sickness is finally past."

Ethan blinked. "You're pregnant?"

Beaming, Judd wrapped an arm around his wife. "We are. Thirteen weeks."

"Congratulations!"

Miranda liked the quick hug Ethan gave Autumn and the hearty handshake to Judd. His obvious pleasure for the couple told her he'd gotten close to them since he'd moved here, that they hadn't just been a case for him.

"This calls for celebration. What can you have?"

Autumn laughed. "Pretty much anything but alcohol."

"Better question: What do you want?"

"I can't seem to get enough cheese fries."

"Then cheese fries the lady shall have. Judd?"

"You can buy me a celebratory beer when you're truly off duty and can drink one with me."

"Fair enough." Ethan flagged down a waitress and put in the order. Turning back to Miranda, he asked, "Do you know what's going on medically with everybody in this town?"

She shrugged. "That's small-town medicine."

"How do you deal with the ethics of it? Of treating people you know and have relationships with?"

"As I said before, there are a lot of blurred lines. I wouldn't do major surgery on anyone I was really close to, but it's hardly a violation to treat my family for bronchitis or whatever the latest viral infection is. If I didn't treat the people I know, I wouldn't have any patients."

"So, if I let somebody else remove my stitches, I could ask you out?"

Delighted, Miranda grinned. "I can give you a good referral for a follow up."

Judd hooted. "Oh, Mitch is gonna love this."

Miranda pointed at him. "No. You are not siccing my brother on me *or* Ethan. This is not fodder for discussion at Poker Night."

"Everything's fodder for discussion at Poker Night."

Miranda rolled her eyes. *Men.* She turned to Ethan, intending to get his opinion, but realized his attention had strayed to something across the bar. She shifted to see what he was looking at—and saw Harley Forbes making his way through the room.

As CONVERSATION CONTINUED at their table, Ethan shifted in his seat for a better view of Forbes. Resentment bubbled low in his gut. He didn't want to waste his attention on this low-life. But this was the job, and he was, technically, still on duty. In truth, he'd been damned lucky to get this long a stretch to flirt with Miranda without interruption.

Was Forbes already drunk? Analyzing his gait, Ethan didn't think the man had come in already lit. He didn't make waves as he headed for the bar, though the usual cloud of belligerence hovered around him. People automatically fell back, as if sensing impending trouble. Ethan almost, *almost* wished he'd get into it with somebody. Just go ahead and do something, *anything* he could be hauled in on. But that meant Ethan would have to deal with it, and he wasn't ready to call it a night with Miranda yet. Another bar brawl wouldn't be enough to hold him for long. Not the kind of hold they needed to get Rene out of that house. He didn't have the same faith in that eventuality that Miranda did. Experience had taught him that people seldom changed, and that meant Harley Forbes was likely to keep beating on his wife, and she'd keep making excuses for him.

Ethan did his best to plug back into the conversation. By the time the appetizers were eaten and another round of drinks were bought—mostly soft drinks and water—Clay was back up on the stage and Forbes was nursing his second beer. Ethan and Miranda made their way back to the dance floor. It was a two-birds, one-stone situation, as he got to touch her and was in a better position to observe his quarry. But Forbes, for once, was behaving like a model citizen. Ethan scowled.

"Sucks having your hands tied, doesn't it?" Miranda observed

Realizing he'd been all but ignoring her, he shook his head. "I'm sorry."

The flirtatious smile she'd been wearing most of the night slid into something far more serious. "No, don't apologize. He's trouble. You know it. I know it."

That was the damned truth. "You heard any more from Rene?"

"No. She's not due in for a follow-up for a few weeks."

"You think she'll come?"

"If for no other reason than to get her cast off, yeah. I'm just hoping she doesn't need medical attention for something else before that. After how everything went down last week, I don't know if she'll come to me." The thought clearly troubled her.

"You did what you thought was right."

"I pushed too hard. It's such a fine line to walk, and I may have strayed too far across it."

"Would you have been able to live with yourself if you hadn't tried?"

Miranda considered that. "No. Believing people can be saved is how I'm wired."

"Then you did what you had to do." Much as he didn't share her optimism, he appreciated her conviction.

At the bar, Forbes finished off his beer and shoved back. Ethan tensed, watching him walk toward the door. He wasn't staggering, wasn't weaving, but something about the whole situation had Ethan's gut twanging. He wanted to follow the guy.

Miranda squeezed his shoulder. "Go."

"What?"

"You want to tail him, tail him. You do what you've gotta do."

Surprised, he searched her face, looking for the resignation or irritation he'd grown so accustomed to in Becca. All he found was understanding. He filed that away to think about later. "You are one helluva woman, Miranda Campbell."

She shot him a saucy grin that had dimples winking in her cheeks. Damn, if he didn't have a soft spot for dimples. "You're a helluva dancer."

"I had a great time tonight."

"So did I."

"I meant what I said. I want to take you out for real." Nobody was more surprised about that than Ethan himself.

Smoothing her hands along his shoulders and down his arms, Miranda stepped back and lifted her hazel eyes to his. "Then I expect, Mr. Ex-Marshal, you've got the skills to track me down later."

That was a pursuit he'd look forward to. "I expect I do." He wanted to kiss her. To lean right on in and take that slightly bottom-heavy mouth with his. But now wasn't the time or place. When he kissed her the first time, he wanted to linger over it, not rush out the door after a sleazeball. So instead, he squeezed her hand and let her go. "Night, Legs."

"Night, Cowboy."

Forbes had already climbed into his truck by the time Ethan made it outside. He waited in the shadows until the man had pulled out of the lot, watching for reckless driving or other signs of DUI. Nothing. He bolted for his patrol car and followed behind, far enough back that he didn't think Forbes would notice him. Either the man had caught on to the tail or he was on his best behavior. He didn't so much as blow a stop sign on the way back to his trailer. Forbes parked by the little rusted out Ford Escort and went inside.

Ethan drove on by, then doubled back, parking just out of sight with his lights off so he could watch the sagging single-wide. The outside light turned off and a few more interior lights came on. Despite the frigid temperatures, Ethan rolled the window down so he could listen. But there were no screams, no sounds of argument. All was annoyingly quiet.

As he sat in the cold, his ass began to ache. The over-the-counter painkillers he'd taken had long since worn off, and he no longer had the distraction of Miranda—those legs that went on for days, that smile that woke up a part of him he'd thought dead and buried. Ethan wanted to see more of that smile, wanted to make her laugh. He loved her laugh. It was big and bawdy and unapologetic. Nothing about Miranda Campbell was small or repentant. He liked that about her, liked how she could go toe-to-toe with him. And he liked the surprise that she didn't seem at all put out when he'd had to leave for the job. After years of festering resentment from his ex-wife, the idea that a woman could understand that sometimes the job had to come first was more than a little shocking. Of course, they hadn't even been on a formal date, let alone in any kind of relationship. She didn't have expectations of him. But it looked like he was gonna get a chance to find out if that acceptance would extend beyond the night. Neither of them had been subtle about their interest, and at the earliest opportunity, Ethan had every intention of following up on that connection.

After an hour, the lights went off in the trailer. Apparently, bedtime in the Forbes household. Nothing was going to happen tonight and, it seemed, he'd cut his evening with Miranda short for no reason. As he cranked the cruiser, Ethan wondered if he'd made the right call. Was he just looking for something to fill the time because he was having some trouble adjusting to small town life? He'd gotten so used to chasing fugitives, enforcing federal laws. This whole scene of small-town policing was a switch, a decision he'd made after losing his wife and nearly his life because of the job. Maybe this focus on the situation with Forbes was out of line.

But Ethan knew, deep down in his gut, that Harley Forbes was a volatile son of a bitch who abused his wife. This kind of shit was a cancer in a small town like Wishful. It wasn't a matter of if something was going to happen, it was when. God willing, Ethan would be able to nip it in the bud before it turned into something for the six o'clock news.

CHAPTER 6

"I heard *somebody* was cutting a rug at The Mudcat last night with our Chief of Police." Shelby Abbott, Miranda's office manager, peered over her bright green cheaters, brows raised in expectation.

"This has nothing to do with our staff meeting," Miranda told her. The staff meeting she was beginning to wish she'd cancelled. After the late night, her ass was dragging.

"Girl, we are your staff, this is a meeting, and we want details," Keisha announced.

"There are no details. We danced. That was it. And then he had to leave to go take care of police business." She'd tossed and turned for quite a while once she'd gotten home, wondering if anything had happened with Harley. She'd wondered, too, if Ethan was going to follow through on his promise to ask her out or if that had just been flirtation of the moment.

"I heard up at The Grind that he couldn't take his eyes off you," Delaney teased.

Miranda gave fleeting thought to throwing her under the bus by mentioning the alleged flirtation at the bowhunter safety class, but the girl had brought coffee for the entire staff this morning, including the triple shot espresso that was the only thing keeping Miranda on her feet just now, so she'd earned clemency. Buying herself some time, Miranda tipped the coffee back and took a long swallow. Not as good as the sex she wasn't having, but definitely on up the list of the best things in life. Who decided businesses were supposed to be open in the mornings anyway?

"Since when is my love life up for discussion?"

"Uh, since you finally show signs of getting one," Shelby pointed out.

Well hell. She'd stepped right into that one. "One night of dancing does not a love life make." Never mind the fact that Ethan was the first guy she'd been legitimately interested in since she moved home.

"You're really not gonna give us *anything?*" Keisha asked.

"I am not because there's nothing to give. Now where are we on strep tests?"

Miranda managed to wrangle her nosy staff back on task long enough to get them through the meeting. Then the doors opened, and the initial flood of patients kept them all hopping. Nobody had time to think about Miranda's love life or lack thereof after that.

Her mood took a distinct nosedive when she checked the next chart to find Ralph Slocombe waiting for her. As a result of an on-the-job accident at one of the now-defunct factories several years back, he had a problem with chronic pain. It was an all too familiar problem, one that was a recipe for opiate abuse. At one time, it had been a lot easier for patients to doctor shop, going from physician to physician and getting separate prescriptions for various narcotics meant to manage pain. Now that the state had implemented an online tracking protocol, identifying drug seekers was a lot easier. The downside was that they were a lot harder to handle.

Before she even went into the room, she pulled up the records. He was ten days out from when his current prescription ought to be finished. Maybe she'd luck out and he was here for something else. Blowing out a breath, Miranda braced herself for a fight and went inside.

"Mr. Slocombe, what brings you in today?"

The whip thin man shifted on the exam table. "It's my back again, Dr. Campbell. It's been giving me fits. Lots of spasms. It's been hurting me so bad, I cain't hardly sleep."

"Have you done anything to aggravate the injury?"

"Just normal livin'. You know it ain't been right since the accident."

For just a moment, Miranda wished she were still in Chicago. At least there, she could point him to alternative means of managing pain. But small-town Mississippi didn't lend itself to acupuncture or medical marijuana. She knew without even suggesting it that Ralph couldn't afford the rates the Babylon Spa charged for massage, and she wasn't sure it would help anyway. "Did you try the muscle relaxers I prescribed you a couple months ago?"

"I'm out. They didn't do a thing to touch the pain. Only thing even made a dent was the Loritab. I came to see about getting more."

"I cannot legally prescribe you more opiates for another ten days. The original prescription I wrote you should have lasted that long."

"It wasn't a strong enough dosage. I been hurting, Doc." The truth of that lay in the glimmer of tears gathered at the corners of his faded blue eyes.

Miranda's heart twisted. "I'm sorrier than I can say about that, Mr. Slocombe, but my hands are tied. We can try some other things to get you through, but no one will be able to prescribe you more narcotics for ten more days."

He exploded off the table. Miranda shot across the room on her stool hard enough to slam into the counter.

"You don't care! None of you." His fists bunched, and he took a step toward her, then blanched and sagged back against the exam table.

"Mr. Slocombe, you need to calm down." Despite the fact that her heart was thundering, Miranda kept her voice calm and matter of fact as she approached him. "Let me help you back up."

He jerked his shoulder out of her touch and shoved himself back onto the exam table. "Ain't nobody out there cares about somebody like me. I didn't do nothing to deserve this. I did my job, never caused trouble. Got hurt. And then the factory went and moved to Mexico. How's a man supposed to survive after that?"

The door opened without preamble and Keisha stuck her head in, Delaney right behind. "Everything okay in here?"

Miranda held up a hand so they'd stay where they were. "Everything's fine. Mr. Slocombe is just a little upset. Give us a few minutes, okay?"

Keisha looked like she wanted to argue. "We'll be right outside if you need anything." She shut the door.

Ralph's shoulders slumped, and he dropped his head into his hands. "I'm sorry. I'm so sorry. The pain about drives me out of my mind."

"I understand." Miranda pulled the stool back and sat down. "Let's talk about what we can do to get you through the next week and a half."

He was calmer by the time he left, and Miranda was already wishing for a cupcake from Sweet Magnolias to take the edge off. She hated when she couldn't help people. The morning continued to roll, with patient after patient, mostly keeping her too busy to dwell on Ralph Slocombe or anything else.

Because her throat was beginning to ache on top of the exhaustion, as soon as Miranda had a moment to breathe, she gave herself a strep test and left it to process as she moved on to the next patient on her list. As she was escorting Winnie Tolleson back for her regular blood work, Ethan strode through the door. He was in full cop mode this morning, large-and-in-charge in the uniform that had never looked quite so good to her. His eyes warmed at the sight of her.

A burst of pleasure and nerves wiped away the suck of the morning and had Miranda waving Delaney over. "Can you go ahead and get Mrs. Tolleson settled in the back for her blood draw?"

Catching sight of Ethan in the waiting room, thumbs hooked in his duty belt, Delaney hesitated. What was that about? General nerves around cops? With her history, Miranda couldn't blame her for that, but Ethan wasn't a part of that past. Maybe she did have a thing for him, too.

"Delaney?"

The girl blinked, shaking her head in apology and offering a smile. "Sure thing, Dr. Campbell." Tucking a hand beneath the elderly woman's arm, she began the slow trek down the hall. "Miss Winnie, how have you been doing these last couple of weeks?"

Assured her patient was taken care of for the moment, she adopted a casual stance. "Morning, Chief. What can we do for you?"

He inclined his head in that Old West nod she found so appealing. "Doc. Had some business to tend to, so thought I'd drop by."

Was that cross speak? Was she the business or had something happened last night? "Oh? Did our mutual friend have problems getting home?"

"No. Ended up being quiet."

Quiet was good, she supposed, in a no-news-is-good-news kind of way. Which meant he had to be here for her. Miranda relaxed.

From behind the counter, the phone rang. "Dr. Campbell's office, hold please." Obviously, Shelby wasn't planning on missing a thing.

Miranda tipped her head toward the hall. "You want to come back?" At least the break room would provide a modicum of privacy.

"Can't stay, and you're clearly busy. I just wanted to see if you were free for dinner tonight."

Painfully aware of all the ears—staff and patient—suddenly tuned in to her answer, Miranda grimaced. "I'm on at the ED tonight."

His brows drew down in confusion. "Thought you already did your rotation this month."

"I did." She resisted the urge to look down at his ass. "But I picked up this shift to help out one of the other doctors in town. What about Friday night?"

"Can't. I'm on duty again. Don't want to get called out in the middle of anything."

Nothing in his tone was remotely salacious, but Miranda couldn't help imagining the possibilities of what "anything" could mean. She liked all of them. "Saturday?"

"Saturday I can do. I've got a thing for a fair chunk of the day, but I'll be free in time for dinner."

"Dinner then," she agreed.

He flashed that slow, molasses smile. "It's a date."

A date. A real, honest-to-God date, with an interesting, attractive man. This new year was starting to look up. "We should probably swap numbers so we can sort out the details without an audience."

The smile turned faintly sheepish as he glanced around the waiting room and caught everybody staring. "I've got yours."

Oh right. From the report he'd taken about the vandalism of her Jeep.

He pulled out his phone and tapped a few buttons. From inside the pocket of her lab coat, her own phone vibrated.

"There, now you've got mine."

For some reason, the idea of it made her giddy as a teenage girl. "Saturday, then."

"Saturday. Later, Doc." With one last look in her direction—he was totally checking out her legs—Ethan turned on heel and left.

The moment the door shut behind him, the entire office crooned, "Oooooooo," like a bunch of middle schoolers.

"Oh, shut up and get back to work," Miranda groused. But she couldn't hold back her own grin as she grabbed the next chart and headed down the hall. She detoured to the lab to check on her strep test.

Positive.

Miranda wanted to thunk her head against the lab counter. She did not have time for this shit. A Rocephrin shot should knock it out. Sticking her head out in the hall, she looked for her nurse. But Keisha was back with Winnie Tolleson. Shelby was on the phone. That left Delaney. She could walk the girl through a shot.

"Delaney."

"What do you need?"

Anxiety skittered over the girl's face as Miranda shut the door. "I need you to give me a shot."

"You what now?"

"I just tested positive for strep and there is no way in hell I'm missing that date. I need an antibiotic shot, and I can't very well give myself one in my own ass. You are the only one with free hands at the moment. Don't worry, I can walk you through it." Moving quickly, she pulled out the necessary supplies and prepped the syringe.

"Are you sure?"

"It's just a shot." Stripping off her lab coat, Miranda unzipped her pants and tugged down so her hip was exposed. "Go ahead and swab it with an alcohol wipe."

Hesitating only a moment, Delaney did as asked. Miranda handed her the syringe. "It's going in the meaty part of the hip."

Delaney eyed the expanse of skin and cringed. "I don't want to hurt you."

"You won't." And if she did, well, small price to pay not to be knocked on her ass by strep for the next week.

Miranda coached her through the procedure, impressed when she barely felt a prick. "Now, slowly press the plunger in."

Delaney did as she was told, delivering the antibiotics with minimal burn. She disposed of the syringe and slapped on the cotton ball and Bandaid combo as if she'd been doing it for years."

"Well done. You've got good, steady hands. I hardly felt a thing."

"First timer's luck, I guess."

"That's not usually a thing. You've got a knack. You ever think about going back to school for something in the medical field?"

Delaney shrugged. "I don't know. I hadn't thought much about going back to school at all yet."

"Something to keep in mind. Thanks. My glimmer of a possible love life thanks you."

She laughed. "You know that means you have to share details of your date."

Miranda narrowed her eyes but smiled. "We'll see."

Since he'd taken the job as Chief of Police back in November, Ethan had rarely had a night off. Their department was small, encompassing only himself, four officers, a day-time dispatcher, and a night-time dispatcher. There were a couple of reserve officers who were brought in from time to time, but, in general, small-town policing meant he was rarely truly off duty. That wasn't all that different from his time with the Marshals. He'd lived his life prepared to be called out on a warrant at the drop of a hat.

But tonight he'd been looking forward to something else. A step in the direction of having that life Clay kept bugging him about. The fact that postponing dinner with Miranda until Saturday had made him twitchy and restless was a sign that he had a long damned way to go before he effectively transitioned.

Maybe he should call Clay, see if they could move up their rescheduled jam session. Or maybe he should just pick up his guitar and give his fingers a workout before Sunday to make sure he could still back up the claims he'd made.

Grabbing a beer and his beloved Taylor acoustic, he headed out to the glassed-in back porch. His rental house faced a scraggly patch of woods and was, in his opinion, way too close to neighbors. He didn't actually want to be able to see anybody else's house or for anybody to be able to look out and see his. But it would do until he decided where he wanted to live long-term. Part of that was deciding this job was for him long-term. He'd needed to get out of the Marshal Service—that hadn't been up for debate—but the jury was still out whether this had been the right move. For all he'd gotten tired of the city, he wasn't sure he was small town anymore either.

Ethan had barely set himself up on the old metal glider before his phone began to ring. Irritation prickled. Just because he hadn't been able to spend tonight doing what he wanted didn't mean he'd put out a call to the Universe to interrupt him. But irritation morphed quickly to pleasure when he saw Miranda's name flash across the screen. He was smiling as he answered. "Hey there. I didn't expect to hear from you tonight."

"Hey, Ethan. I'm really sorry to bother you at home on your night off."

The tension in her voice had him dropping his feet, sitting up straight. "That's fine. What's wrong?"

"Can you come down to the ED?"

Half a dozen forms of crisis scrolled through his mind. Violent patient. Hostage situation. Homicide. "Of course. Do I need backup?"

"No. Nothing like that. Just you, please. And maybe stick to plainclothes instead of your uniform."

"What's going on, Miranda?"

"Rene Forbes is here."

Shit. "I'm on my way."

Ethan's tension cranked up a couple more notches as he stepped through the sliding glass doors into the Emergency Department of Wilton Memorial Hospital. He sure as shit hadn't planned to be here again so soon. But at least he wasn't the one bleeding this time. The shoulder holster carrying the Glock .40 he preferred was a comforting weight beneath his jacket. Overkill maybe, but he wasn't about to be caught unawares.

The staff had evidently been told to watch out for him. A nurse, the same one who'd assisted Miranda last weekend, escorted him through the double doors back to the patient bays. Miranda was waiting toward the back in a little, tucked away corner, a surgical mask dangling around her neck.

Her grim expression lightened somewhat as she caught sight of him. "Thanks for coming."

"How bad?" he asked softly.

In answer, she pulled up her surgical mask, opened the curtain, and nudged him inside.

Holy shit.

Rene Forbes lay on the gurney, her face so bruised and battered, he wouldn't have immediately recognized her, if not for the bright pink cast still on her wrist. One eye was swollen shut and blood had dried in a black crust along her split lip. The arm with the broken wrist was currently bound up in a sling she hadn't been wearing at the clinic. Dislocated shoulder, he guessed. There was no possible way she could blame this on falling or walking into a door.

Rage burst through Ethan. Harley had done this sometime after he'd left last night. Had he caught on to Ethan's tail? Was this some kind of retaliation? A fuck you to the cops who could do nothing? Choking back his own reaction, Ethan kept his voice soft. "Rene, can you tell me what happened?"

Her one good eye slitted open, staring him down before rolling to fix on the ceiling.

From the corner, a gangly teenaged boy spoke up. "He just started whaling on her. No reason. He never has a reason."

"He always has a reason," Rene croaked.

"Bullshit," the boy snarled, his long, narrow hands clenched.

"Johnny." Despite her injuries, Rene's tone still carried the rebuke only a mother could manage.

"Your father did this?" Ethan asked.

"That bastard is no father of mine."

"He adopted you. Gave you his name."

"I'd rather have stayed a bastard."

Rene made a wounded sound at that.

"That's enough." Miranda's voice brooked no argument and the boy subsided. "Rene, we already talked about this when you came in for your wrist. Harley's escalating. You aren't safe with him."

"There's nothing can be done."

"I can get him away from you, get him off the streets." Ethan would relish the chance to haul the asshole in. "You just have to file charges."

Rene shook her head, biting back a moan at the movement. "I'm not filing charges. I brought this on myself. I married him and a woman's place is with her husband."

"That walking sack of shit is no husband," Johnny growled. "And you're stupid if you think he's going to stop just because you stay."

This time it was Miranda's voice snapping like a whip. "Johnny, your mother is not stupid."

Something tender there, Ethan noted. It was the second time he'd seen her go off against the idea of Rene being stupid.

"Then what do you call it?" the boy demanded.

"Scared. And rightly so. But you're not wrong. He's not going to stop. Rene, please let us help you."

Rene swallowed, her throat working as she focused on Miranda. "How do you see this playing out?"

"Simple. You file charges, Chief Greer arrests him, and you move out to the women's shelter."

It wasn't that simple, and Rene obviously knew it.

"And what happens when he gets out again? Harley doesn't give up what's his."

They spent another half hour going rounds about it, but in the end, the woman stubbornly refused to press charges against her abuser. Ethan wished he was surprised, but this was par for the course.

Unwilling to give up, Miranda slipped some information about the women's shelter into the pocket of Rene's purse. "Just read over it later."

Ethan stuck around after Rene was released and Johnny tucked her into the rusted-out Ford Escort he'd seen in the drive last night. The kid was a ticking time bomb. All that rage had to go somewhere eventually. He wondered whether the boy would implode or explode and made a mental note to see if the kid had any kind of record. Wouldn't hurt to have his officers watching out for any changes in behavior, too.

After checking a few other patients, Miranda managed to break away to corner him in an office. Frustration pumped off her in waves as she scooped both hands through her thick blonde hair. "What are we doing to do, Ethan? This keeps up, he's going to kill her."

"She's too afraid to act on her own."

"If we could just get Harley off the street for longer than twenty-four hours, I think I could manage to get her to the shelter and leave his ass. Once she's out of that house, I think she'll start to see."

Ethan wasn't so sure. "Even if you pulled that off, it's unlikely Rene will follow through."

The stubborn jut to her chin shouldn't have been so appealing. "I have to try. And I need you to help me. Harley is an asshole and a troublemaker. There has to be something you can haul him in on."

"Not so far."

"You're a resourceful man, Ethan. Surely you can employ those famous Marshal skills to find out what kind of shit Harley's involved in."

The idea of it sparked Ethan's sense of the hunt, something that had been sorely missing since he'd moved to tiny town Mississippi. If he'd had any reservations about using department resources in the name of his own investigation into the man, they'd been obliterated at the sight of Rene's bruises.

"I promise you, if there's anything to find, I'll make it a priority to dig it out." It was a devil's bargain, one he wasn't entirely sure he could keep. Not every piece of shit was actually involved in anything illegal. But he liked the idea of Miranda Campbell needing him for something. Her idealism and stubborn belief in people's ability to change clashed with his own jaded cynicism, but he found himself wanting to protect that for her, for reasons he didn't entirely understand.

Her face relaxed a fraction. "Thanks for that."

Ethan could see the exhaustion weighing on her and itched to wrap her in his arms and soothe. But she was on-duty and the intercom made it clear her night was far from over, so he shoved his hands in his pockets. "I should get out of here. You've got work."

"I've got work," she agreed. Walking with him toward the door, she dug up the ghost of a smile. "But I'm really looking forward to Saturday when I don't."

"Me, too, Doc. Me, too."

CHAPTER 7

Saturday dawned frigid and foggy. The wisps of white curling over the ground and around the trees as he drove out to Chester's farm gave Ethan the illusion of solitude he'd been craving and dragged out memories of winter mornings on the ranch with his grandfather. There'd be more memories where those came from once he got to work. Temperatures would rise with the sun, and he knew he was in for a day of sweaty labor.

He wished he'd had time to walk the fence line before today. Chances were, there'd be multiple weak points in addition to the ones he knew about. But he'd made an educated guess when he'd picked up supplies at the co-op yesterday. He'd even brought his own tools. Ethan wasn't taking chances that Chester would have what was needed to do the job right.

Horses milled in the paddock when he pulled up. Four beautiful animals in turnout coats that had him detouring to the rail to admire. Houdini lifted his head and bobbed it in the equine version of *hey man.* A pretty little chestnut mare wandered over to investigate and bumped her head against Ethan's hand for pets.

Obliging, he scratched her under the forelock and watched her ears twitch from pleasure.

"That there's Miss Kitty." Chester's gravelly voice was muffled by the lingering fog.

Ethan found himself smiling as he turned to greet the crotchety old man. "You a *Gunsmoke* fan, Chester?"

"Damn straight. Good show."

"This little lady have as much sass as her namesake?"

"More than. Spoiled rotten. She was my wife's. Just got saddle broken right before Jeannie passed."

Ethan pegged the mare at five or six years old. Chester had been on his own for a few years now.

He didn't look at Ethan as he reached out to stroke a hand down the mare's neck. "Thought about selling her, selling them all after that. But couldn't do it. She loved these animals."

Ethan felt a twinge of sorrow. Were these horses all the man had left of his wife? He thought about expressing condolences, but Chester's manner didn't invite them. Instead, he kept his tone matter of fact as he passed out scratches to the other two as they sidled up to the rail. "Well, we'll do right by her today and see the fence is fixed properly so they stay on your property and safe."

Chester finally looked at him. "You're really gonna do this?"

"I really am."

"Why?" The old man's bushy brows drew together in confusion.

"Well, it's clear you could use a hand with repairs, or you'd have done them by now. The horses are a prospective danger to traffic, not to mention the traffic is a danger to them. And because I moved to Wishful for a slower pace than what I had in my last job.

I don't want to go ruining that by getting a call about a homicide because Mrs. Ramsey finally had enough."

A muscle in Chester's jaw twitched. "Well, I reckon there's time for a cup of coffee before we get started. Let a little more of this cold burn off. I feel it in my bones."

He could do that.

Ethan followed him back up to the house, his boots thudding across the floorboards of the porch. The interior smelled faintly of Bengay, with a lingering scent of bacon beneath the coffee. The furnishings were comfortable and dated, with a feminine edge that would've surprised him if he hadn't just heard about Chester's late wife. Everything had an air of being undisturbed, down to the fake flower arrangement gracing a table in the front hall, colors muted with a layer of dust. Wide-planked pine floors seemed to run through the whole first floor. They held a patina of age and wear that he knew people would pay good money to duplicate as a "distressed" look in new construction. Ethan preferred the real thing. It meant the house had been lived in.

In the kitchen, which seemed to have been updated sometime in the 1980s, Chester went straight to the coffee pot and poured two mugs. "How do you take it?"

"Black's fine."

He nudged a mug toward Ethan, then retrieved a bottle of hazelnut creamer from the fridge.

Ethan raised a brow as he dumped several healthy glugs into the mug. "You gonna have a little coffee with that creamer?"

"Like my coffee like I liked my women—blonde and sweet." He sipped and studied Ethan over the rim. "Hear tell you got the same taste."

Hell, even Chester had heard about his interest in Miranda? "Don't know as 'sweet' is exactly the word I'd use to describe her."

The old man threw back his head and laughed. "Doc Campbell's a pistol, that's for damned sure. Woman like her'll keep a man on his toes."

He didn't want to discuss his prospective love life. "Got an appreciation for spirited women, Chester?"

"It's a stupid man who doesn't."

"Your neighbor fits that description."

"I know it. Maudie Bell was good friends with my Jeannie." There was something in his tone that had Ethan's curiosity pinging.

"Then why, exactly, are you going around pissing her off by not taking care of your fence problem? I can see you care about your property, your animals, so this doesn't fit."

A flush crawled up Chester's neck. "I get it fixed, maybe she stops coming by."

Ethan stared. "You're doing all this to get her attention?"

The bony shoulders twitched, and he didn't quite meet Ethan's gaze. "Her coming over and ranting at me is kinda like having my Jeannie back a little bit. She gets a kick out of it, too, since her Melvin died. Not that she'll admit it."

"So, let me get this straight—this whole little feud y'all have going on is some kind of flirtation?"

"It passes the time."

"Man, you can do better than that. You *will* do better than that. Today we're fixing that fence. And next week, you're going down to the nursery to pick up the replacement roses Cam ordered, and you're gonna put them in for her. And maybe when you're done with that, you'll actually apologize and do something radical, like ask her to dinner."

"What qualifies you to hand out advice on anybody's love life?"

Given the divorce under his belt, probably not much. "Apparently a better sense of self-preservation than you've got."

Chester harrumphed. "You any better qualified to fix a fence?"

"Grew up on a ranch in West Texas. I was fixing fences from the time I was five years old."

The old man's eyes lit with interest. "Well, reckon we'll see how good you are with the fence first. Maybe you're worth listening to on the rest."

Ethan's lips twitched. "You don't listen, I can fine you."

"Same song, different verse, son. Let's get to work."

"THIS IS NOT WHAT I EXPECTED." Despite the firm grip Ethan had on her hand, Miranda dragged her feet a little as he pulled her across the scuffed wooden floor of Speakeasy Pizza toward the little stage.

"You said you wanted to hear me sing."

"Yeah, *you*. Not me."

His eyes glinted with amusement. "Maybe I wanna see what you're made of. Karaoke says a lot about a person."

As they joined the short line beside the binder containing all possible song options, nerves kicked in her belly. "That a deal-breaker for you?"

He sobered, bending close to her ear to speak. "Not if you legitimately don't want to do it. You don't strike me as the nervous type."

"I'm not usually totally sober when I do this. And the last time anybody managed to drag me up here was for my friend Piper's bachelorette party."

"How long ago was that?"

"Well, the baby just turned three weeks yesterday."

Ethan crouched down just a little to look into her eyes, as if trying to determine whether he was gonna make her go through with this. It'd have been nice if she knew whether she wanted to do it.

"C'mon, Legs," he coaxed. "I'll let you pick the song."

Bracing herself, Miranda stepped up to the book. "Fine. Let's see what you've got."

He peered over her shoulder as she made her selection of "Islands in the Stream." Not close enough to touch, but near enough the heat of him distracted her.

"Old school. I dig it." He punched the number into the machine himself, removing her last opportunity for escape.

And then they were on the stage, and he was grinning at her as he launched into a damned fine impression of Kenny Rogers. Her voice shook as she added her Dolly to the mix. She could carry a tune, but she was no performer, and this stage was generally ruled by the active community theater members who were. Ethan never once looked at the crowd. A funny thing happened under that complete and total focus—she lost her nerves. So, by the time they wrapped the country classic, Miranda was grinning back and laughing.

Ethan swung an arm around her shoulders as they stepped down. "You give good Dolly. That definitely earned you pizza and beer."

They nabbed a table far enough back from the stage they could talk without yelling and put in an order for a New York style pie with pepperoni and mushrooms. As they waited, they listened to the other performers—good, bad, and heinous—and Miranda entertained him with little anecdotes about each of them.

"Do you know everybody?" he asked.

"Seems like. Other than school and residency, I've lived here all my life."

"Was that always the plan? Or did you want to stay in Chicago?"

She tipped her beer back and considered. "No. Chicago was a means to an end. But I did expect to be there longer than I was."

"Surgical residency, wasn't it?"

"Somebody was paying attention."

"You had your hands on my ass at the time. Hard to pay attention to anything else."

Miranda snorted and hoped she'd get the chance at that again under less professional circumstances. "Fair point. When I started up there, I fully intended to finish out my trauma surgeon training. But Chicago is one of the most violent cities in the country. It started to feel like I lost as many people as I saved. Some of them I managed to patch back together only to have them show up months later from some other thing and end up with a toe tag. It was wearing on me."

"I can imagine."

"I became a doctor because I wanted to make a difference in people's lives. Wanted to see that that difference lasted. Most surgeons have only a peripheral kind of relationship with their patients. Bare minimum contact to do the procedure and follow up. Trauma surgeons often have even less because of the nature of the conditions being treated. My mentor constantly frowned on my desire to get involved beyond medical necessity. He considered me naive. I chalked it up to the fact that he's been a practicing surgeon for nearly thirty years, and in all that time he's developed a wall between himself and his patients out of self-preservation. But I just couldn't live like he did. I give a damn, and that isn't going to change. So, I gave up my residency up there and came home to specialize in family medicine. Even now, he still hasn't forgiven me for walking away. He thinks I'm wasting my skills in a small-town clinic."

"Do you feel like your skills are wasted?"

"No. I love what I do—most of the time. Small town medicine is about healing more than the body."

"Do you miss the surgery?"

"Some. Our head of Emergency Medicine allows me to keep my hand in and assist as the need arises. Keeps my skills sharp."

"Handy, I expect, when medical expertise is limited in the area."

"Exactly." She waited as the waitress slid their pizza onto a rack in the center of the table. "What about you? Why did you decide to become a Marshal instead of a country music heartthrob?"

He laughed, and it was such a heady thing, seeing the usually stoic chief of police unbend a little…for her.

"I grew up on a ranch in West Texas. My granddaddy was foreman—exactly what you imagine an old West cowboy to be. He knew cattle, horses, and men, and he wanted a different kind of life for his only daughter. But she fell in love with a bronc rider on the rodeo circuit, got married at nineteen, had me. So, Pop hired him on at the ranch, hoping he'd settle down. He did, for a bit, but got it in his head he needed one last ride. The prize money would've made a nice little nest egg to put a down payment on a house."

"Would've?"

"He was thrown. Broke his neck. Died on impact."

The idea of it broke her heart, both for him and for his mother. "Jesus, Ethan. I'm sorry."

"I wasn't even two, so I don't remember him. Anyway, Mama and I moved back in with Pop, and I grew up on the ranch. She didn't date much after Daddy. But about the time I was ten years old, there was this guy who hired on. Ranches have a lot of seasonal work, so there's a regular turnover in staff. This one guy—Ray Diffy—he took a shine to my mama. Pop didn't like it, but it was the first time I'd seen her smile like that in forever, so I was predisposed to like the guy. I guess you could say he charmed us both."

Ethan took a bite of the pizza, nodded in approval. "Ray was, as it turned out, a professional charmer. He was a con man on the run from a drug cartel out of New Mexico. He had multiple warrants out for his arrest, and the cartel itself was still looking for him, on account of the fact he stole a fair chunk of their product. They eventually tracked him down to the ranch and figured out they could use my mama for leverage, so they took her hostage."

Pizza forgotten, Miranda leaned toward him. "Oh my God. What happened?"

"The Marshals came in. They had a whole cross agency task force put together for the bust. Deputy Marshal Phil Jenks was running the show, and he took the time in the middle of all the crazy, to assure me that they were gonna save my mama. I believed him. He was that kind of guy. Didn't make promises he couldn't make good on. And he did. They had her out within an hour. Safe and sound."

"So you became a Marshal because that's who rescued your mom?" Who wouldn't have some hero worship going on after that?

"Not exactly. See, when the bust went down, and they got inside the cookhouse—Mama was cook for the ranch—Phil found she'd gone after one of the cartel guys with a butcher knife. She'd been on the verge of breaking out when the task force broke in. I think he fell for her on the spot."

"Marshal Jenks fell in love with your mother?"

"Yeah. He came back after, to check on her. But Mama, she'd had enough of men in dangerous professions, so she wouldn't give him the time of day. He kept coming back, though. Kept checking on her—and me—for years. About ten years after it all went down, he retired and they got married, had my baby sister. They all moved to Florida a few years ago."

"It's nice your mom got a happy ending."

Ethan's lips curved and it was a different sort of smile than the one he used to flirt. Something quiet and powerful, that spoke to his love of family. "Yeah. She sure as hell deserved it. Anyway, I became a Marshal to chase down others like Ray, to get them off the streets before they could wreak more havoc on innocent people's lives."

"You loved it." That wasn't even a question.

"I did. I was good at it."

"Why'd you stop? Why give all that up for small-town policing?"

The pleasure that had lit his face during the telling faded, and he set his slice of pizza aside. "About eighteen months ago, I got shot. Wasn't bad intel or carelessness. Just straight up bad luck and a cheap ass trailer. Perp shot through the wall from a closet in another room. The walls were so thin, they might as well have been paper. I came perilously close to dying right there. Mom, Phil, and Julie were there when I woke up in the hospital. Mom and Julie were worried to death, of course, and Phil asked me why I was still doing it. Why I was out there risking my neck. For the first time since I'd started, I didn't have a good answer." He shrugged. "I saw what it did to my mama to see me like that. I figured she's lost enough people she cared about, so here I am."

Miranda had to appreciate a man who regularly risked his life for others and held deep love and respect for his mother. She had to appreciate a lot of things about Ethan Greer.

After dinner, they strolled arm-in-arm across the town green. She watched the cop in him scanning the quiet streets, never fully relaxed, and her brain circled back around to their earlier conversation. "Do you miss it?"

"What?"

"Being a Marshal. The chase. The need for constant vigilance?"

"Yeah. Slowing down is hard. I went full-tilt for a lot of years. But my fundamental job is still the same. Protect the innocent from the bad guys."

They stopped at the fountain that was the centerpiece to town. The quiet murmur of the water cut through the night. "You want to make a difference, same as I do."

"I suppose I do. But I'm less of an idealist than you. I've seen too much to have that kind of faith in humanity."

God, it was so much like something Stephen would've said. In the wake of that disastrous relationship, she'd promised herself she'd never again get involved with someone who was so fundamentally different from her. It wasn't worth the heartache. Why the hell did Ethan have to be so appealing on every other level?

Feeling a little brittle, she glanced at the constellation of glittering coins in the basin. The hundreds, maybe thousands of wishes people had made over the years. "I guess you think that kind of faith is foolish."

"I think you make me want to do whatever's necessary to protect this little corner of the world so you can keep looking at people like that." He reached out to tuck a strand of her hair behind one ear.

Caught by the sincerity in his eyes, Miranda turned into the touch, so his fingers skimmed her cheek, lighting little fires of anticipation and rekindling the hope that Ethan Greer was different. He couldn't know what that meant to her. "You've got a bit of a hero complex."

"Guilty."

"I find that works for me."

"Yeah? How about this?" The hand at her cheek slid into her hair, tipping her face up to his.

Miranda flowed into him, wrapping an arm around his lean waist and hanging on as he sipped and savored her mouth because this was what she'd wanted. To taste him. To feel him. The unhurried play of his lips over hers made her sigh and press closer. His arm banded around her. Ruthlessly patient, he took the kiss deeper by degrees.

Patience had never been one of Miranda's virtues. It had been so damned long since she'd felt any of this—attraction, arousal, and a heady, gleeful desire to be a little reckless. Opening her mouth beneath his, she dove into the kiss. She felt his pulse of surprise in the fingers that clenched in her hair and the momentary stillness in the body pressed to hers. Then he hauled her closer, devouring her mouth, his tongue stroking against hers in a way that had her wishing for skin on skin.

The approving whistle had him snapping his head up, leaving her feeling unbalanced and bereft without his lips against hers. As he cast a hunting glance around—and God, wasn't that faint predatory gleam sexy?—Miranda struggled to slow her breathing and find her feet again.

Ethan's gaze came back to hers, the gunmetal gray of his irises all but swallowed by black. "That was…"

"I'd go with delightfully stimulating."

One corner of his mouth lifted. "That's one way of putting it."

"And for the record, yeah, that totally works for me."

They stayed that way, wrapped around each other by the burbling fountain for several breaths. What exactly did you say to someone you'd just played a very public game of tonsil hockey with?

"Do you have any change?" she asked.

"Sure. Why?"

"We're at the fountain. We have to make a wish." She already knew what she wanted hers to be.

He dug into his pocket with an expression of good-natured forbearance. "We do?"

"You cannot live in a town that's all about wishes without actually making one."

"Fair enough." He dropped a coin into her palm.

Miranda curled her fingers around it and watched him instead of the water as she mentally composed her wish. *I wish for Ethan's time in Wishful to restore his faith in people and give him back some perspective.* "Ready?"

"Do we share?"

"Nope. Not unless it comes true."

"Okay." He paused, as if to consider, then nodded.

Together, they stretched their arms out. "Three, two, one."

The coins hit the water with a splash.

"All right then, now what?" Ethan asked.

"How do you feel about dessert?"

CHAPTER 8

When he answered the call up at the high school on Wednesday, somehow, Ethan was unsurprised to find Johnny Forbes slouched in a chair in the principal's office. The boy lifted baleful eyes as Ethan came in, then dropped his gaze to the floor again. He had the beginnings of a fresh shiner around one eye. Probably not from his stepfather if the principal was calling.

"Dr. Warner, what can I do for you?"

"Thank you for coming, Chief Greer." The fifty-something woman shook his hand, then circled around to sit behind the big oak desk. She straightened a stack of papers that didn't need straightening before folding her manicured hands. "We have, as you know, a zero-tolerance policy for fighting. Johnny violated that policy by going after another student. First offense is suspension. This is his third for the year."

"Where's the other kid?"

The woman's head jerked back hard enough that her hair, which had been shellacked into a virtual helmet, shook. "I beg your pardon?"

"The kid Johnny allegedly attacked. If you have a zero tolerance, do you not punish both sides of the fight?"

"There were numerous witnesses that Mr. Forbes started the fight."

Ethan wondered whether all those witnesses would've seen the same thing if Johnny Forbes wasn't dirt poor and living in a home with an abusive alcoholic. "I'll still need to talk to the other student."

"He's been sent home."

"Did the school nurse assess his injuries?"

"Some bumps and bruises. Nothing serious."

And yet they'd called the cops on Johnny. "I'll still be needing to get a statement from him regarding the incident. If you could just write down the boy's name, parents' names, and contact information."

After a moment's hesitation, the principal did as he'd asked. Oh yeah. Clear case of favoritism for the other kid. He'd get the boy's statement, but Ethan already knew how this was likely to turn out.

"Have you contacted Johnny's mother?" Ethan hoped like hell they hadn't contacted Harley.

"We were unable to reach her."

"All right. I'll take care of that." He turned to Johnny. "C'mon, son. Let's take a little ride."

The boy rose and held both hands in front of him, eyes downcast.

Ethan laid a hand on his shoulder. "I'm not going to march you out of here in cuffs. C'mon."

The dark eyes flickered with some kind of uncertainty before he nodded and fell into step with Ethan out to the cruiser. The kid said nothing on the drive to the station, only glowered out the window. He still had that powder keg thing going on, and Ethan was afraid today's mischief was only the first spark of a truly spectacular explosion. Though he wondered exactly how much legitimate trouble he'd caused.

Back at the station, he bypassed the interrogation room and led Johnny into his office. "Inez, can I get a couple of Cokes, please?"

The older woman's brows disappeared beneath the fringe of salt and pepper bangs. Okay, so this wasn't standard procedure. It was his damned department, and there was more going on here than a kid getting busted for fighting in school. Ethan waited for Inez to bring the drinks.

"Thanks. I also need you to see about tracking down Rene Forbes, please. Quiet-like. I'd rather Harley not get wind of this if we can help it."

"Sure thing, Chief."

Shutting the door, Ethan passed Johnny one of the Cokes and popped the top on his own as he dropped into his chair. "So, what actually happened today?"

"You heard Dr. Warner. I went after Scott Neary."

"Yep, I heard her version. I want yours."

Johnny said nothing, staring at a spot somewhere over Ethan's left shoulder. Ethan just waited him out, patient. He didn't have anywhere else to be right now.

"I went after Scott Neary."

"Why?"

"What does that matter? I'm suspended either way."

"To my way of thinking, there's a big difference between a guy who starts fights just for the hell of it or because somebody looked at him crossways, and a guy who was provoked. Do you have a history with Scott Neary?"

"We've been in school together since kindergarten. We never liked each other."

Ethan thought about Miranda's lifelong battle with Clarice Morris, then wished he hadn't because thoughts of Miranda inevitably led to thoughts about that kiss. He still didn't know what he was going to do about her. Shaking the memory off for now, he nodded. "Sometimes it's like that. I don't think that's everything though, is it?"

A muscle jumped in Johnny's jaw and his eyes went hard.

"Did he insult you?"

"The fucker insulted my mother."

Ethan let the language pass. "What did he say?"

Those eyes blazed as he lifted them to Ethan's. "That she looked like she'd gone rounds with Floyd Mayweather and wasn't that gonna cut into her being able to make the rent money on her back this month."

"I'd have wanted to punch the little shit, too." His admission made the boy blink. "Look, I'm not interested in policing this town based on a past history of what everybody else says. I'm starting with the now and what I can see with my own two eyes. This right here is, as far as I'm concerned, your first offense."

Suspicion flashed across Johnny's features. "So, I'm getting off?"

"No. I'm guessing there's a good chance Neary's parents are the type that will press assault charges. I've got no interest in seeing you thrown in juvie for defending your mother's honor. I've got something else in mind."

Ethan made some calls. By the time he'd arranged things to suit him, Rene Forbes was hurrying through the front doors of the station. He scanned her with a practiced eye. He didn't see any overt evidence of new injuries, but she wouldn't meet his eyes. Beneath the colorful bruising that was too livid for even good makeup to hide, she was wan.

"Is he under arrest?"

"Why don't you come on back?" Ethan gestured her into his office.

When Rene saw the black eye, she made a pained noise. "We've talked about this! You can't be fighting."

Johnny ducked his head. "Sorry, Mom."

"What was this about?"

"Doesn't matter," Ethan said. "I'm not arresting him. I've already spoken with Judge Carpenter, and we're putting Johnny on community service. As long as he keeps his nose clean and meets his hours, we're calling it square."

"What kind of community service?" Rene asked.

"He's going to be helping Chester Harkin out at his farm every Saturday for the rest of the semester."

That finally got a reaction out of the boy. "I'm gonna be doing what now?"

"Whatever Chester needs help with. He's getting on up there in years and isn't as spry as he used to be. He can use a young back to help with the animals, hauling feed, mucking stalls, doing repairs. It's hard, honest work, and it'll be helping out a senior in need." Ethan hoped to God Johnny didn't repeat that statement. Chester would shit a brick at being called a senior in need.

"But…how will he get there? We don't have an extra car and if I'm working—"

"Don't you worry about that. If you can't drop him off, I'll see that Chester picks him up or I or one of my officers gives him a ride."

Ethan pulled out two of his cards and passed them over. He figured Rene had tossed the one he'd given her that day in Miranda's clinic. "This is my contact info, including my cell. If you need a ride to Chester's, need help, or just need to talk—either of you—you can call any time."

By the looks on their faces as they reluctantly accepted the cards, Ethan knew they'd never actually use them. Settled on things with Johnny, he shifted his attention to Rene. "Have you given any more thought to what we talked about at the hospital?"

She gave one short, sharp shake of her head. "Things are fine. Quiet."

Yeah, that's what Ethan was afraid of. Quiet now. How much longer until the pressure built up enough to blow? And what would be the consequences when it did?

Knowing he wouldn't get any further by pushing, Ethan rose. "You're free to go. When is your suspension up?"

"Monday," Johnny muttered.

Better to keep the kid out of the house this week, then. "All right. Then you can get a head start on your hours tomorrow. I'll be by to pick you up at seven."

"Seven! Dude!" The tone of utter baffled outrage almost made Ethan smile.

"Farm work starts early, son. Be glad I'm not getting you at sunrise." He clapped the boy on the shoulder. "See you in the morning."

~

"I HEAR you're getting all creative in your policing." The remark was punctuated by the familiar tones of tuning as Clay made minor adjustments to his guitar.

Ethan pulled his Taylor out of the case and took the stool across from his friend. "How's that?"

"Hooking up Johnny Forbes with Chester Harkin instead of sending him to juvie."

"That *just* happened this morning. How do you even know about it?"

Clay just laughed. "The only gossip tree faster than the one starting at Dinner Belles is the one at the high school. It's just a microcosm of the broader town. Anyway, I doubt it was what Dr. Warner had in mind, but it was a nice thing."

"I'm pretty sure Dr. Warner would've preferred Johnny be locked up and the key thrown out. She's biased against him. I figure it's my job not to be. Anyway, it was ultimately Judge Carpenter's decision. I just made a suggestion. Juvie isn't gonna do that kid any favors. Some good, honest work might. You know him?"

"Never had him as a student, but the high school's a fishbowl. I see everybody at some point."

Ethan began checking his own tuning. "What can you tell me about him?"

"Probably not a lot more than you already know. He's bottom of the social heap. Target of bullies. Mostly he keeps to himself, no matter what gets thrown at him, but he's been getting hotter under the collar lately. Hence the fight with Scott Neary."

"What about Neary?"

"Entitled little bastard. Apple didn't fall far from the tree with that one. I went to school with his daddy. Thought he was God's gift and no life experiences since then have dissuaded him of that fact."

"Would you say other students are deliberately seeking Johnny out for harassment?"

"That's high school." Clay shrugged. "The popular kids prey on the weak or the weird. I keep an eye out as much as I can, but, as I said, he's not my student."

"You think I made the right call?"

"I think it can't be a bad thing to give a kid another shot. Having somebody give a damn about his situation could make all the difference for somebody like him."

"That's certainly the hope. I just wish I could make a difference for his mother, get them both out of that shitty situation."

"I'm guessing you and Miranda haven't had any luck on that front."

"No."

Clay's eyes turned mischievous. "How about on the dating front? Everybody's been talking about your debut at karaoke night."

Ethan jerked his shoulders in a move he hoped came off as nonchalance rather than irritation. "The date went fine."

"Fine? Surely it went better than fine, given how you had your tongue down each other's throats by the fountain."

Ethan took a measured breath and released it again. He'd chosen small-town life. He'd known that meant he'd be an object of scrutiny. He'd known he'd be under a microscope as the new guy in town. But he'd foolishly believed that would be more for his performance on the job, not his personal life. Apparently, nobody here had any clue about boundaries.

The truth was their date had gone more than fine. It had been damned near perfect. *She* seemed damned near perfect. That sharp mind, that body, that big, compassionate heart. She was the total package, and every cell in his body had urged him to call and ask her out again about five minutes after he'd left her at her door.

He hadn't given in.

"We have chemistry," Ethan acknowledged.

"Duh. And?"

"There is no and."

"When are you going out again?"

"We're not." Maybe saying it out loud would help him stick to his decision.

"You're not? Why?"

"Because of Becca."

Clay hit him with some serious side eye. "Brother, please tell me you are not still hung up on your ex-wife."

"No. Not hardly. But I am not about to make the same mistakes with Miranda as I made with her."

"You're gonna have to explain the logic of that because I'm just not seeing it."

"Everything with Becca was hard and fast. She batted those baby blues at me and took me out at the knees. I was crazy about her from the word go. Wanted to spend every waking minute with her—and did on up until I started working for the Marshals. We got too serious too fast. If I'd kept my head, slowed things down, maybe we wouldn't have gotten married in the first place."

"So let me get this straight—because I'm not at all sure I'm understanding you. You're putting the brakes on with Miranda because you actually really like her, and you're worried you'll fall ass over teakettle in love with her and do something stupid like marry her too fast?"

Put like that it sounded stupid. But it didn't feel stupid. "I like her. A lot. The kind of a lot that has historically made me do stupid things. I'm still on probation with this job until October. I can't afford to do anything stupid. I need to keep my eye on the ball."

"And you think spending time with a sexy, intelligent woman is going to impact your ability to do your job? Dude, that's just sad."

"That's not—" Leave it to Clay to make him feel like a jackass. "That isn't what I meant."

"Fine. We'll table the discussion. You're not going back out with Miranda. End of story." He lifted his hands in surrender. "Since you won't be taking up that free time with dating, it means you can finally get back up on stage with me. And I have the perfect venue for you to start."

"Oh?"

"Tomorrow night there's a big bonfire out at Hope Springs. It'll be a small gathering. A nice, low-key, informal sort of performance.

Nobody's expecting perfection. Just some good music and fun. Think you can handle that?"

Grateful the topic of Miranda had been dropped, Ethan nodded. "Bring it on, Turner."

∿

"THAT'S HEALING up really well. Your range of motion is much improved since I saw you last." Satisfied, Miranda made a note in Brianna Daly's chart.

Brianna laid a hand over the little bump of her belly. "What about the baby?"

"You're coming along just fine. Vitals are good. I want to see you in the office in a month for a more thorough workup and the ultrasound, but for now everything is as it should be." And that was a damned miracle, considering the dislocated shoulder and other injuries Brianna had sustained at the hands of her now ex-boyfriend. The boyfriend who was currently in county lockup in Lawley. Thank God.

The young woman exhaled a relieved sigh. "Good. That's good."

As Brianna was her last patient of the day out at the women's shelter, Miranda began putting instruments back into her bag. "We'll be able to check the sex of the baby then, if you're inclined to find out."

A soft smile curled Brianna's lips as she rubbed her baby bump. "I'll be happy with whatever I get, so long as it's a healthy baby. But I'm hoping for a girl."

"Fifty-fifty shot. Are you good on your supply of prenatal vitamins?"

"All set. I can't thank you enough, Dr. Campbell."

"Think nothing of it. I'm happy to help and glad to see you doing better."

"I really am. It's so hard to think that after where I was just a few weeks ago, but everyone here's been so wonderful. We're really blessed, me and the baby."

A knock sounded at the door.

"Come on in," Miranda called. "We're finished."

Lily Mae Pollard, the founder and head of Monarch House, stuck her head in the door. "Brie, if you're done here, Whitney could use a hand in the kitchen."

"Yes ma'am." She rose from the sofa. "Thanks again, Dr. Campbell."

"I'll see you next month." Miranda waited until she'd made it down the hall. "That girl is a marvel. Such a positive attitude after everything she's been through."

Lily Mae came into the room. "She's a success story for sure. Some you don't know how they're gonna make it outside these walls. Some choose not to stay. But Brianna—she's focused on making a good life for that baby. It helps her to have something else to focus on. Sometimes it's easier to do stuff for somebody else than it is for yourself."

Miranda thought about Rene and Johnny Forbes and wondered if the boy had been younger, if she'd have gotten up the gumption to leave Harley. "Any advice on how to nudge somebody who's reluctant to make a move?"

"People don't move until they're ready. Or until circumstances force them to. You have somebody particular in mind?"

"Rene Forbes. Harley's escalating. She's stopped denying he's behind it, but she's very stuck on the idea that she brought this on herself. I don't know what it will take to motivate her to leave him."

"It's a hard thing, seeing somebody go through that, knowing you can't do anything about it."

Truth. And Miranda didn't know how to channel that sense of impotence. "I keep thinking if we could get Harley locked up for a few days at least, I could convince her. Ethan's going to see what he can find."

Lily Mae arched her steel gray brows. "Oh, Ethan is it? I heard you were seen stepping out with the new police chief."

"We had one date." A date she still couldn't stop replaying in her head, wondering what went wrong. Because he hadn't called her.

"Are you gonna see him again?"

Miranda shrugged with a nonchalance she didn't feel. "I don't know. We've both been pretty busy the past week." That was her excuse anyway. What was his?

Lily Mae hummed a noncommittal note. "You want a tour of the new expansion?"

"I'd love one." Anything to change the subject from the first date that had apparently been their last.

Two stories, the new wing extended off the east end of the house, facing the woods on one side and the gorgeous expanse of Hope Springs on the other. It was a peaceful spot, a healing spot. Lily Mae had chosen well when she'd picked this site.

"You've got good timing. They just did the punch out work a couple weeks ago." She opened the door to one of the empty bedrooms. Everything had that clean, fresh scent of new construction—wood and paint and a lingering odor of varnish from the hardwood floors.

"Oh, I didn't realize it was finished! How soon will you be able to move people in?"

They continued down the hall. "Well, we've already moved some folks in. Sadly, our services are always in demand, as you know."

"It's fantastic that you have the space now. I know y'all were bursting at the seams."

"We've got plenty of space, yes, but it's not ideal. It's not furnished yet, and I don't know when it's going to *get* furnished. We used the full budget on the expansion. So many of my girls and their children come here with next to nothing. Not having properly furnished rooms to give them just highlights that. Right now, folks are sleeping on air mattresses and grateful to have them and a safe place with a roof over their heads. But I want to offer them more than that."

"Of course, you do. I'm sure we'll come up with something." The beginning of an idea was already percolating at the back of Miranda's brain.

"The community has already been so generous with donations, I hate to ask for more. We aren't the only good cause in town."

"Maybe not, but you're one of the best." Miranda gave Lily Mae a squeeze. "Thanks for the tour. I need to be getting on back. If you need anything, don't hesitate to call."

Once she got in her car, Miranda wove her way further down the springs instead of turning back toward town. This close to Norah and Cam's place, she might as well stop by instead of call.

Norah answered the door in yoga pants and the same Ole Miss sweatshirt she'd had since they'd roomed together in college. "Hey! Come on in."

Miranda stepped into the wide foyer and hung her coat on a peg by the door. "I'm not interrupting your dinner, am I?"

"Nah. Cam's got a City Council meeting tonight, so he'll be home late. I'd love a little company. I was just sitting down with a glass of wine. Want some?"

"I'd love a glass."

A few minutes later, they settled in the living room. Norah tucked her bare feet beneath her on the sofa, and Hush, their enormous white dog, curled beside her, laying her massive head in the crook of her mistress's knees. "What brings you out this way?"

Miranda sank down in one of the leather chairs flanking the fireplace and sipped at a very nice petite Syrah. "My monthly volunteer work at Monarch House. Did you know the expansion was finished?"

"I heard! I haven't made it over to see yet, though."

"It's beautiful. A great space. But the whole of what you managed to raise through Dancing With Wishful ended up going to the building. There was nothing left to furnish all the new rooms. People are sleeping on air mattresses, Norah."

"That's awful! What can we do?"

This was why she'd come here. Because Norah would always be the first in line to help.

"Remember how we used the cover for the Valentine's Dance a couple years ago as a fundraiser for the citizen's coalition? Couldn't we do the same thing this year and put the proceeds toward furnishing the new rooms? I mean, it might not get everything, but it would be a big help toward at least getting some proper beds. Unless it's already earmarked for something else."

"That's a great idea! We were keeping things kinda low key, but I can absolutely put together a campaign to bring in some more people for the dance, see if I can't drum up some more bodies to pay the cover." She grabbed one of the notepads and pens that were always in reach.

"Maybe you can get Clay to play. He always packs them in."

Norah grinned. "You'd have better luck convincing him of that. He's still got a soft spot for you."

"High school was a long time ago."

"You could ask your new beau." She waggled her eyebrows. "He seems to have special sway with Clay."

Miranda scowled. "Ethan's not my beau. He's not my anything, apparently."

Norah sobered. "I thought you said your date went really well."

"I thought it did. But I haven't heard boo from him since he dropped me off at home." Furious at the knot in her throat, she took a healthy swig of wine. "It figures that the first guy I'm interested enough to put myself out there for up and decides I'm—well I have no idea what he's decided. And it doesn't matter because I really don't have time for a guy anyway." She absolutely hated the expression of sympathy on Norah's face.

"That doesn't make not hearing from him suck any less. But I saw the way he looked at you that night at the Mudcat. I'm sure there's some kind of explanation."

"There probably is. He's not that long divorced. Maybe he's just not ready to get back out there." Although, if that were the case, the least he could've done was let her know so she didn't waste all this time trying to figure out what *she'd* done wrong.

"You could always call him," Norah suggested. "Maybe he's not sure of how you felt."

"That wasn't an issue." She'd practically climbed him like a tree. And maybe that was the problem. Maybe Ethan didn't like his women that forward. If that were the case, better this happened now instead of weeks or months down the road. Miranda was no shrinking violet, and she didn't want to be with someone who didn't like her exactly as she was.

She drained her wine. "It doesn't matter. We had one date. It was fun, and now it's over. I need to be getting home. If you want me to talk to Clay, I'll do it at the bonfire tomorrow night."

"You're still going?"

"Of course, I'm going. It was one date. I'm not broken-hearted. I'm insulted. What better way to prove it doesn't matter than going on out and having fun?"

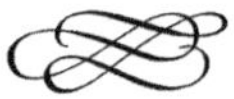

CHAPTER 9

A low-key, informal sort of gig. That's what Clay had said. No frills, no pressure.

The cluster of parked cars big enough to occupy half a football field didn't quite fit with Ethan's expectations. People milled around the big blaze in the distance. Fifty or sixty of them, at a guess, and that was just what he could see from the ambient light of the bonfire.

Was Miranda here?

He tried to tell himself it didn't matter if she was. He was man enough to face her and explain. The truth was, he'd behaved badly. Manners and his own conscience dictated he apologize. But he didn't have the first clue what to say.

It's not you, it's me. Right. Because that always went over so well. He'd just have to trust that the right thing would occur to him.

Ethan parked and pulled his guitar case out of the backseat of the truck. The sky stretched out above, a cloudless blanket of stars. He picked out Orion, the dippers, and Cassiopeia as he made his way to the crowd. Picnic tables sat in a horseshoe just back from the blaze, and camp chairs were clustered along the perimeter. Conversation and laughter carried on the chilly night air. With temperatures hovering in the upper forties, it wasn't at all a bad night for a bonfire. Somebody had music playing from somewhere, and a knot of people were dancing.

Ethan scanned the throng, looking for Clay, automatically registering familiar faces, assessing everybody's level of sobriety. He saw Cam Crawford chatting with Miranda's brother, Mitch. Tucker McGee was there, beside the nurse who'd tended to Ethan in the ER. He recognized one of his other students from the hunter safety class. Damn if he could remember his name just now. He'd been somewhat distracted by having been shot in the ass. Delaney hung a little back from the group, people-watching. Catching his eye, she gave a shy wave. Ethan nodded in acknowledgment. The attention had her dropping her gaze. Was she really that shy? He wasn't here to find out, so he kept moving.

Where the hell was Clay?

A familiar peal of laughter pulled Ethan's attention to the dancers. And there was Miranda, smiling and laughing as she danced with some other guy. Who was that?

"Are you growling?"

Maybe.

Ethan loosened the fingers he'd clenched around the handle of his guitar case and turned to Clay. "Wondered where you were."

"Not dancing with Miranda."

Ethan grunted as he recognized her partner. Ben Rawlings was the head of the Wishful Volunteer Fire Department. He was a good guy, a good firefighter. One Ethan presently wanted to punch.

"Come on and eat something before you go do something stupid," Clay urged.

Ethan followed him over to the food tables and threaded some kielbasa on a skewer. Clay was smart enough not to remark on the fact that he set himself up to roast it where he could keep watching Miranda and Ben. They didn't stop after the one dance. All he could think was that it should've been him.

He knew what it was to dance with her. He'd had her in his arms, had her looking up at him, smiling at him and making him feel about ten feet tall. He'd loved every minute he'd spent with her. Too much. So much that he'd stupidly walked away, and now here she was dancing with another guy.

Dumbass, she was interested in you, *but you blew her off.*

He'd done this to himself, and faced with the consequences of his own fears, he regretted it.

But maybe…maybe he could still have this. Just this. The fun and the laughter. It didn't have to be serious and forever. She hadn't actually offered that, hadn't asked for it. It could just be fun and good. That's what normal people did, right?

Maybe he hadn't blown it completely. He just needed to apologize.

"You're gonna do something stupid, aren't you?" Clay asked.

"I'm gonna risk looking stupid and hopefully do something smart."

Clay rubbed his hands together and grinned. "Oh boy, this should be fun."

As soon as he'd finished his dinner—which he'd burned—Ethan pulled out his guitar. Somebody took that as a sign to cut the music that had been playing. Thank God. He and Clay set up on one of the picnic tables, and folks scrambled to rearrange camp chairs to better hear their performance.

"How you wanna do this?" Clay asked.

"Old school. It's been about a million years since we did an unplugged show."

"All right then. Let's see if you can keep up, old man." He began to strum.

As soon as Ethan recognized Brooks and Dunn's "Neon Moon", he jumped in and found a little piece of home he hadn't even realized he'd missed.

They rolled from one to the next. Alan Jackson. Kentucky Headhunters. Diamond Rio. Garth Brooks. George Straight. They kept it fast and light, fun, in keeping with the tone of the gathering, and as they played, Ethan felt something of his younger, lighterhearted self come back to life. Several people got up to dance. Miranda wasn't one of them, he noted. Others sang along. As they finished their first set, Ethan grinned and offered his fist to Clay for a bump.

Clay returned the gesture. "Good to have you back."

"Good to be back."

Miranda appeared at his elbow, bottles of water in her hands. Now that she was here, Ethan couldn't seem to say anything but "Thanks," as she handed over the water. She looked flushed and beautiful, but there was a layer of reserve he wasn't used to seeing. That was his fault, no doubt. At the very least, he'd pissed her off, and at worst, he'd hurt her with his silence.

His mouth seemed unreasonably dry, so he opened his bottle and tipped it back, buying time to think of something brilliant to say.

"Do you ever sing about anything other than outlaws, drinking, breakups, or exes?" she asked.

Clay laughed and answered for him. "Ethan stopped that a long time ago as a matter of self-preservation."

"Why's that?"

"Because everything else tended to result in either marriage proposals or excessive casseroles." Clay gave a wistful sigh. "Those were the days."

Miranda snorted, some of the unnatural reserve cracking. "Seriously?"

She had no idea. Why should she? She hadn't been in Austin during their heyday. Ethan angled his head to study her. "Is that a challenge?"

"Sure. Why not? Show me what you've got, Chief."

Chief, not Cowboy. Yeah, if he'd needed a clear sign that he'd screwed up, there it was.

He'd wanted to apologize. What better way to do it than this? Strumming his fingers lightly over the strings, he fixed his eyes on hers. "I've been hanging on to this one just for you."

Miranda wasn't sure what she'd expected. He'd said he was the balladeer, so something soulful, maybe. Something blatantly sexy. But as he fixed his eyes on her and her alone and began to play, he sang a prayer. His rich baritone wrapped around her, creating a cocoon from everybody and everything else as he sang of a man who'd hit bottom and lost everything that mattered—including the woman he loved. It was a song of apology, one that seduced her, not only in the simplicity of the plea for a second chance, but in the sincerity of his performance. His gaze never wavered from hers, and the vulnerability he put on display broke through the wall she'd determinedly erected against him.

By the time the last notes died away, Miranda understood that Clay had spoken nothing more than the truth about Ethan's effect on women. That had been a panty-melting performance, as evidenced by the wild cheering from the other women present. Ethan was still watching her, the gray of his eyes almost swallowed up by black. Miranda knew she had to say something, and it had to be something other than, "Come home with me, right now." She needed to lighten the mood somehow and get a hold on her rioting libido.

Taking a firmer grip on the beer bottle she'd nearly dropped, she worked up a casual expression. Or at least one that didn't involve her mouth hanging open. "Well damn. And here I thought Clay gave good smolder."

He remained totally serious, but for the glint in his eyes. "With great power comes great responsibility." One corner of that sinfully sexy mouth kicked up. "So how bout it, Legs? You feeling the urge to bake a chicken pot pie?"

She was feeling the urge to do a lot of things. Most of them naked. Not a one involved a chicken pot pie. "Not a bit."

"Just as well. I need to watch my figure." He set the guitar aside and patted the flat stomach she felt sure sported a six-pack beneath that shirt.

Miranda just shook her head. "I've seen your ass. It'd take more than a few casseroles to make it anything less than a work of art. Medically speaking." She took a sip of her beer to wet her parched throat and managed a real smile this time. "How are your stitches?"

He threw back his head and laughed, a big booming roll of sound. "I'll refrain from making the obvious double-entendre about house calls so you can check."

She tipped her beer in his direction for a toast. "Your heroic restraint is noted and appreciated."

Delaney materialized behind him and mimed fanning herself on the way to the s'mores table. Hot, hot, hot indeed. Miranda dragged her chair a little further from the fire for the next set. By the end of the third, she thought she'd cooled off enough that she could be trusted not to proposition him on the way to her car.

"Give me a second to pack up, and I'll walk you out."

Miranda was counting on it.

She collected her keys from Brody. Ethan joined her, his guitar case in one hand. They headed toward the remaining vehicles. The crowd had thinned out during the last set. And no wonder. It was nearing eleven and a work night.

"What did you think?"

Miranda knew he wasn't asking about the cumulative performance. "As apologies go, that was…something."

"'I'm a dumbass, please forgive me' just doesn't have quite the same lyrical resonance."

She huffed a laugh.

"Seriously, I should've called."

It was gratifying to hear the admission. "Why didn't you?"

"Because of how bad I wanted to approximately five minutes after I dropped you off."

Whatever girly flutter she felt at the fact that he'd wanted to call was overshadowed by the complete foolishness of his explanation. "Ethan, you are seriously challenging my initial impression of you as a logical man."

"Let me see if I can explain in a way that doesn't make me look like any more of a jackass or like a crazy man." He stopped walking and turned to face her. "Everything—our date, that kiss, *you*—it was all more than I was expecting."

"And more is bad?"

"No. Yes. Not exactly."

He was flustered. This capable, intelligent, interesting man was flustered. About her. That was a little more balm to Miranda's wounded ego.

"I'm not looking for more," he said.

She crossed her arms, struggling not to take offense at that. "Ethan, what exactly is it you think I want? Because if I have somehow given you the impression that I am in a rush for marriage, two point five kids, and a picket fence, let me assure you that I'm not. I mean, one of these days, probably, but right now, I don't have time for serious. I am up to my eyeballs in debt. Between my student loans for med school and the business loan on my practice. A practice that's doing well but still requires ninety percent of my time and effort. What I'm looking for is some fun to squeeze into that other ten percent. Which is about where I figured you were, given you're only a handful of months into a new job, in a new town."

His lips twitched and he looked off toward Hope Springs for a moment before bringing his gaze back to hers. "I mentioned the part where I'm a dumbass, right?"

Her mouth gave an answering twitch. A man who could admit he'd been wrong was worth a second chance. "You did."

"Fun and simple is exactly what I'm looking for. *You're* exactly what I'm looking for."

Wasn't that an appealing thought? "Okay then. We're on the same page."

"Looks like. Although I do have one non-negotiable condition."

"Oh?"

"I'm an old-fashioned guy. One woman at a time. So long as we're having fun together, it's just with each other."

"Even if I weren't inclined toward monogamy myself, you're the first guy to catch my interest in two years. That won't be a problem for me."

"Alright then." He finally reached out again and touched her, tucking that hair behind her ear, the pads of his fingers skimming her cheek. "It's late. You should probably be getting home."

Her skin hummed with awareness and the desire he'd kindled with his song earlier. She thought about inviting him home with her, getting started on some of that fun. But it *was* late, and she thought they both needed a little time to be easy with each other again. "Yeah. There's just one thing you should know."

"What's that?"

"I lied earlier."

He went brows up. "About what?"

"Well, a half lie. I don't bake chicken pot pie. I do make homemade tamales."

His smile spread like warm molasses on biscuits. "Time and place, Legs."

"When is your next night off?"

"Sunday."

"Perfect. That gives me all afternoon to roll them. Say six o'clock?"

"I'll be there."

As they reached her SUV, she popped the back hatch and tossed in her folding camp chair. Slamming the liftgate, she frowned. Her Grand Cherokee seemed oddly low. Had she parked in some kind of a dip?

Ethan noticed, too, and flipped on the light on his phone. "You've got a flat."

"Seriously?" She moved around the end of the Jeep to look, pulling out her own phone. "Well, damn it. That's exactly what I wanted to be doing at eleven PM on a January night. Changing a tire in a pasture." She went back to the rear to get the jack and the spare.

"Miranda, don't touch anything." The serious tone had her pausing.

"Why?"

"Because you don't have just one flat. You have four."

"I what?"

From where he crouched by the front driver's side, he looked back at her, expression grim. "Someone punctured your tires."

She made a quick circle around, as if seeing it for herself would somehow change the truth. "Why would anybody do this?"

"You piss anybody off lately?"

"Other than Clarice, who I haven't even seen since that day in the diner? No. I can't imagine pissing anybody off enough for this."

"You haven't had any run-ins with anybody else?"

"No. I—wait." Surely Ralph Slocombe wouldn't do something like this. "I had a patient last week who got upset when I denied him more prescription painkillers when he'd used up his last round too fast. But I don't think he can move well enough to do something like this. He's got a serious back injury and a lot of chronic pain."

"All right, I'll talk to him. Find out if he's got an alibi for tonight. Meanwhile, let me get some stuff from my truck."

Frustrated and upset, Miranda crossed her arms and waited as he did his cop thing, taking pictures of each tire, taking her statement and making notes for a report.

"C'mon. I'll take you home."

"What about my car?"

"I'll see that the tires are dealt with tomorrow."

It was on the tip of her tongue to say she could deal with it herself. She could call for a tow just as easily as he could. But there was something about letting him take care of this annoyance for her. Maybe because it let him be, in a small way, the hero he so clearly wanted to be. And maybe because it was nice to have a hero, for once. "Thanks."

CHAPTER 10

Ralph Slocombe lived in a rundown, single-story ranch built sometime in the 1970s, judging by the sandy yellow tone of the brick. An aging Chevy pickup sat beside an equally well-worn minivan in the driveway, in front of an open garage door. The interior of the space was littered with all the detritus of yard care, covered in a coating of dirt and dust that indicated it hadn't been used in a good long while. The patchy front lawn was more weeds than grass, and the mailbox listed to one side. The whole place looked tired, as did the woman who came out of the house as Ethan stepped out of his cruiser.

She paused the digging in her purse—probably searching for car keys—and stopped by the door of the minivan. "Can I help you, officer?"

"Yes, ma'am. I'm Chief Greer. Does Ralph Slocombe live here?"

Her hands clutched at the purse. "That's my husband. Is something wrong?"

"I just need to ask him a few questions. Is he home?"

"He's right inside." With a nervous flutter of her hands, she gestured toward the house. "I'll just take you to him."

Ethan offered her a smile and followed her into the house, through the garage door. It led into the kitchen, by way of a laundry/mud room combination. Breakfast dishes were piled in the sink, but the room was otherwise spotless. That wasn't the case for the living room Mrs. Slocombe led him to. The sagging furniture matched the man sprawled out in a recliner in front of the TV—threadbare.

"Did you forget somethin', Birdie?"

"The police are here."

Ralph's head whipped toward his wife, then to Ethan. "What's this about?"

"I needed to ask you a few questions, Mr. Slocombe. I'm Chief Greer."

Suspicion clouded the thin man's face, and he asked again, "What's this about?"

"Where were you last night, say between eight o'clock and eleven PM?"

"Right here at home. We had dinner at six-thirty and watched some reruns until bedtime."

"What time did you go to bed?"

Ralph's thin lips pursed as he seemed to consider. "I don't know. Nine-thirty. Ten?"

Ethan glanced at his wife. "Do you happen to remember, Mrs. Slocombe?"

"I went to bed at nine. I don't know what time he went to sleep. He didn't come to bed."

Ethan looked back to Ralph, brows raised in question.

"I been sleepin' in the recliner on account of my back. I got a lot of pain from an old injury, and I don't want to toss and turn and keep Birdie awake."

Birdie nodded. "I can still work, and he doesn't want to wear me out."

"Thoughtful." And convenient. It meant she couldn't truly verify his alibi for the time in question.

"What is it you're pussy footin' around to see if I done?"

"Someone was out at Hope Springs last night, vandalizing a vehicle at the bonfire."

The man looked truly baffled. "And you think I'm the one who done it?"

"It was Miranda Campbell's SUV. I understand you had a bit of an altercation with her last week over your prescription."

Ralph pushed the footrest down and struggled to sit up. Ethan didn't miss the way his cheeks flashed white beneath the hot flush of anger. Pain. The man was definitely in pain. Because he'd overdone it with the vandalism last night? Or had he been in bad enough shape he couldn't have carried it out?

"Did she send you out here after me? I ain't done nothin' to her. I ain't done nothin' wrong."

"I understand from some of her staff that you were pretty upset last week."

"I'm in pain. I'm always in pain and the drugs don't last long enough so I can work. I gotta depend on my wife, when it's my job to take care of her. I ran out, and she wouldn't give me more. Yeah, I was upset. I apologized for it, and I didn't do nothin' against her. She's just doing her job. Ain't her fault the rules are what they are."

Ethan tried a different tack. "May I ask what kind of injury you had?"

"It's my back. Was an on the job injury from a few years ago."

"Where did you work?"

"Heirloom Home Furnishings. They closed well before you got here. Greedy corporate fuckers moved the factory to Mexico. I ain't been able to keep steady work since. Had to go on disability."

Ethan filed that away. "I'm sorry to hear that, Mr. Slocombe." He wasn't gonna get any more out of this interview. "That's all the questions I have. I appreciate your time this morning. Mrs. Slocombe, I hope I haven't made you late for work." He nodded and let himself out. On his way back to the cruiser, he glanced at the Chevy, checking the tires and undercarriage. Dried mud caked them both, but it was red clay, not the dense grayish brown mud he'd heard locals refer to as gray gumbo. As the latter still coated the soles of his own boots from meeting the tow truck out at Hope Springs first thing this morning, he thought it unlikely Ralph Slocombe was their guy.

When he got back to the station, Ethan studied the photos of Miranda's tires as he sucked down a Hot and Sassy from The Daily Grind. He could only hope the double shot of espresso in the drink would make up for the sleep he didn't get last night.

Her tires hadn't just been punctured. They'd been slashed. There was a violence and anger here that niggled at him. This kind of thing tended to be personal rather than random. And that meant someone was very, very pissed off. Was it the same someone who'd keyed her car? Or had that truly been Clarice Morris and this was someone else? Was this the end of it? One destructive burst and done? Or was this just the beginning of something bigger? Something that would target Miranda herself instead of her belongings. Or was it a case of mistaken identity? Hers was hardly the only dark SUV to have been parked at Hope Springs last night.

It had been the only one left when he got the wrecker out there this morning to pick it up, after he'd taken crime scene photos in the daylight. Lou Jenkins had had plenty to say about the issue, none of it actually helpful. But he'd promised to send his nephew to Lawley after four new tires if he didn't have the right size already in stock. Miranda would have her car back today.

Wandering out into the bullpen, he clipped the pictures to the top of the bulletin board. "We had some vandalism last night out at the bonfire. Y'all have been here longer than I have. Do either of y'all remember somebody doing something like this in the past?"

From the desk where she was working on reports, Rowan shook her head. "I don't remember anything." Not surprising. As the newest member of the force and another out-of-towner, she wouldn't be in a position to have heard much.

Inez considered. "Oh, well now, there was that incident with that Newell woman a couple years back."

"Tell me."

The dispatcher eased back in her chair, tapping her chin. "Let's see...she was brought up on stalking charges. Best I can remember, she found out her man was cheating on her. Then he dumped her. Nobody would've blamed her for pulling a Carrie Underwood and carving up his truck—which she did. But she went beyond that and started harassing the new girl. A little bit might have been understandable. But there were phone calls, a fire, and yeah, some vandalism. The girl was scorned right and proper."

"Did she do time?"

Inez shook her head. "No. She ended up getting sentenced to a court-mandated psych eval and inpatient treatment. Must've worked. Haven't heard a word about her since other than gossip rehashing the original story."

"Do me a favor and pull the file."

While he waited, Ethan studied his newest recruit. "How you holding up?"

Rowan shrugged. "Everything's good here. Back in Houston…"

"You don't have too long before the trial."

"No."

"You worried?" Ethan couldn't quite imagine having to testify against former colleagues.

"Less worried, more just ready for it to be over. I'm building a life here, and I'd like to get on with it."

"You adjusting to small town life okay?"

"I'm finding it surprisingly satisfying. What about you? Dallas this is not."

"I'm getting there."

The corner of her mouth tipped up in a smirk. "I expect a certain blonde doctor's helping that cause along."

Was absolutely everybody paying attention to his love life? "Could be."

"Here it is, Chief." Inez came back with a folder.

Ethan ignored Rowan's grin, thanked Inez, and retreated to his office with a Coke. Popping the top, he prepared himself to read all about the escapades of one Delaney Newell. The mugshot had him pausing. Delaney Newell was the red-head from his hunter safety class. The one who worked for Miranda. The one who'd been at the bonfire last night. Did she have some kind of beef with her boss? A quick review of the reports in her file had him grabbing his keys to go find out.

MIRANDA WAS CONSIDERING whether she could just attach the coffee maker to an IV drip by the time Ethan showed up mid-afternoon. Her patient load had been insane, and she was having serious regrets about not making it into bed sooner. Especially as she'd lain awake regretting the practicality that had kept her from having the buzz of good sex to make up for the loss of sleep. But the sight of him swinging through the door of the clinic with that long, rangy gait had her spirits and energies lifting. Then she saw the green and white striped bakery box.

"Afternoon, Doc."

She could hardly tear her eyes off the box in his hand. "Are those cupcakes from Sweet Magnolias?"

"They might be."

"Don't play with me, Chief. I'm a desperate woman when it comes to cupcakes."

"Somebody told me you had a habit. Consider me your dealer for the day." He lifted the lid to reveal a half dozen Better Than Sex cupcakes.

Miranda whimpered—actually whimpered—and grabbed for one. "Sweet baby Jesus, you are my hero."

She bit in and the blend of devil's food cake, caramel, and sweetened condensed milk burst on her tongue, the sugar hitting her bloodstream in a rush that was, despite the name, not quite as good as sex. Still, she gave a little moan and didn't miss the way his eyes darkened. Did he know what these were called, or had Carolanne picked them out?

She peeled away more of the wrapper to devour the other half. "Is this your way of softening the bad news that my car isn't actually ready?"

"Nope." He pulled the keys from his pocket. "Just had Lou drop it off. You're good to go. He said you can settle about the bill later this week."

"You're just racking up all kinds of points today."

He huffed a laugh. "I'll keep that in mind. Is there somewhere we can speak in private for a minute?"

Miranda wasn't sure if she should be concerned or if he was just looking for somewhere to slake a little of the desire still humming between them. She couldn't read him. He didn't have the kind of gravely serious expression she'd come to associate with their conversations about Rene and Harley Forbes. "Come on back to the break room."

He trailed her down the hall to a faint chorus of "oooooo" from the peanut gallery. Miranda was in too good a mood from her cupcake to flip them off. She finished the last bite and shut the door. "Before you say whatever it is you don't want them to hear, I need to say something."

"All right."

"Thank you." Curling her fingers in the front of his uniform shirt, she lifted her lips to his for a lazy, open-mouthed kiss. Without hesitation, his hands dug into her hips, dragging her closer. He angled his head, taking the kiss past a well-intentioned thank you and into *does this door have a lock?* territory.

Because she couldn't quite forget the fact that this was her clinic, and she had staff and patients all over the place—not to mention the fact that she truly couldn't remember if this door locked—Miranda eased back. "There. That should hold me for a few hours anyway."

His expression was positively feral, and Miranda loved it. "Christ, woman, how am I supposed to get through the rest of the day without thinking about taking you to bed?"

Smiling sweetly, she grabbed another cupcake and offered it to him. "Better Than Sex?"

Keeping his eyes on hers, he took a bite and swallowed. "I should write Carolanne up for false advertising."

Rising to her toes, Miranda licked at the icing on the corner of his mouth. "You could. Or you could devote some of your day to carving out time in your schedule to actually take me to bed."

"We need to schedule it?"

"Two busy people, respectively on call a lot of the time? Yeah. Because once I have you in my bed, Ethan, I don't intend to let you out for quite a while."

He groaned. "Have I mentioned, I really love the fact that you're direct?"

"Life's complicated enough without adding guesswork about things that are really pretty basic. I want you. You want me. That's simple. Elemental."

"I'll check the duty calendar as soon as I get back to the station."

"Good. Now what did you actually come here for, besides to deliver my car and cupcakes?"

"To talk to you about who might have slashed your tires."

Well, that was a nice arousal killer. "Did you to talk to Ralph?"

"Yeah. He doesn't have a verifiable alibi. Claimed to be home with his wife, but he's sleeping in the recliner so his tossing and turning doesn't keep her awake. After meeting him, I'm inclined to agree with your assessment that he may not be physically able to do the deed."

"Which leaves us where? I already told you last night, I can't think of anybody who'd do something like that."

She saw the subtle shift into cop mode. "Ralph can't be the only doctor shopper you've had. Can you get me a list of everyone you've had any kind of similar run-in with for, say, the past six months?"

"I'll have Shelby pull something together for you. She keeps the records for that kind of thing. But I'll go ahead and tell you, nobody stands out."

"It might not have anything to do with that, but it's an avenue I want to explore." He paused. "What about Delaney?"

Miranda's back went up in a second. "Excuse me?" She shoved out of his arms. If this was going where she thought it was going, she needed some distance.

"I read her file today. Are you aware she has a criminal record? That she was arrested for stalking and vandalism?"

Miranda lifted her chin. "Yes."

That seemed to surprise him. "You knew all that and hired her anyway?"

"People can change."

"That was some pretty destructive behavior. I saw the crime scene photos of the damage she'd caused."

Irritation began to bubble and stew. He was doing his job, following leads. It was no wonder someone had mentioned Delaney to him. He didn't know her, didn't know Wishful, so it was on Miranda to help balance out that automatic suspicion. If she wanted him to take her opinion on this seriously, she had to remain calm. Taking a firm grip on her temper, she shoved it down and locked it away.

"Some of it was justified, given how that asshole treated her. But that aside, she was ill. The judge sent her to treatment, where she was accurately diagnosed and properly treated for the first time in her life. Since that incident, she's been on the straight and narrow, without a single blip of a problem. That whole sordid mess seriously fucked up her life, Ethan. All she wants is to get everything back on track. I gave her a job and chance when no one else would, and she's never given me cause to regret it. She has absolutely no reason to target me."

"You haven't had any tiffs? Any frustration with rate of pay or problems with her performance in any way?"

"Not a one. She's an exemplary employee. Look, I appreciate that you're being thorough here, and I know you're used to looking for the worst in people, but you're barking up the wrong tree."

She waited for him to tell her she was being foolish, seeing good where there was none. It's what Stephen would've done. Instead, he angled his head, studying her. "She's really got your loyalty, hasn't she?"

"She's earned it."

He lifted his hands in surrender. "All right. Well, until I figure this out, you need to be extra careful. No being on the phone on the way to your car. Pay attention to your surroundings. If somebody is targeting you, you don't want to make it easier for them to attack."

His concern was sweet, but his big city was showing.

"I appreciate the concern, Ethan. I know the drill. I did live in Chicago for a number of years. And a huge part of the reason I came home was so I didn't have to be so vigilant. This is Wishful. More than likely it's some kind of malicious prank. One and done." She had to believe that or what was the world coming to?

"Maybe. Maybe not. There's been a string of robberies in Lawley the last few months. Pharmacies and doctor's offices. So far there's no sign it's expanded here, but you can't be too careful."

Miranda opened her mouth to respond, but the break room door burst open and her brother strode in. "What the hell is this about your tires being slashed last night?"

She fixed him with a bland stare. "Hello to you, too, Mitch."

"Seriously, why did I have to hear about this at The Grind instead of directly from you?"

"Because it's taken care of," she said dryly.

Mitch shifted his attention to Ethan. "You've found the person responsible?"

"I'm working on it."

Her brother made some monosyllabic grunt and turned his attention back to her. "I don't like the idea of leaving the country without somebody watching your back."

"First off, I have absolutely no bearing on your plans to go to that conference in France. You've been looking forward to this for nearly a year. If you cancel over something this minor, you're an idiot. Secondly, I don't need anybody watching my back, as I am a grown-ass woman—"

Ethan interrupted her. "No one's going to lay a hand on her. I'm going to get to the bottom of this. You have my word."

They eyed each other, a couple of big, tall, over-protective males. The testosterone in the room was almost enough to choke her. Miranda rolled her eyes and made shooing motions at them both. "Okay, you know what? I still have patients to see, and I would like to get out of here sometime this century. You two go take your male posturing outside and let me get back to work. I can take care of myself, thank you very much."

Ethan shifted his gaze to her, and she saw a hint of heat under the serious cop expression he'd put on as soon as Mitch barged in. "I'll be in touch, Doc."

"Fine. Fine. Thanks for helping with my car. Now, both of you get out."

CHAPTER 11

*M*iranda's brother followed Ethan out. "She's pissed at us."

"Yep," Ethan confirmed, slipping on his aviator glasses and scanning the parking lot.

Mitch stepped up beside him, hooking his thumbs in the pockets of his khakis and rocking back on his heels. "Is that my sister's lipstick on your mouth?"

Well, shit. He resisted the urge to wipe his mouth. "That a problem for you?"

"Don't know yet." He shot Ethan an appraising look out of hazel eyes that were so like his sister's.

Ethan sighed. "Is this the part where you threaten to break me in half if I hurt her?"

Mitch's look was part amusement, part pity. "Nope. My sister's got claws, and she fights dirty. You hurt her, she'll take care of you herself. I'll just be there to help hide the body."

Ethan couldn't decide whether to smile or scowl. "You do remember I'm the chief of police, right?"

"My money's still on her."

"Good to know. In all seriousness, though, do you know of anybody who's pissed at her? Somebody who'd want to get back at her like this?"

"You don't think this is just petty vandalism?"

"I'm not sure what to think. Somebody keyed her car a few weeks back. Now this."

"You think they're connected?"

"Timing seems pretty coincidental if it's not. Maybe, if there had been multiple vehicles targeted last night, I'd've bought the idea that it was some kind of random vandalism. But all four of just *her* tires? That screams personal to me. I just have to figure out who and why."

Mitch considered. "Miranda's not any kind of a shrinking violet, but she's not the kind of woman who has a lot of enemies."

"It only takes one."

Her brother frowned. "Fair enough. I can't think of anybody. But Norah might have better ideas. Miranda talks to her more."

"She was gonna be my next stop."

"Do you think she's in any legitimate danger?"

"No. It's a long damned way from vandalism and harassment to bodily harm, and I can assure you I won't let anybody lay a hand on her."

"Except you," Mitch observed.

"That's a whole other thing and none of your business."

After a long moment of silence, he nodded. "You might be all right, Greer."

Ethan smirked. "High praise."

"Hey. Take what you can get. Can I ask you something?"

"You can ask. I won't commit to an answer."

"Did you really end up with marriage proposals from your performances back in the day?"

At this Ethan did smile. "Yeah."

"How many?"

"I stopped counting at twenty."

Mitch whistled. "Damn. Were you ever tempted?"

"I appreciate a forward woman on most fronts, but on this, I'm still old fashioned. They were doomed to disappointment."

"Fair enough. I'd best be getting on. I appreciate you keeping an eye out for my sister."

"I'll keep her safe."

After Mitch left, Ethan wiped his mouth and considered his next move. Whether Miranda believed it was a thing or not, nobody went around slashing random people's tires without a reason. They'd already started a list last night of who'd been at the bonfire, but he knew it wasn't complete. With that in mind, he walked the three blocks to City Hall to track down Norah. In his short time in Wishful, he'd learned that the city planner had a mind like a steel trap when it came to people. She ought to be able to flesh out the guest list considerably. Ethan knew the perpetrator might not have been someone everybody saw at the party. Somebody could have arrived and left without ever joining the group, but it was the next logical step.

Man on a mission, he greeted Jerry Noble, the guard stationed at the front of City Hall who was old as Croesus, then loped up the stairs to the third floor. Norah's door was closed, so he knocked and waited.

"It's open! Come on in."

Turning the knob, he stepped inside. "Hey Norah, I was wondering if I could ask you a few questions." The sentence faded by the end because she wasn't alone. Miranda's mother was seated in one of the guest chairs across from Norah's desk. "I'm sorry. You're tied up. I can come back later."

When he made to beat a hasty retreat, Norah just waved him to the other chair. "Sit. Aunt Liz and I were just finishing up. You remember Lisbette Campbell?"

Ethan inclined his head, wishing he had his Stetson to take off, so he had something to do with his hands. "Yes, ma'am."

The woman was a shorter, older version of her daughter, albeit with slightly darker hair and blue eyes. Those eyes were fixed on him with an intense scrutiny that made him wonder if he'd managed to get all the lipstick off his mouth. Was he just going to run into all of the Campbells today?

"You've been seeing my daughter."

The back of his neck itched. "Yes, ma'am."

Liz nodded. "You'll come to family dinner on Thursday."

Ethan recognized an order when he heard one, no matter how much of a smile went along with the delivery. "That's a kind offer, Mrs. Campbell, but I'm on duty Thursday."

She waved that away and rose from her chair. "Nonsense. You have to eat. If you have to leave early, so be it. You should meet the rest of the family."

He'd seen all of them at Norah and Cam's wedding back in the fall. There were a lot of Campbells. It looked like he was gonna get trotted out for their inspection to deem if he was worthy of one of their own. Recognizing there was no graceful way out of the situation, short of manufacturing a call on the day of the event, Ethan conceded. "Yes, ma'am. A home-cooked meal would be nice. I'll look forward to it."

"Good. Miranda will let you know the time and place." She patted him on the arm. "See you Thursday, Chief Greer."

"Yes, ma'am."

Norah's eyes were sparkling with unrestrained amusement as her —What the hell was Lisbette Campbell to her? Aunt-in-law? Was that a thing?—walked out of the office. Once her footsteps had faded, he let out a careful breath.

"You have any survival tips for that?"

Her mouth bowed. "Oh, no. You get to navigate this on your own. I'm just gonna enjoy it all from the cheap seats."

Ethan offered her a bland stare. "Thanks for that."

She laughed. "What can I do for you, Ethan?"

"Were you aware that Miranda's car was vandalized at the bonfire last night?"

All humor fled. "What?"

"Her tires were slashed. I was hoping you could help me compile a list of who all was there last night. I know you left before we did, but I figure you can add some names to the existing list."

"Yes, of course."

He pulled out his little notebook, and they went over the list. She added quite a few more, offering up little vignettes about each person to give him an idea of their character.

"But I can't imagine any of these people doing something like this."

"What about Delaney Newell?"

Norah blinked. "I know she's had some issues. But from what I understand, she's been medicated since her stint in treatment and hasn't stepped a toe out of line."

"What exactly was Delaney treated for?"

"Bipolar disorder, I believe. Miranda would be able to tell you more about it."

"You and I both know she won't."

"True enough. She's very protective of Delaney. Either way, I'd have a really hard time imagining her targeting Miranda like that. Miranda has done a lot for her, when nobody else would."

"That's essentially what Miranda said."

Norah's expression turned thoughtful. "Although..."

"What?"

"It's just that she seemed a little upset last night."

"Upset how?"

"Well, honestly, it was when you were singing to Miranda. Nicely done, by the way. Delaney just looked a little sick and left not long after. Maybe the hot dogs didn't agree with her or something and the timing was coincidental, but I remember thinking it was a little odd. We were all enjoying you and Clay performing."

It wasn't a lot, but it was enough to make Ethan hang on to the suspicion nagging at the back of his brain. He'd do his due diligence to chase down any other leads, but whether Miranda liked it or not, Delaney Newell needed a closer look.

Nodding, he closed his notebook and rose. "Thanks for your help, Norah."

"No problem. If I think of anything else, I'll be sure to let you know."

"I guess I'll be seeing you Thursday."

"I promise Grammy's pie will make the whole experience worth it."

"I'm sure pie would make all interrogations go better."

"Oh, they won't interrogate you. Probably. Aunt Liz knows Miranda would wait forever to bring you around because she never brings guys to family dinner. She's just circumventing for the chance to see the two of you together."

"So, it's a recon mission."

Norah laughed. "Something like that. You're a smart man, and you're legitimately into her. You'll be fine."

"You don't have any warnings to issue? Mitch already had his shot today."

"Nope. I saw everything I needed to see last night at the bonfire."

Ethan realized he had, perhaps, shown too much of his hand with that performance. "She's an amazing and appealing woman."

"Yes, she is. It's good that you can see that. See you Thursday, Chief."

～

"LET me just say again how sorry I am she shanghaied you into family dinner." Miranda bustled around the kitchen, gathering plates and utensils so she didn't quite have to look at Ethan. Of course, *of course,* her family couldn't let her bring him around in her own time. Of *course,* they bypassed her entirely. "I love my family. I really do, but there's a reason I haven't introduced anybody to them in years. It's one of the perils of dating in the same small town where you grew up. I have an enormous family, and they all really like to meddle. I mean, I really shouldn't say anything. I meddled all over the place with Cam and Norah, but I totally had ulterior motives."

Before she could grab the tamales, Ethan stepped into her path, tipping her chin up so he could look into her eyes. "I don't mind, Legs. My interest in you isn't a secret."

And he'd apparently impressed the hell out of her mother with his easy manners. "I know. I just…this doesn't fall under the heading of what we agreed to. Meeting the family is decidedly *not* part of the Fun and Simple Plan, and I don't want you to be over-whelmed." She also really, *really* hoped that her mother's interference didn't blow the *other* plans she and Ethan had for tonight.

Those gunmetal gray eyes warmed. "I'm a big boy." He brushed a quick kiss over her lips and got out of her way. "Anyway, I may have a small family, but because I grew up on a ranch, I had a whole big honorary family who felt it was their duty to look out for me. I don't overwhelm easy."

"Did they try to intimidate the women you brought home?"

"Girls. I was under eighteen for most of it. And no. It was more them looking out to make sure I was nothing more than the perfect gentleman. Which I was, because I knew the second I wasn't, it'd get back to my mama, and I'd live to regret it. The only one they tried to intimidate was my wife. Which, looking back, I probably should've seen as a sign."

Miranda's curiosity sharpened. She'd known he was divorced, but this was the first time he'd mentioned her. "They didn't like her?"

"It wasn't personal exactly. They thought Becca was a perfectly nice woman. Just not right for me."

"Why?"

"She was a city girl, for one. Not that there's anything wrong with that. There was some question of common ground to start. Plus, I already had my eye on the Marshal Service by the time we got engaged. Mom wasn't sure she'd be able to hack being married to someone in law enforcement. And, as it turned out, she was right."

Miranda glanced at him as she loaded tamales and spicy Mexican rice onto plates. "What happened?"

He scrubbed a hand over his face. "She worried, of course. Didn't really understand why I loved the job, and she sure as hell hated that the job so often had to come before her. But the final straw was when I got shot. She had me served with divorce papers while I was still in the hospital."

"That bitch!" The words spilled out before Miranda could stop them. "Oh God, I'm sorry. That was inappropriate."

Ethan chuckled. "Oh, my mama would like you. That's a sentiment she shares, along with Paul, Clay, Julie, and everybody else who mattered in my life at the time." He carried the plates to the table. "I won't lie. It sucked. But at that point it was really just our marriage coming to an obvious conclusion. We weren't well-matched. She kept hoping I'd go back to Clay, back to the music. That I'd finally agree to Nashville. She'd have been a lot more okay with that kind of lifestyle. But that's not me, and I guess it just took us both too long to see that."

Miranda choked back the irrational jealousy that he'd probably played and sung to his wife as he had to her the other night. "That's all well and good, but she could have at least had the decency to wait until you were out of the hospital."

"The papers had already been drawn up weeks before. She'd just been working up the nerve to give them to me. I guess my nearly dying lit a fire under her to get it over with as quickly as possible."

She shook her head. "How do you get over something like that?"

"Is that your way of asking if I am over it?"

"You ought to recognize by now that if that's what I wanted to know, I'd come straight out and ask."

"I do appreciate the fact that you're a straight shooter. And for the record, I am. I mean, I've got a few scars from it. But I don't figure anybody makes it to thirty-six without a few."

"True enough."

"What about you? You ever get close to walking down the aisle?"

She thought of Stephen. "Not really. There was one guy I considered going there with during my residency."

"Another doctor?"

"Yeah."

"What happened?"

He'd shared his story. It was only fair if she reciprocated. "In the beginning it was great. Dating somebody in the same profession, you get each other on a level that someone who isn't an insider just can't. You're both on the same page with the demands of the job, the stressors and the pressures. He knew exactly what I was facing because he faced the same thing every day. He was a couple years further along in the residency than I was."

"Another trauma surgeon?"

"Yeah. Brilliant. We were good together. Until we weren't. We handled the stress very differently. We had a revolving door of all kinds of trauma from violence coming through our hospital. Stephen followed our mentor's example of erecting that wall between himself and his patients. I didn't."

"That was a problem?"

"Yeah. He grew to resent the extra time I spent with patients, trying to help them with linkage to better care, going above and beyond repairing the immediate damage to their bodies to try to save them from whatever shitty situation brought them to me in the first place. He couldn't understand why I'd do that. Why I'd go that extra mile for junkies or gang members or prostitutes, who were just going to go back out there and engage in the same behaviors that got them hurt in the first place. He said I was stupid for putting so much into people who weren't going to change." The memory of that conversation, of the sneer on that aristocratic mouth, had her clenching her hand around the fork.

She dared a glance at Ethan. "I guess you probably wonder the same thing."

He shook his head. "No. I know why you did it. He didn't see them as human, as people. And you couldn't see them as anything else. I may understand where he was coming from, recognizing that most of those people weren't going to change. Doesn't mean I agree with his approach. Your idealism doesn't make you stupid or foolish, Miranda. It makes you a goddamned amazing doctor. And I don't know how all of it works, but I'm willing to bet your patients probably had better outcomes because you gave a damn."

Her throat went thick, her chest tight. This amazing, intuitive man absolutely got it. Got her. At that knowledge, she felt the edges of that long open wound start to close up. Unable to speak, she stood and circled around to his chair, slipping into his lap. Taking his face between her palms, she pressed her mouth softly to his. His arms came around her, an easy, comfortable hold, as his mouth opened under hers. There was heat simmering, as always, but this was about something else.

On a sigh, she rested her brow against his.

"Not that I'm complaining, but what was that for?"

"For understanding me."

Ethan skimmed his fingers over her cheek, into her hair. "I've made something of a study of you the last few weeks."

"You're a very good student."

"I'm looking forward to the practical, hands-on exam."

Heat flared low in her belly, and she straightened to look into his eyes. "Are you now?"

"Been thinking about it an awful lot. But we've got these kickass tamales you worked so hard on, so I'm gonna be a good guest and appreciate them first."

She twined her fingers in the hair at his nape. He was a couple weeks past due for a trim. "Putting on the brakes again, Cowboy?"

"Not brakes. Just pacing myself. Plus, I really love tamales."

On a grin and a laugh, she slid off his lap and returned to her own seat. "Okay then. You'll have to let me know if mine are up to snuff."

The fact that he went back for seconds and thirds was answer enough. Conversation turned to lighter topics the rest of the meal. He earned a whole other set of brownie points for helping her not only clear up the plates, but wash all the dishes involved in prep. There was something unbearably hot about a man who wasn't afraid to roll up his sleeves and do some dishes. By the time she put away the last of the pots and pans, the pleasant little hum in her blood cranked up to a simmer.

"You want coffee? A beer?" *Me?*

He held up a finger as his phone began to ring. "Greer."

Miranda knew by the expression on his face that he wasn't going to be having any of the above.

"I'm on my way." He hung up the phone, his face set in lines of regret. "I'm so sorry."

"Nature of the job, Cowboy."

He snagged his coat and slid it on. "I'm not even technically on call tonight, but I've got several lines set right now, and I maybe just got a bite. I need to follow it through."

"I get it." She opened the door and kissed him. "Go, do your job. Catch the bad guys."

Something flared hot in those smoky eyes. He slid both hands into her hair and laid his mouth over hers in a blistering kiss of frustration and promise that said he wasn't gonna be putting this off any longer than he had to. "I'll see you soon, Legs."

Then he was striding toward his truck.

Blood pumping at more than a simmer now, she stepped out on the porch and watched him pull out of the drive. There was something to be said for all the interruptions. Whenever they did go to bed, the anticipation was going to add a really great edge.

As his taillights disappeared at the end of the road, Miranda felt a chill skate down her spine, poking holes in her warm, fuzzy happiness. Automatically she scanned the area, looking for the eyes she felt on her. She didn't see any of her neighbors out, didn't see any signs of movement in their windows. Of course, it was full dark. There was no telling who—or what—was out there.

Ethan has made you paranoid.

She hated that. Hated the erosion of inherent safety she felt from home. She'd left Chicago to escape all this. To be reminded of all the good of humanity in a place full of decent, loving people. She refused to let her view of home be tainted.

It's probably just Mrs. Gifford's cat. I really hope he's not nosing around the shed again.

Shrugging off the sense of being watched, she went back inside. But just in case, she locked the deadbolt.

CHAPTER 12

The one and only time Ethan had seen all the Campbells together, he'd been putting Cam's father in handcuffs at his and Norah's wedding. Miranda could only hope that this family dinner would be a calmer affair. Then again, she knew her family. She'd spent the last few days thinking up ways to derail prospective interrogation. Ethan might think he had the leg up in that arena, but he hadn't ever faced a meal with the entire Campbell clan.

Ethan's hand pressed into the small of her back as they made their way up Grammy's front walk. "Relax. It's gonna be fine."

Miranda liked the possessive feel of it. She shot him a pitying glance. "Oh sugar, you keep believing that. Don't say I didn't warn you."

She opened the door onto semi-controlled chaos. The din of conversation led them into the living room, where all twelve members of her family—including the latest contingent of fiancées and spouses—were sprawled or perched on the furniture. The crackling of Ethan's radio drew everyone's attention.

With an easy smile, he held up a finger and turned the volume down. "Sorry 'bout that. I'm on duty. Evenin' everybody."

Miranda's mom rose immediately. "Welcome, welcome! We're so glad you were able to make it."

"I appreciate the invite."

Look at him being all polite. Such a good Southern gentleman.

"Miranda, perhaps you'd like to make introductions?"

Miranda recognized an order couched as a suggestion when she heard one. "Everybody, this is Ethan Greer, our Chief of Police. But then y'all already knew that. Ethan, this is the peanut gallery, otherwise known as my family. You already know Cam and Norah; my brother, Mitch; and of course Aunt Sandy and her husband Trey."

Ethan shook the hand of their resident billionaire. "Hard to forget a killer right cross. Good to see you again, sir. And you, Mayor Peyton."

"Likewise."

"Over here is my cousin, Reed, and his fiancée, Cecily Dixon. These are Reed's parents, my Uncle Jimmy and Aunt Anita. This lovely lady over here is my Grammy, Helen Campbell."

Ethan took her hand between both of his and actually bowed a little. "Ma'am."

Grammy simpered.

"I believe you've already had the pleasure of meeting my mother, Liz, and this is my dad, Pete."

Her father gave Ethan a thorough once over and a firm handshake. "Good to meet you, son."

"And you, sir."

Before he could launch into any variation of *what are your intentions toward my daughter?* Miranda mimed dusting off her hands. "There, introductions dispensed with. What are y'all talking about?"

Please, God, let it not be us. Or the vandalism to my car. She'd asked Mitch not to share. Norah, too, though she'd told Cam, of course. Despite the care Ethan had taken to have things repaired on the down low, Miranda knew there was still an excellent chance that the news had leaked from somewhere else.

"We just drew straws to see who gets stuck taking Mitch to the airport in the morning," Cam announced.

Mitch grinned. "Mom won."

"You have to be there at five-thirty. I'd say Aunt Liz lost," Norah pointed out.

"Oh, I never regret time spent with my baby boy." Liz reached up to frame Mitch's face between her hands and dragged him down for a smacking kiss.

"Better you than me," Miranda muttered.

"You weren't even in the pool. Nobody's gonna risk your wrath with a pre-dawn wakeup call." Mitch shifted his attention to Ethan. "This one is liable to shoot morning people on sight and drink coffee while sitting on their cooling corpses."

Miranda grimaced. "What a lovely pre-dinner image."

"Hey, the man deserves fair warning—ow!" Mitch glared down at Norah, who had subtly dug her heel into his foot.

This was why they'd been best friends for more than a decade.

Grammy leapt into the conversational breech. "I can't believe you're going to be gone for three whole weeks!"

"It's been ages since I took a proper vacation," Mitch said. "The conference is nearly a week, and if I'm already on that side of the pond, it seemed like a good opportunity to do some sightseeing. Rhett and I are hitting up as many architectural wonders in Europe as we can fit in."

"This is technically his going away dinner," Miranda explained. She figured she could refrain from doing a happy dance that her brother would be out of the way as her relationship with Ethan progressed. At least until she was out of his sight.

"Speaking of dinner, now that everybody's here, let's eat!" Grammy herded them all into the big kitchen, where everybody grabbed a plate, bowl, or platter and carried it into the dining room.

Liz passed the roasted carrots. "Have you ever been to Europe, Ethan?"

"No, ma'am. I had a few fugitive cases that took me into South America, but they weren't exactly vacations. Not the kind of places you want to sightsee."

"Must've been exciting stuff, chasing bad guys." Her father forked up a stuffed pork chop. "Big change to come here."

Translation: Do you see yourself staying?

It was a question Miranda wanted the answer to herself, but she hadn't felt like they'd quite reached the point to ask it. She wasn't sure he knew the answer yet and didn't want to put him on the spot. They were good as they were, right now. Fun and simple. It was what they both wanted.

Ethan didn't hesitate as he added green beans to his plate. "Yes, sir. I was looking for a change."

"Why small town policing?" Uncle Jimmy asked.

Ethan's lips twitched, the first break in his serious cop expression. "Well, I had hoped it would keep me from being shot again."

"Of all the ERs in all the towns in all the world, you walked into mine," Miranda intoned. "At least it was just a flesh wound." The smile in his eyes unraveled some of the knots in her belly.

"Not complaining. You've got a way neater hand with stitches than my last doctor."

Cecily's eyes had gone wide. "You've really been shot?"

Oh really, don't bring this up over dinner.

But Ethan just nodded. "Couple times. Once in the Army, once as a Deputy Marshal. If tradition dictates I'm gonna get a new scar for every new job, then I guess it's good I got this one out of the way early."

"Where are the other ones?" Grammy asked.

"We are *not* discussing battle scars at dinner," Miranda interrupted. She was certain the other two didn't have nearly as amusing a story to go along with them, and she didn't want to bring up bad memories for him.

Norah—God love her—jumped in to change the topic. "The details for the fundraiser are all squared away, so now we're down to just sorting the details for decorating and set up."

Ethan raised his brows in polite interest. "Fundraiser?"

"We're using part of the proceeds from the Valentine's Dance as a fundraiser to help furnish the expansion at Monarch House," she explained. "It was Miranda's idea."

Uncomfortable with the pride in her friend's tone, Miranda shrugged and forked up a bite of pork chop. "You're doing all the work."

"You'll have your turn when it's time to set up. Speaking of setup, what are you doing on February 12th, Ethan?"

"I don't know off-hand. I'd have to check the duty schedule."

"If you aren't on duty, do you think you could help us with setup at the community center? We can use more strong backs and tall people."

"I'll have to see." Courteous, noncommittal.

Cecily laughed. "Oh, that's cute. He thinks he can dodge you."

Cam smirked and looked fondly at his wife. "You may as well give up now. She always gets her way."

"Nicest steamroller you'll ever meet," Miranda added.

"Resistance is futile," Aunt Sandy agreed. "Why do you think we made her the city planner?"

Norah just batted her eyes, the picture of innocence.

Ethan laughed, and Miranda knew he was going to capitulate. "You are a dangerous woman, Mrs. Crawford. Fine. If I am not on duty or otherwise tied up with police business, I can come haul tables or hang stuff or whatever."

"Excellent."

"But I'd like your help with something, too."

Trey pointed at Ethan in approval. "Oh, quid pro quo. The man has brains."

"I've got a kid who is, shall we say, at-risk. He got into some trouble for fighting, and I convinced Judge Carpenter to put him on community service and informal probation. By my choice, I set it up for him to work off those hours out at Chester Harkin's farm."

"Doesn't he have some kind of feud going on with Maudie Belle Ramsey of the Casserole Patrol?" Norah asked.

"Well, we call it a feud. Apparently, he calls it flirting. Chester and I have already talked about that in a separate conversation. Anyway, I wanted to pitch the idea of a more formal program that links teens with seniors. It wouldn't have to just be juvenile offenders. If the high school has any kind of mandatory community service component, it would be a good way for students to meet that requirement. It'd help keep the kids out of trouble and provide some assistance to older folks who need it."

Norah clapped her hands together. "I love it. Done. I'd do that even if you weren't helping with the dance. But no takesies-backsies."

"Wouldn't dream of it."

"Will you be coming to the dance?"

"That depends." Ethan shifted his gaze to Miranda, and she wondered if anybody else noticed that wicked gleam. "You wanna give me a reason to wear my dress boots?"

Her lips twitched. "You have dress boots?"

Feigning a wounded expression, he laid a hand over his heart. "Darlin', I'm from West Texas." He broadened the Texas twang, until he sounded like something out of one of the spaghetti westerns she loved.

She couldn't help it. She went full on dimples. "Well, you have already proved you can dance, so I'd say you've got a date, Cowboy."

He grinned, even as the radio at his shoulder began to squawk. "Sorry, y'all." Dialing up the volume so he could hear better, he replied, "This is Greer, come back."

"Chief, Raines was sent to respond to a call at the Forbes place about twenty minutes ago. A neighbor just called in a report of shots fired, and I can't raise Raines on the radio."

The bottom fell out of Miranda's stomach. Rene? Johnny?

Ethan shoved back from the table. "Get medical on stand-by, radio all available units for assistance. I'm en route."

"Corbett Raines, that new, young officer?" Aunt Anita asked.

Ethan's only reply was a curt, "Yes, ma'am," as he strode from the room.

Miranda scrambled up after him. "I'm coming with you."

He rounded on her, the humor in his eyes replaced by implacable steel. This was the soldier. The Marshal. The man ready and willing to put his life on the line. "The hell you are."

In another context she'd find the commanding snap of his voice incredibly sexy, but right now she met steel with steel. "It's either my patient or your officer who could be shot. You want medical on standby. I'm medical, and I guarandamntee you that I've got more experience with gunshot wounds than any of the para-medics or EMTs in the county. Do I need to tell you how fast someone can bleed out? How rapidly someone can sink into sepsis if it's a gut shot? Whatever it is, I can stabilize them long enough to get to the actual hospital. Let me help."

For just a few moments he looked like he wished he could throttle her. Or maybe handcuff her to a chair so he'd know she was safe and out of harm's way. But he knew as well as she did that there was no time to argue.

"You wear a vest, and you stay in the floorboard of the car and don't move until I say move. Got it?"

She nodded once. "My bag's in my car."

ETHAN HATED everything about this situation. He hated that his rookie was in there alone and over his head. He hated the lack of backup—though Darius was hauling ass from a call on the other side of town. That he was about to be entering the unknown in another piece-of-shit trailer, exactly like the one where he'd taken the bullet that nearly killed him. Most of all, he hated that Miranda was here because he knew exactly how fast this shit could go FUBAR, and he needed her safe and out of harm's way.

"The vest is too big to fit you properly, but it's better than nothing at all." He'd strapped his spare one on her himself, adjusting as much as possible. It wasn't enough. He saw too many places a bullet could slip through.

Miranda reached up to cup his cheek. "Stop imagining how this could go wrong. I'm not looking to do something stupid here. I'm staying down and out of sight until you say otherwise. Focus on the job, not me."

His hands closed over her shoulders for just a second. He didn't have the time to find the words he wanted to say, not when someone's life was on the line. "We need to have a conversation later."

"Then we will. You can yell at me as much as you want, after everybody's safe."

Yelling wasn't what he had in mind. But he shut it down because he couldn't have her in his head and do his job. Behind her, Darius's cruiser whipped onto the street. Thank God. Ethan hadn't wanted to go in without backup, but another minute or two and he would've. Corbett's life might be counting on it.

In the distance, the wail of an ambulance siren could be heard. Reaching for the radio, he tapped the county dispatcher. "Get on the horn and have the ambulance cut the siren. I want them to stop, just out of sight, and stay put to wait for my order."

A few moments later, the siren went silent.

Darius parked the car at an angle next to Ethan's, effectively blocking the drive. He climbed out. "How you wanna play this, Chief?"

"As far as we know, Raines is still in there, and he's non-responsive. There's a door in front and another in back. You circle around and wait. I'll approach from the front, enter first. If Forbes is gonna bolt, it'll probably be out the back once I breach. If he tries to run, take his ass down. Otherwise, come straight in the back."

Darius nodded and headed into the trees.

Ethan turned back to Miranda. "Into the car. Wait for me."

Her eyes searched his, full of something he didn't dare analyze just now. "Be careful."

"Always."

Once she was safely secured and hunkered down as ordered, Ethan made his way up the weedy walk. Instead of climbing the concrete steps and setting himself up as a target in front of the flimsy ass door, he hunkered close to the trailer's base from the ground and listened. Everything was too quiet. Dread crawled up his spine as he reached over to bang on the lower half of the door.

"Police! Open up."

Nothing moved, but he thought he heard a murmur that might've been voices.

"We had a report of shots fired. Is everyone okay in there?"

He fully expected Harley to offer up a "Fuck off!" or something similar. But there was nothing. Was he still in there? Or had Ethan gotten this wrong? Was it possible he'd been the victim instead of the shooter? The neighbor had reported two or three shots. Had he drawn on Raines? Had they shot each other?

Too many questions with no answers. Too much time had passed since he got the call. Raines could be dead or dying. He was done waiting.

"I'm coming in on five. Five. Four." Ethan listened for the back door to bang open and hoped Darius was ready. "Three. Two." On one, he reached for the knob and yanked the door open. It flew back to crash against the outer wall of the trailer. Ethan pressed himself back against the opposite wall, but nobody came out shooting.

Leading with his gun, he peered into the trailer. A half wall divided the entry space from the rest of the living area, and he couldn't see past it. He knew how these things were built. Like matchsticks. That half wall wouldn't make for any kind of cover.

He could smell the blood.

For just a fleeting moment, he hesitated, feeling the phantom flash of searing pain from the bullet that had nearly taken his life.

Not. Happening.

He went up the concrete steps moving fast and low. No one was in the kitchen to the right. Ethan swung left, toward the living room, and felt his heart stop as he saw Corbett Raines stretched out on the floor in a pool of blood. Rene Forbes crouched over him, some wad of fabric pressed to the wound. She looked at Ethan out of blackened eyes, tears flowing down her cheeks. "He didn't mean to. It was an accident."

Cold rage flooded Ethan's limbs that she'd try to protect Harley, even in this. "Rene, is he alive?"

"For now. He's lost a lot of blood."

Then there was still a chance.

"I couldn't get to the phone to call 911 and Johnny…" She looked toward a corner of the room Ethan couldn't quite see.

Ethan moved further inside and saw her son leaning against the wall, tears streaking his face, a shaking gun clutched in one hand.

Oh fuck. It wasn't Harley Rene was protecting. It was Johnny.

"Johnny, what happened?"

"He hurt her. He's always hurting her. I just wanted him to stop. But he got in the way."

Too many "he"s in that scenario, but Ethan understood well enough. Johnny Forbes had tried to kill his stepfather and the rookie had intervened.

"Where's Harley?"

"Gone. After I…he ran."

"Okay. We'll figure this out. I need you to put the gun down, son." He lowered his own weapon, edging toward the boy.

"I just want him to go away."

The back door flew open as Darius swept in. Johnny's gun snapped straight again, and Ethan lunged forward neatly disarming the kid before he could put a bullet in another officer.

Darius took one look at Corbett and swore.

"He says Harley's gone. Clear the rest of the trailer."

On a nod, Darius moved down the hall.

Ethan clamped a hand on Johnny's shoulder. "I'm gonna need you to come over here and sit down." When he steered the boy to a chair, Johnny didn't resist.

Moving quickly, Ethan dropped into a crouch beside his fallen officer and pressed two fingers against Corbett's wrist. "Raines. Come on now. Stay with me."

The rookie didn't move, but there was a pulse. Weak but there. The hand mic mounted to his shoulder was destroyed. Looked like the bullet had glanced off it and into his neck. The towel Rene had pressed to the wound had already soaked through with blood. Her hands were shaking. "Rene, don't move. I'm getting help."

She offered a trembling nod.

"We're clear," Darius announced.

"Bag the gun. I'm getting medical." Ethan raced for his squad car, thrilled to see the ambulance waiting just past the tree line. He waved it on into the yard and yanked open the door to his cruiser.

Miranda was folded into the floorboard, as ordered. He reached in to help her out.

"How bad?" she demanded. "Who?"

"Corbett Raines. I don't know how bad. He's lost a lot of blood. The bullet hit above the neckline of the vest."

As soon as both feet hit the ground, she was racing for the door, her medical bag in hand. EMTs were right behind. Ethan watched her dive in, taking over pressure from Rene, snapping out orders to the EMTs. With great care, she peeled back the soaked towel to reveal the entrance wound, just above his clavicle.

Oh, Jesus Christ.

Miranda's hands were rock steady. "Let's get an occlusive dressing on here, stat. Help me roll him to the side."

They moved fast, in perfect sync, as if they'd done this before. Everybody else stayed silent, but for Rene, who sobbed quietly. Ethan realized that, as Miranda worked to stabilize Corbett and prep him for transport, she was feeding information to one of the EMTs, who was radioing back to the hospital to have an operating room prepped for surgery on arrival. There was a lot of medical jargon he didn't understand, but the words "carotid artery" and "nicked" stood out. He knew men who'd bled out from that sort of wound on the battlefield and was grateful he hadn't argued when Miranda insisted on coming.

Bare minutes after they'd come in, the three of them shifted Corbett to the gurney and headed for the door. He trailed them out, watching the EMTs lift his officer into the back of the ambulance. Miranda didn't climb in after them.

"You aren't going to the hospital?"

"He's as stable as we can make him. Dr. Phillips is waiting. He was one of the best trauma surgeons in Atlanta before he came here. It's bad but he's not doomed. The bullet went mostly through the muscle. Chad will take good care of him."

They both watched as the ambulance hit the sirens and peeled out of the gravel drive. Ethan stared after the ambulance long after it was gone, wondering if Raines would even make it out of surgery.

Miranda laid a hand on his arm. "He's going to make it."

Ethan sure as shit hoped so. "I have to haul the kid in."

"I know." Her eyes were sympathetic. "Will the judge take into account he was trying to protect his mother?"

"I don't know. He's in deep shit either way. I've got to get a clearer picture of what happened." Had he made a mistake in talking the judge down to community service?

"Is there any reason I can't be with Rene through all of this? She's pretty shaken up."

"Come on."

They went back inside.

Johnny was still a little shocky himself. He hadn't moved from the chair. Ethan crouched down in front of the boy as Miranda ushered his mother into the kitchen to wash up.

"You're gonna arrest me, aren't you?"

"I need you to tell me what happened first. Then we'll sort out what to do."

"If I go to jail, who's gonna protect my mom?" The desperate, miserable fear that shone out of his eyes sliced Ethan deep.

"Jail! No! You can't arrest him." Rene rushed into the room. "I told you. It was an accident."

Ethan shifted his attention to her, feeling exhaustion press down on him. He knew how this was going to go. "Accident or no, he shot somebody."

"He was protecting me! That has to count for something."

Ethan wanted it to count. Wanted it to matter. Because no way did he want to see this kid put away for trying to stop an abuser. So, he'd play hardball.

"Not if there's no means of verifying it. You've consistently refused to press charges against Harley for battery and assault. There is nothing officially on record to back up the claims, though we all know exactly what's been going on. If you want a chance to save your son, give me something to work with, Rene."

CHAPTER 13

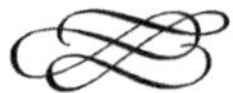

It was coming on three in the morning and Miranda's neighborhood held that perfect silence of deep night. After the chaos of the last several hours, she needed it.

"I can't believe she finally agreed to press charges." Ethan shut the driver's side door and followed her toward the front of her house.

"Sometimes women will end up taking action for their children when they won't for themselves. If Harley had ever actually raised a hand to Johnny, maybe she would've acted sooner."

"Maybe," he conceded.

It hardly mattered now. The important thing was that Rene had acted. They'd taken her statement, filed the charges, and helped her move all her things—which wasn't much—out to Monarch House. There, Miranda and Ethan had stuck around, while Rene had gone over it all again with Tucker McGee, her new attorney. He was filing for an order of protection first thing. And as soon as the police managed to track him down, they would, at last, be arresting Harley Forbes on charges he couldn't skitter out of like the cockroach he was.

Miranda tugged out her keys. "Do you think it will be enough to keep Johnny out of jail past the next few days?" Ethan had already told them he'd be a guest of Wishful PD until his arraignment.

"I don't know. I sure as hell hope so. If Corbett is able to corroborate, that will help."

She unlocked the door and turned back to him. He looked so tired and worn. She wanted to smooth that furrow in his brow. Despite the bloody beginning, tonight had been a win.

He worked up the semblance of a smile for her. "Thanks for pushing to come with me. I don't know that Corbett would have survived if you hadn't." They'd gotten word about an hour before that he'd come through surgery and was expected to make a full recovery.

Miranda slid her arms around him, offering the comfort she knew he needed. "He survived. Period. There's no sense in thinking about what ifs. Not that I'm doing so great with that myself. I keep thinking about how things could've gone so very wrong if Harley had been there. If he'd been the shooter." Even as she'd worked on Corbett, she'd imagined what it would be like if it had been Ethan lying there, bleeding out beneath her hands.

He stroked a hand along the length of her spine. Miranda absorbed the heat of him, the feel of him, and felt the knots begin to unravel.

"That a problem for you? The dangerous aspect of my job?"

"Do I wish you did something that didn't carry those risks? Sure. I don't want to see you hurt. But my need for you to be safe doesn't trump your need to risk yourself for the safety of others. I wouldn't expect you to change that. It's part of who you are, and I like the man you are."

For a long stretch, he said nothing, just continued those long strokes of her back, but she could feel a tension in him ease.

"You know, I've spent half my life going into situations that could get me killed. Afghanistan. Iraq. The Marshal Service. This. There's fear—you're stupid if you're not a little scared. But you learn to channel it, to do what needs to be done. And tonight, for just a second, I wasn't sure if I could do it. I was afraid."

"Because it was similar to the situation where you got shot?" She'd certainly thought of that as she'd been crouched in the floorboard of his police cruiser, not knowing what was going on.

"No." He pulled back and lifted a hand to cup her jaw, stroking his thumb across the arch of her cheek. "Because for the first time in a long time, I have something to lose."

Her breath caught and her heart gave a painful squeeze because— oh—she understood. She felt the same about him, and she wanted —needed—to show him.

"Ethan." She rose to her toes, brushing her mouth to his, then holding there at the edge of temptation. "Stay. Don't go home tonight."

Miranda waited for him to gently set her away, make his excuses. It was beyond late, and they'd both been through a lot tonight. Instead, he reached for the knob himself and led her inside.

Anticipation washed away the bone-numbing exhaustion, as Ethan shut the door. A single lamp was on in the living room beyond the foyer. It cast his face in shadow, but still she could see the hunger as he looked at her.

"I won't ask if you're sure."

"Good." Taking a firmer grip on his hand, she led the way upstairs, not bothering with lights. In her bedroom, she bypassed the bed and went straight into the big master bath with the glassed-in shower and dual shower heads that had sold her on the house. She was still wearing the same blood-stained clothes she'd had on earlier. Releasing his hand, she opened the shower door and switched on the water to scalding.

Ethan removed his duty belt, watching her as she moved around the room lighting candles.

Feeling a little self-conscious at the weight of his stare, Miranda snuffed the match. "I love this bathroom. It's why I bought the house. A candlelit steam or a bath with a glass of wine is one of my favorite ways to unwind at the end of a long day of being on my feet."

"Nothing wrong with a little atmosphere." He set the belt aside and started on his shirt. "I like a woman who knows what she wants."

"I haven't been shy about the fact that I want you." When her fingers went to the buttons of her own shirt, his eyes followed the brisk flick. This wasn't a seductive striptease, but the heat in his gaze said it was having the same effect.

Ethan shrugged out of the shirt and ripped open the Velcro on the Kevlar vest beneath. The sound of it echoed against the tile. "I like that you're a straight shooter." He slipped off the vest, and it was Miranda's turn to watch with avid fascination as he stripped the undershirt up and over his head. The flat plane of his abs was every bit as toned and hard as she'd expected. Her mouth watered at the sight. She wanted to learn every dip and slope, with her fingers, with her tongue.

"Getting behind, Legs." He curved that slow, molasses smile he seemed to reserve just for her, and Miranda realized she'd stopped moving, her hands still on the placard of the shirt.

"Can't have that." She stripped it off, enjoying the way his eyes followed her.

"Very nice. I wouldn't have pegged you for a pink lace kind of woman."

"I'm full of surprises."

He prowled over in bare feet, hooking a hand around her nape. "I look forward to discovering all of them."

Miranda shivered, imagining all the different ways he could explore her. What kind of lover would he be? Slow and thorough? Torturous? Demanding? Maybe a little dominant? The expression on his face promised all that and more, and it thrilled her. He thrilled her, just by looking.

Steam was beginning to fill the room, casting everything in a soft haze with the flickering candlelight. When he drew her against him, she didn't resist, lifting her mouth to his and letting her hands explore as she'd dreamed. Her fingers traced over a scar high up on one shoulder. She knew from the puckered feel of the tissue it was where he'd been shot in the Army. It wouldn't have been a pleasant wound, but it wasn't life threatening. No, that scar was lower, over his ribs. That shot would almost certainly have collapsed a lung and come perilously close to hitting his spine. Her brain automatically imagined the trajectory, the damage, as her fingers traced over it. So close. So close to losing him before they'd even met.

"You're thinking too hard." Ethan's fingers curved around her nape, holding her in place so he could thoroughly seduce her mouth, even as his other broad palm slid up the bare skin of her torso to cup her breast.

Miranda gave a purr of approval and reached for the zipper of his pants. She wanted skin. Wanted to feel what she did to him. To feel the proof that he was very much alive.

He'd dispensed with her bra by the time she shoved his pants and boxer briefs down his hips, and his hands closed over her breasts as hers wrapped around his cock. They both groaned, pressing into each other. He was heavy in her palm, so thick her long, surgeon's fingers didn't quite meet. She ran a slow thumb around the crown. Ethan cursed, abandoning her breasts and making quick work of her pants, stepping out of his own. Then he was hauling her into the shower. He backed her up against the tile, running his hands up her arms and lifting them over her head, as he ravaged her mouth. Her nipples tightened as his chest rubbed against hers, and her legs went loose, with a long, liquid pull low in her belly. The spray battered them both, sluicing over every inch, but Miranda barely noticed the heat of the water. All she could focus on was the feel of his hard, hot body pressed against hers. Close, but not close enough.

"Ethan."

He stopped kissing her—a pity—and watched her with hooded eyes. "Don't move until I say move."

It was the same order he'd given her earlier tonight, and Miranda didn't know what to do with it in this context. She wasn't a submissive woman, but she found she liked the thrum of command in his tone. Her lips curved. "Bossy."

"You'll like it."

The promise prompted another of those long, liquid pulls between her thighs. "Mmm. Okay, I'll cooperate. But just so you know, it's my turn to torture you next."

Ethan's mouth quirked. "We'll see."

Oh damn, now that was a challenge.

But Miranda remained still, her arms still above her head as he released her and reached for the soap. He worked up a thick lather and started at her hands, soaping and stroking every inch, making his way down her arms, across her shoulders and to her breasts. The combination of the slickness and the calluses of his fingers moving over her flesh, rolling her nipples, had her dropping her head back and moaning. The man took his time, his eyes unerringly focused on her, and she realized he was learning her reactions. When something made her breath catch, he did it again, refining and adapting the touch until she was gasping. By the time he slid one hand down to cover the curls at the apex of her thighs, her arms and legs were trembling.

"Ethan."

"What?"

She pressed her hips into his hand, wanting him to part her, to touch her, needing him inside her to fill the ache he'd built. "Please."

"Please what?"

"For the love of all that is holy, if you don't touch me right now, I'm going to beat you over the head with a shampoo bottle."

On a huffing laugh, he slid his fingers between her folds, over her clit.

Miranda's breath exploded out. "God, yes."

He traced slow circles, making her writhe, drawing out the tension until she almost couldn't stand it. Miranda whimpered. When, at last, he slipped two fingers inside her, she nearly wept with relief.

He moved closer, curling those fingers as he bent to her ear. "Miranda, move."

She dropped her arms, wrapping them around his shoulders and hanging on as she pistoned her hips. He watched her as she rode his fingers, and that was almost more intimate than his touch, as he seemed to drink in the sight and sound of her taking her pleasure. As the orgasm whipped through her, he kissed her again. His tongue thrust against hers in the same rhythm as his fingers as he wrung out every last pulse, until she collapsed like a rag doll against him.

~

Ethan switched off the water.

Miranda gasped against his shoulder. "That was…that was…"

"What?"

"A really good start."

Ethan laughed and pulled her with him as he stepped out of the shower. "I like the way you think, Legs. Can you stand?"

"I'll manage."

He reached for the towel, wrapping it around her beautiful body and using it to pull her in close for a kiss. Her sigh had him going impossibly harder, but he held himself in check as he slowly, thoroughly dried her off, steeping himself in the taste of her. At least until her hand closed around him and squeezed.

Her thumb stroked up the underside of his cock. "Ethan."

"What?" he gritted out.

"I really, really need you inside me."

He jumped in her hand. "Condom in my pants."

"IUD. So, unless you have some other objection—"

"I haven't been with anyone since my divorce."

She brushed her lips over his again. "Then make love with me, Cowboy."

Ethan dropped the towel and boosted her up. "Wrap your legs around me."

She complied, tightening those long, glorious legs around his waist and shimmying until his erection was nestled in the drenched folds between her thighs. He gave fleeting thought to just turning to set her on the counter, so he could plunge inside all that waiting heat, but he had control enough to get her the extra ten or fifteen steps to the bed. Probably.

He all but sprinted the distance, turning at the last second so that he fell on his back and didn't crush her. Before he could get another grip on her and reverse their positions, she rose above him and sank down, taking him in in one long, slow stroke.

"Oh God, you feel good."

"Christ." It was all Ethan could manage as her body closed around him like a wet fist.

Miranda leaned forward, pressing his arms above his head and holding him there by the wrists. "My turn."

He could break the hold with little effort, but she kissed him and began to rock, and he forgot why he'd want to. She shoved up, bracing herself against his chest as she quickened her pace. Her breasts swayed with every roll of her hips. He wanted them in his mouth, in his hands. Even as he had the thought, she skimmed her own hands up her torso and covered them, dropping her head back on a moan.

"Damn, you're beautiful." Ethan reached to grip her thighs and surged into her, grinding the base of his cock against her clit.

"Yes, yes. Exactly like that," she gasped.

He did it again, thrusting, rubbing, until her body began to pulse around him. As her climax ripped through her, she bowed back on a cry. Her sex clamped around him, obliterating the last of his control. He rolled, still feeling the ripples of her orgasm as he plunged deep. She locked her legs around his hips, digging her feet into his ass to pull him even closer, and he lost himself, spilling into her on a shout of triumph.

By the time he had more than a single brain cell firing, he noticed the faint vibration of her chest beneath his. "Are you *laughing?*"

"Not at you. I swear. It's just…a few years ago Norah gave me this t-shirt that I've never worn. It says 'Save a horse. Ride a cowboy.' I was just thinking now I finally could wear it."

Ethan propped himself up on his elbows so he could look into her face. She was flushed and gorgeous, obviously sated, with her eyes sparkling, even in the ambient candlelight flickering from the bathroom.

"I can't decide whether to be offended by that or not."

Still chuckling, she wrapped her arms around him and pressed a kiss to his throat. "Be very, very flattered."

He bent his head, nuzzling along the ridge of her collarbone. "I'll think of a creative means of payback for that when I have blood in my brain again." As the scent of him was on her skin, he didn't think that'd be any time soon.

"If there were a few more hours left in the night, I'd gladly spend them keeping you too occupied to actually think."

"You have deep appetites."

"Two. Years. A little more than, actually. I told you I had no intention of letting you out of my bed quickly once I got you in it."

Feeling more than a little smug and pleased that he'd been the one to end her long dry spell, Ethan pressed a kiss between her breasts. "I'm pretty sure I could happily stay right here for the rest of my life."

The hand she'd been stroking along his back froze, mid-motion.

Ethan played his own words over again and cursed his lack of functional brain cells. Lifting his head, he offered a rueful smile. "Not part of the Fun and Simple Plan. Sorry."

"No." Miranda framed his face in her hands. "No, don't apologize for that. I'm all about fun and simple. But this was more than that, and I think we both know it. How could it not be after what we went through tonight?"

It wasn't just tonight. It was her. It had been her from the beginning. And despite his best intentions, he hadn't been able to fight his own nature.

"I have a confession to make."

Her face shuttered, and she dropped her hands to his shoulders, her body tensing beneath him. "Okay."

"I said I just wanted simple and fun. The truth is, I *wanted* to want just simple and fun. I wanted to be able to be that guy who didn't look for more because I didn't think I had more to give. I gave it a damned good try. But that's not who I am. It's not how I'm built. I wanted more the first moment I kissed you. So much more I scared myself and almost screwed everything up. The fact is, Miranda, after tonight, I don't think I can keep holding myself back from that."

It really wasn't fair of him to dump all this on her while they were both naked and he was still buried inside her. Especially not as his cock was ambitiously beginning to campaign for a round two. But to his mind, true intimacy demanded honesty.

"What are you saying? What is it you want?"

She hadn't pushed him away, so he took the leap, admitting what had been circling around his brain. "I want you. A serious relationship. To see where things go for the long term. I know it's not easy looking at long-term with a career cop. It's long hours, interruptions, and it's dangerous. I know that kind of relationship comes with a lot of risk, but—"

Miranda pressed a finger to his mouth. "Stop."

Ethan felt his heart drop into his gut. He'd pushed too far, too fast. He'd screwed up this good thing between them. He'd—

"I don't need a recitation of the downsides. I don't care what they are because I want more, too. With you."

That rogue heart began to pound. "You do?"

Her fingers traced patterns on his nape, which did nothing but stir him further. "I've been telling myself for a long time now that I don't have time for anything but fun and simple. But the fact is, I've let work consume everything else because I didn't have anyone in my life. I've stuck to the party line of fun and simple because I thought it's what you wanted, and I didn't want to scare you off."

"I don't think you could scare me off." Ethan stroked his fingers through the ends of her hair.

"Thank God." She dragged his head down to hers. "Make love with me again. Just one more time before we sleep."

"Anything you want," he murmured, and captured her mouth with his. But he knew one more time would never be enough.

CHAPTER 14

When her alarm went off, Miranda slapped the snooze and groaned, pulling the pillow over her head from long habit. God, she hated mornings. At least today her body felt deliciously used and relaxed. Maybe she could convince Ethan of the merits of quickie shower sex before work. That would sure as hell make up for the indignities of being awake at dawn. With that in mind, she stretched one foot out toward his side of the bed.

But there was no warm, willing man stretched out beside her. In fact, the sheets were cold. Miranda pulled her head out from the pillow and squinted over where he ought to be. He'd gone to sleep with her last night. She hadn't dreamed curling up around him. The scent of him still lingered on the pillow and on her, so where the hell was he?

Angling her head, she listened toward the bathroom. But the shower wasn't running, and she didn't hear any sounds of him puttering around. Surely, he hadn't just left? Unless he got a call and she somehow missed it? But he'd leave a note in that case, wouldn't he?

Dragging herself out of bed, she stretched and slipped on one of the oversized t-shirts she normally slept in. Coffee. She'd make coffee and figure this out. She hadn't set up the automatic timer last night, so she'd suffer through the pod stuff for her first cup, just to kickstart her brain enough to measure beans properly. Her yen was so strong she could smell it. And bacon.

Wait. Bacon? That wasn't one of her normal morning hallucinations.

Shuffling downstairs, Miranda stumbled toward the kitchen and stopped in the doorway. There was coffee in the pot and a barefoot, bare-chested, sexy man cooking bacon at her stove. As she watched, he lifted a couple of slices onto a paper-towel covered plate.

"What is all this?" Well, it was what she'd meant to say. What came out was more like, "Whasis?"

Ethan turned and smiled at her, and it was almost as good as a shot of coffee for taking the sting out of being awake this early. "Mornin', Legs. I made breakfast."

Miranda blinked, wondering if she was still dreaming. Then he reached for the carafe of coffee and poured it into a mug. And not one of the tiny, normal people mugs. The big, holds-two-full cups one with a picture of Grumpy Cat on the side. She whimpered a little prayer. "Coffee?"

He brought it over, setting the mug on the island. Miranda followed its path like a junkie in search of her next fix. Which she was.

When she reached for it, Ethan blocked her path. "Wait just a bit. It'll scald you." He reeled her in instead, lacing his hands behind her back and pressing his mouth to hers.

Because he was warm and solid and way cozier than her chilly kitchen, Miranda melted into him, twining her arms around his neck and wishing they had an hour or three until they had to be at work. This was a much better way to begin the morning.

"Mornin'," he murmured.

"You made me coffee."

His chest rumbled against hers. "Bit of a one-tracked mind first thing, huh?"

"Two. But you weren't in bed when that God-awful alarm went off."

"Sadly, there's no time for that." Ethan released her and went back to the stove, where he expertly flipped some fried eggs. "We've got just enough time to eat, shower, and for me to take you to get your car."

Miranda picked up the mug and brought it to her lips for a long swallow. The taste of the heavenly brew brought another hum of pleasure. The man made stupendous coffee. Another few sips and her eyes felt less like they needed a crane to haul them open.

Ethan plated the eggs and bacon and brought them to the island. "Sit. Eat."

Sliding onto one of the barstools, she gave him a sideways glance. "You're a morning person."

"You say that like it's an accusation of murder."

She took another gulp of coffee. "In this house it normally would be. But you made me coffee and breakfast—after a night of really excellent orgasms, so I'm finding it hard to hang on to my natural mad."

He unsuccessfully hid a smile in his own mug of coffee. "Your brother wasn't kidding about you not being a morning person."

"No. No he was not. And that's on a night when I get normal sleep."

"I probably should've walked away last night. I'm trying to feel bad that I didn't, but I'm having a hard time with that."

"You were exactly where you were supposed to be."

Ethan reached out to tuck a lock of her hair behind one ear. "I was exactly where I wanted to be."

Miranda leaned into the touch, closing her eyes. "Do we have to adult today? Can't we call in sick and stay in bed all day?" She opened her eyes. "Catching up on sleep and…other things."

Those smoky eyes went hot. "I have never wanted to play hooky more in my life than I do right now. But I have about a hundred things that have to get done today. Paperwork to finish, reports to file to make sure everything goes as it should. And much as I want to take you back to bed right now, nothing's going to stop me from arresting Harley."

Well, that was a sufficient mood killer.

"That definitely takes priority. The sooner he's off the streets, the better I'll feel."

"You and me both."

They shoveled in the rest of breakfast in relative silence. Miranda thanked God that he understood she didn't want endless inane chatter in the morning. By the time she'd finished and drained the coffee, she felt like she could face the day. Or at least the next four hours until she allowed herself another caffeine hit.

She showered—alone, sadly—and dressed for the day, while Ethan hopped in after her for what he promised would be a ninety-second rinse off. With a towel still wrapped around her hair, Miranda trotted back downstairs and went to get the paper.

As soon as she opened the door, the stench hit her square in the face.

"What the—"

Miranda looked down and promptly screamed.

Seconds later, Ethan came flying down the stairs, a towel wrapped around his hips, his service weapon in hand. He grabbed her, pivoting to put himself between her and danger. "What is it? What happened?"

She pointed to where the door was still open. "Front porch."

Tightening the towel, he prowled forward and crouched. Miranda trailed behind and wondered that her breakfast didn't come straight back up.

The pile of viscera and fur had once been a raccoon. The characteristic ringed tail was about the only thing still intact.

"Did something kill it and leave it here?"

Ethan's mouth tightened into a grim line. "Not something. Someone. Looks like it was hit by a car to begin with. But somebody gutted it right here on your front porch."

Miranda squelched the rise of nausea. "Who would do something like that? Why?"

"I don't know. To send a message, maybe. I don't like it. The vandalism didn't worry me overmuch. That was petty. This...this is something else. Somebody's targeting you."

The idea of it was utterly absurd. "Why on earth would anybody target me?"

"I don't know, but I'm sure as shit going to find out."

Ethan rose, an incongruous picture with the towel riding low on his hips and a gun in his hand. Suds still clung to his shoulders.

"Is everything okay, Miranda?"

At the sound of the older woman's voice, Miranda swore softly. Of course, *of course,* one of the Casserole Patrol would be out for her morning walk, when Ethan was standing on the porch in nothing but a towel. She stepped around him, shooing him back inside. "Everything's fine, Miss Betty."

"What's that on your porch?"

Miranda automatically shifted to try to block the old woman's view of the raccoon as she came up the front walk. "Nothing you need to worry about, Miss Betty."

"Why Chief Greer. Good morning." Her wrinkled cheeks split with a delighted grin.

"Mornin', Mrs. Monroe." His voice was low and easy, as if he hadn't just raced out of the shower.

"Been wondering who was gonna take you off the market. Good for you, young lady." Bright blue eyes scanned him from head to toe. "If I were younger I'd have made a play for that myself."

"Uh..."

"While I concede he is a fine view in the morning, we've got to finish getting ready for work. You enjoy your walk now." Miranda put an arm around Miss Betty's shoulders and steered her back up the walk.

By the time she got the woman on her way, Ethan had sensibly retreated inside and their reputations were mutually ruined but good. Miranda had a hard time caring. She was a lot more concerned with who'd been prowling around her house after three in the morning, carving up roadkill in some kind of macabre message of…what? Had they been waiting for her when Ethan brought her home? If he hadn't been with her, would they have stopped with just leaving the grisly offering?

Gooseflesh rose on her arms and Miranda hugged herself. *Getting ahead of yourself. It was probably just a vicious prank.* Because this was Wishful. It didn't make sense for it to be anything more serious than that. Ethan's paranoia was rubbing off on her. She'd worked too damned hard to shake off the inherent suspicion of city life and embrace the simple of home to let some asshole drive her back to that stress and misery.

Either way, she was getting really damned tired of whoever wanted to make her life difficult. Casting a searching glance around, wondering if the perpetrator was still watching, Miranda squared her shoulders. No matter who'd done it, this thing was left with the intention of getting to her. So, she wouldn't give them what they wanted. Circling around to the shed in the backyard, she went in search of a shovel. She'd take care of this mess, and they'd both go on with their days, focused on the important stuff. She wasn't going to give this asshole another thought.

"The police chief, on the front porch, in a *towel!*" Clay crowed it as if he'd just won a game of *Clue* when he answered the door.

"Shut up," Ethan groused, shouldering him aside so he could bring in his guitar.

"Oh no. I gotta know how you ended up mostly naked on Miranda's front porch just as one of the Casserole Patrol was going by. I deserve that much explanation since you're late."

Ethan set his guitar case on the sofa. "That's actually related to why I was late." He unpacked his Taylor and began checking the tuning as he explained about the gutted raccoon.

Clay's amusement faded. "Why the hell would somebody do that?"

"I don't know. Just like I don't know why somebody would slash all four of her tires."

"Jesus, when did that happen?"

"Night of the bonfire. They may not be related." Though a knife had clearly been used in both cases. And if they were related, going from destruction of property to mutilation of an animal—even one that had already been dead—showed an escalation Ethan didn't like. "Either way, I spent a big portion of my day tracking down Harley Forbes to inquire about his whereabouts last night."

"I heard that's where Corbett Raines got shot. Is he gonna pull through?"

"Yeah, thanks to Miranda."

"Is it true Johnny was the one who did it?"

"Afraid so."

"Shit. I knew the kid was a powder keg, but I never expected him to do something like this."

"By all accounts and evidence, it was an accidental shooting. Well, partly. Johnny was trying to shoot Harley and Corbett got in the way." Corbett had corroborated that himself when Ethan went by the hospital to see him, in between checking in with Ralph Slocombe and a handful of others on the list Miranda had given him. He'd been beyond relieved to see the rookie sitting up in bed, albeit swathed in bandages. It'd be several weeks before he healed up enough to get back to work, and Ethan had already called in his two reserve officers to help pick up the slack.

"What beef has Harley got with Miranda?"

"None that I know about. And he claimed to have been asleep on the sofa bed at his cousin's place last night between three and six, which his cousin confirmed." Ethan hadn't had any logical reason to tie Harley to Miranda's harassment, but figured it couldn't hurt to ask. He wasn't sure he believed Harley's alibi, but couldn't disprove it. His alibi for the night of the bonfire was equally flimsy. "He was staying there on account of nearly getting shot in his own house."

"I'm not a fan of the guy, but I can't blame him for that."

Strumming his fingers over the strings, Ethan hummed a noncommittal note.

Clay crossed his arms and kicked back against the arm of a chair. "Why'd you go after him?"

"To finally arrest his ass on domestic battery charges." And it had been so satisfying to see that arrogant prick's smirk turn to outrage when he'd realized Ethan was serious. He'd managed a whole host of creative suggestions as to what Ethan could do with his manhood by the time he'd been wrestled into the back of the cruiser. Ethan had been a little disappointed the jackoff hadn't taken a swing at him so he could add resisting arrest and attempted assault of an officer to the list of charges.

"Seriously?"

"Yep. This thing with Johnny was finally enough to push Rene into pressing charges."

"Well, thank God for that. You think the charges will actually stick?"

"God only knows. We're hoping documented evidence of the abuse will help support her son's case and prove he legitimately feared for her safety." What the district attorney would do with that, Ethan had no idea. He hadn't been around long enough to have a feel for the man. "But either way, Harley Forbes is behind bars at County for the time being, and I, for one, feel better having him off the street."

"I'll drink to that. You want a beer?"

"Damn straight."

Clay disappeared into the kitchen and came back with a couple of long-neck Shiner Bocks.

Ethan set his guitar aside, twisted the cap off, and took a pull, feeling the muscles that had been knotted since early this morning begin to relax. "I needed that."

"I reckon an hour or two with your guitar ought to take care of the rest. And whatever's left over can be worked out by the lovely Dr. Campbell."

Ethan leveled him with a glare. "Watch it."

Clay just grinned. "Oh no, it's too late for that, son. You can't be caught all but *in flagrante* on her front porch in a towel—by a member of the Casserole Patrol no less—and not expect to catch some shit. Everybody in town now knows y'all are sleeping together."

Ethan winced. He'd been afraid of that. "It's not just sex."

"Didn't figure it was after that little stunt you pulled at the bonfire the other night. You're stuck on her."

As Clay knew him better than anybody else, Ethan didn't bother denying it. "Seems I am."

Clay tapped his bottle in a toast. "Well, I say good for both of you."

He took another pull and rolled the bottle between his palms. "I didn't plan on this."

"So the hell what? You can't plan for everything. To my way of thinking, finding a good woman's a bit like being struck by lightning." Clay tipped his own beer back for a swallow, then pointed it at Ethan. "And you, my fine fellow, are still smokin' from the strike."

Ethan shot his friend a bland stare. "And are you already planning our wedding and two point five kids, too?"

"Just stating the obvious. I know you. You're a slow mover, but once you set your sights on what you want, that's that."

"Yeah, well, after what happened with Becca, I'm a little more cautious this go round. Trying not to be blinded by lust or anything else." And yet, despite his best intentions, every instinct he had wanted him to throw caution to the wind.

"Miranda Campbell is nothing like your ex-wife. As somebody who's known her my whole life, I can say this with conviction." Crossing the room, Clay picked up his own guitar from the stand.

"In most respects, no. But I don't know if she can handle the realities of being with a cop long-term any better than Becca did. It worries her."

Clay began to pick out some warm-up exercises. "Brother, it worries me. It worries my mama, who considers you a second son. It worries all of us who give a damn about you because we don't want to see you hurt. That doesn't make her like your ex. She deserves more credit than that."

Ethan thought about what she'd said. That her need to see him safe didn't outweigh his need to put himself on the line to save others. That was a concession he'd never have gotten out of his ex-wife. But that was after just one incident. What would happen in a few months? A year? Five years? Would her ability to tolerate it wear down?

No reason to borrow trouble. Where they were right now was very, very good. Ethan could roll with that.

"Let's take the set from the top. I want to get out of here in time to swing by Miranda's on the way home."

"As you wish, lover boy."

CHAPTER 15

"We need more lights!" Norah declared.

Miranda eyed the maze of outdoor cafe lights currently stretched across the floor of the community center gym in a spoke pattern. "You seriously need an intervention for your love of John Hughes movies."

"First off, *Footloose* was not a John Hughes movie. Second, it's going to be beautiful once we get them all suspended. We'll have paper lanterns as accents, and I've got Kendall Westin from the Chadwick Gallery working on origami centerpieces for the tables."

Shaking her head, Miranda slung an arm around Norah's shoulders. "I love you, you know that?"

"I do. And hey, at least I'm not going overboard on the crepe paper streamers."

"Thank God for small mercies."

Cam strolled up, rolling another canister of helium. "Be grateful I talked her out of the Cinderella's coach picture station."

Miranda stared at her friend, aghast. "Oh God. You wouldn't."

Norah pouted. "You have no sense of romance."

"You have always had enough for the both of us," Miranda told her.

"I hear that may be changing." Shelby arched both brows as she grabbed another balloon out of the bag and fitted it over the nozzle of the helium tank.

"I already told you that's not up for discussion. I shall neither confirm nor deny." Who knew she'd be legitimately grateful for an outbreak of strep to keep her staff hopping enough this week *not* to hound her about her love life?

Shelby snorted and tied off the balloon, passing it to Delaney, who attached it to the growing chain that would ultimately be an arch. "I'm off the clock, and honey, Betty Monroe is doing all the confirming you'll ever need."

"I would like it noted that this is me pointedly *not* demanding details for why Ethan was standing on your front porch in nothing but a towel," Norah announced.

"Your restraint is noted and appreciated. Because I'm not gonna talk about it."

Over the past week, Ethan had managed to keep news of the mutilated raccoon from spreading, for which Miranda was grateful. She didn't want her family to worry about who was harassing her. But he couldn't do anything about people's wagging tongues. In the past several days, assorted versions of their encounter with Miss Betty had run rampant.

Time for some deflection. "What *I* want to talk about is who's taking who to the dance."

Norah's eyes lit with humor. "All our crew is paired off, and with Mitch out of the country, there's no speculating to do there. You and Ethan *are* the topic of interest."

"Well, that's no fun. Somebody fill me in. Any interesting matches coming up this go round?"

"Reuben Blanchard is taking Violet," Cam offered.

"That's no surprise. Everybody knows Mama Pearl's been trying to make that happen since Vivian's wedding." Miranda scanned the assembly, looking for who could help dig her out of this hole. "What about you Cassie? Surely you've gotten the latest dirt on somebody at The Grind."

Cassie Callister, everybody's favorite coffeeshop owner, looked reflective. "I heard Charlotte Ballard asked that new guy. The volunteer fireman who used to be a hotshot. Does something with Eli Hamilton with the forestry service. What's his name?"

"Sean Murphy?" Delaney suggested.

Cassie snapped her fingers. "That's the one. He's so pretty, I wonder he's not having to beat the ladies off with a stick."

"Is this really what y'all discuss around here?" Ethan's voice cut through the chatter.

Miranda couldn't stop the automatic grin as she turned toward him. "Oh, we bet on it, too. Omar keeps the official pool up at Dinner Belles."

"I heard something about that. Autumn Hamilton's reigning champion for picking pairings, I understand."

"She is." Miranda confirmed, then squealed in surprise as Ethan simply plucked her off her feet and kissed her until her brain fuzzed over with lust.

When he dropped her back on her feet with a satisfied smile, she was grateful he didn't let go because her legs had turned to jelly. "So, we're that couple now?" He hadn't struck her as a PDA kind of guy.

Ethan bent to her ear. "Considering word of our exploits has already spread far and wide, I didn't see the point in further discretion."

"Fair point. In that case—" She hauled him in, fastening her mouth to his in a claiming kiss—on the off chance somebody had missed the first one. "How was your day?"

His chest vibrated with a hum of pleasure. "Better now."

"Glad to hear it. What took you so long? I figured you'd be here more than an hour ago." Miranda dropped her voice. "Did something go wrong at the arraignment?"

"No. That went about as well as can be expected. Johnny's been remanded into his mother's custody until a further evidentiary hearing. I took him by the house to pick up his stuff and then drove him out to Monarch House myself."

"Then why don't you look pleased?"

He scrubbed a hand over his hair. "Because Harley made bail."

"He what? When?"

"Got out this morning. Since I was in court, I didn't get the message until lunch."

"How did he afford fifteen grand in bail?"

"Hell if I know. But I've got an officer keeping tabs on him. His public defender should have put the fear of God into him." Though he said it casually, Miranda understood that if the attorney hadn't managed it, Ethan would be more than happy to finish the job.

"Well, now that our requisite tall guy is here, let's get started suspending the lights." Norah's voice cut through the chatter, effectively putting an end to the discussion. "Ladies, if you want to keep working on that balloon arch?"

As was usually the case when Norah gave an order, everybody leapt into action. As soon as Miranda came over to help with the balloon arch, Delaney handed over the end. "I'm sorry. I have to go."

The girl's expression was pinched, and she was a little pale.

"Honey, are you okay?" Miranda started to reach toward her, but Delaney simply backed away.

"I'm fine. I'll see you at work tomorrow."

Frowning, Miranda watched as she went, trying to decide if she was upset or ill or if, perhaps, she'd missed her meds. She'd seemed fine just a few minutes ago. Then again, Miranda's focus had been on Ethan. She sure hoped Delaney wasn't getting struck down by a strep infection. They were short-handed enough at the clinic.

After another hour and a half, Miranda was forced to concede that Norah was right. The lights were beautiful. Chinese red paper lanterns hung at intervals along the strands, adding a nice flair to the look. Matching balloons made fun arches over both entries and reminded her of the prom she'd attended with Clay all those years ago. The stage had already been set up at one end of the gym. Tables had been placed along the perimeter of the space, draped with white tablecloths and still awaiting the centerpieces, but overall, it was coming along.

She and Ethan were among the last to leave.

"Are you walking me to my car because you're worried about me walking around in our bustling metropolis after dark or because you're hoping to wrangle an invite to come over?"

"Can't it be both?" He brought the hand he held to his lips. "I missed you today."

They'd both had crazy schedules the past week. And yet somehow, no matter how busy they'd been, he'd made it a point to find his way back into her bed every night. She'd made it a point to keep him there until morning.

It wasn't sustainable. Miranda really needed some sleep. Tomorrow would be an early day, with appointments booked solid until early afternoon, when she was cutting out to get a much-needed haircut for the Valentine's Dance. But she knew she wouldn't say no. She didn't think she'd ever say no to him.

"Well, as you're a responsible public servant, it's only right that you see me home. Just to make sure I get there all safe and sound." She punctuated the statement with a flirty smile.

"I am the epitome of responsibility." To demonstrate, he leaned in to fasten her seatbelt himself, pausing for a lingering kiss while he was at it.

"I do find that unwavering sense of duty incredibly sexy."

"Good. I'll be right behind you." On that, he shut her into the car.

Blowing out a breath, Miranda fought to focus for the drive home. It wouldn't do to be pulled over for driving under the influence of lust. Grinning at the thought, she pulled out of the parking lot.

She'd barely made it two blocks before sirens split the night. A fire engine came around the corner, lights flashing, gaining speed. Miranda pulled her car off to the side of the road, allowing it to pass. The sight got her blood pumping the same way it did when a new case hit the ED. As it flew by, she wondered where they were headed and whether it was a fire or medical call. Either way, she sent up a quick prayer it wasn't serious.

The engine turned north, and she began sifting through everyone she knew on that side of town as she trailed somewhat behind.

Not my business.

But as the engine took yet another turn in the direction of her own neighborhood, she found herself picking up speed. Maybe she'd just do a drive by, in case it was a medical call. She could help.

As the fire engine turned onto her street, Miranda gave up even pretending to watch the speed limit. She had several elderly neighbors. Was it Miss Betty? Mr. or Mrs. Gifford? Her brain raced through all their known medical conditions, then stalled out entirely as she made the corner and saw firemen spilling out of the vehicle, leaping into motion.

In front of her own house.

MIRANDA WAS ALREADY sprinting for the house when Ethan screeched to a stop. He threw open the door and raced after her, catching her before she reached the porch.

She kicked and bucked in his grasp. "Let me go! That's my house that's on fire!"

He only tightened his hold. "No. Stop and look. They're going around back."

She stopped struggling and followed his gaze to where the fire-fighters were hauling hose into the backyard. He could smell the acrid tinge of smoke on the air, hear the shouts of the men as they coordinated. Even as they stood, more volunteer firefighters pulled up at the curb, tugging on turnout coats and pants before throwing themselves in to help.

"Get another line going. Wet down the deck and roof so it doesn't spread to the house!"

"See, it's not the house."

"I have to see. I have to know." Miranda spun away from him, running around the opposite side of the house. Ethan followed, determined to keep her out of harm's way.

Miranda pulled up short at the corner of the house. The shed in the back corner of the yard poured smoke. Flames shot through a hole that'd been burned in the roof. But even as they watched, the water began to beat back the blaze. A second hose opened up, catching both of them in the blow back as the fire fighters doused the deck and roof.

Ethan tugged her back. "It's just the shed. The house is okay. C'mon. Let's let them do their job." He kept his tone calm and matter of fact, though his brain was firing a mile a minute, considering the implications, wondering if it was arson. And if it was, what the next escalation would be.

The fire was out in a matter of minutes. One of the men broke away, tugging off his helmet as he came toward where they stood on the front lawn. Ethan recognized him from the bowhunter safety course.

"Dr. Campbell, I'm Sean Murphy. We've got everything taken care of. Fire's out. You were really lucky your neighbor saw the smoke and called it in. We were here in time to put out the fire before things got really bad. The shed is pretty much a loss, but it didn't spread."

"Thank you." She blew out a breath, obviously struggling to find some composure. "Any idea what started it?"

"Things are still cooling, but we found a can of linseed oil tipped over on a shelf. At a guess, the top wasn't adequately sealed, and it set up a slow drip on the stuff underneath and eventually spontaneously combusted. Linseed oil is highly flammable and gets hotter as it evaporates. It's a really common cause of fires."

"How long would something like that take?" Ethan asked.

"Hard to say. Depends on how bad the can was leaking. The cold weather would've slowed things down some. Might have been hours. Might have been days to build up enough concentration."

"Could it be arson?"

Miranda's head whipped toward him, and Sean's gaze sharpened. "If the can was tipped over deliberately, then yes, it could be. But usually if arsonists go this route, they'll use oily rags. We aren't seeing evidence of that. Most fires caused by linseed oil are accidental."

Most, but not all. The timing of this one just seemed a little too coincidental, given everything else going on.

Beside him, Miranda stiffened, her face going ashen. "Oh God. Did you see any evidence of…of a cat inside?"

A cat? She didn't have a cat.

"We haven't been through everything yet, but we didn't see anything right off," Sean assured her.

"What cat?" Ethan asked.

"Percy. The neighbor's cat. He's always getting into the shed to go after mice. I had to shoo him out the other morning after I put the shovel away. I didn't look to see if he'd messed anything up, just nudged him out and locked up again. He jumps on everything. He could've knocked the can over, and I wouldn't have known."

"Sounds like your most probable fire starter," Sean agreed.

"The damned cat drives me nuts, but I wouldn't want him to die like that. I just wish they'd keep him in the house and off my property."

"We'll do a more thorough inspection once everything cools. If there's anything concerning, you'll be the first to hear about it, Chief."

"Thanks, Sean."

The cat was a logical explanation. It should have put Ethan at ease. But it didn't. Once they got into the house, he couldn't settle until he'd checked the whole thing from top to bottom, looking for… well, he didn't know what he was looking for. Something out of place. Some evidence someone had been inside. He found nothing. That didn't make him feel any better either.

Miranda found him in the living room. "I just got off the phone with Mrs. Gifford. Percy is safe and sound at home, and he'll be staying that way. She was horrified her little angel caused all that damage."

"If he caused it."

Her mouth pulled into a frown. "Of course, he caused it. I saw him in there days ago. You heard Sean. It makes the most logical sense."

It did. Based on Occam's Razor, the cat was at fault. But Ethan's gut was still clanging. He had to credit that for the crazy that spewed out of his mouth. "I'm moving in."

She stared at him. "You're what now?"

He hadn't thought it through, but the idea was out there now. "If you don't want me in your bed, I'll sleep in the guest room. Or you can move into my place. But I don't want you alone until I figure out who's behind all this."

"I don't need a bodyguard because of some vandalism. And certainly not because of a shed fire caused by a stupid cat. You are totally jumping into this ridiculous hyper-protective mode over nothing."

Her breezy acceptance that the cat was at fault made him want to punch something. It wasn't nothing. He'd seen too much as a Marshal, spent too much time on protection details, where things turned to shit on a dime. That leap from opportunistic harassment to premeditated violence was completely unpredictable. It could come at any time, and he didn't even know which direction to look. The lack of progress on finding the person targeting Miranda had him on edge, trying to anticipate what was coming. He'd fallen into bodyguard mode as easily as he'd fallen into her bed.

He could tell her all of it, share the hair-raising tales of the shit he'd been through to very clearly show her how situations exactly like this could blow up. But would it work? If he told her this stuff, just to prove his point, he ran the risk of alienating her. With her rose-colored glasses view of Wishful, she might continue to cling to her perceptions. She had that nostalgic need for it to be safe. A small town retreat from the big city life she'd left behind. He also ran the risk that she would believe him. Did he really want to be responsible for permanently ruining that optimistic outlook that helped balance his cynicism?

Ethan needed more evidence than just his gut before he went down that path. Struggling to shove down his frustration, he crossed over. "I'd rather worry about nothing than risk you getting hurt." He combed her hair back with his fingers. "This isn't just me being a cop and going the extra mile. You matter." It was a dim expression for what he was coming to feel for her.

When she only continued to stare at him in stunned silence, Ethan's gut sank. Here he was pushing too far, too fast. Again. Hadn't he promised himself he wouldn't do this? That he'd take it slow and easy? And here he was again, getting ahead of things. Maybe he could've stuck to the plan if she hadn't been in danger. But that wasn't the reality they faced. He wondered what he could do or say to salvage this situation. Honesty won.

"I know this is another big step away from that Fun and Simple Plan we were on. But I think we already established that got shot all to hell. This thing between us isn't casual."

Miranda dropped her gaze as she reached out to curl her fingers around his waist, sucking in a slow breath and letting it out again in a sigh that had Ethan all but vibrating with dread. "No, it isn't." She looked up again. "Tell me something. You've been here every night for the past week. Was that because you felt the need to play bodyguard or because you wanted to be with me?"

His answer mattered. If he said the wrong thing, he had no doubt she'd kick him out and send him on his merry way. But he didn't want to lie to her.

"I came because I couldn't stay away. Because I think of you all the time. And because I can't imagine a better way to end the day than being next to you."

Her eyes softened, and she brought her hands up to frame his face. "Then I think you should pack your stuff."

Her acquiescence had him blinking. "Really?"

"You matter to me, too. I think about you all the time, and I can't think of any better way to start the day than waking up next to you. So yeah. Really. I think we should give this whole living together thing a trial run."

Having his words reflected back left him feeling more than relieved. It felt right. And as she tipped her face up to his, he vowed he'd do whatever it took to keep deserving this. Deserving her.

CHAPTER 16

Miranda stepped out of the shower and reached for a towel. She'd shaved, rubbed, buffed, and moisturized every inch for tonight. She, who claimed to eschew romance, was positively giddy at the prospect of this dance. It was ridiculous. She hadn't been this excited in high school. God help her if Norah got wind of it—she'd never let Miranda hear the end of it. There might even be chanting along the lines of "Miranda and Ethan sittin' in a tree..."

From the bedroom, she could hear him on the phone. He needed to get his own shower if they were going to make the dance on time. Wrapping the towel around her body, she strode out of the bathroom to tell him so.

His eyes zeroed in on her and heated, though his tone didn't waver. "I want extra patrols out at Monarch House."

Miranda sobered, shooting Ethan a questioning glance. He just shook his head in a nothing-to-worry-about gesture.

"No, Cleveland. I am officially not on duty and not on call tonight. I do not want to hear from you for anything short of alien invasion or the zombie apocalypse." He paused to listen as he trailed a finger along her still damp shoulder. "No, not for that either. The Sheriff's Department is on notice to help out with anything that Darius and Rowan can't handle on their own."

Almost faster than she could blink, Ethan's hand shot out and yanked away the towel, spinning her naked body against him. Miranda stifled a giggle and fought to give him a stern look.

"Mmmhmm. That's right." His hand skimmed down her back, over her butt, and squeezed.

Two could play at this game. Miranda pulled his shirt free and efficiently unzipped his pants, sliding her hands into his boxer briefs to cup his very fine backside.

"That should cover it. I gotta go. I better not be talking to you later." Ethan clicked off the phone without a goodbye and tossed it on the dresser. "You smell amazing." He buried his nose against her throat and continued exploring down to her legs. "Mmm, very nice."

"What was all that about?"

"I was doing whatever I could to ensure we aren't interrupted tonight."

"A nice idea. What about the extra patrols out at the women's shelter?"

"Lily Mae called earlier today and said one of her ladies thought she saw a prowler the other night. Might be nothing or might be something. There are any number of lowlifes who could be sneaking around out there to cause trouble for those women. I'm not taking any chances with them. But for tonight, all that is someone else's problem. I gave orders."

"Think it'll work?"

"Hell if I know. But I've given everything to the job since I started in November. It's time for you to come first. In more ways than one."

When his hand headed up the inside of her thigh, Miranda shoved away. "As appealing an idea as it is to take you up on that right now, we don't have time. You need to shower, and I've got to finish my hair and makeup before I get dressed."

"You could come join me in the shower." His voice dropped to that gravelly range that had her knees going weak.

"I am wise to your ways, Ethan Greer. If you get me in that shower, you will spend half the night making me scream, and we'll never make it to the dance."

His lips curved in a self-satisfied smirk. "You like it when I make you scream."

"So much." No sense in denying what he'd been proving on a regular basis. "But screaming can wait until later. Go get cleaned up, Cowboy."

Ethan huffed out a sigh. "Fine. But I'm just gonna be devising more ways to torture you when we get home."

Miranda moved over to her underwear drawer. "Promises, promises."

Laughing, he headed for the shower. When it cut on a few moments later, she shot a glance at the bathroom door and gave in to the urge to heave a girly sigh.

He'd called this home. Maybe it had been just a slip of the tongue. She kept waiting for the idea of it to freak her out. She'd never cohabitated with a boyfriend before. She hadn't even had a roommate since Norah. But the panic never came.

Ethan had slid so seamlessly into her life here. First into her bed, then into her house. Over the past couple of days, she'd made space in her closet, emptied some drawers. His razor and toothbrush sat on the bathroom counter, very clear reminders that she had someone occupying her space. And they looked right, somehow. Just as the boots that sat neatly by the chair looked right, as if they'd always belonged in that spot. The sight of them made her unreasonably happy. And that was just stupid.

Ethan living here was temporary. A trial run. Softer emotions aside, it was meant as a protective measure until he caught whoever was behind the vandalism. A necessary—to his mind— step for her safety. Was he enjoying the side benefits of that? She'd made sure he was. But that didn't mean it was the legitimate next step in their relationship. She understood him well enough to recognize that he couldn't separate her as a case from her as a woman. Oh, she absolutely believed he cared for her. But she couldn't help wondering if they'd be here now if he didn't think she was in danger.

Miranda didn't like second guessing herself. It wasn't like her not to just straight up ask where they stood. But she'd passed the point where the answer to that didn't have the power to hurt her. She'd passed a whole helluva lot of points with Ethan, rushing headlong into lo—no, she wasn't in love with him. Was she?

You practically have cartoon hearts and little chirping birdies circling your head over the sight of his boots on your floor.

Oh God. She clutched the matching bra and panty set to her chest as her heart began to pound.

The shower switched off.

She shimmied into her underwear, willing her hands not to shake. This was only a disaster if he didn't feel the same way. But what if he didn't? What if this was all really just his protective instincts and they dissipated when he finally figured out who was harassing her and put a stop to it?

He came out of the bathroom, a towel wrapped around his hips. "Is that what's going underneath your dress? Damn, that's gonna have me hot all night."

Miranda forced her lips into a flirty smile. "That was the idea." She could do this. Realizing she was in love with him didn't change how they interacted. She'd just hang on to that piece of information until such a time as it made sense to tell him. When she was more certain of his feelings.

Ethan frowned at her. "Something wrong, Legs?"

"Not a thing. I was just thinking I should call the answering service and make sure they direct any calls to the hospital tonight." Look at her thinking on her feet.

Actually, she should totally make that call. He'd gone the extra mile to try and block off tonight. To put her first. He'd told her about the problems he'd had in his marriage because he'd always put the job first. She understood the realities of that and accepted them, just as he accepted the same about her. But still, he made the effort. That had to mean something, didn't it? Or was it just that their relationship was new, and he was still in that best-foot-forward phase? God, she hated being so uncertain.

"Good plan. Because once I get you back out of that dress, I may have to shoot anybody who dares interrupt us."

"I do love your commitment." With a wink, she sailed past him, back into the bathroom to finish getting ready.

~

"I HAD a meeting with a focus group at the senior center earlier this week. They're pumped at the idea of the teens with seniors program," Norah announced. "Of course, the Casserole Patrol wants the option to select their teens—which in their world means some hot young athletes to ogle."

"Does anybody else feel dirty?" Cam asked. "I feel dirty."

Ethan made a non-committal noise of agreement. His focus was on Miranda, who stood nearby, in conversation with Delaney. She smiled and laughed and otherwise behaved normally, but he couldn't shake the feeling that something was off with her. Was she feeling the pinch of having him invade her space? He hadn't exactly given her a choice in the matter. She'd seemed fine about it, and the transition had gone remarkably smoothly, considering. Maybe that little honeymoon period was over.

"Earth to Ethan."

Realizing he hadn't heard the last couple minutes of conversation, he dragged his attention back to the Crawfords. "Sorry. You were saying something about the Casserole Patrol?"

Norah looked amused. "We'd moved on a bit from that. I was asking how things were going with you and Miranda."

"It has not gone unnoticed that you've been staying nights." Cam interrupted.

Ah, so Cam was going to step into the role of protector in Mitch's absence. Ethan had wondered when he'd hear something from her family. He wanted to tell them it was just as a safety precaution, but that'd be lying. It was a safety measure, but it certainly wasn't only that. Was Miranda doubting that? Was that what that little funk was about?

"That a problem?"

"Seems kinda fast."

Norah popped her husband on the arm. "Oh, stop being such a fuddy duddy, Cam. I think it's wonderful."

Cam's flat stare said he was reserving judgment about that. That was fine. Ethan wasn't concerned with proving anything to him. The only one he needed to prove anything to was Miranda herself. At the sound of her laughter, Ethan looked back in her direction. Her honey blonde hair flowed in waves down her shoulders, glowing a bit beneath the canopy of cafe lights above. Her cheeks were flushed, and her smile was conspiratorial as she shared some private joke with Delaney.

She was beautiful, smart, compassionate. How the hell did he get so lucky?

Norah rolled right on without input from either him or Cam. "When it's right, it's right, and I don't see the point in pussy footing around about it."

Why indeed?

"You know what? You're absolutely right." Ethan shot a quick smile at Norah. "I'll be right back."

Stepping up to Miranda, he pressed a hand to the small of her back, pleased when she automatically leaned into his touch. "Sorry to interrupt, ladies." He bent his head to Miranda's ear. "This should say what needs saying."

She frowned in confusion. "What?"

Ethan pressed a quick kiss to her cheek and cut through the crowd toward the stage, where Clay was coming up on the end of the first set. His buddy caught sight of him as he wrapped the Tim McGraw cover. With a series of quick hand gestures, Ethan made his request and had his answer.

"I'm about to step down for a quick break here, folks, but don't you leave the floor because our very own Chief of Police Ethan Greer is about to take the mic."

Ethan hopped up on the stage, accepting the guitar from Clay with a nod.

"Go get her, buddy," Clay murmured.

Ethan slid the strap over his neck, feeling the familiar weight settle around his shoulders. He felt the performer persona slide into place just as easily. "Evening, Wishful. How're y'all doing tonight?"

There were a few hoots and hollers.

"Come on now. Y'all have been listening to Clay Turner. Let's give him a warm round of applause for keeping you in the arms of your sweetheart for the last forty-five minutes."

That got a reaction. The whole room began to clap, with a few enthusiastic whistles thrown in for good measure.

"That's more like it." Ethan strummed a few fingers over the strings, absently adjusting the tuning. "You know, I've never been a fan of Valentine's Day before. The chocolate, the flowers, the cards always seem more about commercialization and profit than an actual expression of your feelings. So, I thought I'd do something a little different tonight for my girl." He sought her out in the crowd, finding her still back by the refreshment table with Delaney, Cam, and Norah. Oh, he had her attention now. "Miranda, this is for you."

The lights, the crowd, it all faded away as he began to sing. When he'd done this at the bonfire, it had been about proving something and showing off. But this was for no other reason than to reassure Miranda of his feelings—the ones he hadn't actually said aloud because he had some kind of timeline in his head for when the right time would be. And that was just stupid. He felt what he felt —and life should've taught him by now not to take such things for granted. He could be killed tomorrow, and he didn't want her uncertain of where they stood.

In his periphery, Ethan saw Delaney's face twist in something that might've been pain and she slipped back, melting into the crowd. He filed it away but didn't tear his gaze from Miranda. Nothing was going to interrupt tonight. The dancing couples parted for her as she made her way toward the stage. Ethan barely heard the wild applause when he finished.

He didn't even glance at Clay as he handed back the guitar. His eyes stayed on Miranda alone as she stepped onto the stage, plucked his Stetson off his head, and pressed her mouth to his—a feat more easily accomplished in her sky-high red heels. Ethan scooped her up and spun her in a circle. Whistles and whoops split the air.

Miranda laughed. "That is never, ever going to get old."

"Guess I felt the need to make a public statement."

"That, my dear Cowboy, is what we call a spectacle, and this one will have people talking for a while."

"That worry you, having your name linked to mine?"

"Not a bit." She settled his hat back in place and curled her fingers through his. "Come dance with me."

As Clay took the stage again, they found an empty space on the dance floor and lost themselves in each other. He loved holding her like this, feeling the subtle give of her body as she followed his lead. He hoped he'd be able to do this for years to come.

"You feel better?"

Miranda lifted her head from his shoulder. "About what?"

"Us. You seemed a little off when we left the house. Like—I don't know—you'd been too much in your own head and were over-thinking things."

"I suppose I was. I was worried we were suffering from The *Speed* Effect."

"From the what now?"

"You remember that old Keanu Reeves movie, *Speed*? The take-away lesson is that relationships that develop under extreme circumstances don't last."

Ethan tried to remember anything about that movie, but all he could bring up was something about a bus that had to be main-tained at a certain speed or a bomb would detonate. "There was a romance in that movie?"

"Exactly." She nodded, as if that explained everything.

"Legs, I've been crazy about you pretty much from the moment you plowed into me at Dinner Belles. Maybe before that, when you tried to tell me off for driving into the ambulance bay that first time I saw you. That's got nothing to do with my wanting to protect you from whatever trouble's got you in its sights."

He felt the subtle relaxation of her body. "It's nice to have that confirmed."

"We're okay?"

"Cowboy, we're way better than okay."

Smiling, Ethan bent to kiss her again.

"I'm so sorry to interrupt, Miranda, but your phone was ringing." Norah handed over Miranda's little purse.

Miranda winced as she dug out the phone to check the readout. "I'm sorry. The answering service isn't supposed to call me tonight. I gave them explicit—"

The frown had Ethan going on alert. "What?"

"It's the alarm company I use for the clinic."

Ethan led the way, weaving through the crowd until they passed beneath the balloon arch and out into the hallway, away from the worst of the noise.

Miranda hit redial. "Yes, this is Miranda Campbell. I had a missed call."

Ethan listened as she confirmed her information and knew their fun night was over before she'd even hung up the phone.

"Something set off the alarm at my clinic."

"Let's go."

Two police cruisers sat in her parking lot, lights reflecting off the building like a garish red and blue disco ball. Darius Greeley and Rowan Beale stood in front of the open door. None of the interior lights were on, so it was just a gaping, dark hole. What would she find inside? The grim set to the officers' faces extinguished any lingering hope that it had been a false alarm. Miranda closed her eyes for just a second and prayed it wouldn't be too bad.

Ethan squeezed her hand. "Whatever it is, we'll deal with it."

She could only nod. When he pulled a gun from a lockbox and armed himself before sliding out of the truck, Miranda said nothing. They walked over to join his officers.

"Doctor Campbell, I'm real sorry about this," Darius said.

"Have you already cleared the building?" Ethan asked.

Rowan nodded. "Yes, sir. Whoever did this is long gone."

"Are there cameras?"

Miranda tore her attention from the open door. "No." It hadn't seemed necessary. This was Wishful. But she thought about the robbery at the pharmacy as she followed him inside. Using a pen, he flipped on the lights.

The waiting room was largely undisturbed, though the potted plants Shelby babied had been upended all over the floor. She was going to have a hissy fit. Together, she and Ethan moved through the door to the back, turning on more lights as they went. Miranda hissed in a breath as she saw patient files ripped and scattered all over the floors. It seemed all of them had been yanked from their shelves behind Shelby's desk. The front desk computer monitor had been smashed and the tower lay cracked open on the floor. The phone was tipped over, the handset dangling by the cord. The automated voice of the operator echoed in the otherwise quiet space. "We're sorry. You must first dial a one or—"

One by one, they checked the patient rooms. With each and every one, Miranda felt herself closer to absolutely losing it. Rolls of paper had been yanked from the exam tables. Glass jars of supplies were shattered on the floor. Exam instruments were scattered everywhere. Each would need to be examined for damage and resterilized. The x-ray room was blessedly locked, so at least the most expensive piece of equipment was probably safe, but everywhere she looked, Miranda saw dollar signs adding up and flowing out of the accounts that were already taxed by the weight of her student loans and the cost of her business loan on the practice. Even with insurance, this was going to be a huge blow.

"Where do you keep the drugs?"

"In the lab."

"Show me."

Miranda led Ethan to the back, clinging to her control by a thread. A lot of good the lock had done. The vandal had simply smashed open the glass case. The contents of the case were scattered across the floor, along with the bottles and boxes of other medications and testing supplies. More money, down the drain.

Keep it together. Keep it together. She didn't want to lose her shit in front of Ethan. She didn't want to stress him out or make him feel like this was somehow his fault for not doing his job. He'd been frustrated enough with this case, and no one could've predicted this. Except he'd been telling her for days this was more than she'd made it out to be. She hadn't wanted to believe him.

"Do you have an inventory?" Ethan's calm, matter of fact voice pulled her back to the present.

"Yes. We reconcile it at the end of every day."

"So, you can check what's left against that to determine what, if anything, was taken?"

"Yes."

"Do you keep much on hand that would appeal to thieves?"

"Not a ton. The injectable pain meds would be about it."

Ethan glanced around, his mind clearly churning through possibilities. "There have been a string of robberies of pharmacies and doctor's offices over in Lawley. Judd's team had a bust a couple weeks ago. Didn't catch the guy but seized most of his stash. It's possible the thieves have expanded their territory."

Miranda crouched down in her heels.

"Don't touch anything," he warned.

"Either the vandal didn't know what he was after or this wasn't about drugs. The Demerol is still here."

"Maybe. Maybe not. Can you tell if anything's been taken?"

Miranda looked around at the chaos that had been her nice, pristine clinic and wanted to weep. This...*this* was where she lived. This was the heart of her. "Not offhand. I'll need to bring in my entire staff to help deal with all of this. The mess has to be cleaned up, and Jesus God, the files. Shelby's gonna murder whoever did this. It's going to take...I don't even know how long it's gonna take to put them back to rights."

"It's possible someone was after particular medical records. Do you have any means of determining what's been taken there?"

"I bought this practice from Dr. Klein, so there are paper records going back a ways. We're required to keep them for seven years from last service. When I bought the practice, I invested in an electronic data management system because most insurance requires electronic filing now. We've been working on digitizing old patient records so that the electronic record is complete, but that's not finished yet."

"Is there an off-site backup of those digital records?"

"Yeah." And thank God for that.

"Okay. I know there's a lot of work to be done. We're going to finish working the scene. You'll need to contact your insurance company, I expect."

Miranda scooped a hand through her hair. "Yeah." Would they even be able to send someone out before Monday? How long would she have to stay closed in order to deal with this mess? Loss of revenue aside, her patients needed her.

"I'm gonna go talk to Darius and Rowan, get the ball rolling on this."

Miranda nodded and stayed where she was as he moved back down the hall.

There'd be no keeping this quiet. Her family was sure to hear about it by morning. That was both a blessing and a curse. They would help deal with the chaos as soon as the police were finished doing their thing. And they'd be all up in her business in the name of protecting her.

Much as she didn't care what anyone else thought of Ethan moving in with her, she wasn't exactly thrilled with facing down her parents over that fact. Her mother would probably already be knitting baby booties and her dad—well, he was an old-fashioned Southern daddy. He might be able to willfully overlook the signs that she and Ethan were sleeping together, but living together was a whole other thing to Peter Campbell. She didn't need that stress on top of everything else.

Ethan came back a few minutes later. "I'm bringing Judd in to assist in the investigation. He'll be here as soon as he can. I've sent Darius out to check on Harley."

"Harley? You think he did this? Why?"

"I don't know. Maybe because you were helping Rene. It may not be him, but I want to verify his whereabouts." Ethan ran both hands down her shoulders. "I'm so sorry about all of this."

Because she wanted to lean for just a minute, Miranda moved into him. "Are we cursed?"

"Cursed?"

"We just wanted one night where our jobs didn't interrupt everything. And we can't even have that."

He exhaled and pressed a kiss to her brow. "It won't always be like this."

Quiet footsteps sounded in the hall. "Chief, they're here."

"Thanks, Rowan."

"Who's here?" Miranda asked.

"Cam and Norah."

Shit. "Why?"

"Because I called them. I'm sending you home with them."

Miranda pulled back, feeling the first flames of temper lick through the upset. "Excuse me?"

"Honey, there's nothing you're gonna be able to do here tonight. I need to stay here to do my job, and I don't want you home alone. You're staying with them out at Hope Springs tonight."

"This is *my* clinic, *my* livelihood."

"I know. And you're justifiably upset and not thinking clearly. Go on home with Cam and Norah. She'll help you devise a plan of attack for getting everything sorted as quickly as possible with the clinic, and you know she'll set up whatever work details are necessary to get you back in business. The sooner I finish here, the sooner y'all can get started on that."

Miranda's hands curled to fists. She hated feeling powerless, hated someone else calling the shots. But what choice did she have? He didn't trust her judgment right now. The idea of it rankled.

You're not being fair. You're just being too sensitive because of your experience with Stephen. Ethan's not like that.

And hell, maybe he was right. She *was* upset and perilously close to a break down. She'd just as soon have that away from him. Stuffing all that simmering rage down, she took a breath. "Fine. I'll go tonight. But Ethan, I'm not going to stop living my life just because some asshole decided to have a tantrum at my expense. If I do, that means he wins."

"There's something here, somewhere, that's going to tell us who's behind this. And I'm going to find it."

She didn't doubt him, but she sure as hell hoped it was soon. She didn't know how much more she could take.

~

"You think this is your guy?" Ethan asked.

Judd kicked back against the break room counter and chomped down on a donut. "I don't know. None of the other hits had this kind of vandalism. That wastes valuable time. Up to now, every single one has been in and out, clean as a whistle. Why would he change now?"

"Could be the thief broke in, hoping to replenish his supply, expected to find more than he did, and lost his temper when he didn't find much."

"Maybe. Criminals are often stupid, so I'm not ruling it out, but it seems unlikely. Even if he didn't find what he wanted, he's smart enough to know what he could take. Why leave that behind?"

"Time? Or maybe he realized it wasn't gonna be the haul he wanted, and he decided to cut his losses and get the hell out."

"Do you really believe that?" Judd asked.

"It's a theory. But no, it doesn't ring true." Ethan didn't like the idea that it wasn't a failed drug theft. Because if it wasn't about that, then it was more likely about somehow striking at Miranda.

"Well, it wasn't Harley." Darius strode in and reached for the coffee pot. "Nearly a dozen witnesses place him at The Mudcat."

Ethan mentally calculated the distance, both on foot and by car. "The whole time?"

"Before, during, and after. And guess who he was drinking with?"

"Who?"

"Ralph Slocombe."

"Which knocks Slocombe out for this, too." Ethan scrubbed a hand over his stubbled jaw. "Are the two of them known friends?"

"I don't know. I think they used to work together. They were bitching about the factory closing with some other guys. Nothing illegal about that."

Maybe not, but it seemed damned coincidental. Then again, as he was increasingly reminded, Wishful was a small town. It seemed most everybody knew everybody else in some form or fashion. "Hmm."

"Are you trying to make a connection between my guy and Forbes?" Judd asked.

"Probably just wishful thinking. He's a bad son of a bitch, and I want to put him away for something he can't raise enough bail to get out of. He may not have been the vandal, but he's not innocent. Where are we on that list of his known associates?"

Darius shrugged. "There's nobody on it with a blinking red sign that says criminal here. A few with criminal records, but it's all for minor stuff. Misdemeanors. No worse than Harley's own record up to now. A lot of them are in the same boat as Harley and Ralph. Trouble finding work since the factories closed."

"Anybody who seems to be living beyond their means under those circumstances?" Ethan asked.

"That'll take some more digging."

"It can wait. The vandalism at the clinic takes priority." Ethan poured his own mug of coffee. He'd lost count of how much he'd had since last night. "Are the prints scanned in?"

"Yeah. But we'll need to get prints from everyone on staff to weed them out. Everybody's been notified already, so they should be swinging through the station sometime this morning to get that taken care of."

"Good. I want to question all of them. See if there's anybody or anything that sticks out in their memories. Something Miranda's not thinking of."

"What about the kid? Harley's stepson. Do we know his whereabouts last night?" Judd asked.

"I haven't checked yet," Darius admitted.

Ethan crossed his arms. "What motive would he have for targeting Miranda?"

Judd finished off his donut. "Maybe he's mad she didn't convince his mama to leave Harley sooner? I don't know. You said yourself the kid was a powder keg. Hell, he shot Raines while trying to kill his stepfather. That doesn't exactly scream stable."

"Darius, follow up on it. Verify his whereabouts. Maybe I'm being biased. When you're finished, take yourself home. You've been up all night."

"So have you." Darius lifted his mug in a toast before draining it. "I'll bring back my findings."

Judd set his mug into the sink. "I'm gonna be getting on, too. Heading into Lawley to check in on some things. If I hear anything useful, you'll be the first to know."

"Thanks, man."

As soon as they were gone, Ethan took his coffee into his office to review the crime scene photos. As big a mess as the place was, most of it was just nuisance stuff. The glass could be cleaned, the supplies replaced. The files were a disaster. Unless some turned up missing, that was probably just more mess. The computer was the worst of it. But why destroy just the one up front? Why not the ones in the patient exam rooms? Lack of time? Assumption that they weren't on the same system? What was the purpose of the vandalism? Distraction? A tantrum like Miranda suspected? Was it meant to upset her? Scare her?

He continued to click through the photos, scanning details.

"Chief?"

He looked up at Inez in the doorway. "Yeah?"

"Delaney Newell came in to be printed."

Ethan rose. "I'll take care of it. Thanks."

Delaney was dressed up, clearly on her way to or from church. Her gaze flitted around the station, taking it all in, as she twisted the strap of her purse.

"Miss Newell. Good morning. Thanks for coming in."

Her attention swung to him and she seemed to settle. "Oh, of course. I just can't believe somebody would trash the office like that."

"We just need to get your prints, then I'd like to ask you a few questions, see if there's anything you can think of that Miranda hasn't."

"Sure."

Quick and efficient, Ethan finished the fingerprinting—not mentioning the fact they already had her prints on file from her previous arrest—then led her back to his office. "Have a seat, Miss Newell."

Delaney sat in one of the chairs across from his desk and checked her watch.

"Somewhere you have to be?"

"I was stopping in on my way to church. The service starts in half an hour."

"I'll try to be brief. Have you noticed anything odd at work the past few weeks or months? Any patients giving Miranda trouble? Or any talking about her behind her back?"

The woman considered. "Well, she had that tussle with Ralph Slocombe, but you already knew about that. There's always some fussing from people when she tells them something they don't want to hear—like that they're going to have to give up bacon because their cholesterol is too high or something. But for the most part, everybody loves Miranda. It's why her practice is thriving."

"The clinic wasn't the first incident. Her tires were slashed out at the bonfire. You left early that night. Did you see anything that seemed off to you?"

"Not that I can remember. There were people in and out all evening."

"Why did you leave early?"

"I wasn't feeling particularly well."

"How about the night of setup for the dance? Did you see anything or hear anything that would indicate somebody's upset with Miranda?"

"No, everyone was just talking about the dance itself."

"You left right about the time I got there."

"I did."

When Ethan didn't pursue that and instead asked, "And last night?" she frowned.

"What about last night?"

"You left the dance early."

Delaney's eyes narrowed. "Are you watching me, Chief Greer?"

"I watch everybody."

Still frowning, she said, "Yes, I left the dance early."

"You seemed upset. Why?"

"Because that song you sang Miranda upset me. It reminded me of my ex. It used to be our song, and I just didn't want to stay after that."

"That whole situation was a pretty bad one, finding out your guy had been cheating. That's enough to piss anybody off."

Delaney's lips thinned. "You already know I was more than pissed off or you wouldn't be pursuing this line of questioning. I don't love Bryce anymore. I don't care what he does or who he's with. I am over him and over that whole situation. I haven't missed my medication. I was upset, yes, because I was at a Valentine's dance *alone*. But I am not stupid or crazy. Why would I take anything out on Miranda? She gave me a chance when no one else would. Why on earth would I repay her with meanness?"

"Maybe you're tired of her being so vocal in defending you. Her getting angry and fighting about it just brings all of it back up in everybody's minds."

A quick flash of temper crossed her face before she got herself under control again. "People will gossip no matter what. I'm hardly going to criticize her for defending me. Almost no one else has been willing to stick their neck out to do that."

"Maybe you feel threatened by Miranda like you felt threatened by Gina Draper with Bryce."

Delaney just shook her head, confused. "Why would I feel that way? The only person she's seeing is you."

Ethan just looked at her, waiting.

Her cheeks pinked. "You think I have a thing for *you?*"

He crossed his arms. "Never shot a bow before?"

"Oh, for the love of—" She rolled her eyes and huffed a breath, obviously struggling with the desire to tell him he had a big head. "I *hadn't* shot anything like you had for the class. I hardly think the summer I spent at camp in Alabama when I was twelve actually qualified me for anything."

"You're awfully good with a bow for just that."

"Tell me something, Chief. Do you shoot something other than your service weapon? Hunting rifles? Shotguns?"

"Yes."

"And do you not find that your marksmanship translates to some extent across weapons?"

"Are you saying you've got some other kind of marksmanship experience?"

"Two-time finalist in the state riflery championship in high school. And before you ask, no, I do not currently own any firearms. Now look, you seem to be a mostly nice guy. Miranda wouldn't be with you if you weren't. I get that you're just doing your job and at some point since you arrived in town, somebody told you about my sordid and unfortunate past. You wouldn't be doing due diligence if you didn't follow up on that. But I did not do this. So, unless you have sufficient cause to charge me—and I'm assuming you don't since, as I said, I *didn't do this*—I need to be getting on to church. If there are no further questions?"

The little mouse has a spine after all. "Just one. Since you say you didn't do this, can anyone verify your whereabouts after leaving the dance?"

She pressed her lips together. "I went straight home."

"Alone?"

"Yes, alone."

Convenient. "Did you see anybody? A neighbor? A roommate? Somebody who can confirm round about what time you got home?"

"I live in an apartment above my aunt's garage. Maybe she noticed when I got home. I don't know. But I'm sure you'll ask her."

"I will. Thank you for your cooperation, Miss Newell. That's all for now. But don't be leaving town. I might have more questions later."

Eyes sparking with temper, Delaney shoved up out of the chair. "I won't be leaving town. I'll be helping Miranda put the office back to rights so we can all get back to work." With one, final fulminating glare, she sailed out of his office.

He waited until she'd gone before heading to the file room. It took him only a few minutes to find the folder Inez had pulled for him mere weeks ago. Back at his desk, he opened the file, flipping through the printed crime scene photos and reports until he found the one he wanted. There, in damning black and white, was the proclamation of County Fire Marshal Charlie Hammond that the fire at Gina Draper's residence was, in fact, probable arson by means of rags soaked in linseed oil.

Ethan reached for the phone.

The other man answered after only two rings. "Hammond."

"Charlie, this is Ethan Greer down in Wishful. I need you to come analyze the scene of a fire for possible arson."

CHAPTER 18

"Please tell me I can get back into my clinic to start sorting this mess out." The words were out of Miranda's mouth before Ethan had even shut the front door.

"Hello to you, too." He looked exhausted. At some point since last night, he'd changed into his uniform. Had he been back to the house or changed into the spare he kept at the station?

"I'm sorry. You haven't slept." Miranda crossed over to slip her arms around him.

His lifted in response, but the gesture felt automatic. "No, I have not."

"You want coffee?"

"Cassie sent over an assortment. I believe I'm currently being fueled by a Ja Mocha Me Crazy. If I add more caffeine on top of that I might *be* crazy. How long have you been home?"

"Cam and Norah dropped me off on the way to church this morning. What did you find out?"

He skimmed his hands down her arms and focused in on her. "Let's sit down."

Miranda tensed. "You've figured out who's behind all this."

His expression grave, he just folded her hand in his and pulled her toward the couch. "C'mon, sit with me."

She tugged free, resenting the softness because it made her feel like he thought she was breakable. She was upset, but she wasn't weak. "Don't coddle me, Ethan. Just spit it out. What did you find out?"

On a sigh, he seemed to accept she wasn't going to join him and sank down on the sofa. "We've finished processing the scene, so you can get in this afternoon to start cleaning up."

"Great. The sooner that's sorted, the better. Now who is making my life difficult?"

"You're not gonna like it."

Miranda had a bad feeling about all this, but she waited.

"I've had my suspicions, and this morning I brought in the fire marshal to look over the shed more thoroughly. I wanted a more expert opinion on the likelihood that it was arson."

The knot of dread grew heavier in her stomach. "And?"

"There's someone in town who's already committed arson under the guise of an accident. Someone who's had a history of unstable behavior."

Don't say it. Don't say it.

"Delaney."

The refusal was instant. "No. It's not her." It couldn't possibly be her. Delaney was a friend and the last thing she needed was to be dragged through the mud again by having her past mistakes spotlit as part of a new investigation.

Ethan rubbed a hand over his hair. "I'm not making this accusation lightly. Just hear me out."

Though every instinct shouted in rejection of the idea, Ethan had a reputation as a good cop. If he said he had evidence, he had some kind of evidence, and she owed it to him to listen. Crossing her arms, she nodded at him to go on.

"She was at the diner the day your car was keyed, and she's frustrated that you're so vocal in defending her, keeping all the gossips fueled rather than letting the whole thing lie."

Was that really what Delaney thought? Would she rather Miranda say nothing to contradict the asshats like Clarice Morris? "Even if that's true, she left before I did that defending."

"Let me finish," he snapped.

Miranda clenched her teeth but nodded.

"She was at the bonfire the night your tires were slashed, and she left early after witnesses noted her seeming upset after I sang to you. She was at the set up for the dance, and again, left early, seeming upset after seeing you and me together. Based on the evidence Charlie Hammond found, it's unlikely that fire was a result of a slow buildup of linseed oil. And there's documented evidence from her original arrest about a fire started with linseed oil beneath the deck at the home her ex shared with Gina Draper. She left the dance itself early, also seeming upset, during my performance. She had just enough time to get to the clinic and trash it before we were notified. Apart from the alarm, there were no signs of breaking and entering, suggesting either someone extremely good at picking locks or that the perpetrator had a key. And she has a history of retaliatory behavior against a woman involved with the guy she was into. She had means, motive, and opportunity and no verifiable alibi for any of those occasions."

"Retaliatory behavior? What the hell are you talking about? All of this stuff has, as you've consistently pointed out, been directed at me."

He just looked at her, apparently waiting for her brain to connect the dots. When she did, she simply couldn't contain her incredulity. "Are you kidding me? You're seriously basing her motive for these crimes on the idea that she has a *crush on you?* Jesus Christ, Ethan, how big is your ego?"

"This is not about my ego. It's about evidence."

She couldn't stay still and began to pace the room. "Evidence? Everything you've just tossed out is purely circumstantial supposition. You say she had opportunity. I can list off at least eight people who also had the same opportunity at all of those locations. It's a small town. We all hang out together. You haven't proved anything but that she's part of our crew."

His lips thinned. "It's an ongoing investigation."

"An investigation that's going to destroy what she's managed to rebuild of her life. Do you have any idea what she's had to go through to get to where she is now?"

"Frankly, right now, I don't give a damn. My job is to protect people and prevent crime. I'm here talking to you about this because I'm trying to protect *you* from being the victim of further escalation because you aren't willing to see the truth."

Miranda sucked in a breath.

"Delaney Newell is a woman with a history of unstable mental health and rash, violent behavior. This entire string of events fits her pattern."

No. He was wrong.

"So that's it? You're just going to write her off based on past behavior and circumstantial evidence because you can't fathom that someone can actually change."

"Most people don't."

Ethan certainly hadn't. He'd shown his cynicism that first day outside the diner, and she'd foolishly believed that Wishful would work its magic on him. That he'd learn the world wasn't what he imagined it to be. Apparently, the fountain couldn't grant all wishes.

"Delaney didn't do this. I know she didn't. You looking at her is going to be noticed. It's going to wreck any progress she's made in town, and not only is it spurious, but all the grief she's about to get will be partly your fault. Not only are you wrong, not only is this...focus of yours going to hurt her, but you're making me a part of that."

Miranda shook her head. She didn't want to be party to any of this. "I thought you were a better cop than to go around making accusations on evidence this flimsy."

He'd been a man of unflappable calm the whole time she'd known him, and she'd wondered if anything could rattle him. But as her barb struck, his gray eyes turned hard as flint and a muscle began to jump in his jaw.

"Damn it, Miranda, stop being a Pollyanna about this. If it looks like a duck, quacks like a duck, and walks like a duck, it's a damned duck. Believing anything else out of some misguided sense of optimism about people is dangerous and stupid."

Oh, hell no.

"Get out." The words were barely audible, though she wanted to scream.

Ethan blew out a breath, obviously searching for some calm. "Miranda, I know you're upset—"

"Upset? Upset. Oh, of course, because I'm the naive optimist, whose judgment can't be trusted." The temper that had been simmering for weeks kicked up to a full-on boil, until all the frustration and upset and anger she'd been shoving down simply erupted.

"That's not—"

"No. Just stop. I've been in a relationship where my beliefs were belittled. I won't do it again. I won't share my life, my home with someone who makes me feel like less."

Some of the hardness in his eyes faded, replaced with shock. "Miranda—"

She held up a hand. "I'm not doing this anymore. I shouldn't have done it in the first place, but I let myself believe that you'd be different. That we could balance each other. But the truth is, your narrow-minded insistence on seeing the worst in people makes *you* stupid. You're wrong." Because her hands wanted to shake, she curled them to fists. "Get whatever gear you have to have and go. You can get the rest later. I want you out."

He rose slowly, his hands clenching and unclenching, as he stared her down. "I don't want to leave things like this."

"I don't care. Out."

Without another word, he went up the stairs. Miranda stayed where she was. Waiting. She was going to lose it, utterly and completely. But she'd be damned if she'd do it while he was still here.

When he came down a few minutes later, he held a duffel bag in one hand. In the foyer he stopped and turned to her. "I don't like you being here alone."

"That's not your concern anymore."

He sucked in a slow breath through his nose. "Lock up after I go."

In answer, she marched to the door and yanked it open, gesturing for him to take his ass through it.

With one last look at her, he went. As soon as his boots hit the front porch, she slammed the door and shot the deadbolt.

She stood there, hands braced against the wood, listening as he got into his truck and cranked the engine. It idled in the driveway for a long minute before he backed out and drove away. No spinning tires for him. For some reason that made her even angrier. She felt like hurling things. Preferably at his head.

Needing to move, to act, she scooped up her keys and purse. He'd said she could get into the clinic. She'd work off some of this mad cleaning up. But she had a feeling it would take a lot more than a broom and dustpan to set her life back to rights.

ETHAN WAS GENERALLY a man of calm and control. He'd had too much training, spent too much time in dangerous situations where anything else risked deadly outcomes. But he didn't feel in control right now.

How dare she strike out at the core of him in a fit of temper, just because she didn't like what he was telling her? He was a good cop. His record proved it. He had means, motive, opportunity, and probable cause. But Miranda was so damned certain that Delaney would never betray her, she couldn't look at the truth sitting right in front of her face. He wasn't even sure she'd believe a direct photograph of the woman with a smoking gun in her hand. She'd probably argue the thing was Photoshopped. But because he sure as shit didn't want to risk making a false arrest, he spent the rest of the afternoon going over every shred of evidence, every list, every crime scene, every interview, looking for anything that pointed to someone else.

Miranda wasn't entirely wrong. There were, in fact, nine other people who'd been at all three locations at the time in question. Two of them were Cam and Norah, who obviously had nothing to gain from harassing her. As to the rest, she'd been over those lists before and said she didn't have any kind of history or bad blood with any of them. But people didn't always know when someone else had a beef with them. Needing some perspective, he called Clay and asked him to meet for a late dinner at the diner.

For once, Dinner Belles wasn't packed to the gills. Good. Maybe the entire contents of their conversation wouldn't be all over town by tomorrow morning. He'd just as soon his business be private for a little while longer. And maybe Miranda would calm down and realize she'd overreacted and this whole thing would count as their first fight instead of their last. But Ethan couldn't help but see that quick flash of hurt that had flickered over her face before her temper went supernova. In retrospect, losing his own temper with her hadn't been the best way to handle things. But Christ, he hadn't slept in nearly forty-eight hours, and she wasn't being rational about her own safety. If anything happened to her...

"You look like shit," Clay announced as he slid into the corner booth.

"Feel like it, too." Ethan's gaze tracked over the diner, noting the two other tables of customers. Deciding to ensure they had a little more privacy, he slid out and headed to the vintage jukebox. He popped in some quarters and made his selections, figuring the lineup ought to give them enough time to get through the particulars.

Clay just arched a brow as he sat back down.

"I'd just as soon not everybody in town be privy to what we're talking about."

"Fair enough. What are we talking about? Your case? Miranda?"

"Both."

"You any closer to figuring out who's behind the vandalism?"

"Thought I was. Still think I am, but Miranda's convinced I'm dead wrong, so I want some outside opinions to see if there's something I'm missing."

"Alright then." Clay broke off with a cheerful smile at Mama Pearl as she ambled over to take their order. "And how are you, my dearest, darling girl?"

"Still not fallin' for yo flirtin', Clay Turner. What'll you have?"

Clay just winked. They both gave their orders without glancing at the menu.

"Mama Pearl, can you come back by when you get our order back to the kitchen? I'd like to pick your brain a bit," Ethan told her.

"Sure thing, Chief."

When she came back, he'd pulled a sheet of paper and pushed it toward the edge of the table. "Everybody on that list was known to be in the vicinity the night of each vandalism. My question to both of you is whether you're aware of any ill will or bad blood between Miranda and any of those people—old or new."

Clay scooted over and Mama Pearl sat down, both of them bending over the list. After a few moments, Clay shook his head. "I can't think of anything."

"Most of these people would be at the head of a lineup to string up whoever's behind this. Especially this one." Mama Pearl tapped her finger against Delaney's name.

"Why's that?"

"She got herself into some trouble some time back. Miranda helped her out of it. And Miranda's first in line to defend her when anybody tries to start up the rumor mill again. That's what she was doing that day you bumped into her when she was tellin' off those busybodies."

"You don't think, given the girl's history, that something might could shift her loyalties?"

"That girl's had a helluva time getting past what happened. I have a hard time imagining her doing anything that might bring it back up again—to Miranda or anybody else. She's worked hard, kept her head down, and her toes on the straight and narrow."

Which was more or less what Miranda had said. Ethan scrubbed a frustrated hand over his face. Was she right? Was he looking so hard at Delaney because she was the perpetrator or because she was the most obvious and he wanted this case closed?

Clay looked at the list again. "You said this was everybody who was at all three locations. But the fact is, these were all public events, and in this town, it wouldn't be hard to find out Miranda was going to be at any of them. Seems like limiting your suspect pool to who was visible is possibly cutting out some options."

The same thought had occurred to Ethan. "Have either of you heard any rumblings in the past few months about anybody who might have a thing against her? A disgruntled patient? Anything. Because I'm running out of viable leads to follow."

Clay looked thoughtful. "What if it's not about her?"

"What do you mean?"

"I mean...if you toss out the keying of her car, which you can't absolutely tie to everything else, this all started the night of the bonfire when you basically took out a billboard announcing your interest in her. What if it's actually about you?"

"I had thought of that. Which was why I had so strongly considered her." He tapped Delaney's name.

"Oh no, honey, she's got a thing for that new firefighter. What's his name...Sean Murphy."

Sean Murphy. He'd also been one of the students in that bowhunter safety course. Had he been standing nearby during that demonstration with Delaney? Ethan couldn't remember. But he had been at the bonfire.

"Are you sure?"

Mama Pearl gave him a pitying look. "Child, I wouldn't say it if I wasn't sure."

"Yeah, I saw her watching Sean and Charlotte at the dance and looking like she'd swallowed a box of razor blades. There were definite shades of I-wish-that-were-me," Clay said.

If that were true and Delaney didn't actually have some kind of crush on him, then that killed her only viable motive for targeting Miranda. Which meant Miranda was probably right.

"Okay, circling back around to the original question: Why would somebody targeting Miranda be about me?"

"If somebody's pissed off at the attention you're giving her. Maybe they figure a strike at her is a strike at you." Clay shrugged. "It wouldn't be the first time you had a crazy fan."

"I hadn't even performed here before that night."

"You and I both know sometimes it only takes once."

Was that really even a possibility? Was he looking at this whole thing from the wrong angle? Had he really already acquired some lunatic fan? Delaney had been the only one he'd suspected of having leanings in that direction and it seemed he'd been wrong about that. Miranda's scathing remark about his ego echoed through his head again. What if it had nothing to do with attraction or obsession? What if someone was striking out at him through Miranda for reasons that were related to *not* liking him? That would seem to suggest it was something to do with the job, someone he'd crossed as police chief. He hadn't been in town long enough to make enemies of a personal nature.

"Order up!"

Mama Pearl shoved up from her seat and went to retrieve their supper. As she slid it onto the table she gave Ethan a long look. "Seems like you got a lot of ponderin' to do. A fair bit of groveling is probably in order, too."

"Excuse me?"

"You gon' tell me you not planning to fix whatever you broke to send her in here for a breakup pie?"

Ethan swore. Apparently bad relationship news traveled even faster than the good.

"You two broke up?" Clay asked.

"I pissed her off about Delaney. She lost her temper and kicked me out. I figured she'd cool off, and we'd talk about it like rational adults." Ethan wasn't willing to believe she'd really, truly ended it.

Clay shook his head. "Oh brother, no. That is not how Miranda Campbell is built. She has a temper, but she keeps it tightly in check. Normally she has no problem, but if you actually made her unleash that temper, you are screwed in the worst possible way. Groveling is the only solution."

As something that might've been panic lodged itself under his sternum, Ethan swore again. "Mama Pearl, can I get a to go box?"

CHAPTER 19

*B*roken glass hit the pile of detritus in the big garbage can with a crunch that had Miranda grinding her teeth as she emptied the dustpan for what felt like the hundredth time. Turning back to the patient room, she shone a flashlight across the floor, looking for stray shards of glass. Finding none, she declared this room done and shoved the garbage can back into the hall. The floors would get mopped later. Striding back to the counter, she made a notation to the ruthlessly organized list about what needed to be done to that particular room, then stuck a fork into the turtle pie she'd picked up from Dinner Belles earlier in the afternoon. It was half breakup pie, half self-pity for the state of her clinic—all self-medication with sugar. She'd been working her way through it as, room-by-room, she set her clinic to rights. Alone.

She could've called a dozen people to come help. Her staff. Her family. Her friends. They were all just waiting for her to say the word. But she'd needed to be by herself to stew and lick her wounds. She was far too raw to see anyone else. At the slightest show of sympathy, she'd crack. Better to be alone when she broke.

She'd started in the back, with the lab, looking around at the destruction and the mess, feeling her fury rise all over again at whoever had done this. And as she'd thrown stuff away, put things back on shelves, and begun the inventory needed to determine whether anything had been taken, she wondered if she'd had a wolf in her midst. Had she been blind? Had her desire to see the best in people made her a dupe? She started mentally reviewing all her interactions with Delaney, looking for something she'd missed since she'd been all wrapped up with Ethan. And then she was furious with him all over again for making her doubt Delaney. It had taken an entire slice of pie to calm her down from that enough to move on to the scattered patient files.

"Miranda?"

She closed her eyes, unsurprised that Norah had come to track her down. She'd been ignoring her phone all afternoon. "I'm back here."

Note to self: Should have locked the back door.

But she'd been going in and out with bags of trash as she restored order to chaos.

Norah came around the corner. "Jesus. Have you cleaned all of this up on your own?"

"I have." There was some small satisfaction in that. In proving she wasn't beaten.

"Why didn't you call us?" Norah's gaze strayed to the pie, and she immediately understood. "Oh no. Tell me that's not a break-up pie."

"That would make me a liar." How could admitting it out loud hurt worse than actually kicking him out of her house and watching him drive away?

"Oh honey." Norah flew the rest of the distance, wrapping Miranda in a tight hug. "What happened?"

A hot, prickly ball of emotion lodged in her throat. "I made a mistake. I thought we could be something more than a fling. That our differences wouldn't matter. But I knew better. I knew better, and I rushed headlong into things and now it's over." Her shoulders shook as the tears spilled over.

Norah held on, stroking her back. "I don't understand. Why is it over?"

Miranda sniffed and scrubbed at her cheeks. "I made a choice between my feelings and my principles. My principles won." And she didn't regret that. If Ethan couldn't respect something so fundamental about her, they hadn't ever stood a chance.

"You're going to have to explain that one."

"He thinks Delaney is the one behind all the vandalism and harassment."

"Seriously? Why?"

Miranda told her what had happened, laying out the evidence as he'd presented it to her. When she'd finished, Norah looked thoughtful.

Miranda scowled. "Don't you dare tell me you agree with him."

"No. I don't think she'd do anything against you. You've been one of her greatest champions. But I can see why he'd think as he does. He's still an outsider here. But how did that lead to y'all breaking up?"

"Because he said I was being stupid for not believing what was in front of my face, and I kicked him out."

Norah winced. "He actually said that?"

"Loud and clear." Shaking her head in disgust, Miranda forked up another bite of pie. She'd be sick as a dog tomorrow from all this sugar, but who the hell cared? She felt sick anyway. At least she'd found her mad again. That was far preferable to the tears. "I knew he wasn't an idealist. I knew he had a dim view of humanity because of his job. But he at least seemed to respect my viewpoint, which was more than Stephen ever did. But he was clearly just humoring me."

"It sounds more like he was frustrated with you."

"Yeah. Stephen was frustrated with me, too. Every damn day. And all those little digs ate away at me. Made me doubt myself. I'm never, ever going there again." She stabbed the pie and left her fork in it, vibrating with the same frustration coursing through her body.

Norah quietly plucked the fork from the pie and nudged it out of reach. "Sweetie, just because the two of you disagree on this doesn't mean he's like Stephen. He cares about you—that's more than obvious to anyone with eyes—and he's worried about something that's a clear threat to your safety. From his point of view, the evidence points to Delaney."

Miranda crossed her arms. "The evidence is wrong. Or incomplete. Or something. It's not Delaney."

"I'm not saying it is. But if he believes it is, and you're allowing her to stay close, to his mind that's a potential danger to you. That's got to be a little crazy-making for him, so maybe he spoke out of turn."

It made a kind of sense. God knew, she understood what it was to say things in the heat of the moment that you came to regret. But

Miranda wasn't in a place where she wanted sense. She wasn't ready to let go of her anger because once it was gone, she'd be left with nothing but the grief. "Why are you defending him?"

Norah reached out to curl her hands around Miranda's upper arms. "Because, honey, you're in love with him, and I don't want to see you throw this away because you lost your temper."

She hissed in a breath, but Norah rolled on. "I'm not saying you're wrong to defend Delaney. I don't believe she's behind this any more than you do. But I think Ethan just wants to protect you. He's not Stephen. He's so much a better man than that."

Miranda pressed her lips together as a fresh knot of tears replaced the fury she'd been riding for hours. "I want to believe that. Before the last couple of days, things were great between us. And then everything just went to shit. We hit maximum stress level, and we just…broke."

"It happens. It happened to me and Cam. But it doesn't have to stay that way."

"Are you suggesting I'm the one who owes him an apology?" Because hell would freeze over first. She wasn't wrong.

"You two are great together. He's made you happier than I've ever seen you. I'm saying y'all's relationship deserves a legitimate conversation, not just a fight when you're both tired and pissed off."

"That's certainly my vote."

Though she jolted, Miranda didn't turn toward the sound of Ethan's voice. Not until she could get herself under control. "What are you doing here?"

"I came looking for you. You shouldn't be here with the door unlocked."

Miranda whipped around, but before she could go off again, Norah jumped in.

"That's my fault. I left it unlocked when I took the last load of garbage out."

Ethan set a styrofoam box on the counter beside the pie, not even showing a flicker of surprise that a third of it was gone. His face was drawn, the lines around his eyes and mouth more pronounced. He probably still hadn't slept yet.

She was still furious with him. But a part of her was so glad he'd shown up, that he wasn't willing to leave things where they were. Because maybe Norah was right. Maybe they didn't have to stay broken.

"What's that?" Had he brought her some kind of peace offering?

"My dinner. See, I was under the impression that this afternoon was a fight, and we'd circle back around to discussing things when we were calmer. Then Mama Pearl mentioned how you'd been in for a breakup pie, and Clay informed me that if you'd actually lost your temper with me, I was all kinds of up shit creek, so I figured I'd best come deal with that before things got any more out of hand."

Norah made a sound that might've been a laugh, but she wisely turned it into a cough. "I'm just gonna leave you two to talk."

Miranda didn't try to stop her. One way or the other, she wanted this resolved tonight.

Miranda watched him with shuttered eyes as Norah made her escape. Ethan missed the usual open humor, but he understood she was pissed. More than pissed, she was hurt. He could see she'd been crying, and the idea of that gutted him. But it also gave him hope that maybe not all was lost.

The door shut behind Norah, and they were alone with all the temper and hurt feelings and take out. "Look, can we sit and talk? Really talk? I'd say we can do it right here, but I'm not gonna lie to you—I'm exhausted. I've been up for two days, and I really don't want to face plant into what's left of that pie."

The corner of her mouth twitched, as if she'd started to smile, then stopped herself. Without a word, she scooped up the pie and headed down the hall to the break room.

Ethan grabbed his own food and followed, glancing around at the progress. "You've gotten a lot done."

"Rage cleaning is very efficient."

"Certainly more productive than a lot of the alternatives." If he'd had the time—and the actual energy—he'd have been going several rounds at Blanchard's Gym in the boxing ring. "Are you planning on opening tomorrow?"

"By afternoon, if we can. My staff will be here in the morning to finish the reorganization and sterilization. I needed to do this part myself." She dropped into a chair and set the pie on the table.

Ethan sat beside her. "Taking control of a situation where you've had none."

She nodded and forked up a bite of pie. "You wanted to talk, talk."

Straight to it then. After a moment's hesitation, he turned off his radio. For the next little bit, he wanted to focus on nothing but Miranda.

"You said something earlier that's been gnawing at me all day. That you'd been in a relationship where your beliefs were belittled. That you couldn't share your life with someone who makes you feel like less. It kills me that I said or did anything that made you feel like that. The last thing I ever wanted to do was hurt you. I was frustrated and worried, and I just don't see the situation the way you do. I have no problem with your idealism." Her expression hardened, and he realized he'd said the wrong thing yet again. "But I felt like you weren't willing to take necessary precautions for your safety. That makes me nuts, and I made just about the worst possible choice in words to press my point."

He leaned forward, staring into those hazel eyes and willing her to believe him. To let him in. She didn't back away, but she didn't lean toward him either.

"You're not stupid. I would never think of you as stupid, ever. You're smart and compassionate and beautiful, and one of the bravest people I've ever known. It takes guts to believe in people. To put yourself out there knowing you might not get anything back. You do that every day because you don't know any other way to be. I don't have that kind of courage. I've let my experiences define me. I've let them limit me. And I tried to use them to limit you. I won't apologize for trying to protect you, but I will apologize for how I did it."

Miranda stared at him for a long moment, eyes still glistening—shit, he didn't want to make her cry again—before she set the fork aside and laced her fingers together. "I appreciate that. I do. I certainly never got anything close to an apology from Stephen. But this isn't just about me and my sensitivity to being called stupid. It's about a fundamental difference in how we see the world. A difference that's led to you making accusations that could absolutely destroy the life of someone I care about."

"I was wrong. It's not Delaney."

That set her back in her chair. Her eyes narrowed. "What changed from this afternoon?"

"You ever heard her mention Sean Murphy?"

Miranda frowned. "The firefighter?"

"Yeah."

"I've heard his name somewhere recently. I mean besides when he was at my house." She snapped her fingers. "He went to the dance with Charlotte Ballard. We were talking about it just before you got to the community center for set up. And Delaney was upset when she heard it and left right after. I didn't connect the two because I didn't know who he was at the time."

Ethan blew out a breath. "Mama Pearl says Delaney's got a thing for him. I'd say that confirms it. He was also in my bowhunter safety class."

Miranda crossed her arms with an unmistakable air of I-told-you-so. "So, you're dropping her as a suspect?"

"She had a prior history, opportunity, and motive. But I was wrong about the motive, so I have to look elsewhere because I *am* a good cop."

Her eyes dropped, and she grimaced. "I'm sorry. I should never have said that. You put as much into your job as I do, and it wasn't fair of me to lash out because I was angry at how you were focused on my friend."

Ethan waved that off. "The point is, she's no longer a suspect, and I'm not going to make trouble for her. And that means I am officially back to square one with this investigation."

Her breath gushed out. "Thank God. I mean, not thank God, but you know what I mean."

"That's about all I know." Ethan ran a hand through his hair. "I don't presently have any other viable suspects." And it was lowering to admit that. Not that he hadn't had cases that took weeks or months—years even. But none of them had been personal.

"You don't think this has anything to do with that string of robberies in Lawley?"

"I can't rule it out conclusively, but you were being targeted already, and none of the other vandalism fits with the robberies. Judd doesn't think this was his guy. Clay theorized that it might not be about you at all but somebody trying to get at me through you."

Her brows drew together. "I don't understand. How does targeting me attack you?"

How could she not understand what she meant to him? "If the answer to that doesn't immediately occur to you, then I've done a shitty job of showing it." Leaning toward her, he braced his arms on his knees. "I'm in love with you."

All trace of combativeness melted from her expression. "Ethan."

He took a chance and grasped her hands. "Look, I know I'm not perfect. I know I've been overbearing and overprotective. I know we've butted heads. But I never expected to be here again. After my marriage imploded, I never thought anybody would tempt me enough to take the leap into love again. You did. Almost from the first time I saw you. And I don't want what's between us to be over."

The hands in his tightened, and hope leapt in his chest.

"Neither do I."

The knot that had been lodged beneath his heart the last several hours finally unclenched. They'd survive this, and they'd be stronger. But he wanted to make sure there was no room for misunderstandings. "You'll give me another chance?"

"I'll give us another chance. Because I'm in love with you, too."

Just like that, his world tipped back into proper alignment. There were a hundred questions he didn't know the answer to, but right here, in this moment, he knew she loved him, and that was the only thing that mattered.

Ethan slid his hand around her nape and drew her mouth just a breath away from his. "I'll make sure you don't regret it."

When he tugged, she flowed into his lap without resistance, wrapping her arms and legs around him as if she wanted to eradicate all the emotional distance they'd endured. Ethan could absolutely get behind that idea. He took her mouth and drank in the taste of her, as if they'd been apart for years instead of hours. A fresh urgency began to beat in his blood. She wiggled, putting just enough space between them that she could reach the buttons of his shirt.

"Wait just a sec," he gasped. With quick, efficient fingers, he unhooked the radio mic from his shirt and removed his duty belt.

She went back to work, stripping him out of the shirt and the vest, as he tugged her sweatshirt up and off. He yanked off his undershirt as her hands fought with his belt, his zipper. He freed her breasts from the plain cotton bra. Then she had her hands around the length of him, and he dropped his head back on a curse.

"Got a logistical problem here," he rasped.

Miranda glanced down at her yoga pants, then back up at him. "Counter."

He didn't need to be told twice. Gripping her thighs, he surged to his feet and carried her the short distance to the break room counter. Almost as soon as her butt hit the surface, he was reaching for her waistband, dragging down the pants and her underwear. For half a second, he tried to slow down, to find some measure of control.

But she reached for him. "Now. Hurry."

Bracing his hands on the counter, Ethan slid inside her. As her body closed around him, he groaned out her name. She wrapped those long, long legs around his waist, digging her heels into his ass to pull him even deeper.

"Ethan." She pressed her brow to his, skimming her hands over his shoulders.

For a long moment, they held there, all the distance gone. Then she kissed him again, and he began to move. Past the doubt, past the hurt, chasing the heat that built between them, until there was nothing left but need. He took her screaming over the edge and emptied himself.

She trembled in his arms, pressed her lips to the thundering pulse in his throat. His own legs shook, but nothing on Earth could've gotten him to move just yet. For the first time in a long time, he felt whole. As if she'd filled all the empty places inside him. Burying his face in her hair, he tightened his arms around her. "I love you."

She stroked his nape. "I love you, too. And I really want you to take me home so we can do that all over again in a bed."

It turned out he could make himself move if properly motivated.

They dressed and set the room to rights. She cleaned the counter-tops and put the rest of the pie into the fridge. As they stepped into the hall, she paused and peered at the door.

"What are you doing?"

"Checking to see if this door really *does* have a lock." Her dimples winked. "We might need it again someday."

Ethan found himself grinning. "Legs, I like the way you think."

CHAPTER 20

"Jd like to get my hands on whatever asshole did this."

Miranda felt the same way, but also about a million times lighter than she had during her rage cleaning the night before. She swung an arm around Piper's shoulders, giving her a squeeze. "I appreciate you taking time away from the baby to come help sort things out."

"It's fine. Myles is working from home and pacing his office wearing her in the sling. He's under the impression he's already training her for journalistic greatness, and it's the cutest thing ever. As I have zero plans to give her a brother or sister any time soon, my ovaries needed a break. So, what's the plan here?"

"Patient rooms and sterilization are priority. I did the drug inventory last night, so that's taken care of, but we still need to finish reorganizing and inventorying the other supplies, and deal with the nightmare that is the files." Before Ethan had arrived last night, she'd scooped them all into boxes for sorting.

Shelby cracked her knuckles. "I'd like a half an hour alone with the asshole and your surgical instruments."

Ethan straightened from his position against the wall. For once, her staff hadn't commented on her police escort to work. "I assure you, I'm doing everything I can to find out who's behind this. With that in mind, I'll be talking to each of you individually this morning. Delaney, I'd like to start with you, if you don't mind. Miranda, you too."

Delaney's cheeks paled, but she didn't argue. The poor girl already had reason to be nervous around cops. Ethan's accusations hadn't helped.

Miranda couldn't resist slipping an arm around her. "It'll be fine."

Because it was one of the few rooms that didn't need touching, they retreated to the break room and shut the door.

"Have a seat." Ethan gestured toward a chair, an air of polite expectation on his face.

Reluctance in every line of her body, Delaney sank into one of the other chairs. Ethan and Miranda took two of the others.

It took everything Miranda had not to look at the counter. Less than twenty-four hours ago, she'd sat there, bare-assed, with Ethan buried inside her. Her body heated at the memory and her cheeks flushed.

Ethan didn't look at her. Probably for the best. He pulled a notepad from his shirt pocket and flipped it open to a clean page. "Before we get started, there's something I need to say to you."

Delaney's gaze darted from him to Miranda and back again. "Okay." The tone was measured, and her shoulders were stiff, obviously bracing for a blow.

He folded his hands. "I'm sorry."

The utter shock on her face was almost amusing. "Excuse me?"

"I'm sorry for accusing and upsetting you. Given what you went through before, I'm sure all that was difficult. I never set out to do that. I won't apologize for looking into you or asking the questions—that's my job—but I wanted you to know that you're no longer a person of interest in this case. At least not from the standpoint of being the perpetrator."

"I don't understand. What changed your mind?"

"Two things. One: You have a staunch champion."

Miranda smiled as his gaze turned to her, the corner of his mouth lifted in a rueful smile.

"She didn't doubt you. Not once. She made very convincing arguments that sent me looking elsewhere."

Delaney's blue eyes were suspiciously shiny as they shifted to Miranda. "Thank you."

Miranda reached out to grasp her hand, wanting to comfort. "No need to thank me for telling the truth."

"You and I both know you've done more than that. I don't know what I did to deserve that."

"You've been a solid employee, and you've worked your ass off to make up for what you did. I believe people can change, and you did. That's it. I knew the woman you are now would never have done the things somebody's done to me. All I did was tell him so." Which, okay, was probably glossing over some of the realities. But in the end, that's what she'd done.

The girl's throat worked. "You are so awesome." She swallowed back tears and looked back to Ethan. "So…what was the other?"

"Somebody told me about your interest in Sean Murphy."

At the mention of the firefighter's name, Delaney's cheeks went pink. "Oh God, is it that obvious?"

"Well, let's face it, Mama Pearl knows all. But no, I didn't think it was, which is why it hadn't occurred to me. Why didn't you just *say* you were interested in him when we talked the other day?"

She looked at Ethan as if he'd lost his mind. "You already had me pegged. If I'd admitted my interest in Sean, you'd have seen it as an excuse."

He ducked his head. "I deserve that. And again, I'm sorry. I hope we can move past it."

"I will if you will."

This girl had such a generous heart. Maybe that's what had drawn Miranda to her in the first place.

Ethan inclined his head. "Thank you."

"If you're not looking at me anymore, what is it we're getting started on?"

"There's a reason I suspected you. There is a possibility, however remote, that somebody may be setting you up to take the fall for this."

"What?"

"The details of your case are fairly widely known. Except for the origins of the fire. That was something straight out of the crime scene report and not—as far as I'm aware—common knowledge. I don't have any reason to suspect any of my officers, so who, other than yourself, would have known about that?"

"I..." Delaney shook her head. "I don't know. Bryce and Gina, certainly. The fire department would've told them about the oily rags they found under the porch. Anybody who was with them when they were told." She straightened and fixed Ethan with a hard stare. "To be clear, I did not deliberately set that fire. I deliberately used oil-based stain to write my opinion of Bryce's manhood all over his prized deck. But they got home sooner than I was expecting, and I stashed the rags under the porch so I could get out in a hurry. I had no idea they could spontaneously combust, and I can't tell you how grateful I am that they caught it before it spread to the house."

"Noted. Do you think either of them would target you?"

"I don't see why. Or at least, I don't see why they'd try to get to me through Miranda."

Miranda had been thinking about this herself since Ethan mentioned the theory at breakfast. "Maybe because I gave you a hand in helping you get your life turned around? Is that something that would piss them off?"

"Probably. Gina was never satisfied with the fact that I didn't do actual time. But the idea that either of them could be behind this? I don't see it. Frankly, neither of them seems that smart."

"Do you know what sort of work they do?"

"Gina is a hostess out at Tosca, and Bryce has been commuting to Lawley for some job since the plant closed."

Ethan's gaze sharpened. "Heirloom Home Furnishings?"

"Yeah."

"Did he associate with Harley Forbes?"

Harley? Where was he going with this?

"Not that I'm aware of."

"Did you ever hear him mention Harley?"

Delaney frowned. "Maybe once or twice in a telling-stories-about-work kind of way. Why?"

"Maybe nothing. Maybe something." He scribbled something on a notepad. "Is there anybody else you can think of who might want to get back at you for something? Was there anyone else you might have crossed or offended before your arrest?"

"All my focus was on Bryce for cheating on me and Gina for being the other woman. I can't think of anybody else who'd actively try to throw me under the bus like this."

"Keep thinking. If anybody or anything pops for you, I want you to let me know."

She promised she would, then hurried out to get started on the inventory.

"You're coming back to Harley with this?" Miranda asked. "I thought he had alibis for all the times in question."

"He does. Allegedly."

"If he has alibis, how would he have pulled any of this off?"

"He couldn't have done the vandalism here. Too many people saw him drinking with Ralph Slocombe at The Mudcat that night. But I find it more than a little coincidental that a patient who had a beef with you is all buddy-buddy with Harley, who is pissed his wife left him and may rightly blame you or me both, and they both happened to work with the ex-boyfriend of the woman who's prospectively being framed for harassing you."

"Heirloom was the primary employer in town before they closed a couple years ago," Miranda interjected. "You're going to find a whole lot of people who used to work there. It's not exactly a smoking gun."

"No. And it may be nothing. But it's another thread to pull. I think, after I get done questioning the rest of your staff, I'll go track down Bryce Kelso and Gina Draper for a little chat."

Miranda pushed back from the table and crossed over to wrap her arms around his shoulders, loving the way he leaned into her. "It was good of you to apologize."

"I can admit when I'm wrong, Legs. I was wrong about her, and she deserved to know it. From what you've said, she had a pretty rough go of it, and I'd as soon she not be afraid of me just because I'm a cop."

Miranda cupped his jaw and bent to brush her lips to his. "You're going to figure this out. I have faith in you."

His hand curled loosely around her wrist. "I intend to see that faith is justified. Go ahead and send Keisha in."

"Yes, sir, Chief."

~

ANOTHER DEAD END.

Ethan ought to appreciate that. Those were threads he didn't need to keep tugging. But Gina Draper and Bryce Kelso had been the best possible leads he'd come up with today. He'd even worked late so he could talk to Kelso once the guy got back from his job in Lawley. Both of them had alibis that weren't each other for each of the different crimes. Kelso claimed he couldn't stand Harley Forbes, calling the man a lazy son of a bitch who'd contributed to the company's decision to up and move production to Mexico. Ethan was inclined to believe him. Which meant yet another night he had to go home to Miranda and admit failure.

But at least he got to go home to her. That was the lone bright spot in all of this. They'd both had a long day. The clinic parking lot still hadn't emptied when he'd driven back to the station half an hour ago, but surely, she'd be finishing up soon. He ought to check and see what kind of take out she'd like for dinner. They could spend the evening relaxing. Maybe watch a movie before bed. Hopefully he'd be clearer in the morning after a good night's sleep.

Ethan was reaching for his phone when the perfunctory knock sounded on his door. Cleveland stuck his head in. "Chief, Chester Harkin is here to see you. He's got the Forbes kid with him."

Ethan knew from the set of Chester's jaw that he wasn't gonna be going home any time soon. "Chester, Johnny. Why don't we go on into the conference room?"

The boy looked almost gray as he shuffled ahead and sat. He didn't meet Ethan's eyes. Chester looked as if he'd aged another ten years since Ethan saw him just days ago. He shut the door.

"What's going on?"

"Show him," Chester demanded.

Johnny flinched at the harsh tone. Slowly, he pulled his hand out of his hoodie pocket and laid a box on the table. Celebrex. One of the drugs that had turned up missing from Miranda's clinic.

Shit. Maybe it wasn't what he thought. "What's that?"

"Arthritis drugs," Johnny mumbled.

"Why?"

"I thought Mr. Harkin could use them."

So, Ethan hadn't been the only one to notice Chester's debilitating arthritis. "Where did you get them?" He knew there was no good answer to that question.

Johnny's shoulders rounded, and he muttered something.

"Speak up, boy," Chester ordered.

"From Doc Campbell's clinic." The kid's tone was edged with tears.

Ethan shut his eyes for just a moment, wrestling with his own disappointment. He'd gone above and beyond to give this kid a chance. Now this. This is what he got for believing people could change. For going against his training, his experience. Accepting what he'd have to do, he sat. "You're the one who broke in and trashed the place."

The dark head bobbed once.

"Your friend who provided your alibi. Owen. Was he with you?"

"No. I just used his truck." If possible, Johnny's voice got even smaller.

"Tell him why, son." Chester prodded.

"Harley threatened me and my mother." Tears spilled over as the boy looked up. "I didn't want to do anything. I swear. But when he got out of jail, he came out to Monarch House. Snuck in and cornered me. He said I had to do what he told me. That I'd tried to kill him, and he could press charges any time he wanted. He said that, on top of shooting Officer Raines, meant I'd be put away, and as soon as I was gone, he'd come after my mother. Show her what happened to women who leave their husbands. He'd already made it past the security system out there. What was to stop him?"

The prowler Lily Mae had reported. It must've been Harley.

Ethan struggled for patience. "Me, Johnny. That's the entire point of my job. Why the hell didn't you come to me with this?"

"Because you said you'd put him away, and he just got out again. Like he always does."

It was a failure of the system. Ethan knew that. But he couldn't quite shake the sense of personal failure. He'd made a promise to this boy, to his mother, that he'd protect them. "Let's let that go for now. Tell me exactly what he wanted you to do."

Johnny sniffed and scrubbed the tears from his face. "The first time it was setting a fire. He wanted it to look like what Delaney Newell did to her ex."

"He said that?"

"Yeah. He gave really specific instructions."

"Why would Harley want to frame Delaney Newell? Do they know each other? Have any kind of history?"

"I don't know. I think it's just 'cause everybody knew what she did. He thought it would take suspicion off of him."

And it had. If not for Miranda's staunch refusal to believe it, Ethan probably would've charged Delaney.

"What about the dead raccoon?"

"What dead raccoon?"

"Somebody left one all carved up on Dr. Campbell's front porch."

The boy's face went impossibly paler. "I didn't have anything to do with that either. I didn't do anything before the fire, and I haven't done anything since the clinic."

"Okay let's talk about the clinic. What exactly did he say?"

"He demanded I break into the clinic and trash the place. I tried not to do too much damage. Just to make it messy. She's a nice lady. I didn't want to do anything against her. You have to believe me. I didn't want to do anything. But he threatened my mother."

Harley had blackmailed Johnny into acting on his behalf so that he had a couple of very public, very convenient alibis. Tried to throw suspicion elsewhere by framing Delaney. That was a helluva lot of planning for a guy who was allegedly just pissed off and acting out. What was he leading up to? What was Ethan missing?

"Did Harley say why he wanted any of this done?"

"He was pissed she finally convinced Mama to leave. He blames both of you. You, especially."

"Why?"

"He found your card in her purse when he was looking for money. It's what set him off that last time I took her to the ER. He said—" The kid hiccupped. "He said how you'd taken his woman, and he was going to make you pay. Show you what it feels like."

Ethan's instincts began to jangle. Escalation. This whole thing had been an escalation, exactly as he'd thought. "When? When did he say that?"

"After I called to tell him I'd finished with the clinic."

"Has he asked for anything else?"

Johnny shook his head. "I told him I wouldn't do any more and to leave us the hell alone."

Ethan yanked out his own phone and hit Miranda's number. He had to warn her. He'd had Darius sitting on the clinic since he left this afternoon, but that wouldn't be enough. She wasn't going anywhere without a police escort until Harley was brought in for good.

CHAPTER 21

At 6:35, Miranda shut the front door of the clinic behind her last patient and locked it. Thank God. Her feet ached, she hadn't had anything resembling lunch, and all she really wanted to do was fall face first into bed and check out for the next ten hours. Everything was almost back to normal. Cam had sent over new plants for the lobby this morning, bless him. The whole day had been accompanied by a soundtrack of Shelby's muttered threats and curses against whoever had tossed the clinic, as she'd laboriously put files back together and back in order. That process would take another day or so, but at least they'd been able to open the doors to patients just after noon. Probably they'd all have been able to go home earlier had there not been a steady stream of Lookie Lous wanting to hear all about the break-in.

Keisha slipped out of the last of the patient rooms, already having prepped for tomorrow. "Are they gone?"

"They're gone," Miranda confirmed.

Delaney popped out of the lab. "Truly? We're done?"

They all looked as exhausted as she felt. "We are done. Thank you all for sticking it out past closing time. Let's go home."

"You don't have to tell me twice." Shelby was already shutting down the computer that had been moved from one of the patient rooms and pushing her chair under the desk.

The four of them went out the back together, using the buddy system as Miranda locked up. Darius waved from the driver's seat of the police cruiser parked across the street. Ethan had said he'd be keeping an officer posted on-site once he left, but she'd been so covered up with patients, she hadn't noticed. Relaxing into the front seat of her Jeep, she pulled out of the lot, relieved not have to think for the rest of the day.

Her stomach growled. Okay maybe she'd have to think long enough to figure out sustenance. Ethan hadn't left work yet either. Was he done questioning Bryce Kelso? Had he found anything useful? The idea of the asshole doing anything to cause more trouble for Delaney had Miranda even more furious than the vandalism itself. She'd been working so hard to get her life back on track. Going after her felt like a cheap shot. The move of a bully. Miranda despised bullies.

Ethan would sort it out. She knew it was wearing on him that he hadn't been able to pin down the vandal. He'd taken a vow to protect this town, and he felt like he was falling down on the job. He had to be at least as tired as she was. They'd both feel better after a good night's sleep. Maybe he could pick up some kind of takeout on the way home.

It was another of those domestic thoughts that made her stupidly happy. She was beyond relieved that they'd worked out their differences and he'd be *coming* home. It didn't feel like he was just staying with her. Hadn't since the day he moved in. Should she bring up the idea of formalizing that arrangement? Or was it too soon? That probably wasn't a discussion to be had while they were both sleep deprived.

But he loved her.

She hugged the knowledge close, knowing she wore a sappy grin. The police chief and the doctor. Who'd have thought they'd fall so hard and fast? Who'd have imagined he'd feel the sting of her temper and still think she was worth fighting for?

Pulling into the garage, she exhaled a sigh of relief. Home. Grabbing her purse, she waved to Darius, who gave a friendly beep of acknowledgment as he pulled away from the curb. She hit the button for the garage door and watched it lower behind her. On her way into the house, she flipped on lights, her mind already turning to a glass of wine and a bath. Yeah, one of those nice, hot soaks that would leave her fingers and toes pruny as she dozed. Her legs were long enough that she wouldn't slip below the water if she fell asleep. With that goal in mind, Miranda dumped her keys and purse on the little desk in the kitchen and opened a bottle of Cabernet. Maybe she could talk Ethan into pizza. Even the lousy frozen kind would be good after a day like today. Or, even better, maybe she could talk him into joining her in the tub for a soak himself—and whatever consequences that might entail —before pizza. Yeah, that sounded like the ultimate way to relax.

Shoving the phone into her back pocket, she headed up the stairs, sipping at her wine and stripping out of the cardigan she'd worn under her lab coat. She dropped the sweater into a chair and toed off her shoes, already dreaming of fragrant bubbles. The phone began to ring. The flash of Ethan's name across the screen and had her smiling.

"Hey Cowboy, I was just—"

"Where are you?" The urgency in his tone had her going stock still, one hand stretched toward the faucet.

"I just got home. What's wrong?"

"Stay put and make sure the doors are locked."

Had she locked the garage door on her way inside? Miranda couldn't remember. Doing an about-face, she went to check. "I'm going to check the door. What's going on?"

He blew out a breath. "I found out who trashed your clinic."

"Who?"

"Johnny."

The shock almost had her stopping again. "You're kidding."

"I wish I was. Harley coerced him into harassing you by threatening his mother."

"That bastard." She checked the front door. "Front door is locked with the deadbolt. Why the hell is Harley harassing me?" She hurried into the kitchen.

"Short version: He's pissed we convinced Rene to leave him and is targeting you to get back at me."

The door into the garage wasn't locked. She twisted the knob and quickly threw the deadbolt before making a beeline toward the den. "Garage door is locked. What does he hope to gain from all of this?"

"I don't know. But even if he's been acting through Johnny as proxy, he's escalated. I don't want you alone until I can bring him in."

In the den, she started to reach for the light and hesitated, the hair on her arms standing up. Something was wrong. Miranda scanned the room. In the ambient light spilling out of the kitchen, she could just make out the glitter of shattered glass on the carpet. One of the panes had been broken out of the French door.

Her hand tightened around the phone. "Ethan, someone's—"

A hand clamped over her mouth and yanked her off balance, up against a solid male body. The glass dropped out of her hand. Miranda felt the splash of wine on her leg as she automatically reached for the hand. She struck out at her assailant with the phone. It connected with his head, causing the fingers to loosen just enough for her to get out a short, sharp scream.

"Ow! Stupid bitch."

Harley.

Snaking another arm around her throat, he cranked down. The phone fell from her fingers as her oxygen was cut off. Her hands scrabbled at his arm, unable to slacken his grip.

Think. *Think!*

She struggled to remember anything from the self-defense course she'd taken years ago, when she'd moved to Chicago. But there was no thought, only panic. She began to hit, kick, and claw, aiming for whatever she could reach. But her blows just bounced off him, causing nothing more than grunts, even as pain radiated up the elbows she tried to jab into his ribs.

Harley hauled her backward, jerking her off her feet. She kicked out, hoping to meet the wall for some kind of leverage. As they struggled, her foot connected with something solid. It hit the floor and shattered. On a snarl, Harley squeezed harder, applying pressure to her carotid.

Miranda felt consciousness begin to flicker

Ethan. Ethan was on the phone. He'd come for her.

But as her limbs stopped cooperating, her brain starved for blood and air, she wondered if he'd make it in time.

~

"Ethan, someone's—"

At the abrupt cutoff of her words, Ethan's stomach dropped. "Miranda? Miranda!"

Something thumped, and Miranda screamed. The sound sent ice cascading through Ethan's veins, already propelling him into motion, as a muffled male voice growled, "Stupid bitch!"

His heart all but stopped. Harley was at the house. He shouted orders on the way to the door. "All units to Miranda's. He's got her. The son of a bitch has got her."

Bursting out of the station, he pelted toward his police cruiser, hearing sounds of a struggle over the line. "Hang on, baby. Keep fighting. I'm coming. I'm coming."

He threw himself into the driver's seat, peeling out of the lot, sirens blaring. Drawing on every shred of defensive driving he'd ever learned, he flew through town, skidding around corners, flying around cars, coaxing every ounce of speed from the engine.

Something shattered. Then the only thing Ethan could hear was the roaring in his ears. Fear gripped him by the throat. Had the line gone silent?

Too far. He was too goddamned far away.

Why hadn't he insisted she work on some self-defense? Why hadn't he installed that alarm system? Why hadn't he posted a full-time guard on her? He'd known in his gut that this whole situation was going south. That it was more than just vandalism.

Seconds stretched out like hours as he closed the distance, not knowing what he'd find. Backup was en route, but he didn't wait, whipping into the driveway on screaming tires. There was no sign of another car or of Harley's beat-to-shit truck. Only a handful of lights were on inside.

Drawing his service weapon, he headed for the front door. Two swift kicks had the door slamming open, cracking against the interior wall. Shoving down the terror, he stepped into the house, forcing himself to follow protocol and clear each room, even as he listened for sounds of struggle or escape. A lamp lay broken on the floor. A few feet beyond that, a glass lay on the carpet, a dark stain splattered out from it. The scent of wine was sharp in his nose. A pane was broken out of the French door. Obviously, the point of entry. Moving into the kitchen, he saw the open bottle of wine and the corkscrew on the counter. A light was on in the garage. The empty garage. Miranda's Jeep was gone, the garage door down. Not letting himself think about that yet, Ethan raced upstairs, heart pounding with every step. Nothing appeared disturbed up here, save for the shoes and sweater Miranda had obviously ditched when she got home. Whatever had happened had gone down in the den and hallway.

"Chief!" Darius called out from downstairs.

He met his officer halfway down. "She's not here." A part of him had known that as soon as he entered the house, but he'd needed to clear it, needed to make sure there wasn't a body.

Harley hadn't killed her. Yet.

Terror and fury over what the bastard had planned for her all but brought Ethan to his knees. All his training, all his skills, and the son of a bitch had still managed to kidnap his woman. He hadn't been able to keep her safe.

But he'd sure as hell be bringing her home.

Darius watched him, expression horrified. "I shouldn't have left her. I thought she'd be safe in the house, and I got a call—"

"Not your fault. I didn't give you orders to stay."

Ethan let out a long, slow breath, locking away emotion. He'd be no good to her if he was freaking out. He needed to be calm, cold, and collected—a hunter of men. He'd spent the better part of his Marshal career doing exactly that against criminals far smarter and far deadlier than Harley Forbes.

"Secure the scene."

"Yes, sir."

Rowan hustled across the yard as Ethan hit the porch.

"Beale, I want you canvassing the neighborhood. Find out from the neighbors if they've seen a beat-up GMC pickup or Miranda's Grand Cherokee. In particular, I want to know if they saw her vehicle leave in the last fifteen minutes, and if so, which way it went. I also want to check with the neighbors on the street behind her house. He broke in through the back, which means he slipped through somebody's yard to get there. If anybody saw anybody, I want to know about it."

"Yes, Chief." She fell into step beside him as he skirted the cruiser. "Do you know who we're looking for?"

Ethan held up a finger as he reached for the handset of the radio. "Cleveland, this is Greer. Come back."

"Yes, Chief."

"Issue a BOLO for Harley Forbes."

Rowan hissed and nodded before hustling toward the nearest neighbor.

"Pull his details from his file," Ethan continued. "The son of a bitch is wanted for kidnapping and should be presumed armed and dangerous. His victim is Dr. Miranda Campbell." Ethan's voice skipped a beat on her name. "Caucasian female, dark blonde hair, hazel eyes. 5'10", approximately 170 pounds. Presumed to be injured or under duress. It is believed he may be in her vehicle, a black Jeep Grand Cherokee." He reeled off the license plate.

There was a beat of silence, and Ethan could hear Cleveland audibly swallow. "Yes, Chief. Anything else?"

"Call Clint and have him track down Rene Forbes. She's probably out at Monarch House. Have her brought into the station. And bring in Nash and Reuben. I want every able-bodied cop in this town working on this."

"On it."

Replacing the handset, Ethan grabbed his cell phone. It was still connected to Miranda's. For a fleeting moment, he wondered if she had it on her, if they could triangulate her position. Then he heard Darius call his name, heard the echo of the other man's voice through the speaker, and knew it had been left behind.

Hang on, Legs. I'm coming.

Hanging up the call, he popped the trunk and grabbed some gloves and booties before returning to the scene. Then he made the call he'd prayed he'd never have to make.

Judd picked up on the second ring. "Hey man, what's up?"

"I need you. Miranda's been kidnapped."

"I'm on my way."

CHAPTER 22

Miranda struggled to keep her breathing slow and even, so he wouldn't know she was awake again. Fighting through the fog of pain, she took stock. Her mouth was covered. Taped. Flexing her numb fingers, it seemed her wrists and ankles were bound with that as well. The son of a bitch had hog tied her with duct tape. He might even have used the big roll in her garage. Some kind of blindfold was tied around her eyes.

Another bump threw her body. They were moving. In a car? Then he was probably in the driver's seat. She shifted, feeling a roughness against her face. Carpet. Trunk or the back of an SUV? The road noise didn't sound as muffled as she imagined a trunk would. As they continued jolting down what she now recognized as a rutted gravel road, she strained, trying to hear past the ringing in her ears.

Was that Harley breathing? Surely if she could hear him breathing, she was in the back of an SUV instead of a car. Maybe her own Jeep. Didn't Harley have a truck? Miranda couldn't remember.

How long had she been out?

Where were they going?

With aching slowness, she rolled her ankles and wrists, struggling to get the blood flowing again without making noise. If an opportunity to escape presented itself, she'd never be able to run like this. Her limbs felt like painful blocks of ice. How was she going to get free? Duct tape was universal, utilitarian, and damned near impossible to tear.

Think.

What had Ethan said? Harley was angry they'd finally convinced Rene to leave him. He'd been targeting her to get back at Ethan. Every harassment had been an escalation, and nearly every one had involved a knife. Would Harley go so far as to use it on her? What exactly was his plan here? Did he even have one? Kidnapping wasn't something he'd get out of. If he'd been smart enough to coerce his stepson into acting on his behalf, he'd be smart enough to know that. Which meant he probably didn't plan on her surviving to press charges.

A fresh dose of adrenaline dumped into her system. Harley Forbes was going to kill her.

The vehicle turned, skidding to a stop a few seconds later. A driveway?

It took everything she had not to whimper when Harley got out of the vehicle and slammed the door.

How long did she have before he came around to get her? His footsteps seemed to go away from the car. For a few frantic seconds she struggled against the tape, feeling it dig into her wrists. There was no way she'd get out of this without a knife or something sharp. If this was her Jeep, did she keep anything in the back that might be useful? Could she even reach it if she did?

Something loud scraped outside, as if a large door were being shoved open. The sound of returning footsteps had her going still again, fighting to slow her breath.

The back hatch popped. Even behind the blindfold, she could see the rear cabin light pop on. Hands grabbed her arms and legs, dragging her to the edge of the cargo compartment. She briefly considered thrashing, but what good would that do? If he dropped her, she'd just get further injured and would probably piss him off. Better to keep playing possum for now.

He tapped none too gently at her face, then ripped the tape from her mouth. It took everything she had not to scream. Apparently satisfied, he threw her over his shoulder, and she forced herself to be deadweight, despite the steadying hand on her ass. Every muscle screamed at the awkward strain of the hold.

Steps moved from gravel to dirt. The scent of moldy hay tickled her nose. A sneeze built at the back of her throat.

No. No no no no. I can't—

She sneezed.

Harley dumped her unceremoniously on the ground. "Glad to know you're back among the land of the living. This will be a lot more fun with you awake."

Miranda turned her head and tried to spit out the dirt in her mouth. "What the hell are you doing, Harley?"

"Just taking my due. You're an interfering bitch, you know that? A man's got rights to his wife. But you just couldn't leave well enough alone. Had to go giving Rene ideas." He said the last word as if pronouncing a venereal disease.

"You're the one who beat her." The words were out before she could think better of them.

Harley slammed his booted foot into her stomach in a swift kick that drove the air from her lungs and made her whole body seize up.

"You drove her off. She was a proper, well-trained woman." He emphasized every last descriptor with another well-aimed kick to her gut.

Tears poured from her eyes, but she didn't make a sound. Couldn't. She couldn't seem to suck air into her lungs. Not even when Harley yanked off the blindfold and she saw the knife in his hand.

This was it. She'd always been told her smart mouth was going to get her in trouble. Now it finally had.

Harley crouched down, turning the blade in the flickering light of the old barn, as if admiring its craftsmanship. Then he quickly sliced through the tape connecting her wrists and ankles.

If there'd been any breath left in her body, she'd have exhaled it in a gush. Instead, she wheezed.

Stepping over her, Harley opened another door. Scooping her up like a sack of feed, he carried her inside, dumping her into a chair. Her back almost screamed with relief. Using a length of rope, he attached her bound hands and wrists to the spindles of the chair. With her arms pinioned behind her back, her breasts were thrust forward.

Harley's eyes raked over them. "You drove her off," he repeated, following his gaze with a drag of the knife. The blade sliced open her shirt, revealing the swell of one breast. "So now you're gonna pay. You and that chump cop."

Ethan. Where was Ethan?

He'd know something was wrong. He'd been on the phone. He'd have been coming. How much lead did Harley have? How far away from home were they? He knew it was Harley, so he'd narrow his search from there. But how the hell would he find her?

He was a U.S. Marshal. He hunted fugitives for a living. He's going to find you. You just need to buy yourself some time for him to get here.

"I don't understand. You had an alibi for the clinic and for the fire." *Play dumb, get him talking.* TV villains always liked to talk about their superiority.

A satisfied smirk crossed his face. "I had my boy take care of that for me. He's been getting ideas, too, but I set him straight. Reminded him who's in charge in our family. Gave the little bastard my name. He owes me."

"The harassment started before Rene left you. Was that you, too? The slashing of my tires?"

"Lot of fun, that one. It was a favor to a friend. You know Ralph. He was pretty pissed you denied him more drugs, so I helped him out with that—as I often do—as a thank you for being a good client."

"You've been supplying Ralph with opiates?"

"Him and anybody else who don't like the new laws. It's a lucrative business. Had to do something once the factory closed, and I wasn't much keen on traditional employment. Too much stress for too little pay."

Was he involved with the drug thefts over in Lawley? Was that how he had the idea to trash the clinic?

"And the raccoon?"

"I thought that was obvious. Dead meat. It was a warning, after you'd moved my wife out of our house. Your cop boyfriend understood, but not you. You just assumed everything was fine. Stupid, naive bitch. Not that it would've made any difference. I've been watching you for weeks. Just waiting for my chance. And now here we are, all alone. No bodyguard in blue in sight." He reached out with the tip of the blade again, drawing it down her cheek in a slow caress. "We're gonna get to know each other real well, Doc. Just you wait and see."

ETHAN SAW the fist flying at his face and made no move to stop it. Peter Campbell's right cross slammed into his jaw, whipping his head back and rocking him back a step. Blood flooded his mouth. The older man had a helluva punch.

Several women gasped, and Liz Campbell tried to grab her husband by the arm.

"You were supposed to keep her safe!" Grief-stricken hazel eyes bored into him from a face reddened with anger. Fists still clenched, Pete took another step closer.

Reuben Blanchard, Ethan's other reserve officer started toward them, but Ethan held up a hand, staying the former SEAL's progress. He spit blood into a nearby trash can and turned back to Miranda's father. "You get one for free because I understand you're upset, and there's nothing you can say or do to me that I haven't wanted to do to myself. But kicking my ass the rest of the way is going to have to wait because I have a job to do, and I don't have a moment to waste going over my failures."

Liz stepped up beside Pete. "What are you doing to bring our daughter home?"

Ethan had dispatched a team to search Harley's residence, another to his cousin's place. Rene and Johnny were currently waiting in interrogation, and at least a half dozen county deputies were en route and awaiting orders. But Miranda's parents didn't need to know the details. "Everything."

At the grim determination in his voice, Pete gave a slow nod and stepped back.

Ethan swept a gaze over the collected Campbell clan, knowing he wouldn't be able to focus with all of them crowding his station. But before he could say so, Judd emerged from the back.

"I know y'all are concerned and you want to know what's going on, but we have law enforcement personnel coming in from all over the county. It's best if y'all go home and let us do our jobs."

"But—"

A pale-faced Norah stepped up and put an arm around Liz. "He's right. They don't need us in the way. Let's go back to the house. As soon as they know anything, I'm sure they'll tell us." She looked to Ethan for confirmation.

"Of course."

They turned collectively, as Norah began to herd them toward the door.

Cam lingered behind, searching Ethan's face. For what, Ethan had no idea. At length, Cam nodded, evidently seeing what he needed to see. "You love her, so I know you'll do whatever it takes."

The words twisted something Ethan had locked away at the scene. He shoved down the softer, painful feelings and felt the cold rage strain for release. "I swear on my life."

Cam clapped a hand on his shoulder. "Bring her home."

No other outcome was acceptable here.

As soon as they'd left, Ethan strode into the single stall bathroom. Switching on the water, he scooped some up to rinse out his mouth. He'd have a bruise on his jaw in a few hours. A good reminder. Not that he needed one. Bracing both hands on the sink, he took a few seconds just to breathe, trying to stop the parade of horrors about what Harley could be doing to Miranda right now from marching through his brain.

Judd spoke from behind him. "Shut it down."

"I spent most of the last ten years chasing down the worst of the worst. I know what can be done to a woman." With each minute that ticked past, his blood chilled just a little further.

"You're no good to her if you're crazed with fear and rage."

"I want to kill him." Ethan had shot and killed men in his career. But it had never been personal before.

"Preaching to the choir, man. You kept me calm when that lunatic had Autumn last fall, so I'm gonna return the favor. I'm with you, every step of the way."

Ethan blew out a breath and splashed more water on his face. Yanking out some paper towels, he dried off and headed for interrogation, Judd trailing behind.

"You've filled Rene in on what her son's been up to?"

"Yeah."

That would save a little time.

Inside the little room, Rene knit her hands. "—just can't believe you'd do all this."

"I was trying to protect you." Johnny sat, head hung low, not looking at her.

Tears spilled down her cheeks—clearly not her first. "I should have left sooner. I should have put you first. I should have—"

"You should have done a lot of things, Rene. But right now, we don't have time for your self-revelation and lack of focus." Ethan tossed a notepad onto the table.

The woman flinched back in her chair as if he'd slapped her. He had a hard time feeling bad about it.

"Wh—what's going to happen to my son?"

"I don't know, and right this second, I don't care. Your violent, piece of shit husband has Miranda Campbell. He broke into her house and attacked her, kidnapped her, while I was *on the goddamned phone with her*. I need to know where he'd take her."

Rene began crying harder. "I don't know."

"Does he have access to any kind of property? A hunting cabin? Maybe through family members, like his cousin, Terry. The one he stayed with after the attempted shooting. There any kind of property you know about? Somewhere out of the way, where it'd be easy for him to hide? Somewhere he'd maybe go to fish or drink? To get away from things?"

"He didn't have anywhere special to go to drink. He just...drank. He'd be gone a lot, but I don't know where. I was just happy for the quiet."

Ethan struggled with impatience. "Did he inherit any kind of property? Buy some?"

"No, no we didn't have the money for anything like that."

"Yeah we did." Johnny spoke up.

Rene stared at her son. "What?"

"Explain," Ethan growled.

The boy lifted his head. "He was selling drugs on the side. I saw him meeting with his supplier once. I don't know what he did with the money other than drink it away. We sure as shit never saw any of it. But he had some."

The bail money.

Ethan had known Harley had to be into something. If only he'd pressed harder, found something sooner, maybe Miranda would never have been taken.

"Drugs?" Rene squeaked. "No. You must be mistaken."

"I'm not mistaken about anything, Mom, and I'm not blind like you."

Judd pulled out his phone and swiped at the screen. "You said you saw his supplier. Was it this man?"

Johnny studied the picture. "Yeah. That was him."

Judd met Ethan's gaze. "My guy from Lawley. Eugene Willig. We've suspected him, but this is my first solid confirmation. I've just been waiting for sufficient grounds for a search warrant. If they've been working together, maybe he knows something."

"Find him. I want to talk to him."

"On it." Judd slipped out of the room.

"What else do you know, Johnny? About Harley's association with Eugene Willig? About the people Harley dealt to? Anything. Do you know what he was dealing?"

"Prescription shit, I think. The stuff I saw in Doc Campbell's clinic looked a lot like what he got from that guy. I don't know who all he was selling to, and I only saw him with Willig the one time. I was too afraid of what he'd do if he caught me."

Ethan could hardly blame him for that. "Why didn't you tell me any of this before?"

"You couldn't manage to do anything to him when he was clearly beating the shit out of my mother. Why would my word that he's probably dealing drugs be enough to do something?"

Ethan absorbed the blow and scrubbed a hand over his face. Now was not the time to explain. What was done was done.

"Fugitives need three things. A way to communicate, money for food and travel, and a place to stay. At this point, I don't believe Harley's on the run. He's gone to ground somewhere with the intent to do God knows what to Miranda. We have to figure out where." Ethan shoved the notepad and pen toward Rene. "Make a list of every known family member or friend Harley's got. It'll be a start."

"Can you triangulate cell phone signals like on TV?" Johnny asked.

"Depends on whether the phone is on. We can have the phone company ping the nearest tower. We've already done that for Harley's phone, but it's switched off. Why?"

"When he sent me instructions, he didn't use his regular phone." Pulling his cell from his pocket, the boy tapped to bring up a series of text messages. "It was one of those prepaid deals."

Chances were, the phone was also off or tossed by now, but it was another line to tug. Ethan took the phone. "Good thought. I'll look into it."

Judd opened the door and waved Ethan out.

"Keep working on that list, Rene. Anything or anyone you can think of."

Out in the hall, Judd was fairly vibrating with energy. "Willig's grandparents had a farm about ten miles out of town, halfway between here and Chapel Creek. They died about six years ago, and he's been paying the property taxes ever since. He keeps an apartment in Lawley, but he hasn't been back to it since the last robbery. There's a good chance he's laying low at the farm. I've already called Judge Carpenter for a warrant. You want in?"

"Hold that thought." Ethan handed the phone to his dispatcher. "I've got another number for you to check. Different carrier than Forbes' primary line. I want location and call history for the previous two weeks."

It took five minutes and an official fax to the phone company to prove exigent circumstances, but they got what he asked for. As predicted, the phone was off, but Ethan plugged the last known coordinates for the burner phone into a mapping program. Harley had been out into the county in the general direction of Chapel Creek. "Where's the farm?"

Judd checked the address and pointed at the screen not far from the GPS coordinates. "Looks like your boy's been visiting with my boy. And recently."

Ethan straightened and cracked his knuckles. "I'd say that merits a conversation."

CHAPTER 23

"You don't have to do this, Harley." Miranda knew her voice shook, betraying the fear clawing its way up her throat, but there was no help for it.

He lifted a brow but not the knife currently poised between her breasts. "Do what?"

"Whatever you're planning. Everything up to now has been harassment. Vandalism. Petty stuff. You haven't done anything more than scare me." They'd leave off the kidnapping charges for now. "You can still walk away from this."

Amusement curved his lips. "Why would I want to walk away?"

"Because you have a choice. You have a reputation, Harley. Wouldn't you rather be known for an act of goodwill and compassion instead of as the town drunk and a wife beater?"

Harley sat back on his heels and stared at her. "Are you really trying to give me a speech about being a better man?"

"You can always make the choice to be better."

He frowned, tossing the knife on the little table covered in dust and cobwebs and a handful of some kind of farm tools. Pulling a flask from his pocket, he took a long swig. "You really believe that?"

A glimmer of hope sparked in Miranda's chest. "Yes. People can change." She'd seen evidence of that before, so many times. If she could talk Harley Forbes down, then she could do anything.

"Damn woman, you really are a fool."

"Am I? Think about what you're doing, Harley. Because the moment you cross the line to hurt me, there's no coming back from that. Ethan's coming for me. He's going to find you. And if I'm hurt or—" Dead. No, she wouldn't say that. "—worse, he will hunt you down, and you're going to end up locked away for the rest of your life or dead. Is that really what you want?"

The open-handed blow caught her across the check. Pain exploded in her face and tears flooded her eyes as her head snapped to the side hard enough to make the whole chair tip over. She crashed into the table before falling over, crying out as she landed on one arm.

"What I want is to capture the arrogant son of a bitch and string him up so he can watch while I carve you up. Maybe while I fuck you, since you ran my wife off. Might be nice to have a woman with some spirit again." He reached down and rubbed himself, as if testing that idea.

Miranda struggled not to vomit.

Harley crouched down. "And when I'm done, I want to gut you both like that little ol' raccoon. You can bleed out together. Your last act as a couple, since I'm feeling magnanimous. That is what I want."

Pure malevolence glittered in his eyes.

"He's going to kill you."

Harley just smiled. "He can try."

When he reached toward her, Miranda cringed back. Then he stopped, looking toward the door.

Was that another car?

Rising to his feet, Harley grabbed more duct tape, slapping another piece across her mouth, and left her where she lay. As soon as he'd stepped out of the tack room—taking the knife with him—she began to wriggle. The crash had loosened the spindles of the old chair. Maybe she could get free of the ropes. Her shoulders screamed as she tugged, but she thought she felt a little give. Frantic, she jerked again and again, hearing a little crunch as the spindle broke free.

Miranda went still as voices sounded outside the tack room. Should she try to make noise? Was it friend or foe? Before she could decide, the door swung open. Another man stared inside.

She screamed behind the tape. *Help me. Please.*

"Jesus Christ, Harley. What the fuck are you doing?"

"Just some personal business. I needed somewhere to bring her where we wouldn't be disturbed."

"What the hell are you thinking? You can't do that shit here. I can't risk exposure of my operation. I already lost one stash. Do whatever you need to do but get her the fuck out of here." He slammed the door and Miranda felt hysteria beginning to take root.

No time. Get your ass moving.

Struggling with the ropes, she felt the spindle pull free of the chair. No longer held in place, the ropes that had been twisted unwound until she was able to pull her hands loose. Now how the hell was she going to get free of the duct tape?

Rolling to her knees, she managed to bring herself level with the top of the table. Most of it was old tack cleaning supplies. But at the end she spied a hoof pick. It was old and rusted, but the tip still looked sharp. Sharp enough to pierce duct tape.

Tears streamed down her face as she forced her abused limbs to standing, carefully pivoting her back to the table and groping with numb fingers for the pick. When they closed around it, she wanted to sob with relief. But she was a long way from safe. It took three tries to pick the tool up properly and another six to get it dug into the tape. She scratched her wrists in the process and the blood slicking her hands made her fumble and almost drop the pick. But at last she felt the tape begin to give. With one more mighty wrench, she broke free.

Her arms ached. Her breath heaved through her nose so loudly, she couldn't hear anything else. How long until Harley came back? How long had he been gone?

Hurry. Hurry.

She ripped the strip free from her lips and sucked in lungfuls of air as she attacked the strips around her knees and ankles, poking holes with the tip of the pick and pulling. It went faster because she could see what she was doing.

Outside the barn, she could hear the sound of a car door. Whose? Probably not Harley. He didn't intend to leave her.

Didn't matter. She needed to get out of here.

Keeping hold of the pick, she crept toward the door on sock feet and listened. Where was Harley? If he was outside, watching the other guy drive off, she might only have seconds before he came back in the barn.

Taking a chance, Miranda cracked open the door and slipped into the main aisle of the barn. No Harley. Lurching into a stumbling run, she made a beeline for a smaller door at the back.

Gripping the edge, she pulled. The door didn't move. Casting a desperate look behind her, she shoved the pick into her pocket and used both hands to tug. *C'mon. C'mon!*

But the door didn't budge. It was blocked or locked or something. She couldn't get out this way.

Desperate, she grabbed the pick again, looking for somewhere to escape or hide. But the only way out was the front, where Harley surely was. He'd see her, and with the cramps in her legs she couldn't move fast. Where was the light?

She saw a switch on the far side of the barn, near the open front door. Turning, she scanned the back wall, finding another switch near the locked door. Would it turn off all the lights? Only one way to find out.

Knowing she might not get another chance, Miranda hit the switch.

The barn went dark, and she ran.

Service weapon drawn, Ethan circled around the dilapidated house with the sagging roofline. Light flickered behind the blinds in what was probably the living room. Somebody was watching TV. A deputy closed in from the opposite direction. If Eugene Willig was home, there was a good chance he'd bolt out the back when Judd and another deputy knocked on the front door.

Voice low, Ethan radioed Judd. "We're in position."

"Get ready for some action."

A minute later, a loud pounding could be heard from the front of the house. "Police! We have a warrant. Open up!"

Less than fifteen seconds later, the back door opened, and a skinny figure darted into the night.

"Freeze! Sheriff's Department!" At the deputy's shout, the man careened toward Ethan.

Ethan bolted to intercept him, dropping his shoulder and catching the guy in the midriff with enough force that they both tumbled to the ground. The little weasel began to flail. A kick caught Ethan in the gut, and the runner nearly got away. But Ethan wrapped a hand around his ankle and jerked him back. With a quick roll, he straddled the guy, pounding his fists into the other man's face and releasing some of the simmering rage.

"Ethan, stand down! You can't question him if he's unconscious!" Judd's voice pulled him back from the edge.

Breathing hard, Ethan sat back, rolling the man over and cuffing his hands.

The deputies hauled him up and marched him back into the house. They shoved him onto the sofa, where he'd clearly been lounging before being interrupted. A can of Bud Light had tipped over on the low coffee table, half soaking the spilled bag of potato chips.

Eugene Willig was a wiry man with thinning black hair and a scraggly goatee. He glared up at Ethan from his position on the couch. "What the fuck, man?"

Judd spoke first. "Well, I'm Detective Judd Hamilton of the Wachoxee County Sheriff's Department, and as I said out front, we have a warrant to search the premises for illegally obtained prescription medications. My friend, Chief Greer, has some other business with you."

"Chief of what?"

"Wishful PD," Ethan answered.

"You're outta your jurisdiction, ain't you?"

Ignoring that, Ethan continued. "I'm here to ask you some questions about a friend of yours. Harley Forbes."

"Don't know no Harley Forbes."

"We've already got witnesses placing the two of you together. We know he's one of your dealers, so start talking."

"Dealers for what?"

"Maybe for the prescription narcotics you've got hidden in plastic bags in the tank of the toilet," Deputy Nichols suggested. He stepped into the room, a Ziplock bag dangling from his gloved hand.

Judd offered a pleasant smile that fooled no one. "You're caught, Eugene. We've got enough here to shut you down, so you might as well cooperate."

Eugene's face reddened, and he began to swear. "Goddamn it. I knew this would happen. I fucking knew as soon as he brought that woman here, you cops would come sniffing around."

"What woman?" Ethan demanded. "What do you know?"

Sensing he had something of value to trade, Willig smirked. "What's in it for me?"

Ethan grabbed him by the throat, hauling him to his feet. "I don't snap your neck right here."

Willig's eyes bugged out, and he gasped.

"Ethan, if you kill the bastard, it's going to mean a helluva lot of paperwork," Judd said mildly.

"He…he…"

Ethan relaxed his grip, so Willig could speak.

"He had her in the barn. Trussed up like a goddamned turkey. I told him he had to leave."

"When?"

"I don't know. Maybe half an hour ago."

"Did he leave?"

"I don't know."

Ethan squeezed.

"I don't! I didn't get involved. I just wanted him gone," Eugene rasped. "The fucker had a knife. He knows how to use it. I wasn't about to go up against that. Not when he was looking so… cr…crazy."

A hand gripped Ethan's shoulder. "He's turning purple, man. Let him go."

Ethan threw Willig back to the sofa, where the little man coughed and wheezed.

"Crazy how?"

"Crazy like he'd be happy to stick me like a pig if I got in his way anymore. The only reason I had any leverage at all is he's been working for me and he likes the money that comes with being one of my dealers. I didn't like the look of him, so I came back to the house and locked the fucking door. I swear that's all I know."

Ethan was already headed for the door. "We have to check the barn."

Leaving Willig with Deputy Nichols, Ethan, Judd, and Deputy Rickett headed for the dilapidated structure a hundred yards away that passed for a barn. Moving fast and low, they circled the building. No vehicle outside. No lights shone through the gaps between the boards. The whole damned place had an air of abandonment that did nothing to quell Ethan's fears about what could be waiting inside.

Converging at the front, the deputy gripped the wide door. Ethan and Judd pressed against the side, ready to slip in and clear the space. At his nod, Rickett hauled the door open. Ethan slipped inside, going left as Judd went right. He cleared the row of stalls as Judd did the same. The deputy headed up the ladder to the hay loft as Ethan and Judd converged on the closed door of what was probably a storage or tack room.

Ethan kicked it in, sweeping inside. But there was no one in the room. "Empty. The whole place is clear. Get some lights on."

As ancient fluorescent lights flickered to life, he squinted and took in the space. His gut twisted.

A chair lay on its side, spindles broken, a length of dirty rope still partly attached. Wads of duct tape littered the floor. Blood glimmered against the silver of the tape.

"She was here." And she was hurt. Probably from her bindings.

He was going to kill Harley when he found him.

Judd crouched down but didn't touch anything. "Looks like she got loose. There's not enough blood here to suggest she's bleeding out or seriously injured."

Had she managed to escape? A flare of hope sparked. He knelt, dabbing a finger against the bloody tape. "It's still mostly wet. She hasn't been gone long." He and Judd exchanged a look. "Fan out."

No clear tracks showed in the hard-packed dirt floor. Heading back to the door, he shouted. "Miranda!"

No answering shout or even a whimper came back. Only the quiet of the night.

If she'd gotten free, which way would she have run? To the house, hoping for help? Or to the overgrown fields, thinking to hide? This time of year, there was nothing growing. Not a lot of cover either way. Not until the treeline another hundred yards away. She didn't have shoes. None of this terrain was easy on bare feet. The crushed gray gravel around the barn would probably have sliced them. He panned his flashlight in a widening arc from the door of the barn, looking for traces of blood.

"Over here!" Judd shouted.

Ethan sprinted for him. He knew before he reached Judd's side that he hadn't found Miranda. The ground was churned up, as if someone had been tackled.

Judd pointed with his own flashlight to a hoof pick a few feet away. "There's blood spatter. Best guess, she got a piece of him when he took her down."

"Not a big enough piece to kill him." Which meant Harley was that much more pissed off. What would he do to punish her? "Shit! Where the fuck has he taken her?"

CHAPTER 24

Miranda came to in agony. A sharp pain radiated from her temple and nausea roiled in her stomach. Her whole world felt fuzzy. Some part of her brain catalogued injuries. Concussion. Multiple contusions. Abrasions. One eye would barely open. Her limbs were numb with pain. She couldn't breathe properly, and copper coated the back of her throat. Blood.

The relief of unconsciousness dragged at her like a riptide. Everything would feel better if she could just sleep... But there was some reason she couldn't do that.

What the hell had happened? Had she been in a wreck?

Something dinged. What was that? Some kind of monitor? Was she in the hospital?

"Son of a bitch."

The angry male voice had her one good eye going wide.

Harley.

She'd come so close to escaping, but he'd caught her at the edge of the fields, taking her down with a flying tackle worthy of Super Bowl Sunday. She'd fought back, slashing with the hoof pick and catching him in the shoulder. But she hadn't hit anything vital, and he'd struck her full in the face. Given the pain radiating out, he'd probably broken her nose. Jesus, it was a miracle she hadn't choked on her own blood.

Now she was back in the rear of her Grand Cherokee, bound again, beneath a blanket. From the front, Harley continued to curse, muttering something about irresponsible women and proper car maintenance. What was he talking about?

The low-fuel light. She knew she'd been getting low, but she'd intended to wait until morning. He didn't have more than forty miles left in the tank. Either he'd have to stop to refuel, or he wouldn't be able to go far.

Surely everyone would be looking for her by now. They'd know he had her Jeep. He'd be sticking to back roads, and there was no way he'd return to his own place in search of gas. Ethan would undoubtedly have it under surveillance. So where could he go?

Judging by the amount of cursing going on, his original plan had been screwed. Was that a good thing? No time for the long, drawn out torture session he'd apparently been imagining. And surely, no opportunity to set up any kind of sophisticated trap for Ethan. But did that mean he'd cut his losses and kill her quickly? She knew he wouldn't just let her go. He was in too deep, so he had to finish this, one way or the other.

Her brain felt sluggish and the temptation to slide back into oblivion was huge. She just wanted to stop feeling the pain.

Must. Stay. Awake.

The caution did nothing to stop her drooping eyes. The next thing she knew, a crash yanked her back to consciousness as a shudder ripped through the Jeep. The engine revved high as Harley swerved and skidded along the road. Miranda's stomach rolled as she tensed, waiting for the car to flip. But Harley managed to right it. What had he hit?

A minute later, he rolled to a stop and turned off the motor. For a few seconds, Miranda panicked, trying to come up with something, anything she could use to fight. But there was nothing. She'd lost her one chance.

The back hatch opened. Harley flipped the blanket back and chill night air rolled over her, cooling her heated skin. He grabbed her ankles and dragged her to the edge.

"Sit up. I know you're awake."

Miranda struggled to move, her abused limbs refusing to cooperate. The pain in her side had her gasping. She added bruised ribs to her inventory. Probably from the kicks.

"I ain't gonna ask again." The unmistakable sound of a gun being chambered punctuated his statement.

Her mouth went impossibly drier, but she made it more or less vertical.

Harley grabbed her roughly by the arm and hauled her to standing. She almost went down in a heap the moment her feet touched the ground. Only his vise-like grip kept her upright. This time he'd only bound her knees together, leaving her ankles free. "Walk."

Walk? Walk where?

He navigated her around the end of the Jeep and toward a long metal building. As best as she could, Miranda scanned her surroundings as she shuffled along with her captor. He'd parked in the lea of a loading dock. She could just make out a chainlink perimeter fence. Was that what he'd hit? Had he driven straight through a gate?

If they were still near Wishful, this had to be one of the defunct factories. Which one was it that Harley had worked for? Heirloom Home Furnishings. The place had stood empty for more than a year and a half since the parent company moved manufacturing to Mexico. Miranda knew Norah had been trying to find some means of repurposing the space, but so far, there'd been no bites. It was about five miles out from town proper. It backed up to woods on two sides and had a long stretch of empty space between it and the roads, with no farms or neighborhoods nearby. There were some isolated houses, but even if she managed to get off the gag, there'd be no one to hear her scream, and she'd never make it back to the main road before he caught her again. Her only hope was that there was some kind of alarm system that he'd set off when they went inside.

The trip up the stairs was slow and painful, with regular prodding from the barrel of the gun against her back. When he simply lifted a broken padlock off the door and shoved it open, she gave up on the idea of an alarm. The sound of her scuffing steps echoed in the empty space. Except, no. It wasn't empty. Hulking shapes rose up in the gloom. Apparently, the company hadn't seen the need to take its equipment when it left. She had no idea what any of it did, but surely with furniture manufacture there were saws, industrial staplers, and other machines and sharp implements that could tear up a human body. Was there still electricity turned on out here?

Harley paused, studying the place. "Nobody comes out here much anymore. Should've thought of it sooner. It'll do nicely for what I have in mind."

And what is that? But Miranda didn't give voice to the thought.

He didn't seem to need any input from her, just steered her through the dark with a familiarity that suggested he'd spent a lot of time here, probably since the factory closed.

He shoved her back against one of the empty industrial racks that had once probably held pallets of materials. When he grasped her bound wrists and started to fasten them to the rack above her head, she bucked, trying to catch him with her feet. His answer was a backfist to her face that left her ears ringing. Then the gun was in her mouth, the metallic oily taste coating her tongue.

"Cooperate. I'm gonna be real pissed if you make me kill you before I've done what I need to do."

Tears streaming down her cheeks, Miranda pressed back against the cold metal support.

Ethan, where are you?

ETHAN MADE it back to the station first. Judd and his deputies were tied up at Willig's place, waiting on a forensics team and one of the other Wachoxee County investigators. A crowd had gathered outside the police station. Media and a shit ton of locals. He laid on the horn and they parted like the proverbial Red Sea so he could make it into a parking place. Questions were hurled at him from every direction, as soon as he stepped free of the car.

"Do you have any leads?"

"Have you found Dr. Campbell yet?"

"Do you know who took her?"

Ethan ground his teeth and ignored them all, stalking toward the door. Clay was near the front, expression as grim as Ethan had ever seen it. Without a word, Ethan took his friend by the arm and towed him inside. They stopped just past the vestibule because the station was a hive of activity, with officers and people of interest all over the place. Ethan hoped like hell somebody had decent, actionable intel.

"I don't have much time."

"I know. I don't wanna get in the way. I just wanted to check in, like everybody else, I guess. How are you holding up?"

"How's it look?"

"Like you're ready to chew through furniture and spit nails like a machine gun."

"Sounds about right."

"You're going to get this fucker."

"I wish I had your conviction. I feel like I'm always one step behind this guy. I underestimated him."

"You won't do it again. Look, I know I've always given you shit for choosing law enforcement over music. But it was the right choice for you. You're a great cop. Your record speaks to that. You're going to find Miranda, and you're gonna bring her home."

Ethan dredged up the ghost of a smile. "You were supposed to be playing the *Rocky* theme while you delivered that speech."

"It was totally playing in my head." Clay squeezed Ethan's shoulders. "You've got this, brother. Go find the bad guy."

With a short nod, Ethan turned into the chaos. "Somebody give me a sit rep!"

"Harley's truck was found a mile away from Miranda's house. Rowan went over it. No evidence Miranda was ever in it. It looks like he parked and walked. Nash found a laptop," Inez reported. "Jay's holed up in your office seeing what he can pull off it."

Ethan walked in without knocking. Jay Quimby, the local tech guru, was hunched over the desk. "What do you have?"

"Nothing good. Videos. Short clips probably made with a cell phone. He's been watching Miranda for weeks."

Ethan's blood chilled a few more degrees. "What kind of videos?"

"Mostly of her coming and going. Some through windows Peeping Tom-style. Nothing that indicates he was in her house before tonight."

"What else?"

"His search history is nothing unexpected. Porn. Some gambling sites."

"That explains where the rest of the money went. Anything else of note?"

"Not yet."

He clapped Jay on the back. "Keep digging."

Back out in the bullpen, he checked with Reuben and Clint, who'd been tasked with interviewing the people on the list Rene had generated. "Status."

"Cousin Terry reports that Harley has been more of an asshole than usual, more erratic and angry," Clint said.

"He say anything about the drugs?" Ethan asked.

"I asked if Harley had been partaking of what he's been selling, but Terry denies knowledge of the drugs. Says he suspected but didn't know and didn't ask."

"What about everyone else on the list?"

"No one else has turned up anything useful," Reuben reported. "Just more reports of Harley being pissier than usual. Most folks figured that was because his wife left him and his kid tried to shoot him."

"Anybody give you any trouble about coming in?"

Reuben consulted the list. "We're still waiting on a couple of people, but so far everybody came straight down wanting to help. Darius should be finishing with Ralph Slocombe any minute now. Maybe he had better luck."

The door to the station opened again and Judd marched in with Willig in cuffs. "Can I borrow a cell for a while? I didn't want to take the time to haul his ass to county lockup while the search was ongoing."

Ethan jerked a thumb toward the two cells in the back. "You know where they are. Appreciate the help." He spied the bruising on Judd's knuckles as his friend shoved Willig into motion. "What happened to your hand?"

"He tried to run again, managed to slam my hand in a door. Mostly just pissed me off."

As Judd hauled the drug dealer down the hall, the door to interrogation opened and Ralph Slocombe stepped out.

"Eugene? What the hell are you doing here?"

Ethan's gaze narrowed on the two men. "You know each other?"

"We used to work together," Ralph said.

Willig only glared.

"Get his ass in lockup then come join me. Ralph, go right on back and sit down." Ethan all but shoved the older man into the room.

Ralph sat at the table, looking nervous. "I'm sorrier than I can be that all this is happening to Doc Campbell. But like I told Officer Greeley, I don't—"

"Save it. I know you've been buying illegal opiates from Harley."

Sweat broke out on Ralph's temple. "It weren't no regular thing. Just when I ran out and couldn't get more the usual way. I told you how it was. I saw Harley after I couldn't get another prescription. Sounded off some about the whole situation, and he said as how he could send her a little message. Cause her a little trouble. I told him there was no point in that. It wouldn't change the system. I...I heard about her tires, but I didn't know he'd actually done something."

Didn't want to ask, more like.

Ethan had never fully trusted Harley's alibi for the night of the bonfire. "So, he was doing a favor for a friend."

"I wouldn't call us friends."

"You were drinking buddies. Plenty of people saw you down at The Mudcat together."

"We knew each other from the old days at the factory, same as Eugene—although he got fired well before the place closed. We'd get together and bitch about it on the regular. Fact is, our whole lives changed because of that place. That's where everything went to shit. It was the start of Harley's drinking, the start of my pain problem. The start of everything."

The start. The idea of it struck Ethan. "Do you know if he's been back out there after the plant shut down?"

"Sure. He took pride in breaking in and pissing around the place. Literally."

Ethan met Judd's gaze and jerked his head. He followed him out of interrogation and out to the massive county map mounted beside the dispatcher's desk. "The factory."

"You think he's holed up there?"

"It's isolated. Empty. It was a place that held significance to him." Ethan found it on the map. Where else would a rat go if all its other escape routes were cut off?"

They studied the area.

"Limited road access. Plenty of places to bolt if he hears someone coming," Judd observed.

"If I were still with the Marshals, I'd surround the place, make a half mile perimeter. But we don't have the manpower for that. And if I'm wrong—"

"Chief!" Cleveland's voice had them all turning. "Delaney Newell is on the phone. You need to take this."

Ethan snatched up the receiver. "Delaney?"

"He's at the old Heirloom Home Furnishings factory." The woman's voice was barely above a whisper.

"What? How do you know that?"

"I don't live too far from here. I heard a noise and came to check it out. The gate's busted open, and I saw a black Grand Cherokee parked by one of the loading docks, so I snuck in to check it out. It's Miranda's Jeep!" she hissed.

"Where are you right now?" Ethan demanded.

"Hiding in the bushes on the north side of the factory, near where reception used to be."

Dear God. The last thing he needed was for another civilian to get dragged into this and hurt. He signaled to his officers to get ready to roll. "We're on our way. Do not go inside. Do not engage. No heroics. You stay hidden and don't make a sound. Understand?"

"Yeah. I can't tell for sure, but I think he's in the main building, where distribution was located."

"How do you know that?"

"I used to work here, too."

Of course, she had. "Which building is that?"

"The big one connected to the loading dock where Miranda's Jeep is parked."

"Okay, we're coming. *Don't move.* Don't talk but stay on the line with Cleveland. If anything changes, you try to let us know if it doesn't endanger your position."

"Yes, sir."

Ethan handed the phone back to his dispatcher and turned to his waiting team. "We just got confirmation that Harley's holed up at the Heirloom factory. Let's go bring Miranda home."

CHAPTER 25

Harley paced, one hand pulling at his hair as he made rounds of the warehouse. Miranda watched him, grateful he wasn't paying attention to her for now. But he was getting more agitated by the minute. He'd said he wanted Ethan to pay, wanted to make him watch while he hurt her. It seemed he was beginning to realize that was easier said than done.

Oh, he could hurt her more than he already had. But there was too much open space here and no easy way to lay any kind of a trap. Certainly not for a seasoned ex-Marshal, who'd undoubtedly show with backup when he came. Which meant...what? Was Harley realizing that and having doubts? Maybe she could talk him down, convince him of the foolishness of his course of action.

"What are you going to do?" she rasped.

His head shot up and he glared. "I'm going to make him pay."

"Yeah. You've said that. You want him to watch. But how are you gonna set that up here? Are you planning to leave me here, while you trap him somehow?" If he left, could she manage to get loose again? Given the state of her injuries, that seemed doubtful.

Harley tipped back the flask again. "Shut up, bitch."

"In what reality do you think you're going to get what you want and walk out of here alive?"

"I said, *shut up!*" Harley punctuated the order with another open-handed strike to Miranda's face.

She barely had the energy to cry out as another wave of pain swept through her. Slaps and punches seemed to be his preferred way to exact pain. She'd lost count of how many times he'd hit her, and she'd stopped begging. He liked it when she begged. Miranda didn't want to give him the satisfaction, and she didn't have the energy to waste. At least he hadn't tried to rape her. Yet, anyway. At this point, she wasn't sure her injuries would allow her to fight back. She should probably listen to him and keep her mouth shut. But that simply wasn't her.

"He's coming for you, Harley, and hell's coming with him." Miranda had no doubt of it.

He gaped. "Are you seriously quoting *Tombstone* at me right now?"

"Seemed appropriate. Look, there's nowhere else for you to go. It's just a matter of time before Ethan shows up with every available cop in the county. How are you gonna fight off all of them?" Surely the man could be made to see some kind of logic.

"They charge the place, I'll kill you. That simple."

Maybe it was that simple for him. Miranda swallowed, wishing she had some water. "But that's not what you want. Then you don't get the satisfaction of watching him suffer. Because as soon as I'm dead, so are you. There's no way out."

She was gambling with her life.

He pulled a cell phone out of his pocket and stared at it. "What's the pretty boy cop's number?"

Miranda stared. "What?"

"What's his fucking phone number?"

"I...don't know. It's just programmed into my phone, back at the house."

Harley scowled.

"But...if you dial 911, it'll get you to the police station, and they can patch you through." If he wanted to talk to Ethan directly, she'd do anything she could to facilitate it. If they could confirm where she was, they'd send help. She didn't see Harley as being open to hostage negotiation, but she'd take whatever she could get.

Harley narrowed his eyes, as if trying to decide whether she was full of shit or not. After long moments of silence, he punched the number into the phone.

Miranda could hear the faint voice of the operator. "Nine-one-one, what is the nature of your emergency?"

"I need to talk to Chief Ethan Greer. This is Harley Forbes."

Closing her eyes, Miranda began to pray.

"THERE'S DELANEY." From the woods just outside the chain link fence, Ethan aimed a flashlight toward her and flicked it on and off three times.

An answering flash came back, presumably from her cell phone.

"What's the plan?" Judd asked.

Ethan spoke into the radio. "Anybody have eyes on the inside?"

"Negative."

"There are multiple entry points to the entire facility, but Delaney believes them to be in this main building, here. There are, best I can tell, three entries to it, not including where it's attached to the next warehouse. There are seven of us. If we do a systematic, simultaneous breach, we might—"

The radio crackled. "Chief, I've got Forbes on the phone."

The three men looked at each other. "You what now?"

"He's called in to dispatch. He wants to talk to you."

"Is it actually Forbes or some nut job trying to capitalize on the chaos?" Ethan asked.

"I'm pretty sure it's actually Forbes," Cleveland said.

Were they about to get ransom demands? "Patch him through." There was a click. "This is Police Chief Ethan Greer."

"You took something that belongs to me, Greer, so I've returned the favor."

The cocky sneer in Harley's voice made Ethan's hackles rise, but he kept his voice level. "Where is she?"

"Oh, she's alive. For now."

Ethan ground his teeth. "What do you want, Forbes?"

"You. Come out to the old Heirloom Home Furnishings factory. *Alone*, or she dies."

"How do I know she's there with you?" *How do I know she's alive?*

"Your boyfriend wants proof you're here."

"Ethan—" Miranda's exhausted voice was interrupted by the crack of fist against flesh, followed by a pained whimper.

He wanted to reach through the phone and strangle Harley with his bare hands. "Don't lay another hand on her. I'm coming."

"Alone," Harley ordered again, then disconnected.

She's alive. Just focus on the fact that she's alive.

"How you wanna play this?" Judd asked.

"He thinks I'm coming from town and has no idea we're already here. Okay, new plan. Darius and Judd, I want you covering the loading dock. The rest of you split into teams of two. I want you to breach on the north and south sides, quiet as you can. I'm taking a cruiser and driving in as he expects. I'll come in with sirens. That should cover the sound of your entry and draw his attention to me. Each of the buildings is connected, so you should be able to move quickly to his location. Reuben takes point, as our resident SEAL. I guarantee he'll expect me to disarm when I get there."

"You're not really going to give up your gun," Judd said.

Ethan lifted his pant leg and checked the compact Sig Sauer 1911 Ultra strapped to his ankle. "Not this one. But I'll lose precious seconds if I have to go for it, so I'm gonna need additional cover."

Judd flexed his injured hand. His gun hand. "I wish I could go in to back you up properly."

"You have a pregnant wife at home. You were staying out here to begin with," Ethan told him. "Let's move."

He hiked back to where he'd left the cruiser, doing his best to slow his breathing and detach himself from the situation. But this wasn't just another day on the job, wasn't just any victim inside. It was the woman he loved, and she'd been hurt because he hadn't been fast enough or good enough to protect her. That wasn't a mistake he'd make again.

Because he knew Harley would expect it, he came in hot, flying through the gates and around the building on squealing tires, siren blaring.

Pay attention to me, you son of a bitch.

Exiting the vehicle, he caught the quick on-off of a flashlight from the perimeter. Judd's sign that the breach was successful. Backup would be working their way into position. Drawing his Glock .40, he tugged open the door. He didn't really think Harley would shoot him on sight, but he took the time to clear the entry and search for cover—almost none.

A scuffle of footsteps drew his attention toward the back of the warehouse.

Harley hauled Miranda to her feet, using her as a human shield. "Got here awful fast."

"I was in the neighborhood. Let her go, Harley." Ethan edged his way forward, his Glock at the ready.

"Put the gun down, Greer." The order was punctuated by a hiss from Miranda, and Ethan realized the bastard held a knife to her throat.

Instantly lifting his hands in an I'm-no-threat gesture, Ethan crouched and laid the pistol on the ground, automatically flipping the safety on.

"Kick it away."

Ethan did as he was told, keeping his eyes firmly fixed on the two of them. "I did what you asked. Let her go."

"I'm the one who gives orders here." He yanked her more firmly in front of him, backing them both into a shaft of moonlight from one of the high warehouse windows.

Ethan got his first good look at Harley's handiwork. She looked like she'd gone ten rounds with a prize-fighter. One eye was swollen shut, and her entire face was a mask of blood and bruises. And that was just what he could see. Given the pained way she moved, he knew that was only scratching the surface. Vision going red, he struggled not to rush Harley. He could slit Miranda's throat well before Ethan could tear him in two.

A quick movement in his peripheral vision told him his backup had arrived. Keeping his focus on Harley, he kept moving forward. "Okay then. What is it you want?"

"What I *wanted* was for both of you to keep your noses out of my business. Neither of you had any right to interfere with my wife, my life. But you just couldn't leave well enough alone."

Ethan continued toward them. "What kind of resolution are you imagining here?"

"Resolution? *Resolution?* Do you think this is some kind of fucking negotiation?" The knife moved a fraction away from her throat, as if he was having trouble fighting the urge to talk with his hands.

"You want something or you wouldn't have asked me to come here, so what is it?"

"I want you to pay. I want you to know what it feels like to have your woman taken from you while you can only stand and watch."

"What good is that gonna do you, Harley? You kill her, I kill you." As he spoke, Ethan shifted his weight to the balls of his feet, ready for action. He was almost close enough. Even if you manage to take me out, others will catch you, and you'll be prosecuted for capital murder. You *will* get the death penalty. Is a few moments of retribution worth your life?"

Harley whipped the knife away, using it to point as he shouted, "Don't you fu—"

The shot rang out and everything tripped into slow motion. Harley screamed. Blood sprayed. The knife fell from what remained of his hand. His grip on Miranda loosened, and Ethan dove forward. Miranda drove her bound hands into Harley's gut. As he released her, she fell to the floor, and the other man stumbled, reaching behind his back and pulling a gun, aiming it directly at her. Ethan collided with Miranda, wrapping his body around her and taking her to the ground, even as all hell broke loose in a hail of bullets around them.

CHAPTER 26

Miranda's ears still rang from the echo of all the shots, and she could barely breathe from the weight of Ethan's bulk over her. Dimly, she realized a bunch of men had moved in, with guns trained on Harley.

"Dead," one of them pronounced.

Ethan shifted, starting to push off her. "You okay?" he wheezed.

"I'm alive." Thanks to him. She needed her hands free so she could wrap her arms around him and never let go.

His face blanched as he shoved up and off her, flopping onto his back in a graceless heap.

Miranda rolled toward him. "Ethan?"

Reuben Blanchard crouched beside him. "Shit. He's been hit. Three shots. At least one pierced his vest. Radio for medical."

"Cut me loose. Cut me loose!" Miranda demanded. As soon as they'd sliced through her bindings with a tactical knife, she scrambled over to Ethan. Blood was pooling beneath him. She reached to tear open his shirt but couldn't make her abused fingers work for any kind of fine motor skills.

"Get his amour off. I need to see the wound. One of you go out to my car. Break in if you have to. Unless Harley moved it, there should be a medical bag in the backseat."

They burst into a flurry of movement.

Ethan coughed. "I'll be fine." But his breath was going shallower by the second.

"Don't talk." She'd wondered as she'd worked on Corbett Raines what it would be like to have Ethan's life in her hands. Now it was, and she couldn't actually use her training. Not the way she needed to.

They pulled away the vest. Miranda shoved up his undershirt and saw the entry wound midway up the left side of his torso, toward the bottom of his ribcage, only inches from the scar of the last time he'd been shot. She allowed the terror to pulse through her for one, single beat before shoving it and the agony in her own body down and away.

Pointing to Clint, she began snapping more orders. "Roll him over. I need to check for the exit wound." The bullet could have been deflected at a weird angle because of entry through the vest or ricocheted off a rib. She needed a set of steady hands.

Desperate, she scanned the gathering of cops. "Do any of you have medical training?"

"First aid, CPR and the like," Clint said.

"Judd," Ethan rasped, groaning as they moved him.

Judd Hamilton was trained as an EMT.

"Where is he?" Miranda demanded, examining Ethan's back. No exit wound. Which meant the bullet was still lodged somewhere inside him. Nothing any of them could do about it here, and it wasn't the most pressing problem.

"Outside. I'll get him."

But Judd was already racing in, Delaney right behind him. Delaney? What the hell was she doing here? Miranda didn't care because her medical bag was in the girl's hands. Thank God something was going her way. But not enough. As she looked back at Ethan's face, he'd gone dead white, and his breathing was too fast.

"Chest hurts."

"You've got a tension pneumothorax. Air is filling your chest and collapsing your lung." And if she didn't get the pressure relieved, it would go beyond collapsing the lung and begin to compress his heart. He wouldn't survive long enough to make it to the hospital.

His gray eyes met hers with a grim understanding. He'd been through this once before. He knew exactly what that meant.

Miranda gripped his hand tight. "I love you. And you are not going to fucking die on me. Understand?"

Ethan squeezed her fingers. "Love y—" His words were cut off with a fit of coughing. The veins in the side of his neck bulged, and she could see the beginning of the displacement of his trachea.

Delaney dropped to her knees with the bag. "What do you need?"

Miranda began pawing through the bag, grabbing disinfectant and gauze pads and passing them to Judd where he knelt beside her. "You're going to have to sterilize the wound." As she continued to dig, Judd did as ordered. She yanked out the dressing for open chest wounds and handed it to Delaney. "Peel off the backing."

Working fast, Judd followed her instructions, prepping the site and applying the occlusive dressing. But Ethan was still deteriorating. His eyes had drifted closed. Pressing her fingers against the pulse at his throat, she felt it stutter.

"Ambulance is five minutes out," Clint reported.

He was going tachycardic. He didn't have five minutes.

"His lung is collapsed. I need to perform a needle decompression, but my hands aren't steady enough. Judd, you're going to have to do it."

"I can't." He held up a hand with swollen knuckles. It shook almost as much as her own.

Damn it.

Miranda looked at Delaney. "Let me see your hands."

Her eyes went wide. "What?"

"Your hands. Now."

The girl held them out. Not a tremor, despite her obvious nerves. Good.

"You're going to perform this needle decompression."

"Are you crazy?"

"It's the only way to save his life."

After only a second's hesitation, Delaney reached for gloves.

Miranda handed her the package with the 14-gauge needle angio-catheter, then leaned over Ethan, thanking God she had enough feeling left in her fingers to identify the second intercostal space. She looked back to Delaney.

"Okay, you're going to place the needle here, just above the rib, perpendicular to the skin." Moving as quick as she dared, she guided Delaney to the correct position. Given the size of the needle, it was probably a good thing Ethan had passed out, otherwise he might fight and that would make things worse. "Keep hold of the hub and firmly press to pierce the pleura."

Worried blue eyes flashed to hers.

"You've got this, Delaney. Steady hands."

The girl nodded, and the group watched in total silence as she followed orders. Her face twisted into a grimace as the needle sank in. A rush of air burst out of the catheter and Ethan sucked in a shaky breath, his eyes flying open again. Miranda almost collapsed in relief.

"Okay. Okay, carefully pull the needle and leave the catheter in place. We're going to secure it with tape. This should keep him stabilized long enough for the ambulance to get here."

Delaney sat down hard on her ass. "I feel a little dizzy."

"That's exactly the way. Hold your shit together until you've done what needs doing. Good job."

"Is he gonna be okay?"

I don't know. There were a hundred other problems that might be going on internally, dozens of complications that could kill him en route or in surgery. But Miranda couldn't think about any of that. Because there was no other alternative but that he survive. She took a firmer grip on his hand and looked into his unfocused eyes, infusing her voice with total command. "Yeah. He's gonna be okay."

THE BEEPING WOKE HIM. Ethan recognized it as a heart monitor. God knew he was familiar enough with that sound. He felt like shit, which was par for the course after being shot. But he was fuzzy on the details. A faint sense of dread weighed him down, kept him from wanting to open his eyes. Not that they didn't already weigh four hundred pounds on their own, but there was something…he wanted to avoid.

Becca. Becca was going to be pissed.

He didn't want to see that look of disappointment and panic, didn't want to have that argument about the dangers of his job. Again. He thought about just sinking back into sleep, but a hand was curled warm around his, so she at least deserved the effort from him, proving he was still among the land of the living.

Ethan forced his eyes open. The room was dim, the walls painted a neutral beige. Low-profile fluorescent lights lit the perimeter. As his vision cleared, he managed to turn his head.

A second hospital bed was butted up to his. The side rails between them were lowered and a woman lay stretched out beside him, her hand curled around his in sleep. Her wrists were bandaged, and her face was a riot of bruises, with the telltale bandaging across her nose that indicated it had been broken. Not his wife—ex-wife. Miranda.

The beeping sped up as he remembered. Harley Forbes. The gun. Getting shot—again. Shit, he'd thought he was done with that. He'd managed to save her, but not before Harley had brutalized her. Every bruise, every scrape, made him hurt worse. He should've been faster. Should've figured it out sooner. Should've—

Vinyl creaked from the opposite side of the room. "You're awake."

Ethan tipped his head back toward the soft voice that rasped as if he'd been up all night.

Clay leaned forward in a chair, forearms braced on his knees. "You gave us a helluva scare, brother."

"Miranda." Ethan's voice came out at a whisper, though he hadn't been aiming for that. He couldn't seem to take a deep breath.

Clay smiled over at her. "They wanted to put her in her own room, but this was the only way she'd consent to staying put."

"Is she—" There'd been no time to take in the full extent of her injuries before all hell broke loose. What he could see now was bad enough.

"She's okay."

"*She* can speak for herself."

By the time Ethan managed to look back toward Miranda, she was rolling toward him in her own bed, wincing. "I've got a concussion, bruised ribs, broken nose, countless abrasions, contusions, and scratches. I win the contest for most injuries. You win most severe."

"Lucky me."

The one eye that wasn't swollen shut was serious as she reached out to lay a hand against his cheek. "Very lucky you."

"I'm just gonna give y'all some privacy, let everybody know Ethan's awake."

"Thanks, Clay."

The door swung shut behind him.

Miranda swallowed hard. "You want the update?"

"It can wait." He was too muzzy headed to follow it right now. "Harley's dead."

"Yeah. He is. And I'm not, thanks to you. That's the important part."

If he'd been a fraction of a second slower… "I should have gotten him off the streets sooner." He'd be second guessing every decision he'd made about Harley Forbes for a long while to come.

"I'm sorry I didn't take the threat seriously."

Ethan stroked a knuckle softly down her bruised cheek. "I'm sorry he had a chance to do this."

"You found me in four hours. You may not have that badge anymore, but once a Marshal, always a Marshal. And a Marshal always gets his man."

"This Marshal is more concerned with getting his woman."

Tears glimmered in her eyes. "You took bullets for me."

Because she seemed to need it, he managed to tug his mouth into a smile. Pain radiated from the bruise on his jaw. "Maybe that means you'll keep me around."

He phrased it as a joke, but he tensed, waiting for her reaction. Becca hadn't been able to handle the realities of his job, and now Miranda had been through the worst of it herself. He wouldn't blame her if she wanted to walk away.

She huffed a laugh, then winced again as her chest jolted. "I'm definitely keeping you. But just so you know, this makes three gunshot wounds for you. That's your lifetime max. You're not allowed to get shot anymore, okay?"

"From your mouth to God's ear."

With painstaking care, she shifted over until she could rest her head on his right shoulder. "I love you. Thank you for saving my life."

Ethan pressed a kiss to her brow. "Back atcha, Legs."

"Actually, Delaney saved you."

"What?"

"My hands weren't steady enough. She's the one who did the needle decompression on you."

"She's the one who confirmed you were at the plant."

"I'm giving her a raise and the biggest cupcake ever."

"I'm pretty sure that's what they call a cake."

The door swung open again.

"Oh, my baby!"

Ethan managed to turn his head in time to see his mother rush the bed. "Hey, Mama."

Tears were streaming down her cheeks. "Oh my God. Can I touch you? Will it hurt?"

"It's okay. I'm fine." If he'd been able to pronounce it at a volume higher than a whisper, it probably would've gone over better. But he reached out a hand to her.

"Ethan McMurtry Greer, you are not *fine*." Despite the snap in her voice, she squeezed his fingers gently.

"Now, Brenna, you heard what they said at the nurse's station. You have to keep calm." His stepfather's low rumble of a voice filled the room.

"I know he looks bad, but he really will be okay."

Everybody's attention swung to Miranda. It was a mark of their concern over him that they hadn't seemed to notice he was practically sharing a bed with another patient.

Ethan's mother covered a gasp with her hand. "Oh my."

Miranda flashed a pained smile. "Yeah, I know. I look worse than he does. I'd hoped I'd be healed up by the time I met you."

"Mom, Phil, this is Miranda."

More people slipped into the room. "Oh, you're finally awake!" Trailed by her husband, Lisbette Campbell curled her hands around the foot of Ethan's bed. "We just don't even know how to thank you for saving our daughter's life."

"She saved mine right back, so I'd say we're even."

"I'm sorry, who are you?" Brenna asked.

All the parents launched into introductions, seeming to forget for a few moments that they were in a hospital room. Miranda took that opportunity to whisper, "McMurtry? Like *Lonesome Dove* McMurtry?"

Ethan winced. "I cannot be held accountable."

She gave a faint chuckle. "I think it's perfect."

Miranda's father edged around her side of the bed. "How you feeling, Peanut?"

"Like I've been run over by a semi. But I'll live. Thanks to Ethan."

Pete frowned, ducking his head before meeting Ethan's eyes. "I'm sorry I punched you."

"You did *what?*" On the last word, Miranda reared up, hissing in pain. "Shit." She sank back against the pillow, glaring up at her dad. "That bruise on his jaw. That was you?"

"It wasn't my finest moment."

"It's fine," Ethan said. "You were missing. He was upset."

She twisted toward him. "It is *not* fine. We're going to talk about this." Somewhere in the room, a heart monitor was speeding up.

Ethan gently cupped her bruised cheek so she couldn't look away. "You are safe. That is the only thing I care about. Everything else is water under the bridge."

Somebody—he thought maybe Miranda's mom—gave a watery, "Aww."

Miranda turned her face into his hand. "I don't get a say in this, do I?"

"No."

She exhaled and the heart monitor slowed. "If I had his right cross, we might not have gotten into this mess."

"We'll work on it." He was putting her through self-defense training as soon as she was able-bodied enough to take it.

"Wow, he's like, the Miranda Whisperer," Cam observed.

"Shut up, Cam," Norah told him.

Behind her, the entire Campbell clan filed in. The room was far too small for all these people, and he was pretty sure there were rules about that.

"How the hell are all of you in here?" Miranda demanded. "This is the ICU. There's not supposed to be more than one visitor at a time."

"Oh, Clay's smoldering at the nurses on duty." Norah grinned. "They weren't paying attention."

In the wake of that pronouncement, more introductions were made and well wishes were offered. Ethan lost track, hearing nothing but a bunch of chaos. But as Miranda settled back against his shoulder, he decided it was a good chaos, one he looked forward to getting used to.

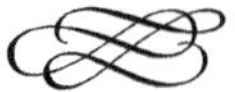

"Well, it's official." Miranda sat on the arm of the sofa and sprawled back into Ethan's lap. "I just accepted an offer on my house."

His arms snaked around her, holding her tight against his chest. "Yeah? How are you feeling about it?"

"Good. Maybe I could've eventually overcome the bad juju of living there, but I just didn't love it enough to try." In the wake of her kidnapping, she hadn't been able to bear a single night in her own house, so after they'd both been sprung from the hospital, she'd moved into Ethan's place.

"Nothing wrong with that."

"Anyway, I hope you're still okay with having me as a roommate because in sixty days, I've got nowhere else to go."

He put on a mock-serious face. "I don't know. We might have to revisit the terms of your lease. A no-escape option might just mean more regular shower sex."

"Oh, well, if I must, I must." Smiling, she fell into his kiss, enjoying the pleasant bump of her pulse as his mouth played over hers. When he shifted, tipping her back on the cushions, she went willingly. Already anticipating getting naked, she was left frowning as he pulled back and stood up. "Excuse me, that is not how that conversation is supposed to end."

Laughing, he held out a hand. "C'mon. Get your boots on."

"Boots? Clearly your brain and my brain are on vastly different paths right now."

"They'll converge again later." To speed her along, he grabbed the cowboy boots she'd kicked off the other day and set them by the sofa. "We've got somewhere to be."

"We do? Where?"

"I've gotta see a man about a horse."

"A horse? Are you serious?"

Ethan grabbed his Stetson off the wall rack and settled it on his head. "Completely."

God, she loved him in full cowboy mode, which made it even more frustrating that she couldn't redirect him to the bedroom. He refused to say anything else, just grabbed the Stetson he'd bought her a few months back and plopped it on her head, before hustling her into the truck. Well knowing that her man wouldn't say a peep until he was good and ready, Miranda settled back and enjoyed the drive with the windows down, October breeze blowing in her hair.

He drove up into the hills outside town. She'd always loved this part of the county. Close enough to town for convenience but far enough out you didn't feel like your neighbors were on top of you.

When he turned onto a long, tree-lined drive, a big black horse wheeled and began to run, pacing the truck. Ethan grinned like a kid in a candy shop. "Isn't he a beauty?"

"He's big."

"That's Houdini."

"Houdini? Like Chester Harkin's Houdini?"

"The very same."

Ethan parked beside the barn, lifting a hand in an answering wave to Chester, who stood grooming a chestnut mare. "He's down to the two. Sold the others a couple months back."

They slid out of the truck and wandered over to Chester.

"How you doing, Doc?"

"I'm well, and you, Chester?"

"Can't complain."

They both watched as Ethan met Houdini at the fence, offering a carrot on his palm. When had he grabbed that? He looked so in his element—a man and his horse. Or maybe that was just because of the Stetson, boots, and extremely well-fitting Wranglers. The gelding followed him back along the fence as he came over to look over the mare.

Miranda stood back, amused, not really understanding half of what the men discussed. Ethan ran his hands all over the mare, checking for who knew what that indicated soundness in a horse. Then he climbed through the fence and did the same to Houdini, who tolerated the handling with a demand for another carrot. Because she seemed to resent the loss of attention, Miranda edged up to the mare and stroked her warm, glossy neck.

"Well, you're just gorgeous, aren't you?"

The mare bobbed her head and practically batted those long lashes. Miranda laughed.

"Do you like her?" Ethan asked.

"I don't know squat about conformation or whatever, but she's got sass."

"As all good women should," Chester agreed.

Ethan nodded. "I'll take them. I think Miss Kitty will do nicely for Miranda."

Miranda gaped as the two men shook on it. "Wait, seriously? You're buying me a horse?"

"And me. That way we can ride together." He said it easily, as if that made all the sense in the world.

"But you...I...horses? Really?"

Chester chuckled. "I'll just let you two hash things out." The old man took himself off to the barn.

"Ethan, you just bought horses."

Grinning, he stepped up on the fence rail and rubbed Houdini's nose. "Yes, I did. I've missed having them since I moved off the ranch all those years ago. I feel like I can finally settle and be in one place long enough to have them."

In the face of his obvious delight, Miranda hated to be the practical one. "So... where are you going to put them? Are you going to be looking around for somewhere to board them?"

Instead of answering, he stepped down and leaned back against the paddock. "What do you think about the house?"

"The house?" What was he on about? Miranda looked over at the farmhouse. It was a little worn around the edges, but work had obviously been done to spruce it up. "Looks like it's had a fresh coat of paint on the porch and trim."

"Yeah. Johnny's work. He did a good job on those and the window boxes over the summer. I think shutters are next up on the list."

"He's still doing community service out here?"

"He's done with his hours. Now he's actually working for pay, so Chester's been having him fix things up."

She'd seen the state of Chester's arthritis. Having a pair of younger hands had to be a huge blessing. "Well, the work's paying off. It's lovely. Comfortable." It was the kind of house that had obviously been a home.

"Chester and his Jeannie spent a lot of years here. It's not easy for him to leave it."

"Leave it?" Had Chester's health declined that much?

"Yeah, with his arthritis, it's gotten too hard for him to keep the place up the way he needs to, so when Maudie Belle asked him to move in, he decided to take her up on it."

Miranda held up a hand. "Wait, I'm sorry. Did you just tell me that Maudie Bell Ramsey has asked Chester to move in with her?"

"Sure did. They've become quite the item."

She looked back toward the barn, where Chester had disappeared. "I'm not sure I want to wrap my brain around that."

Ethan laughed. "Yeah, well, the only way he felt okay doing it is if the place passed on to somebody who'd love it like he did."

"You want to buy it," she realized.

"Yeah. See, the horses are just a part of that whole settling down, thing. I wanted land and a house of my own. Stuff Matt Dillon never really had."

"Stepping away from your Marshal roots?"

"Well, I reckon I'm smarter than Matt Dillon."

"Yeah? How's that?"

"If he'd had an ounce of good sense, he'd have asked Miss Kitty to marry him and settle down. I've got more than an ounce of good sense." He dropped to one knee, right there in the barnyard, a ring in his hand. "I want land, a house—this land, this house—with you. I want to marry you, Miranda, and build a life together. I'm hoping you want all that, too."

Her heart threatened to beat straight out of her chest. A new life and a new home with the man she loved. The man who'd risked his life to save hers. There was only one possible answer.

"Well, I did always want a horse growing up."

A laugh burst out of him. "The horse goes with the ring and everything else. You gotta marry me to get her."

Miranda offered him her hand. "Then I guess we're getting married."

He slid the diamond onto her finger and pulled her in close. "Just so you know, this ring doesn't come with an escape clause."

"Then we should probably talk about renovating the bathroom, so I can keep up my end of the bargain."

"God, I love you."

"Back atcha, Cowboy. Back atcha." Wrapping her arms around him, she tipped her mouth up to his.

Choose Your Next Romance

Good gracious! After all that, I know you want to read Delaney's story. *Burn For You* is a friends to lovers tale with sexy firefighter Sean Murphy. Yeah, that crush totally isn't one-sided and Sean lets her know that in very…satisfying fashion. But their road to happily ever after isn't an easy one.

Or maybe you'd like some lighter Campbell fare? You may remember that Miranda's brother Mitch was headed overseas? In *You Were Meant For Me,* Book 10 in the Wishful Romance series, you find out exactly what happens as a result of his vacation fling! Fans of accidental pregnancy stories are gonna LOVE this one because you'll never believe who that fling was with.

Can't decide? Keep turning the pages to reach sneak peeks of them both!

BOOK #4 WISHING FOR A HERO

Delaney Newell knows what it means to be powerless. Against the family who wouldn't support her. Against the man she loved who betrayed her. Against the gossips who won't let her forget it. But after years of struggling, she's finally getting her life together.

Sean Murphy has spent years fighting forest fires. The former hotshot turned forester knows the growth that can sprout from unfathomable destruction. That's what he sees in Delaney—someone who got leveled by life but didn't stop growing. He's spent the past several months watching the shy red-head blossom, and he really likes what he sees.

When Delaney is accused of a crime she didn't commit, everyone is willing to believe the worst of her. Everyone except Sean. The woman he knows couldn't possibly be behind the rash of fires that are keeping the volunteer fire department hopping. Someone is deliberately framing her. Will Delaney trust him enough to help her find the real culprit?

CHAPTER ONE

*I*t's just drinks.

But as she stepped out of her car, Delaney Newell smoothed her sweaty palms over the skirt she'd worn like she was on an actual date.

No. I wore a skirt like a girl who likes skirts.

Never mind that she hadn't actually *done* that in years. She did like skirts. When she wanted to look nice and show off her legs. It was just…there had been nobody she'd wanted to do that *for* in a long time. Nobody except Sean Murphy, her study buddy and the object of the deep and embarrassing crush she didn't have the courage to do anything about. The gorgeous, sexy firefighter, who hadn't seen her as anything but a classmate. Or so she'd thought, until he'd asked her out for drinks to celebrate the completion of their EMT certification.

She'd said yes. Of course she had. And then she'd spent the last few hours working herself up to an absolute dither analyzing what the hell it meant. Was it just a friendly gesture or was it more?

It doesn't mean anything.

But oh, Delaney wanted it to mean something.

It's not going to mean a damned thing if you don't march yourself through that door to meet him.

She didn't see his truck, but the parking lot of The Mudcat Tavern was packed, and the overflow stretched on down the street. For just a moment, she quailed at the idea of walking in, alone, in front of all those people. The very notion of so many eyes on her made her physically ill. The stares and the whispers—and the not whispers—had dropped off over the past several months. It wasn't like it had been. But it still went against the grain to do anything that potentially drew attention to herself.

It's busy. Nobody will notice you.

She'd gotten good at making herself invisible the past couple of years.

Squaring her shoulders, Delaney went inside. For a night without live music, the bar was unusually busy. The chalkboard hanging in the entryway announced *Beat the heat! $2 Pitchers,* with a list of beer brands underneath. That would do it. The August heat was still oppressive, even this close to sundown. The roar of conversation pressed down on her as she made a slow circuit, scanning tables and booths for Sean without actually meeting anybody else's eyes. After two laps through, she admitted the truth. He wasn't here.

He didn't stand you up.

For all her lack of confidence, Delaney knew Sean well enough to be certain of that. He wasn't cruel. If he wasn't here, it was because he got delayed. Maybe he caught a fire. The Wishful Volunteer Fire Department had been hopping with the drought conditions hanging over this part of Mississippi since May.

She checked her phone for a text. Nothing. Well, she was obnoxiously punctual, so maybe he was running a little late. She'd just get something to drink at the bar while she waited. Slipping through the crowd, she found a little open spot and bellied up to the long, polished stretch of wood. Adele Daly, the owner of The Mudcat, moved like a whirlwind behind it, pouring shots and pulling pints as if she had six arms.

"What can I getcha?"

Delaney started to just order a water. But on the off-chance that Sean wasn't able to make it, she didn't want tonight to be a total waste. She'd come out to celebrate. "Whatever hard cider is on tap, please."

By the time she had the drink in her hand, there was still no Sean. After a few moments' debate, she sent a quick text saying she was here. If he was running late, maybe that would prompt him to say so. Although, if he was still at a fire, he certainly wouldn't be checking his messages.

Delaney sipped at her cider and wished she didn't feel so ill at ease. Maybe she should've talked one of her girlfriends into coming as a buffer. Just in case. Not that the list of possibilities there was long. She'd been dropped by most of her so-called friends and cut herself off from the majority of the rest. Keisha would've come, but Delaney remembered she had that out of town wedding this weekend. And anyway, she hadn't wanted a buffer in case this was actually meant to be a date.

"Why Delaney Newell, don't you look a picture?"

Her shoulders tensed at the oh-so-familiar voice. This was not the easy drawl she'd been expecting. This was the stuff of nightmares. Ruthlessly forcing herself to move slow and steady—the picture of unaffected—Delaney sipped at her cider and turned. "Hello, Bryce."

Her ex made a slow perusal of her body, from head to toe and back again, lingering on the legs bared by the skirt she now regretted wearing. Once upon a time, she'd have found such attentions flattering. Once upon a time, she'd loved him. That had been Before. Now that hungry look just made her skin crawl. His smile spread, slick and oily. Had he always had this creeper vibe and she just hadn't seen it?

"Want some company?"

"I really don't." She couldn't even regret the bite to her tone.

"Oh now, don't be like that."

"I'm waiting for someone."

An expression of *yeah sure* flickered over his face. "I just wanted to talk."

"I have nothing to say to you." *Please, please let Sean get here soon.*

"I know we didn't part on the best of terms."

"You cheated on me. And unless something's changed, you're still with Gina."

Bryce dialed up the sleazy smile. "She never has understood me as well as you did."

This man represented the worst time of her life. She didn't want him back. Didn't want to associate with him. She didn't want anyone to even see them together because that would just start the gossip engines up anew. She'd worked too hard and too long to overcome all that.

Seeming to realize his current tack wouldn't work, Bryce shifted gears. "You've been doing well for yourself. I heard you went back to school."

Delaney's fingers pressed so hard against her glass, she wondered the thing didn't shatter. "Why do you care?"

"I always cared about you, sugar. And I just wanted to say how proud I am of what you've done with yourself the past couple of years."

So he'd destroyed her life, and now that she'd started to get everything back together, he was sniffing back around? Words, harsh and hateful, clogged in her throat. But she didn't let them fly. That would make him too important, and giving them voice would draw to much attention to herself and the situation. With a dawning horror, she watched him reach out a hand to brush the hair from her cheek. She wanted to stumble back, not to let those fingers skim over her skin. He didn't have the right to touch her anymore. But the bar was packed and she barely had room to move. Warring with the cringe was an equally strong desire not to cause a scene. As her instincts battled, her feet remained rooted in place, and she understood that despite the bar full of people, she was utterly alone, with no one here to save her.

SEAN WAS LATE. Almost unforgivably so. Wishful wasn't even big enough to be able to blame it on getting caught in traffic. Well, unless there was some kind of funeral procession. Which there hadn't been. He'd spent way too long at county headquarters, going over the map he'd been maintaining of the fire threats in the region and trying to convince the powers that be to take an offensive rather than defensive position in the face of the months-long drought. The best he'd managed was to get the boss man to temporarily reinstate use of the fire towers to watch for threats. It was a small victory, but he'd take it.

The interior of The Mudcat was loud. Exactly the kind of atmosphere Sean knew Delaney hated. He hoped she hadn't given up on him and bailed already. He'd spent too many months coaxing her out of that shell to blow it now. He scanned the throngs of people, searching her out. There, on the other side of the bar. The red hair that had been haunting his dreams shone in the dim lights. His automatic smile froze as he realized she wasn't alone. Some guy was all up in her personal space, reaching out a hand to touch her. Every muscle of her body was poised to flinch away, but she didn't move, seeming frozen like a deer in the headlights. This guy was the kind of asshole who wouldn't back off without a fist to the face or some other guy pissing to mark his territory. Since he didn't think Adele would appreciate a bar fight, Sean went with Plan B.

Cutting through the crowd like a hot knife through butter, he reached Delaney's side in a half-dozen strides, managing to insert himself between her and the douchebag, as if he hadn't seen the guy reaching for her, hadn't been able to see anything but her.

"Hey, babe."

He caught the flash of relief and gratitude in her eyes, the confusion at the endearment, then saw the flare of surprise when he didn't simply stop. Riding on instinct, he slid his hand beneath the fall of that hair, tipped her face up to his, and kissed her.

Sean meant it to be just a gentle peck. Something chaste, like a high school freshman at the end of his first date. But the moment his lips touched hers, Delaney gasped. Her mouth opened under his and Hercules himself wouldn't have been able to resist taking just a little taste. He got a hint of sharp apples and spice, like an apple pie. Sean freaking loved apple pie.

For one beat—two—he waited to see if she'd push him away. Instead, Delaney's body, which had been straining away from the other guy, melted into him, her hand coming to his chest before skimming up over his shoulder to curve around his nape. His body was giving a whole lot of *Hell yeah*. And then she sighed—a contented purr of a sound that absolutely did him in and made him forget that they were in a very crowded bar and this was about proving a point to somebody else.

It was the cheer and wolf whistle that pulled him back, had him lifting his head.

Delaney's big blue eyes slowly blinked open. Her pupils were blown wide and her kiss-swollen lips parted in a way that had him wanting to taste her again.

There was a reason he shouldn't be doing that. Sean was sure of it. While he waited for his brain to finish rebooting, he just said, "Hi."

"Hi."

God, he liked knowing he'd caused that slightly breathless tone.

"Sorry I'm late." Remembering why he'd started this, Sean shifted, sliding an arm around her waist as he turned toward the douchebag. "Is this guy bothering you?"

Delaney cleared her throat. "He was just leaving."

Douchebag eyed him with considerable hostility. Sean just arched a brow in a *You-wanna-try-me?* gesture. Years of wrangling fire hoses and hauling other heavy equipment meant Sean easily had an extra thirty pounds of muscle on the other man.

Douchebag took a step back, gaze shifting to Delaney. "I'll see you around."

"No, you really won't. You lost whatever shot you had with me a long time ago, and as you can clearly see, I've moved on. Get lost, Bryce."

Sean pulled her a little closer and flashed a smug smile at Bryce to back up her words. Nostrils flaring, he turned away. Sean didn't move, watching as the guy moved through the crowd and straight to the exit, metaphorical tail between his legs. Good.

As soon as Bryce was out of sight, Sean reluctantly let Delaney go.

She was looking everywhere but at his face, and spots of color flew high on her fair cheeks. "So, um…not that I'm not grateful for the assist but…why did you do that?"

Damn it, he'd embarrassed her.

"I'm sorry about that. I saw him bothering you when I came in. I know his type. They won't back off just because a woman asks, and that seemed to be the most expedient means of shutting him down that wouldn't end up with me getting arrested for assault."

"Oh. Well, thank you?" It came out more of a question than an expression of gratitude, and she was frowning somewhere in the vicinity of his left shoulder.

Sean told himself to leave it there and say something to get them back on even footing. To the friends they'd slowly become over the past several months. But then he thought about how she'd kissed him back.

"And at the risk of coming off like an opportunistic asshole, I also did it because I've been thinking about it for the last four months."

Her head snapped up at that, those eyes going wide with surprise, that kissable mouth dropping into an O.

Sean offered a rueful smile. "I guess inviting you out tonight was not as obvious a clue in that direction as I'd originally thought." He'd played things so slow and close to the vest, apparently she hadn't even realized. *Great job, Murphy.*

The blush got deeper. "I didn't want to make assumptions. I... months? Really?" A timid, hopeful smile curved her lips.

Sean relaxed. He hadn't blown it. "Really. Let me buy you that drink and I'll tell you about it."

He hunted up a table in the corner, one where she could sit largely out of view. Over the months he'd hung out with her, he'd learned she was pretty uncomfortable in public. He'd never asked why and wasn't sure if it was some kind of social anxiety or something else. But he didn't want her to be any more nervous than she already was.

Once they'd put in an order for their drinks and an appetizer sampler, Sean leaned forward in his seat, lacing his hands together on the tabletop. "I have a confession to make."

One delicate brow winged up. "Another one?"

"Well, it's part of the first. I didn't actually have to take the EMT course."

Delaney frowned. "But I thought you had to be recertified."

"I did. But recert courses tend to be much shorter. They're refreshers, not the whole enchilada. I took the whole thing over again to hang out with you."

"That seems…kind of extreme."

Too late, Sean wondered if that made him look like some kind of stalker. It had seemed like a good idea at the time. "I didn't mean it in a creepy way."

She laughed. "No, I mean, that seems like an expensive and time consuming option. Why didn't you just ask?"

"Oh. Well, honestly, I thought you might bolt. You're shy. Getting to know you in a group context through school stuff seemed like it'd be less threatening."

Something that might've been consternation flickered over her face and was gone. "God, you're a sweetheart. I've never felt threatened by you, Sean." In a tone so low he could barely hear it, she muttered, "I know what it is to be threatened."

Yeah, he'd been afraid of that.

When he'd been a kid, he and his brother, Collin, had found a dog out at the baseball field a couple miles from their house. It had been skinny as a rail, with a thin, whip of a tail, and ears that seemed permanently lowered. After begging and pleading with their parents, they finally got permission to bring the dog home. But it had taken weeks to coax it close enough. And even years later, Flash had been skittish around strangers, hunching into shadows and hiding whenever somebody came over. Delaney reminded him of that dog. There was a deliberation to her attempts to be invisible, and he wondered what she was hiding from. But tonight wasn't the time for asking about it, so he let the comment slide.

"While we're in confession mode, I have one to make myself." Delaney dropped her gaze again, rubbing a finger up and down, through the condensation on her glass.

Sean couldn't stop thinking about what that would feel like on him. Shifting in his seat, he dragged his attention firmly to her face. "Oh yeah?"

"I took that bowhunter safety course back in January to spend time with you."

"Really? How did you even know I was taking it?"

She jerked her shoulders, still not meeting his eyes. "That day you were at the clinic for your physical, I overheard you talking to Eli about it."

"We'd just met. You didn't even know me yet."

The color was up in her cheeks again. "You kinda rescued me that day, when I almost dropped the vials from that bloodwork in the hall. Our patient has terrible veins and bloodwork is always hard on her." The look on her face was far more serious than a simple catch seemed to warrant. Then she banished it with a smile that skated the edge of flirty. "Besides, have you looked in a mirror?"

He flashed a grin. "I was too busy looking at you that day." At her look of skepticism, he added, "No, really. You had your hair all twisted up with those stick things, and they slipped when you dropped the vials. Your hair came half down around your shoulders."

She snorted in self-derision. "I was a mess that day."

"You were gorgeous." He'd spent the rest of that week wondering what she'd look like with all that red hair loose and mussed from his hands. He hadn't known her then. The desire had only grown stronger over the months he'd spent working his way under that careful shell.

She was still blushing, but now it seemed underscored with a glow of pleasure. Sean vowed to make it a priority to elicit that glow on a regular basis. He lifted his glass. "To confessions. And getting out of our own way."

Did he imagine that shadow crossing her face? Surely it was a trick of the light.

With her first truly honest smile of the night, Delaney lifted her glass and clinked it to his. "Cheers."

Get your copy of *Burn For You* today!

WISHFUL ROMANCE BOOK #10

"Just a fling," she said...

Tess Peyton wanted to do something fun and reckless and wholly out of character. A steamy weekend with a Scotsman seems like a plan. When her Scotsman turns out to be a good Southern boy, that's a minor deviation. Then one night turns to two, two turns to more, and suddenly she knows she's in way over her head. This is why one should always stick to the plan.

"Bachelor for life," he said...

But that was before all of Mitch Campbell's friends, cousins, and even his little sister started pairing off like someone was building an ark. No wonder he fell, and fell hard, for his "no attachments, no last names" European fling. And just when he's ready to tell the woman of his dreams that he wants to change that arrangement, she disappears, leaving him with no means of tracking her down, and a big ol' hole in his heart.

And then Fate stepped in...

Because, guess what? The guy Tess ran out on in Edinburgh shows up at family dinner. He's her dad's new wife's brother's son. What does that make them? It makes them "on again," according to Mitch and the explosive chemistry between them. Tess feels it too, along with a side of awkward, continued uncertainty, and some kind of stomach virus that seems to bother her most in the mornings...

∼

Chapter One

"*P*lease fasten your seatbelt, Miss Peyton. We're heading into some turbulence."

Tess's French-manicured fingers clenched the arms of the leather seat as the plane shuddered and bucked. Not because she was afraid of flying—her father's pilot was ex-Air Force and could fly anything—but because the Indian food she'd gotten from that sketchy takeaway on the drive to Heathrow was making a bid to come back up.

You will not throw up. You do not have time for food poisoning.

The evidence of her packed schedule was laid out on the table before her, in all its painstakingly bullet-journaled glory, in the pages of the planner that dictated her life. If it wasn't in the planner, it simply didn't happen. Puking her guts up somewhere over Alabama wasn't in it. Ergo, she would not be sick. End of story. And what Peytons wanted, they usually got if they worked hard enough.

She breathed through the roiling of her stomach and tried to focus on the reports she needed to get through before they landed. Her father would expect an update on the latest London project, and she needed to be on the ball to prove she had not only handled the additional responsibility he'd given her, she'd waded into the shitstorm and made it come up aces. That would be important when she proposed what she really wanted: that he allow her to take a greater role in operations of the home office in Denver.

Not that either of those things was the point of this trip to Mississippi. No, her powerful, successful, brilliant father had moved there to be with his new wife. Tess still couldn't quite wrap her brain around the fact that her dad had gone to *Vegas* of all places. Sure, Peyton Consolidated had a hotel on the strip. But absolutely no one expected multi-billionaire Gerald Peyton, III to be married by an Elvis impersonator wearing *gold lamé.* Video footage had been leaked by a gossip blog and gone viral. Speculation had run rampant. Tess had her own concerns about the haste of the marriage, but during their brief meeting a few months before, when the newlyweds had swung through London on the way home from their Paris honeymoon, she couldn't deny that Sandy seemed to adore her father, and he was likewise smitten. He was *happy*. Happier than she'd ever seen him. It wasn't in her to begrudge him that after the misery of his marriage to her mother.

Hell, she'd envy him if she truly believed a commitment like that was really real and could really last. But she didn't believe it. Not deep down. Six weeks ago she'd had her own shot at that kind of happiness. She'd been looking for adventure. Romance. A chance to step outside the tower walls and be someone besides Tess Peyton, someone without all the attendant responsibilities that went along with the family name. So she'd gone up to Scotland for the weekend, in search of her own hottie Highlander. Except instead of a kilted Scotsman, she'd found an ex-pat American, with a voice like honeyed whiskey and a mouth made for sin. He'd given her everything she'd wanted—and so much more. One night turned into two, then two turned into four, and before she'd known it, a week had gone by. The best damned week of her life.

But her uncharacteristic bid at recklessness, at going off-plan, hadn't ended with wedding bells. It had just ended. She'd seen to that, hadn't she? Nowhere in her planner did it spell out 1) Meet the man of your dreams. 2) Fall in love. Therefore, it hadn't happened. So there was no sense in dwelling on it. No sense remembering the taste of him or the feel of his hand in hers. No sense thinking about how he'd looked, sleeping and sated, the last time she'd seen him. When she found her fingers stroking over the delicate filigree of her necklace—the necklace he'd given her—Tess dropped her hand, shutting down that line of thinking with the same ruthlessness she used to hold back the nausea, and went back to the reports.

By the time she'd white-knuckled her way through half a dozen more pages, the air had smoothed out and so had her stomach.

Jon came over the onboard intercom. "We're about fifteen minutes out, Miss Peyton. Starting our descent."

Thank God. It would still take time to get from the county seat of Lawley out to the tiny town of Wishful, but God willing, she could be face down on the glorious bed in the penthouse at The Babylon in another hour, falling into blessed unconsciousness. Right this moment, nothing sounded better than that.

Flagging where she'd left off, Tess made a few more notes on things to follow up on when she called to check in with her team tomorrow morning. Then she gathered up her paperwork, stowing it neatly in the relevant folders and squaring the edges before sliding the pile into her Italian leather briefcase, alongside her favorite fountain pens. The tidy little MacBook went next, and finally her planner in the outside pocket. By the time the jet touched down, she had her game face on, ready for whatever got thrown at her next.

At least until she stepped off the plane.

Her father was waiting on the tarmac wearing jeans and a long-sleeved polo shirt. On *a work day.* As she descended the short flight of steps, he took off his aviator sunglasses and hooked them into the neck of his shirt, a broad grin lighting his face.

"There's my baby girl!" He scooped her off her feet, all but squeezing the breath out of her.

"Wait a minute!" Her jet-lagged brain was having trouble shifting to seeing the weekend version of her dad during business hours.

He set her down, frowning. "Problem?"

Tess relinquished the briefcase and threw her arms around him, squeezing back. "That's better. Hi, Daddy." She nuzzled her cheek against his shoulder, feeling some of the stress knots relax at the strength of his embrace. She'd cut off a limb before admitting she needed some of his strength right now, but she'd soak it up nonetheless.

"Good flight?"

"Productive. I've got the latest figures on the Piccadilly project and some ideas of how we might cut costs without sacrificing quality."

He waved that off. "All that can wait."

Tess blinked. "Okay then." If he wasn't going to jump immediately into business mode, neither would she.

"Your bag, Miss Peyton. Good afternoon, sir."

She worked up a smile. "Thanks, Jon."

Her father shook the pilot's hand. "Thanks for delivering my daughter safely."

"Always a pleasure."

Tess shouldered the briefcase. "I'll see you next week."

The pilot saluted and headed to do the post-flight check of the jet. Her father grabbed her suitcase and led her toward the terminal.

Tess fell into step beside him. "Is Sandy with you?"

"At home putting together a big family dinner in your honor. Everybody's coming."

"Who exactly is everybody?" She hoped she didn't sound as wary as she felt, but the idea of peopling after the long flight wasn't remotely appealing.

"The whole family. Sandy's mom, Helen—you're gonna love her. She's a spitfire. Not at all like Grandmother Peyton. Both Sandy's brothers and their wives. Sandy's son and his wife, and all the cousins and their respective significant others." Seeing the wince she couldn't hold back, he laughed. "I know, it's a lot for us, but I promise, you'll get used to it. They're great people, and they can't wait to meet you."

Resigned to the fact that face planting was going to have to wait, Tess looped her arm through her father's. "Then you had better give me the Cliff's Notes bios of everybody so I can keep them all straight."

MITCH CAMPBELL TOOK one look at the coconut cream pie on the diner table and swore. "This is a pie kind of emergency?"

Judd Hamilton laid a protective hand over the clear plastic dome. "Touch this and die. My pregnant wife had a craving, and I am doing my husbandly duty."

Mitch ignored the twinge he felt at the mental image of Judd and Autumn wrapped in connubial bliss. If anybody deserved happiness, it was those two. He slid into the booth on the opposite side. "Then why am I here?"

"Just wait. Liam's on his way."

"Fine." Mitch folded his hands loosely on the table and dug up a smile for the little brunette waitress who sidled up to take his order. The smile took way more effort than it should have. "Hey Hannah, can I get a cup of coffee and a slice of—what else do we have today in the pie department?"

"Apple, chocolate icebox, and Judd here got the last coconut cream."

"Apple is a classic for a reason."

"Warm and a la mode?"

"Is there any other way to eat apple pie?" Dimly, Mitch was aware of the flirtatious grin Hannah shot his way, but he couldn't summon the energy to reply in kind.

"You got it."

As she walked toward the counter, he realized Judd was staring at him. "What?"

"You didn't flirt with her."

"So?" He didn't feel like flirting. That wasn't a crime.

Frowning, Judd shook his head.

"What are we really meeting about? Is this about the design for the nursery? Because I think Liam will kill you if you change it again. You, not Autumn, because we all like your wife."

"He's right," Liam announced, squeezing into the booth beside Mitch. "Your ass I have no problem beating."

"Not the nursery either," Judd said. "It's nearly finished, and she cried buckets over it."

Mitch braced himself. "Good cry or bad cry?"

"Good cry. I think. The preggo hormones make it hard to tell sometimes. Right now, she and Mom are putting their heads together on how to create a girly *Star Wars*-themed room."

"Now *I* might cry. That's beautiful, man." Liam mimed wiping a tear. "You married a helluva woman."

"Yes, yes, I did."

"Looking forward to joining your ranks." Liam relaxed back against the booth, the picture of contentment. "Though I'm starting to think you had the right idea proposing and marrying the girl on the same day. It seems a helluva lot less complicated than planning a wedding."

"I thought your mom and Riley were taking care of all of that," Judd said.

"They are. But I'm expected to have opinions on shit."

Hannah came back with Mitch's pie and coffee and took Liam's order, interrupting the wedding discussion and distracting them from the fact that Mitch had stopped contributing to the conversation.

What could he say? *I wish I could follow you both over that cliff? I want what you have? I thought I had it, but it slipped through my fingers?* None of that was what they expected of him. He was the flirt. The unrepentant lover of women. As all of his friends and cousins had fallen into their forevers, he'd looked on with an increasing sense of bemusement. He'd never be felled so easily.

And yet he had. Hard and fast and irrevocably.

"Afternoon gentlemen." Mama Pearl Buckley, the much-beloved, opinionated heart of Dinner Belles, slid Liam's milkshake onto the table. Her gaze skated over to Mitch's, those dark eyes assessing. After a moment, she nodded to herself, as if confirming something, and Mitch realized she knew. Not the who or the how, but she knew at long last he'd toppled. She'd predicted it right here two years ago, hadn't she?

One of these days, Mitch Campbell, you gonna find yourself one that ruins you for all others, and we all gonna enjoy the show.

Except they didn't get the show because the curtain had already fallen. A week's performance. No reprisals.

Because he'd been the dumbass who'd taken one look at Anna on that tiny pub stage in Edinburgh, singing "Dancing Queen" for all she was worth, and slid right over the edge. When she'd proposed a no strings, no last names affair, he'd agreed without question. She'd dazzled him, plain and simple. Neither of them had planned on more than one night. Neither of them had planned anything. And it had been the freest, most unapologetically himself he'd ever been. By the end of a week, he'd known to the marrow of his bones that he wanted more than just her last name. He wanted everything. But when he woke, intent on convincing her that they were so much more than a simple vacation fling, she'd been gone. His anonymous Anna had disappeared into the ether, as if she'd never been. Except for the indelible mark on his fractured heart.

Judd narrowed his eyes. "Dude, are you humming…ABBA?"

Aw hell, he'd been humming "Dancing Queen" under his breath.

"Is that what that is? I've had an ear worm for days." It was the only lie that might allow him to save face.

Liam angled toward him. "Okay, let's get down to it."

"Yeah, let's." The sooner they finished with whatever this was, the sooner Mitch could get the hell out of here and go…try to find something that would distract him from his misery. Which was becoming increasingly hard to do given he was surrounded by enough new couples to people Noah's freaking ark. Maybe he should think about getting a dog.

"This is an intervention," Judd announced.

"You have not been yourself since you got back from that conference in Paris," Liam added.

Mitch stared at them. "Seriously? This is about me?"

"We're worried about you, man. You're not flirting, not dating, and you skipped poker night." Judd pronounced it like an indictment.

"I had work." They didn't need to know that the plans he was working up were for him and not a client.

"What's going on with you?" Liam asked.

He wasn't telling them about Anna. If he did, it would get back to his large and very nosy family, and there'd be no end to the questions. Not to mention he had no intention of explaining why he'd thought a no strings, no last names affair was a good idea. He could just see his mama shaking her head and tsking, "I raised you better." Yeah, that was not a conversation he wanted to be having. Especially not as gossip moved faster than the speed of light in Wishful, and he was expected at a family dinner in a couple of hours.

But Anna was only part of his funk.

"Excuse me for being less than my usual charming self when I get home from a trip to find out my sister was kidnapped. And that everyone—*everyone*—kept it from me." He still hadn't gotten past that. He'd known somebody was harassing Miranda before he'd left. But she'd insisted it wasn't a big deal, and she was romantically involved with the chief of police. Ethan had given his word nothing would happen to her. So he'd taken the trip. And while Mitch had been abroad, having that life-changing affair, his baby sister had been kidnapped and beaten. Finding out that happened, that he hadn't been home to protect her…it messed with his head.

"The whole thing was over in four hours. There was nothing you could've done," Judd assured him. Not for the first time. As he'd been in on the takedown, he was in a position to know. Not that it made a whit of difference to Mitch.

"And when I called home to say I was extending my trip? Nobody thought I should be read in about the fact that Miranda was in the hospital." He didn't have to manufacture the bitterness in his voice.

"Because the guy who put her there was already dead, and she wanted the chance to heal a bit," Judd continued, as if it was the most reasonable thing in the world. "You know she hates it when you hover. The rest of your family was doing enough of that."

Mitch stabbed up a bite of pie hard enough to send the slice halfway off its plate. "I should have been here."

"What is it you think you could've done that Ethan didn't already do?" Liam asked. "Do you blame him for what happened to her?"

"No." Mitch wasn't arrogant enough to believe that if he'd been home his sister never would have been taken in the first place or that she'd have been found any faster. Ethan had taken a bullet for her. It was hard to think that while they'd both been suffering, he'd been with Anna. Cheerfully oblivious.

"Then what is your deal?" Judd demanded.

If they'd told him, if he'd come home on his normal schedule, he never would have met Anna, and he wouldn't have this damned crater in his heart. Because the Bard was a hundred percent wrong. Loving and losing sucked ass.

"I don't appreciate being cut out." How could she have just *left?*

"Are you seriously going to be a drama queen about this? Because the decision wasn't about you," Judd said.

Not talking about Anna. Pull your head out of your ass.

"I know. Intellectually, I get that. But all of you were here, you went through it, and you processed it. I'm just still working my way through all of that. I'm her brother. I've spent my whole life protecting her. I can't just shake it off." The sense of failure was too great.

Liam nudged him with an elbow. "It wasn't your fault."

"I know that, too. I'll get past it." And he knew he would get past the complicated snarl of emotional shit with his sister, at least. "I'm just…not feeling like any of the things I cared about before matter anymore, and I don't want to just go through the motions."

His friends were silent for a long moment, watching him. Mitch wondered what they saw. Did they really buy that this was all about Miranda?

Judd blew out a breath. "Okay then. Take the time."

"We're here if you need us."

A little of the pressure to perform, to rise to expectations, slid off Mitch's shoulders. He let the corner of his mouth curve. "Are we done with the touchy feely shit now? Because I really just want to finish my pie."

Get Yours Today!

OTHER BOOKS BY KAIT NOLAN

A complete and up-to-date list of all my books can be found at https://kaitnolan.com.

∼

THE MISFIT INN SERIES
SMALL TOWN FAMILY ROMANCE

- *When You Got A Good Thing* (Kennedy and Xander)
- *Til There Was You* (Misty and Denver)
- *Those Sweet Words* (Pru and Flynn)
- *Stay A Little Longer* (Athena and Logan)
- *Bring It On Home* (Maggie and Porter)

RESCUE MY HEART SERIES
SMALL TOWN MILITARY ROMANCE

- *Baby It's Cold Outside* (Ivy and Harrison)
- *What I Like About You* (Laurel and Sebastian)
- *Bad Case of Loving You* (Paisley and Ty prequel)

- *Made For Loving You* (Paisley and Ty)

MEN OF THE MISFIT INN
SMALL TOWN SOUTHERN ROMANCE

- *Let It Be Me* (Emerson and Caleb)
- *Our Kind of Love* (Abbey and Kyle)

WISHFUL SERIES
SMALL TOWN SOUTHERN ROMANCE

- *Once Upon A Coffee* (Avery and Dillon)
- *To Get Me To You* (Cam and Norah)
- *Know Me Well* (Liam and Riley)
- *Be Careful, It's My Heart* (Brody and Tyler)
- *Just For This Moment* (Myles and Piper)
- *Wish I Might* (Reed and Cecily)
- *Turn My World Around* (Tucker and Corinne)
- *Dance Me A Dream* (Jace and Tara)
- *See You Again* (Trey and Sandy)
- *The Christmas Fountain* (Chad and Mary Alice)
- *You Were Meant For Me* (Mitch and Tess)
- *A Lot Like Christmas* (Ryan and Hannah)
- *Dancing Away With My Heart* (Zach and Lexi)

WISHING FOR A HERO SERIES (A WISHFUL SPINOFF SERIES)
SMALL TOWN ROMANTIC SUSPENSE

- *Make You Feel My Love* (Judd and Autumn)
- *Watch Over Me* (Nash and Rowan)
- *Can't Take My Eyes Off You* (Ethan and Miranda)
- *Burn For You* (Sean and Delaney)

MEET CUTE ROMANCE

SMALL TOWN SHORT ROMANCE

- *Once Upon A Snow Day*
- *Once Upon A New Year's Eve*
- *Once Upon An Heirloom*
- *Once Upon A Coffee*
- *Once Upon A Campfire*
- *Once Upon A Rescue*

SUMMER CAMP
CONTEMPORARY ROMANCE

- *Once Upon A Campfire*
- *Second Chance Summer*

ABOUT KAIT

Kait is a Mississippi native, who often swears like a sailor, calls everyone sugar, honey, or darlin', and can wield a bless your heart like a saber or a Snuggie, depending on requirements.

You can find more information on this RITA ® Award-winning author and her books on her website http://kaitnolan.com. While you're there, sign up for her newsletter so you don't miss out on news about new releases!